P9-DDS-678

07/15

# HEADLONG

WITHDRAWN

**Also by Simon Ings from Gollancz:**

*Hot Head*
*Hotwire*
*City of the Iron Fish*
*Painkillers*
*Wolves*

# HEADLONG

## SIMON INGS

FIC
ING

Copyright © Simon Ings 1999
*All rights reserved*

The right of Simon Ings to be identified as the author
of this work has been asserted by him in accordance with
the Copyright, Designs and Patents Act 1988.

This edition first published in Great Britain in 2014
by Gollancz
An imprint of the Orion Publishing Group
Orion House, 5 Upper St Martin's Lane, London WC2H 9EA
An Hachette UK Company

1 3 5 7 9 10 8 6 4 2

A CIP catalogue record for this book
is available from the British Library

ISBN 978 0 575 13112 5

Typeset by Deltatype Ltd, Birkenhead, Merseyside

Printed in Great Britain by Clays Ltd, St Ives plc

The Orion Publishing Group's policy is to use papers that
are natural, renewable and recyclable products and made
from wood grown in sustainable forests. The logging and
manufacturing processes are expected to conform to the
environmental regulations of the country of origin.

www.simonings.com
www.orionbooks.co.uk
www.gollancz.co.uk

*This one's for Daniel,*

*who, with glazed eyes, a white smile, and a voice like he
was speaking from inside an empty aircraft hangar,*

*showed me the steps*

# 1
# UNPLUGGED

# 1

No one knew where George Ballantyne kept his secret clinic. I only ever went there in the throes of EAI delirium, strapped into a canvas stretcher in the back of an unmarked ambulance. The windows were frosted, and the shadows that flicked past were indistinct. I couldn't tell treetops from rooftops.

And once I arrived at the clinic, they injected me with ResponsIV; that stuff kicked me so far into never-never land, I found it hard enough to remember my own name. That is why my memories of the clinic and its staff are so fragmented. The sound of the sea on a pebble bank. Aeroplanes landing. A child's balloon floating past the window. A cloudy night's sky, lit up sodium-orange by streetlights. Nurses in long red gowns. Doctors with cameras for eyes. Nonsense.

My self would sew itself back together eventually; but by then I'd been moved elsewhere. The clinic rented safe-houses from country-living magazines and tourist-board lists. They picked lonely railwayman's cottages, miles away from anywhere, in regions rarely visited by the police, their scopes and their scanners.

Waking from the treatments, I was blind for a while, as helpless as a puppy. When my sight did finally return, I found myself looking at the world as through a dirty windscreen.

Late one October, two years into my treatments, I opened my eyes on a place I'd not seen before.

Grey felt-like curtains framed a mottled grey space which I guessed was a window. Slowly my eyes adjusted to the light in the room. A shapeless fawn sofa sat near the window. Boils of whitish foam had burst from splits along its back and arms. A folding-leaf dining table stood near the door. It was spindly, and the veneer was splintered, as though something had been chewing on it.

The clinic had surpassed itself this time. Nauseated, I turned away. My head felt huge and hollow like a Halloween pumpkin.

'Ballantyne?'

*'Peckham Motors, Janny speaking.'* It was the clinic's favourite cover.

'I want to speak to George Ballantyne.'

*'Who's calling?'*

'Christopher Yale.'

*'Christopher!'*

'I'm calling with urgent medical information.'

*'We met last Thursday, remember?'*

'No. I was in treatment. You're mistaken.'

*'Costa's, in Portobello. Hilda was there.'*

'There have been side-effects.'

*'When is your appointment?'*

'He'll want to know.'

*'There's a free space next Wednesday afternoon.'*

'My teeth are loosening.'

*'We should get together again soon.'*

'There's a sucking sound in my ears.'

*'Will you speak to Hilda or shall I?'*

'I don't even know what I look like.'

*'Have you tried a mirror?'*

'It doesn't help.'

*'I'll pencil you in, then.'*

I wasn't bed-ridden, but the recent illness had sucked the colour out of everything. I felt greasy and delicate, like a shed skin.

I dreamed a lot, and it was hard for me sometimes to know when I was awake and when I was asleep. One night, I remember

4

I shrank back to a child again, and returned to my birthplace: a suburban enclosure south of Toronto. I was sitting by a child-proof stream. Spring sunlight broke gently on the chlorinated, fluoridated, iodized water. The light played across my face, filtered by the foliage of climb-resistent trees. I looked around me, looking for bearings in these ersatz woods. Every few yards or so there were red signs nailed to the tree trunks:

WARNING: Pebbles Can Choke Small Children

CCTV cameras watched me from the tallest branches, their lenses concealed behind bright, comforting shapes, plastic clowns' heads and animal masks.

The light faded, leaching the poster-colours from the masks. Their avuncular smiles became sinister. At dusk, they resembled the gap-toothed lantern ghosts of a Japanese fairy tale. In the silence of the night, the cameras set deep in their gaping mouths whined like gagged men. The branches weaved in the night like skeleton fingers. In autumn, swarms of dead leaves blew by the houses bordering the wood, triggering porch lights. They flooded the wood with a cruel glare like the searchlights of an advancing enemy.

I ran from them, hurtled through the dark, and came to the perimeter road. Bark chips covered the compacted earth to discourage weeds. On the far side, through the chainlink, I saw the campfires of the poor. They threaded the starry night sky with columns of smoke, solid as rags. A long way away, someone strummed a guitar.

A patrolman's jeep rounded the corner. Its tyres made a popping sound against the bark chips. The light from its door-mounted searchlight flashed on. It whited out the hill-side, the encampments and the stars. The bright, plasticated chainlink under my hands fluoresced. The jeep stopped. The idling engine sounded like an old man in the middle of a coughing fit. A safe male hand closed over my shoulder. 'Come on home, master Yale,' he said, in the curious, characterless falsetto typical of castrati. 'Mrs Yale is worrying about you.'

With a shout, I was free. Like the looking-glass Alice I grew, eyeblink-fast, into my mid-twenties. Free of enclosures, free of Toronto and my parents, I looked about me, screwing my eyes up against the glare of the snow.

Above me loomed the broken mouth of Kokanee Glacier. Melt-water gushed over rocks the size of cars. Below me, the tree-line was dark and threadbare. The rock was exposed in places, mottled with lichen and red moss. An elk and two young were stumbling myopically down into the valley, towards the log cabins where I lived and studied. My mentor, the architect and designer Louie Huichang, had chosen a truly inpirational location for his school. The locals – the nearest, an ex-convict, lived thirty miles away – thought we were all completely mad.

It was here, among the spruce and the elk, that I learned how to draw and to build.

And how to love.

'Pull the blanket up, Chris.'

'No, please, Sunshine, let me see.' The bed lay under the window. Her shoulders flexed in the starlight coming through the dirty glass. Her black hair shone in the glow from the open wood-stove.

The generator had packed in again. Smoke tickled my throat. The air was dry; I could hear the click in her throat when she swallowed.

'Christ's sakes make me come, love, I'm freezing.'

So I did. She bent over me and tightened her legs around mine. Her nipples were stiff with the cold. They felt like pebbles under my hand.

'Pebbles choke small children,' I said, breaking the dream into heartbreaking fragments. Ellen, who got an abortion, and a few months later flew to Brisbane; got married, built bridges, became famous, and led a good life; who still wrote me sometimes—

—Best of everything yourself, Sunshine, I thought, sliding Ellen's latest postcard into the drawer.

The lights were off in the Sea of Serenity apartment. Earthlight flooded the pristine window-glass, turning everything in the room a cool marine blue. I looked at my watch. My wife would be home soon. I looked out the window, searching for the dust trail from her buggy. But the lunar sky was clear as indian ink.

Perhaps, I thought, I have time to make her something. A present. A surprise.

A palace, I decided: a palace for my love.

In this dream, my head was still chock-full of Apolloco's accessories. The draughting tools, the rendering wetware, the neural cache. Silently, I recited the mnemonic to transport me to my virtual office. There was a tearing sound. Bright spots of grainy colour sandpapered my eyeballs. The next I knew I was hovering disembodied over a grey, gridded landscape. A mathematically smooth plain of dark grey clay receded evenly and endlessly whichever way I looked. The sky was an ungraduated light grey. There was no sun.

I smiled (though I had no mouth) to be back at the drawing-board: to be working again.

I wondered what to make. Something simple to start with, I thought. A palace. I pointed with my mind: *Let there be stuff.*

Beneath me, the dark grey clay curled and folded in on itself, making foundations for my palace. The trenches filled with fine white stone, soft as putty. Trees of iron, delicate as fern, sprouted from the soft stone.

With a flourish, I summoned up a river and sent it plunging through the building's skeleton. The river fluxed and beat against the iron underbrush. The twiggy mesh gave under the water's weight, thickening and exuding tar; then it set, forming a watercourse of black marble.

Elsewhere the iron trees grew thick and white, gummed with a stony mould. The stone stretched toffee-like from branch to branch. It swelled and popped like boiling mud and hardened into walls, pilasters, embrasures, here and there an ogive window, balconies, dressed stone and decorations—

With a hundred super-sensitive fingers I pruned my creation, snipping back the metal growths the stone had not covered. I balanced windows and doors and stairways, making of the wild architectural growth a thing of balanced lines. Marble I rendered solid black or white. Water, I made pencil grey. Floors were charcoal-coloured wood. I summoned up no colours. Colour would only distract me. Right now I cared only for light: the impossibly pure light of an architect's dreams.

The river plunged and twisted through the palace, making the views from every window and courtyard and balcony spectacular. Brightness scoured the palace's many atriums. I smiled, seeing how the receiving marble splashed dove-grey light down the most remote corridors.

Satisfied with my creation, I slept.

When I woke, the palace had evaporated. There was no sign of it.

The ideal light of my dream was drowning bloodily beneath a frayed horizon. The plain itself was shrivelling like burning paper. I floundered, caught up in the conflagration, and felt myself carried like chaff along a river of sour dreams.

Every day at noon I heard a car drive up outside the house. Below me, the front door banged open. Ten minutes later a thin Asiatic girl in a print dress entered the room. She plumped up my pillows, and fed me thin Campbell's soup and white bread. I didn't know who she was or who she answered to. Sometimes there were tear-tracks down her face. She moved with stiff, bent precision.

There were times her sadness touched me strangely. Every one of her gestures expressed submission. When she walked, it was with a martyred pride, as though she were submitting herself to difficult principles.

At other times, her silent misery aroused my resentment: I never asked her where she came from, and she never offered to tell me.

Once, as she was leaving, I screwed up my courage and asked her where I was.

'Long Lover,' she said.

'Long what?'

'It's what it says on the map.'

The improbable place-name disorientated me still further.

I kept forgetting how I'd got here, and what I was here for. I kept waking up in the middle of the night, sweating with fear. Then I'd call George Ballantyne's office. His secretary kept mistaking me for somebody else, some friend of a friend. 'I don't know any Hilda,' I kept saying. It never made any difference.

One day, without warning, the girl stopped coming. I missed her face, her mouth drawn down in lines of severe beauty, the arch of her eyebrows. Her face had stuck itself in my mind like an emblem. Absent, her image began to obsess me.

I lay in a sulk the whole day, waiting for her, carefully rationing the water in the jug by my bed.

On the second day, hunger seized me. It was a strange sensation, a raw signal from the gut. It missed my mouth entirely. I wasn't even salivating.

I lay there a while, the still centre of a febrile drugscape, exploring my body. The skin over my stomach bunched under my congested fingers. There was nothing about that loose and unfamiliar sac I recognised.

Slowly I put my feet to the floor and stood up. I felt very tall, my legs as thin as stilts. I stepped forward. The air moved around me. It must have been cold – I could see my breath – but the draughts had no more impact on my skin than ripples in a tepid bath.

I crossed the room and opened the door. The hallway beyond seemed as smooth and grey as felt. My brain still wasn't paying proper attention to my sense organs. I was blind to detail. Edges, cracks and textures were simply invisible to me.

*

Look up at the stars. Then, look into a bright light. Look up at the stars again. They have disappeared.

Prick your lip with a pin. Naturally, it hurts. Now slowly, firmly, bite your lip. Make it bleed. Now prick it with the pin again. You can't feel a thing. The greater pain of the bite has numbed you to the lesser pain of the pin-prick, just as the brightness of the light bulb blinded you to the stars.

Now imagine someone gives you other senses, beyond those you were born with. Imagine you can see the full gamma spectrum, hear the harmonic whine of tensile stress, feel electric flow, and smell magnetism. Imagine you have whole new ways to see the world, new avenues of pain and pleasure. Next imagine that, several years later, that same someone takes those senses away from you.

You've got used to them. What you're left with – the old signals of sight, hearing, taste, smell and touch – seem weak and washed out. Sometimes, they hardly seem to be there at all.

That's Epistemic Appetite Imbalance. The metaphors are sound except in one detail. Night-sight recovers in a quarter-hour or so. Sensitivity returns to a torn lip in less than a day.

But EAI doesn't go away. Not for good, anyway.

The numbness keeps coming back.

I found the bathroom and washed the sleep out of my eyes. My face felt like crumpled polythene. There was no way I could tell, by touch or taste or in the mirror, just how bad I looked. Maybe the gray and granulated skin and the sucking sound in my ears were illusory; maybe they weren't.

In the kitchen I looked round for something to eat. The freezer was stacked to the brim with processed white bread. In the pantry I found a Morrisons carrier bag full of UHT milk, tinned tomatoes and pasta twirls.

'*Oh fuck off*,' I said. But the words came out flat and broken, reminding me of those machines in lifts that stick words together into artificial sentences.

I looked out of the window. The ground was a sodden grey carpet. Mud? Stone? Water? There was no way to tell. The landscape beyond was all pumice, the clouds a thin lather, sticking in scraps to the stone.

# 2

The weather grew cool. The sky was permanently over-cast. It drizzled in the afternoons. I tried walking into Stone Chair. The road descended steeply into the village. Lacking much sense of my movements, I felt as though I was being buffeted along like a half-inflated balloon. I stuck my legs out to either side of me like poles to guide my absurd, bobbing progress.

There was a school at the foot of the hill. A high chainlink fence surrounded the playground. It swayed drunkenly over the footpath whenever a football or a child collided with it. The children crowded up against the fence and watched me totter by. They jeered and pointed. I studied their grey faces. I didn't know whether to smile or snarl, or whether, with my face so sallow and sucked in, it would make any difference.

I turned the corner. The children ran round for a better look, gathering at the corner of the yard. I studied them as they pushed forward. Something strange was happening to them. They were somehow – *separating*.

Bodies moved and volumes stretched, spreading substance thinly through time. Leading edges had a greenish cast; trailing edges were tinted red.

Abruptly, everything yawed into focus: the green school jackets, red piping round the collar; amber faces, black shoes, white socks; the blue markings on the ash-grey yard. I grinned at this sudden return of colour vision. A boy, thinking my smile was an attempt at ingratiation, stuck a finger up at me. It was a dark finger, and the pinkness of the nail shone like a jewel.

Quickly, I doubled back past the playground. I wanted to be back in bed, watching the walls and the furniture take on their proper colours. It would be a rite of passage for me, I thought. An earnest of my recovery.

The children began to chant. *Metal-head*. A girl, meaner than the rest, pressed her face into the chicken wire and gobbed at me. Fascinated, I watched her phlegm spin and sparkle against the light. It fell short of me, and I let my gaze pass up into the brilliant red trees.

I returned home. As I'd feared and half-expected, the colours faded out as I walked. Once again I began to float wildly about the narrow road. I didn't seem able to control my legs. They felt as though they were being guided by something outside me. Subtle shifts of the earth's magnetism drew them this way and that. But this first hint of recovery excited me. I decided to call Joanne.

I entered the bedroom and looked round for the phone. I couldn't find it. There wasn't even a socket for it to plug into.

There never had been a phone. I remembered that I didn't know my ex-wife's number. Come to that, Ballantyne didn't have a secretary. My stomach yawed as I grasped the extent and detail of my night-time hallucinations.

I wondered about the girl. That tall, stiff, heart-rending Asiatic misery with her plates of watery soup. What if she was imaginary? I stopped myself, remembering something from my childhood.

Every time you say there are no fairies, somewhere a fairy drops dead.

My strength returned. Soon I was eating lunch every day in a pub in Stone Chair. I passed whole weeks this way, walking from farm to pub and from pub to farm, as restless as a Jersey cow, chained by its horns to a stake in the ground.

The lounge bar was laid out like a sitting room, with frayed easy chairs and magazine-laden coffee tables. Farm workers and a smattering of lapsed muslim travelling salesmen drank warm, weak ale from earthenware mugs. The barman was in his late teens and always wore the same thing: acid-blue sweatshirt and grey jogging pants. His mother – wearing a shift that looked as though she'd sewn it together out of pink check dish-wipes – looked on suspiciously from a dark corner. There were rings on all four fingers of her right hand and she was continually testing their musical properties against her mug.

To start with, I talked about the moon to anyone bored or drunk enough to listen. 'After a day spent blasting through new galleries,' I said, 'the streets smell of patchouli. But more often the air blows into the Domes from ports to the east. Then the stench of mould and pepper overlays everything like smoke from a burning tyre factory.'

I said, 'We were newly married. We were full of ourselves. We treated the place like a playground – an amusement arcade of concrete panels and blue-tinted glass blasted by dust-devils howling up from the spiced honeycombs of the interior.'

I stopped saying these things after a while. I found it increasingly hard to believe what I was saying. Sometimes, forgetting some nuance of my life on the moon, I'd run trembling fingers through my hair, feeling for the plugs. Often a bitter tearfulness overwhelmed me, when I thought of how much I had lost of myself.

I wondered where Joanne was. I toyed with the idea of tracing her through her family. One day, walking back from the pub, I entered a public kiosk and dialled Paris. When the international monitor asked me the purpose of my call, I replaced the receiver.

A few days later, I received another visitor.

'Police! Open up!'

George Ballantyne stood on the bottom step, grinning up at me. 'How're you doing, lad?'

'George.'

He was a big man in his late fifties. He had the look of a labourer: someone who had never seen the inside of a gym, but had got a massy, disorganized kind of strength from hammering iron or juggling feed sacks. Much of this muscle had turned to fat, but there was still enough tone in his arms and his torso to make him formidable.

'Let me in, let me in, in the name of the Prince Regent.' George Ballantyne's Dumfries accent was more acute today, though no more accurate. As though driving North had reminded him dimly of his birthright.

I stood away from the door. He bustled in, Morrisons shopping bags straining to be free of his large, soft hands. 'I know you like books!' His face was gentle, as if to contradict the evidence of his body. His mouth was full and feminine. His long, receding red hair lay slickly across his scalp in a half-hearted comb-over. And while the ridges of bone under his brows gave his blue eyes a hint of animal menace, they also made him look stupid. He played on that; but I wasn't taken in.

I sat in the parlour and pulled out a handful of books from the bag. Ballantyne must have grabbed them at random off a market stall. Collingwood's *The Meaning of History*. A Playfair Cricket Annual for '56. A coffee-table book about window boxes.

'You've not been eating hardly,' he observed. He was restocking the larder with UHT and beans.

There was no point me explaining again about my diet. He would only start on about red meat or protein or haggis or something. I said: 'I've been lunching at the pub.'

Ballantyne came through from the kitchen, throwing his booted feet out to left and right. He told me once he'd lost his toes to frostbite. This was back in his army days, defending Karelia against the Finns. 'Christopher,' he said. 'I hope you're joking.'

I shrugged.

George sighed. 'I bring you to a place like this to *disappear*, lad.'

'I know all that.'

'You know what the police round here are like. I hope you've been discreet.'

I picked a book from the stack and started leafing through the introduction.

Ballantyne sat down opposite me. He took the testing kit from his jacket pocket. Casually he laid out needle, dishes, swabs. He'd grown used to my moods.

14

'There are one or two corners in every garden where plants simply refuse to grow,' I read. 'You plant all kinds of things there and in a matter of weeks they fizzle out and disappear.' I set the book aside and rolled up my left shirt-sleeve. I knew the routine.

'You let yourself get in a bad way before you phoned in,' said Ballantyne, sliding the cannula neatly into my vein.

'I have to be careful with money,' I said, looking away as he drew off a few CCs of blood.

'It's your health we're talking about. You mustn't take chances with it.'

'Yeah, yeah,' I drawled.

Ballantyne withdrew the needle and taped a swab over the puncture. I watched in silence as he fussed over his samples and reagents. In a few seconds, we would know if I could switch to the lower dose of ResponsIV.

Ballantyne nodded sagely over his watch, measuring some reaction or other. Satisfied, he packed the kit away. 'You're here a while longer, I'm afraid.'

I sighed. 'I really do have to get back.'

Ballantyne shook his head. 'You know how careful we have to be about this.'

I knew. I was a post-human: a metal-head. By international law, government authorities could demand a scan and a sample off me at any time. Plus Leeds was the capital now, and spot checks of this sort were common.

In lower doses, ResponsIV metabolises quickly, but higher doses linger – something to do with the chemicals buffering the solution. Finding that stuff in my blood stream would send alarm bells ringing all the way down the Headrow. 'How long until I can go?'

'A couple of days,' said Ballantyne. 'One more full hit should do it.' He prepared the needle, jabbed me, pumped the clear liquor into my vein with a steady hand. 'I'll come see you Monday, if you like.'

'Sure,' I said, without enthusiasm. Since I'd first succumbed to his illicit treatments, I'd kept contacts with George Ballantyne to the minimum. Beneath his bumptious, spivvish exterior, I sensed something to be afraid of.

Ballantyne, notwithstanding his day-job with the London Met, made most of his living trading in pirated post-human accessories. I knew this because he was forever offering me deals on the most defective and infected-sounding packages. Somewhere along the line he had got it into his head that I must be secretly very well off. As though every lunar settler must, at some point during their stay, have discovered the burial chamber of a long-lost insect king. Or had, if not a bucket full of emeralds, at least a weathered map marking its location.

This time, though, Ballantyne's advice seemed more heartfelt. 'You have to look to the future, Chris,' he said. His spoonlike fingers weaved about each other on his lap like worms. 'If you come to London I could put you in touch with people.'

'I know your sort of people, George.'

Ballantyne looked at me blankly, then burst out laughing: 'Oh laddie!'

I winced. Being 'laddied' by George Ballantyne reminded me of every one of my forty-three years.

'The Met's not so bad! Did I tell you? I've moved division.'

'Really.'

'Special technologies,' he said, savouring each syllable.

'Supplying?'

'*Advising*,' Ballantyne corrected me, moueing to show how his feelings were hurt. It was an oddly effeminate expression for that big slack face. 'You know, you're wasting your talents in Leeds.'

'Headingley,' I amended, automatically.

'You don't belong there! With what you've done and what you've seen: a post-human, stuck out here in Sheepshaggerland—'

'I chose to live here, remember?'

'Stuck in that silly granny-flat of yours. Ticking by on Welfare ...'

'I read a lot,' I replied, nettled. I was proud of my flat. I'd spent a lot of money on it. My life was how I wanted it.

'You're still a young man!'

I shrugged. I'd no illusions of that sort left.

'Look.' Ballantyne stared into his lap. His fingers span, weaving a cat's cradle out of air. 'If you're in London. Any reason. Call the clinic.'

'George, I left London. I'm not going back to London.'

'No.' Ballantyne accepted my brush-off with a smile. He stood up. 'No. Of course not. Still. Who knows, eh?' He slapped me on the shoulder and made for the door.

'George?'

George turned.

'Who was it looked after me? Some girl.'

'A girl was here?'

'Feeding me soup.'

Ballantyne looked blank. Reflexively, he ran his blunt fingertips through his comb-over, ruining it. 'I've no idea.'

'I thought maybe it was my imagination.'

'It must have been,' he said. Then, 'What did she look like?'

'Asian. Young. Hacked off about something.'

'One of the nurses might have sent someone over.' He was trying to sound casual. It wasn't working.

'Is something wrong?'

'Only that nobody told me. Forget it.'

Ballantyne's car was slung low. Gravel pinged against its belly as it swung toward the gates. I watched it go.

# 3

Textures came back. A few muted colours. At the pub, the beer started tasting of soap, and I remembered why I never drank it.

I slept less. I explored the house, and found a canvas daypack in a cupboard under the stairs. Two or three times a week I got up before dawn and hired taxis to take me to the railway station. I ate chocolate from the platform vending machines until a milk train arrived heading west or north. Sometimes I was able to catch an extra hour's sleep as I rode, tucking the sack between my head and the carriage window.

I'd end up in Settle as likely as not, and ate breakfast at a cafe near the railway station.

I walked the bridleway to Langcliffe and back, and ran my hands along the dry-stone walls until they were raw, willing them to feel something. As the days went by, so the numbness in my fingers eased. The feel of moss, soft and congealed under my fingertips, was delicious and surprising. I picked at it, discovering thin fibrous soil. I rubbed it to a mulch between my fingers.

I sniffed my soiled fingertips, but detected nothing. Smell was always the last sense to come back.

I headed east, up close-cropped banks to Attermire Scar. It had been raining and the rise was steep. Small stone outcrops poked out the turf at long intervals, and I slithered from one to the other, panting and grinning, trying to get a foothold. I reached the top. Black Hill lay to the south; to the left rose fractured limestone crags, overgrown with lichen and turfs.

There was a natural shelter in the rock nearby. The map called it a cave, because around here people have to make the best of what they have. The walls were rough and dry, angled towards each other to make a Gothic arch. The ground was puddled. Crisp packets poked out from behind a rock. I crawled in and found a dry patch and sat, waiting for the sky to clear. It wasn't long after dawn, and the sun had yet to breach the heavy cloud. A feverish pink haze banded the horizon. I wondered wearily how much that dead fluorescent light was real, how much a product of my faulty vision.

I awoke around noon, excited for no reason. It had stopped raining. There were breaks in the cloud. I'd planned to head south towards Malham Tarn; that way I'd be home by nightfall. Instead, sensing some important change in my condition, I climbed north, over long stretches of ankle-breaking limestone pavement. There were plants growing between the ridges: ferns, red grasses, odd blooms with serrated leaves.

The terraces closed in on either side: The map called this place Yew Cogar Scar. I smiled the smile of a connoisseur. On the moon, I'd often had the job of assigning names to the places where we raised our settlements. I walked through the Scar and came to a valley, steep and grass-banked. At last the sun came out; it lit up the stream at the valley bottom like a shaft of steel.

The valley led straight into Arncliffe. I descended the heather-heavy slopes, racing the declining light. When I reached the village I looked back, surveying the terraces down which I'd climbed. Their outlines appeared mathematically precise in the oblique light, like a series of gigantic gold coins stacked one on top of the other. I counted them, noting their serrations and their flaws.

*Yew Cogar Scar.*

The air smelled faintly of manure and rape-seed. I turned my face to the setting sun and let its antique light flood my eyes. My feet were sore, I could feel new blisters forming, and I smiled, because I could feel these things.

I was getting better.


I walked into Kettlewell and waited for the bus to take me home. The wooden seat was covered in rusty moss. Where the sunlight struck it, it blazed with reds and russets. The colourful bodies of horseflies popped and flashed in the brassy light like soap bubbles.

The bus emerged from over the brow of the hill, its plastic hide white from the narrow roads as though it were dusted with sugar. I stood: sun-dried thistles crackled under my feet.

The windows of the bus were tinted turquoise: it was as though we were being driven deep under the waves, to a land reflected in mirrors of cold green water. I leaned back and closed my eyes, and though the roads were rough, only the faintest vibration troubled my dreams ...

Luckily the driver remembered my destination. Woken by his shout, I sat up; confused, still half asleep, I looked out of the window. I saw the school – empty now – and the hill up to Long

Lover farm. The sky was the colour of ale. I pulled myself out of the seat. Exhaustion had set my joints like solder. I climbed off the bus. The pavements, blasted by the furnace of the afternoon, were hot as kiln bricks under my feet.

I walked up the hill, past the playground, and ran my fingers along the chain-link fence. The rust stuck to my fingertips, tacky like pollen. Trees overhung the road at its steepest section and plunged me into twilight. The air here was as sweet and molten as a berry. I thought of my bed, and of the simple solitary comfort of my hermitage. I yawned, and laid my hand on the gate. It swung open.

It had been unfastened.

I stopped dead. There was a vehicle in the yard. A Land Rover, with its lights off.

I approached as quietly as I could. The vehicle had army drab paintwork. Stencilled on the door in bronze paint was the crescent of the District Sheriff's office. It was empty.

Where was the driver? Was he waiting for me in the house?

I walked back down the drive. It would only take a few seconds, I thought, then I'd be safe behind the screen of the hedge. Then I might be able to think of something. Like who had given me away.

*How had they found me*? Who, other than Ballantyne and his nurses, knew I was here?

My heart trembled. The fear was exhilarating. I felt absurdly fit and young.

'Mr Yale!'

I stopped.

'It is Mr Yale, isn't it? Christopher Yale?'

I turned around. 'It is,' I said, affecting casual surprise. I tried to remember what Ballantyne had told me to say, if I was ever questioned about the treatments.

The sheriff's skin was the mucky, yellowish sort common to the area: milky Lancashire curdling in Bangladesh. He was short, and his head was too big. 'I am Sheriff Anwar Mukut.' He laid a thick, ugly, carefully manicured hand on my sleeve. It's warmth penetrated the flocking of my anorak. 'Please, I must have a word.' The little man led me towards the house. 'I hoped it might be you, sir. I've come—' He stopped in the middle of the path. I tried to meet his eyes, but he kept shying away. 'This is very distressing,' he said.

I pulled away and climbed the concrete steps to the front door. I turned the key, and wondered if I was entitled to shut the sheriff out.

But Mukut made no move to enter. He folded his hands meekly over his stomach. 'I really have to tell you some very bad news, sir.'

'Really.'

'Mr Yale,' he said, 'I've been asked to accompany you to London, sir.'

So.

'What on earth for?' I blustered, playing for time.

The little man gaped, as though I'd somehow misunderstood him. 'Oh Mr Yale,' he said. He made a brushing gesture with his hands, as if to sweep away whatever misunderstanding had come between us. 'We've found a body, sir.'

I stood there stupidly, straddling the threshold.

The sheriff extended his hands in a plea.

'We think it's your wife,' he said.

# 4

Sheriff Mukut called for me early the next morning. It was a smooth journey, and the rhythms of the Land Rover sent me back to sleep for a time. When I woke, the sun was high in the sky. The wet three-lane dazzled me with lemon light. I was cold. My clothes felt damp.

'How are you?' Mukut asked. 'Turn the heater on.'

Later, as casually as I could, I said, 'How did you know where to find me?'

'The message on your answerphone,' Mukut replied, he was surprised that I'd needed to ask.

*What message?* I hadn't recorded any message. I pressed my hands between my knees to stop them trembling. Mukut, thinking I was cold, turned the heater up some more.

The sky was a flat, ungraduated blue. The motorway cut through forested land and the trees glistened green and gold, as though the leaves were sprayed with metallic paint. The light had a burnished quality that made my eyes ache. The road was wet in places, and shone like hammered chrome.

The road's easy curves abolished geography; only the road signs gave us any sense of forward movement. Industrial parks and rural housing developments passed by, indistinguishable from each other, as prepackaged and predesigned as any lunar structure. We stopped finally at a motorway service station outside St Alban's, where we were due to meet officers from the Principality of London. Mukut led me into the lobby. At the foot of the stairs I held back. 'I need the men's.'

'We're meeting in the cafeteria up on the bridge,' the Sheriff said; he pointed the way.

'I'll be up in a minute.'

When Mukut was gone I crossed to the phones. I dialled my flat in Leeds. A woman apologised for my absence and read off my secret address. I didn't recognise the voice; one of Ballantyne's nurses?

I figured Ballantyne must have arranged this. He must have heard what had happened. Then, somehow, he had got a message on to my answerphone. Quick work, but to what end?

Most likely, he wanted to save the police trouble. He wouldn't want them prying too far into my affairs, in case they stumbled upon the clinic – but why hadn't he tried to warn me? Then I remembered. There was no phone at Long Lover.

It made sense, in a paranoid fashion.

I climbed the stairs, looking for Mukut. There was a restaurant built into the bridge straddling the motorway. It was separated from the linoleum-floored walkway by head-high perspex panels, stuck over with signs advertising Stonking breakfasts and Ginormous cups of coffee. The fixed seating was arranged in space-efficient bays: plastic shelves bearing potted plants ran above and behind the moulded benches. Mukut waved to me. The carpet tiles sucked at the soles of my shoes like a rubber compound.

The sheriff was sitting with two men wearing the ostentatious resin body armour of the Principality: all Graeco-Roman ripples with a soft velveteen sheen. The age gap between the two Met officers was huge: they might have been father and son. The younger one was finishing a round of toast.

Mukut ushered me on to the banquette seating. 'Would you like something to eat?'

I shook my head.

'Are you sure you won't have something?'

'I'm sure.'

'An all-day breakfast?' Mukut was hungry, but felt embarrassed to order for himself. He thought his appetite might affront me for some reason.

A little toast, perhaps,' I said, to let him off the hook. My voice came out weak, like I was ill. I didn't feel ill – I didn't feel anything.

The men from the Principality had arrived early, and maybe the wait had made them skittish. The least thing was enough to set them off.

'Shall we get a cafetiere?'

I'll get it.'

'Do you want it all?'

'Did I say that?'

'It holds two cups.'

'All right, you can have one.'

I was only asking.'

Occasionally a lorry grumbled by beneath us. The tremors passed up through my feet into my stomach, and the sounds of sizzling fat and rattling cutlery were like a war film in my head.

The waitress came over. 'Two breakfasts?'

'I only wanted—' I began, then the smell of bacon hit my nostrils. Shamefaced, I accepted the plate.

The 'son' – they told me their names and I immediately forgot them – had his head buried in the road atlas. Surely there was nothing complicated about the Ml ? The 'father' tore open a sachet of sugar and added its contents to the white ring in the ashtray. 'I do know the way,' he said.

The atlas trembled. 'I want to drive now.'

'I'm more than capable—'

'I want to,' the son said, and clapped the atlas shut.

'Why you have to make an issue out of it,' the father grumbled, pushing the filter down on the cafetiere. Without asking, he reached for the son's cup and filled it up.

'Can you tell me anything?'

It came out so suddenly, it didn't feel as if I'd spoken. The father and the son looked at each other. 'It's your wife,' the son said. 'He knows that.'

'How did she die?'

'A wound to the head,' said the father, like he was quoting something; like it was a legal term.

'A wound?'

'Yes.'

'An accident?'

'No,' said the son. The father glared at him.

'Then what—'

'This can wait,' said Mukut. He crumpled up his serviette in a single, fussy gesture.

'No. Please. How—'

'There were no signs of struggle,' the son said. 'But someone moved the body.'

'We're not supposed to tell him that,' the father said.

'What happened to her?'

Mukut laid a hand on my arm. 'Mr Yale.'

I pulled away. There was a rushing sound in my ears. There was an ocean in my head. 'Someone moved her body? So someone—'

The father leaned forward over the table. 'There was no funny business,' he said. His tone was apologetic. As though it was his fault. As though he'd been there.

I was getting all confused.

The son joined in. 'No indecency.'

They meant rape. They meant that Joanne had not been interfered with sexually. 'What sort of head wound?'

'We can't tell you,' the father said.

'We don't know,' the son added.

The father shot the son a wounded look.

'Someone was there? Someone did it to her?'

'There were no signs of struggle.'

'Mr Yale,' said Mukut, 'do please try to eat.'

I picked at my food.

'Do you want any sauce, Mr Yale?' Mukut asked.

I nodded and reached for the ketchup. It was so thick it wouldn't leave the bottle. I prised at it with my knife, but the neck was too narrow. I stifled a sob.

'Are you all right?' Mukut asked me, concerned.

I beat the bottle with the heel of my hand.

'Mr Yale?'

'She was murdered,' I said. I set the ketchup back on the table. 'I mean, that's what you're telling me. Someone murdered her.'

The father and the son exchanged awkward glances.

'Here,' said Mukut, handing me a starched white handkerchief.

I stared at it. I didn't know what to do with it. 'Here,' he said, and he took it from my hand and used it to wipe away my tears, like a mother would a child.

# 5

The officers' police ID gave us easy passage through the Bricket Wood checkpoint and into the Principality of London. We eased along the overpass at the required ten m.p.h., kerb-side detectors snuffling the gasohol-candied air for Semtex and

ZB15. Below us, the old M25 snaked through its overgrown cutting. In the early days of London's autonomy, machine-gun towers lined the disused four-lane, and every weed concealed a mine. But these warlike preparations had since given way to sheepfolds and allotments. Along the terraced cuttings, late flowering dog-rose wound round the stems of peas and runner beans and tomatoes. Its simple white flowers set everything sparkling. The bucolic scene disorientated me, as though we had fallen through a hole in time and come out in the wrong season. I had lived for so long among the dour conservative farmsteads of Yorkshire, I had forgotten how strange London was.

The EU regulations controlling the spread of man-made DNA did not apply in London. Since the war of separation, imports of new plant strains had flooded unchecked through Tilbury Docks. In London, the most delicate houseplant was designed to resist extremes of cold and drought. Allotments and market gardens flourished with hectic growth. There were sugar cane fields on the Isle of Dogs. Prize-winning artichokes grew as weeds in Kensal Green.

Viral contamination had carried this genetic revolution into the city's soil, making everything unnaturally hardy and fruitful. Buddleia bloomed from every cracked wall. Tree suckers took root between cracked paving stones. Dog-rose bloomed throughout the year; it clung to everything.

Bad roads doglegged towards Hampstead Heath. High fences topped with razor wire bordered in the road. Behind the fence ran dirt tracks patched with compacted refuse. Brick slums listed in the dirt. They were so crude, children might have built them. Their doors, those that had them, were corrugated tin. The windows had no frames, and clear plastic sheeting took the place of glass. Sunlight had fogged much of it, and many windows were as bleary as cataracted eyes. The bottom floors were old and cracked. The upper floors were more recent; the occupants simply piled them one on top of another as the need arose. Some houses were four storeys tall. Here and there walls had collapsed, revealing rooms lined with mismatched paper, pages torn from magazines and religious prints: as we turned on to Spaniard's Road I glimpsed a wall-sized poster of Good King Wills.

It was about two in the afternoon, but the settlement appeared deserted. A dirt road ran parallel to the fence for a while. A lame dog loped from shack to shack, a leash of green plastic rope tangling round its legs. Avenues of sickly birch ran between the flat-roofed houses, producing an unconscious parody of Highgate's leafy and expensive terraces.

Sheriff Mukut talked constantly, as though the scenery was something he had to apologise for personally. 'Circumstances required it,' he explained. He rubbed his hands together as though he were washing them under a tap.

'Where did you find her?' I asked.

'Four days ago, as far as we can gather, somebody dumped your wife's body in the central reservation of the North Circular just outside Amos Grove. We're collaborating with London on the investigation because we think she died somewhere outside the Principality's borders.'

'How do you know?'

'She was inhaling Republican air. We found characteristic pollens in her airways.'

I nodded, buffeted by the information. Mukut was a decent man, quick with his explanations; I just wasn't ready for them.

We headed south down Finchley Road, into the more cosmopolitan districts around Regent's Park. The fractured streets had an overcoloured look: a theme park built over a bomb site.

London had paid dearly for its autonomy. Breaking free of the Union, London – now a freeport and Principality in its own right – had had to bootstrap itself out of its rubble unaided. Much of the Western part of the city remained blasted and uninhabitable, and work gangs of young royalists had decorated the ruins with anti-European slogans, icons of Oliver Goldsmith and William Haig, battlescapes of Railtrack Waterloo.

An Honour Guard, their bearskins polar white crisscrossed with red to signify Saint George, goose-stepped round

Buckingham Palace. Trumpets blared fealty to the Principality's Prince Regent. Tourists jammed Buckingham Gate, today as every day, hoping perhaps for a glimpse of the idiot Prince in his ermine bib. My gaze lingered incredulously on the toy soldiers strutting raggedly behind the gates: there was so much gold braid on them, you could barely see the lilac of their uniforms.

Sheriff Mukut winced. 'I'm sorry we had to bring you here,' he said yet again. He shrank back in his seat to shield himself from the moral pollution of the metropolis.

'Joanne and I used to live here,' I said.

The younger of the two policemen said, 'We want to talk to you about all of this, Mr Yale. It'd be best if you didn't volunteer too much now.'

Raw from shock, I felt warmed by the gentleness of the young man's voice. Then it dawned on me that he was cautioning me.

We were heading south down Southampton Row towards the Thames. Traffic was heavy on Waterloo Bridge and it took us some minutes to cross. Ahead of us, on the south side of the river, a helicopter in vivid medical livery settled like a huge and blundering wasp on the roof of the Apolloco hospital.

Apolloco has hospitals like this all over the EU, but none of the others I've seen announce themselves quite so brutally. It's an ugly, stupid building, all poster-paint colours and soft adobe lines, like a Lego construction worn smooth by the sea, and there's a faux-Mansard roof on the eastern wing which I hope was a joke. I saw it first about three months before they flew me to the Moon. I thought, if that's their idea of good architecture, what's the Moon going to look like?

But I was tired, and frightened, and I wasn't alone. There were about a hundred and fifty of us in that group. Apolloco had spent about a year flying us from medical centre to medical centre. At each stopover, doctors and technicians made us less and less what we were, more and more what Apolloco wanted us to be.

Drugs in Milan, surgery in Berlin, interfaces in Prague.

Plugs in London.

And after my years on the Moon I returned here, of course. When we left the Moon, Apolloco brought us back to their hospitals, as international law said they must, turning off and sealing up the plugs they'd given us when we upwelled.

I remember little of that time. Back then, lurching about in near sensory collapse, my sense of time narrowed to a pinpoint, I was deaf and blind to all but the most brute stimuli. It was my first, pre-emptive taste of EAI: the condition that had seized control of my life.

There was the usual bureaucratic delay when we arrived. While the police hunted out the coroner I waited by the tinted windows of the hospital lobby, gazing out. Mortar fire had savaged the West End so badly during the war, no one had yet begun to build there. It had become so overgrown it had lost all connection to the current city. It seemed to belong to an ancient time, as though a bizarre geological accident had spat the ruins of the Roman town of Londinium to the surface.

The view made me uneasy. I scratched absently at my scalp, feeling for the plugs. Scar tissue almost covered them now, hard and glossy to the touch. I was conscious of my own hollowness: my skull, a bony shell, contemplating shells of stone.

Across the Thames, through a screen of ash and red-twigged lime, I could just make out the milky, fluted ruins of Somerset House. The stubs of dressed stone poked out from the bushes like teeth from a blackened gum. I wondered if similar growths were wrapping themselves around the pins and threads inside my head. My brain might in time become as overgrown and riotous as the West End itself, I thought. A birthplace for psychological flowers, wild and delicate ...

I went back to my seat.

There was a box of toys and games in the corner of the room. A small serious boy in a grey school uniform was working through them grimly, as though they were a chore. A four-year-old girl with rounded, sensuous features was reading a book with her mother.

'Oh, look!' her mother said. 'Little people!'

'Little people!'

Since the abandonment of the Moon, Apolloco's hospitals had lost their special function: they doubled as public clinics, and most of the people sitting with me now were mothers and children.

The boy in the uniform sighed and slipped to his knees and crawled under the table. A cardboard dispenser spilled leaflets about cold sores over the smoked-glass surface.

'No, Anton.'

The girl stabbed feverishly at her book. 'Dog!'

'That's not a dog.'

I picked up a magazine and glanced through it, pausing at the photograph of a porcelain shepherdess. 'It's not, it's a polar bear.' I read: *Be inspired for less.*

Something nudged my shoe.

'Anton! People's feet!'

'Dog!' the girl shouted. 'Dog dog dog!' Her halo of wispy, gingerish hair suggested chemotherapy. 'Mr Yale?'

Between the two London officers stood an elderly black man. They told me he was the coroner; his wrinkled face had never smiled much. He led us to a lift. At the second floor, the doors opened and the officers stepped out. I made to follow them. The coroner took my elbow gently, drawing me back.

'Where's Sheriff Mukut?' I asked. I'd only just noticed he wasn't around.

'Probably on his way back to Yorkshire.'

'Yorkshire?'

'He's not part of the investigation.'

The lift doors opened at the seventh floor. I hesitated. 'I didn't say goodbye to him,' I said.

'Come on,' said the coroner. He took me by the arm. 'This way.'

We came to a door like any other in the featureless, fawn hallway. I felt the gentle pressure of his hand on my back. 'Don't be afraid,' he said. 'It's not so bad.'

I opened the door.

The pine-panelled room was furnished like a chapel. It had a careful smell, an inoffensive floral fragrance that had never seen a flower. Unvarnished benches surrounded the mortuary table, which was draped with a blue cloth. On the table, hidden by the cloth, lay an unmistakable shape. I followed the folds and swells of the cloth. I was nodding my recognition even before the coroner lifted the sheet.

Hope shot through me, an absurd bolt of lightning. They had prepared Joanne so carefully, binding her broken head with bandages, cleaning her fine boned Algerian-French face to an unnatural sheen. I imagined her, cared for so well, rising turbaned and radiant to a new, more exotic life. I returned her mischievous smile, forgetting the effects of rictus: that it was usual for the dead to look this way.

'Mr Yale?'

Hope poured away again: a wave drawn back by a jealous sea. 'Yes,' I said.

'Is this Joanne Mabelle Rynard?'

'It is.'

'Thank you.'

The coroner drew the sheet back over the body. 'I can give you some moments alone, sir.'

I did not move.

The door closed softly, and I was alone. I hadn't expected this. To be left here, to be given time. Was this usual? Were all the police shows wrong? I wondered how long I had in here, and if I was being watched.

Gingerly, I took hold of the sheet. I pulled it back. They had dressed her in a long sleeveless paper shift. Her head was bandaged.

With trembling fingers I stroked the dressings binding her broken skull. Above her left ear, where her plugs had been, there was a depression. A hollowness: it gave under my fingers. Was this the wound which had killed her? The fracture was colossal: it would have taken several blows with a lump-hammer to put a hole of that size in her head. More likely, the coroner had widened the original head-wound during his postmortem. I imagined the police, splitting her head like a coconut, searching for pirated accessories ...

And they had gutted her: orange spots stained her shift where disinfectant had leaked from the postmortem incision.

I touched her cheek. I remembered holding her face, holding it tight, holding her mouth and her forehead still against me, gripping her there, as I performed my own wet exploration of her. I let out a groan, revolted by my imagination. Hollowed, Joanne smiled her idiot smile.

I kissed her. The coldness of her flesh tattooed itself into my lips. I fought a shameful urge to rub at them, pummel away the deadly cold, undo the unwise gesture.

Behind me the door opened, and I pulled the sheet back to cover her face.

# 6

A new policeman was waiting for me in the lobby. He had been sent to drive me to police headquarters.

There was something wrong with his face. The skin was creased and stretched, as though he had had a plastic bag pulled over his bones and painted the right colour. With a lurch, I realised I was probably right: that this was a casualty of the war of separation. His eyes were blue and indistinct, as though they'd been poached. They shied away from me when he spoke.

Police headquarters lay off Belgrave Square, he said: not far, but the journey took the best part of an hour. Cyclos and bicycles jammed the street, and the road surfaces were worse than I remembered, pocked and channelled as though small animals had been burrowing through them. Rainwater had collected in the deeper holes, and black mud exploded from under the heavy treads of the army vehicles ahead of us, as they rumbled unconcerned over the broken tarmac. Grit and sand span off their treads into our windshield. They turned off along the embankment, and traffic over the Thames sped up a little before narrowing to a bad-tempered stream between roadworks that looked long-abandoned. Then the siren of a fire tender far behind us froze the whole traffic stream as though it were the Last Trump.

So the light was failing as we crawled round Hanover Square. The traffic was so dense the driver pulled up by the pavement and pointed me to a green glass monolith without signs or insignia, and I walked the rest of the way. The lobby was cool and smelled faintly of roses. The officer at the desk was helpful enough and showed me into a small waiting room with pink striped wallpaper. Green plastic seats were arranged around three walls. I sat down. Twenty minutes went by. Forty. I stepped into the corridor. It was empty. I looked at my watch. It was ten past seven. I felt weak and dizzy. I hadn't eaten since St Albans. I hadn't eaten then. I wondered if I could remember my way back to reception. I took two steps down the corridor when a woman hailed me.

I turned.

'We've been looking for you,' she said crossly: a police sergeant, I saw by the flashes on her sleeve.

'I was—' I began.

'Come with me.'

I hung back, expecting to follow her.

'Come on, Mr Yale!' She wanted to keep me in sight: to shepherd me. 'Down here, down here.' Greenish light dribbled through lichen-stained skylights into a large open-plan office; its walls were brown with age.

The sergeant left me sitting in front of a high steel desk. It was bare but for a terminal and a pristine pad of sticky-notes. I spun the chair round idly, wondering where everyone was. The office must have held about twenty people, but I was alone. I imagined them handing round cigarettes at a high-level meeting in the basement; strapping on absurd body-armour; signing out guns.

Ten minutes passed. The other desks were as bare, every one the same. There were none of the scraps of personality you'd

33

normally find in a place like this -mugs, photographs, pin-ups, pens.

Twenty minutes. Bright, rectangular patches on the old walls showed where charts and calendars had hung for a time. A few of these remained. I was disorientated, and it took me a while to make sense of them.

They were anatomical sections. Blood vessels, lymph ducts and nerves were picked out in primary colours. I went to examine them more closely, and passed a desk covered with photographs. Blow-ups of shaved and broken heads lay piled one on top of another.

The shots were pink, luscious, and strangely pornographic. Plastic retractors held sheets of skin and muscle away from the incision. Whole sections of skull had been removed, and the meningial layers within glittered like sheets of dirty plastic. In some photographs, the meninges had been peeled back and pinned in place with steel clasps. The brains within were greyish pink, wrinkled like coral. Thin probes, like an acupuncturist's needles, stuck up out of the spongy mass at irregular intervals. I wondered if the subjects in the photographs were alive or dead.

I looked about me, seeing the room with new eyes. Chunky flatscreens squatting on anonymous, bare desks. Charts of human CNS on the walls. This wasn't a police room: it was something special, something that tasted of Apolloco.

I looked back at the table. In one corner there was a pile of diagrams. I leafed through them: half-recognising them. They illustrated the sorts of accessories Apolloco had installed in my head. Tissue and electronic circuitry folded round each other, clinging together in fistulae of nerve and conductive fibre.

'Quite a display.'

He was about a foot shorter than I was, and about twice as wide. He had on brown shoes, the pointed toes polished to a high sheen; green wool trousers; a yellow waistcoat that had the quality of old gold in the room's lichen-stained light. He glanced at the table and said, 'Sometimes I think we should start up a gallery.' If it was a joke, I couldn't unpack it. 'Come sit down, Mr Yale.'

He moved with a strange, rounded bebop rhythm, as though he wanted to dance. He waved me back into the chair I'd first sat in. He perched on the edge of the desk and folded his arms, leaning over me like a friendly but critical relation. 'D.I. Rence,' he said, introducing himself.

There was a gold fob-watch on a chain in his waistcoat pocket. A bow tie hung loosely round his heavily starched white collar. In this scrubbed, pallid room, he looked like the eruption of something fey and primeval.

'Christopher Yale,' I said.

Detective Inspector Rence smiled, wisely. There were lines of dark blue stubble like soil in the creases of his mouth. His whiskers came down to his jaw and sported several months' growth.

'I've been waiting here more than an hour.'

'Let's get this over with then,' he said, as though all I'd had to do was ask. He angled his computer monitor towards us and hit the record button. While he waited for the application to load he scratched vigorously at his low, wide sideburns, as if to draw attention to them. 'Please state your full name for the record.'

'Christopher Alain Yale.'

'Age and birth date?'

'I'm forty-three on February nine.'

'Nationality?'

'Canadian.'

'You were married seven years to Joanne Rynard.'

'Yes.'

'And you and she returned from the Moon – less than two years ago.'

He wasn't using notes for this. He had it all in his head. 'Twenty months,' I said.

'May fifteenth.'

'Yes.'

'Why?'

'Why what?'

'Why did you leave the Moon?'

'We were made redundant,' I said. I didn't understand what he was getting at.

'Why? In your own words.'

'There was nothing left for us to do,' I said.

'What did you do?'

'I'm an architect.'

'And Joanne?'

'A city planner.'

I don't remember how long it went on like this. It seemed like an age. I answered his questions as best I could. There was nothing difficult about them. None of them seemed to have any bearing on Joanne's death. They were vague, personal, as though he was writing an obituary and needed a few extra details.

'How did you feel about coming home?'

'Home?'

'Back to Earth.'

'Like everyone else. Like we'd lost our future.' I was weary now; I was answering with cliches. But cliches seemed to be what he wanted.

'When you came to London, did Joanne make new friends?' I bit my lip. 'Mr Yale?'

'She met other post-humans,' I said.

'Ex-lunar post-humans? Plugs in their heads?'

'I guess so. I never knew them myself.'

Rence smiled. 'Not one?'

'No. Not one. She kept herself to herself.' I was telling the truth.

He sat further back on the desk, his buttocks flexing for purchase on the polished surface. 'What I can't understand was why you two settled in London when you downwelled.'

'We could have gone anywhere, I guess,' I agreed. 'Joanne has family in France. I carry a Canadian passport.'

'But you set up home here. You shared a flat.'

'Yes.'

'Eleven Colville Mews.'

'Yes.'

'We searched it last night.'

'Yes?'

'As part of our investigation. You do own the flat still?'

'Yes.' I thought about it. 'What sort of investigation?'

He looked at me oddly. 'Into how your wife died. What did you think?'

'I mean, was she ...' I couldn't bring myself to finish the sentence.

'Killed?' He wiped his large, hairy hands along the creases of his trousers: a dismissive gesture. 'No, I don't think so.'

'No?'

He looked at me. His eyes were an unnatural green. They shone. 'I think she did it to herself.' I stared at him.

'We've put a new lock on the door.' He dug in the pocket of his waistcoat and handed me a plastic sliver. 'Here, have a key.'

'The flat's stood empty since she left,' I said.

Rence shrugged. 'We didn't have a current address for her, so we searched where we could. Please tell us if you find anything damaged. We'll be happy to compensate you.'

'How could she have done that to herself?'

'Tell me about the flat,' he said.

'What did you mean?'

'You separated – eleven months ago.'

'Yes.'

'And you left London for the Republic. Why there? Why Leeds?'

It was another question for which he already had the answer. He didn't even look like a detective. He had the dwarfish look of someone who hoards secrets, rather than someone who uncovers them.

'Well?'

'It felt dangerous to stay in London,' I said. 'If you've plugs in your head, there are people – pirates – they want a piece of you.'

'You didn't want the temptation,' Rence elaborated. All those networks just waiting to be surfed.' I could see from his eyes that he was enjoying himself. His hand was starting to show.

'Post-humans are commodities to these people,' I said, anticipating the way things were going to go. 'We have a street value. I didn't want to be bought. I didn't want to be used.'

Rence's smile was brutally cynical. It was just the usual prejudice – an unadorned man's suspicion of a metal-head. 'Did you try to persuade Joanne to go with you to Leeds?'

'Yes.'

'Why did she refuse?'

'Our marriage was already dead.'

'So Joanne stayed on at the flat.'

'For a couple of months. She told me she was moving out, but she wouldn't say when or where. I wanted to sell the flat. She never returned my calls.'

'Was she jacking pirated 'ware into her head?'

He had wanted to catch me off guard. But he had been enjoying himself too much. I already knew what he was thinking. 'No,' I said, levelly. 'She would never do that.'

'Really?'

'Pirated accessories had no attraction for her.'

'But on the Moon—'

'She shared minds with AIs. What would she be doing with the crap the pirates deal in?'

Rence nodded at the table, the forensic photographs. Something dropped inside me. 'Maybe she felt she needed a stopgap,' said Rence. 'Something to help her as she adjusted to her old senses.'

'Not that rubbish,' I said, with a confidence I didn't feel.

Rence held my gaze a second. His eyes were very strange. 'No,' he said, and smiled. 'No, not rubbish like that. But something—'

'I don't think so.'

'Right.' He paused, glancing at the monitor to see that the voice recognition software was parsing the interview correctly. 'After you moved to Leeds, did Joanne visit you?'

'No.'

'Did she phone you?'

'No.'

'Did you visit her in London?'

I shook my head.

'Why not?'

'When she left the flat, I didn't know where she'd gone.'

'Were you worried for her?'

'Of course.'

'What did you do?'

'I rang people. I called the hospitals one night. I guess she just wanted to disappear.'

'Did that surprise you?

'A little.' I bit my lip. I felt like an imposter, answering questions about a woman I didn't really know.

'Did her family know where she was?'

'Joanne never called them. They didn't even know we'd separated until I rang them for help finding her.'

Rence leaned back and hit the return.

I felt that I'd failed a test of some kind. I let out a ragged breath.

'Officers Prowse and Salgado will talk with you now.'

So there was more. Of course there was more. I rubbed my eyes.

Rence said, 'There are questions about the flat, about where she lived, about her movements. Friends and acquaintances—'

Dizzily, I wondered why Rence hadn't asked those questions himself.

If Rence noticed my exhaustion, he gave no sign of it. He led me out of the room, down a dingy, linoleum-floored corridor. It wasn't anything like the rest of the building. Institutional brown paint covered the walls. There were pinboards on the walls, but all the notices had yellowed through. Dusty bowls of frosted glass hung from ornate ceiling roses. They glowed with weak, bluish light, like gas-lamps. Rence rolled before me, occupying almost the whole width of the corridor with his wide, syncopated gait. I imagined these corridors were his alone. His lair: all earth tones and dust. The place of secrets.

'When did you go to work for The Hague?' I asked him.

He glanced at me, amused that I'd guessed. 'They seconded me six months ago,' he said.

'Are you a court agent?' I knew all the stories of course, what metal-head didn't? The Court of Human Rights in the Hague were in the business of confiscating contraband accessories, and they weren't over-fussy about how it was done. Hacksaw. Blunt teaspoon ...

'I told you; I'm a policeman. I write them unofficial reports. They can't use their own people since Prince Edgar tore up the EU convention.'

'And you think Joanne was plugging into something.'

He said nothing.

'Don't you?'

'I don't know.'

'I saw her head. Who put the hole there? Forensics?'

'She died of a head wound,' he said.

'And you say she did it herself?'

'When we know more, then I'll let you know.'

'What sort of wound? What did it?

'We don't know.'

'A gunshot?'

'Here we are,' he said. Bright light issued from a frosted glass panel in the door. Stencilled over the glass in black paint was a single word: INTERROGATION. In the hard, glare, Rence's face was as pale as stone.

'She wouldn't kill herself,' I said. 'After you.'

'She wouldn't.' It was the only piece of real information I had to offer, the only thing I was sure of. But he wasn't interested in it. 'I mean it,' I said. 'I know her – knew her.'

He blinked at me. 'I didn't say she killed herself.'

Now he was talking in riddles. I watched him a moment. His eyes glistened like pebbles in a stream. 'What game is this we're playing, inspector? Why do you suspect me?'

'After you,' he said.

I looked through the frosted glass. I saw figures moving against the brightness. They were pacing about like cats.

Something seized me; I couldn't go through with it, not straight away. 'I need the men's,' I said.

'Third on your right.'

I hesitated. I assumed someone would have to accompany me. I was taking my cue from police procedurals; the way the arresting officer escorts a suspect. For a moment we stood, facing each other out. Rence smiled, breaking the spell; blushing hotly, I made for the lavatory.

As soon as I was alone again a great pressure lifted, as though a balloon inside my skull had deflated. Standing at the urinal, I had a few seconds to collect my thoughts.

Coming here, talking to Rence: in a perverse way it had helped to be somewhere impersonal, to be talking. I wondered why my heart was beating so fast. And then it came to me, in an appalling flash: I was excited. Rence's suspicion had flattered me. It had made me feel important. Had Rence known the effect he would have?

I crossed to the sinks and splashed cold water over my face. I looked in the mirror. Something impish and hysterical stirred in me: *I've got the eyes for this*, I thought. *Star-witness-for-the-prosecution eyes, strong and grey. A real Fuck You smile—*

I shied from my reflection, sickened with myself, and fumbled my hands under the dryer. There were too many things going on inside me: too many contrary reactions. The mortuary, the interrogation – they were like explosions in my skull. Bits of my personality were flying off in all directions. I wondered if there would be anything left of me when the barrage ended.

And if there was, if I would like it very much.

# 7

When I woke the next morning I was blind. I couldn't see anything. I lay still a second, waiting for my eyes to adjust to the darkness, and nothing happened. From outside came the shrill cacophony of bicycle bells; radio stations blaring; all the sounds of a sunny morning.

My heart hammered against my chest. Panic soured my mouth. It was EAI. It had to be. How could I have relapsed so soon? I turned wildly, legs tangling in the sheets. I screwed my head round, aching for the light. Out of the blackness came a pencil-thin red line. I flung myself at it, overbalanced and fell out of bed. The line bent and swung before me. I forced myself to be still. I was so disorientated, it took me several seconds to focus properly. A few feet away, a thin bleed of sunlight seeped between thick curtains. Relief flooded me – and embarrassment, that I'd panicked so badly.

I knew now where I was.

I had awoken in the flat Joanne and I had bought when we left the moon. It was lightless because we had hung rubber-backed blackout curtains over the windows. They weren't much use. Towards the end of our life together, nothing could ease Joanne's worsening insomnia. But they blocked the light well enough; enough to have put the fear of God in me just now, at any rate.

I got up off the floor and dragged the rubber curtains back. The overburdened rail shook and threatened to peel away from the wall. The street was strewn with the ragged discards of royal birthday celebrations. The crushed shells of fire crackers poked through the patched and cracked road like colourful weeds. Spent Chinese lanterns hung from every lamp-post. Street-corner bonfires had left black, greasy heaps in the gutters. I opened the window. The air was clogged with the smell of carcasses being delivered to a halal shop across the street. The memories I had of this place weren't good. Maybe I should have stayed at a hotel. But Rence had given me the key, and I'd wanted to check the place for damage.

I hadn't found any sign of the police search. In fact, arriving so late at night, I'd found the flat oddly welcoming. I'd forgotten how much stuff we'd left here: furniture, curtains, crockery, lampshades. There was even my old toothbrush in the mug in the bathroom.

This morning, though, the place had a different ambience. It glared back at me, a hostile jumble of colours and surfaces. It had been our battleground, this bedsitting room. Every clash of stripe and solid colour, velvet and leatherette, brushed chrome and polished teak, spoke volumes about our haemorrhaging marriage.

Joanne's insistence on bright, contrasting colours. Her refusal to buy sets of anything but to make of every object, even down to the teaspoons, something eccentric and individual. The way she had mixed satin and matt paints so that, in the morning light, the walls looked as though gigantic snails had left slime-trails over them.

And then the shoddiness of everything. Her disintegrating patience had made a listing mockery of our cheap, self-assembly furniture. Once I came home and found her slamming nails at random into a set of dresser drawers because she couldn't work out how to tighten the retaining screws.

I remember I watched her and I thought, Not more than a year ago, we were building cities. It was then that I knew it was over. That our great adventure was done for, and so were we.

I pushed through the transparent membrane curtain into the kitchen. The linoleum tiles were cold and the edges had lifted. I kept catching my toes on them. I poured myself a glass of water from the bottle I'd bought the night before. My pale grey tweed jacket lay balled up on the kitchen counter. I shook it straight, and from an outside pocket I dug out a half-empty packet of seaweed crackers. I chomped on them listlessly, and cast around hopelessly for some sign of myself in that garish, makeshift room. Joanne's psychosis was written into its fabric

43

like a palimpsest. I tossed the empty cracker packet aside and headed for the bathroom.

There were a few drops of stale lavender oil in the bottle by the taps. In the scented water, I began at last to relax. Or maybe it was only an echo of yesterday's shock, deadening my sensitivity to things. I picked up the shampoo bottle and unscrewed the cap and felt, beneath my thumb, a thread. The hair was Joanne's: long and black. I picked it off the bottle and, feeling foolish, wound it around my finger. I stared at it a while. So many feelings welled up in me, for a time I lost all sense of myself.

I wondered if it was too late to get a lock of her hair. The idea was so pitiable, so inadequate, I found myself smiling. It was a melancholy smile, the smile of a sad clown. Then it seemed only natural, since I was making a fool of myself in front of who knew what God, to kiss the hair around my finger. Then – hell, not even God was looking – I began to cry.

I told myself, I will remember something good. I told myself that what had passed between Joanne and me had its own reality; that past happinesses remain happy. But at times like this you know it's all bullshit. Memory's a liar or at very best a trick; a convention, like perspective drawing. There's no more a past to life than depth to a canvas. Or if there is, then it's a past of damages. Wounds shape a self as kisses don't: Darwin's bitterest bequest.

I tried to think of something good. Instead, I recalled how one day I'd been in the bath, and Joanne had hammered on the door because she needed a piss. But I didn't let her in. I'd just returned from Ballantyne's clinic. Although my sight was back, I was still shaken up and disorientated, afraid of the noise Joanne made and the quickness of her movements. Everything had been boiling up over the day; now I was too frightened to open the door. She kicked it: it boomed. She hammered on it with her fists: I imagined rock-falls, collisions, bombs landing.

Finally the bolt snapped. She fell into the room. Her mouth was all puffy from some trouble she wouldn't talk about. A fight last night in that pirates' dive in Bow. She squatted over the toilet and pulled down her slacks. There were bruises on her thighs. Big fat thumby bruises. I was afraid to ask how they'd got there. Crouching there, bent forward in furious concentration, her grey-white knickers round her ankles, she appeared at once shockingly alien and shamefully familiar. Huddling at the far end of the bath, my arms wrapped protectively round my shins, I wondered which of us in that moment was the more humiliated.

Next I remembered how, when she was done, she climbed into the bath with me. She held me so close, so tight, so desperately, I thought my back was going to break. While she cried I stroked her hair and face, impotently, too spaced out to understand what she needed from me.

'You just lie there,' she sobbed, helplessly.

'It's the treatments,' I said.

'He's turned you into a fucking worm.'


'Jesus,' I said, when I'd no more tears left to shed. I leaned forward and rinsed my hair and put the top back on the shampoo. I imagined myself spending the day like this, collecting evidences of her. Hairs, stains, odours, bad memories.

'Jesus Christ,' I said again, disgusted not so much with myself as with my predicament. There wasn't anything you could do at a time like this that wasn't either heartless or mawkish. There wasn't a thought you could think that didn't stink of inadequacy. (I was drifting off into generalities again, shock knitting over my wounded thoughts like a scab.)

I pulled out the plug and stepped from the bath. Grabbing a towel I walked dripping into the bedsitting room. It looked warm outside: one of the last days of Indian summer. I picked out some clothes from my overnight bag – a pair of stone-washed black jeans, a dark blue pocket T. Over them I shrugged the pale grey tweed jacket I'd travelled in the day before. I was hungry, but though I'd brought in some food the previous night, I couldn't face cooking here. Instead I went to search out a cheap cafe.

The queue for meat stretched down Westbourne Grove almost to Ladbroke Gardens. An outbreak of CJD in Little Venice had triggered a spate of import bans, and meat was hard to come by. A few doors further on there was a juice bar. I stopped and ordered a sugar cane juice. The sweaty Latin proprietor started up the pulper. The grinding of the huge machine set my teeth on edge. Shoeshine boys and pickpockets sucked up glassfuls of Calpico laced with cocaine and watched me warily. What with my height, the years of lunar gravity and the numbing effect of my illness, I must have looked like some great alien bird: everyone's idea of a moon-man. I drank the juice straight off – there's an undertaste to British cane that they swear has nothing to do with the engineering – and as soon as the sugar rush hit me I moved on.

On Portobello Road the boys and girls were already sprawling on fun-fur throws and dentist's chairs before the plate-glass windows. Half of them were hiding their faces behind magazines, ignoring the potential clientele. Anyone hungry for it this early could bloody well knock. I walked by, embarrassed and disturbed by them, but unable to take my eyes away from the fetish gear strapped tight round their pale, amphetamine-tight flesh. Neglected instincts kicked in. It was the blonde that did it finally: the one tapping her stockinged feet to a Walkman's beat, short white hair like a spiked helmet over her skull, her underwear silken and soft like the insides of a shell...

I stared at the ground, willing the feeling away. But wasn't that always one's first response in the presence of death: to fuck and replenish? Women walked by me carrying pails on their heads: washing water for the unplumbed slums of Notting Hill. Children played in the puddle by the standpipe, scooping the water up, straining the grit out with reddened, chapped fingers. Hostesses called to passers-by to try the coffee shops and leaned into the street to show off their *decolletage*. But they retreated into their doorways when they saw me. The Northern reticence of my Yorkshire neighbours had made me complacent, and I had forgotten the oddness that set me apart from other people, the glamour even. My lunar reserve. My prematurely grey hair cut short so that, if you looked for a second, you could make out the plugs.

Now and again a boy, seeing me for what I was, called out the usual names. 'Beat the Meat!' laughed one, to my face. His smile was open and innocent, as though he expected me to join in the joke.

It still unsettled me, the way we post-humans had become bogeymen. Children feared us. They passed this story round and round, how we'd left our souls behind on the moon. They said our spirits were trapped there, and only the meat had come back. Maybe they saw something we didn't.

I came to a quiet Japanese cafe and slipped inside. I was relieved to be off the street. There was nothing to fear this morning. Nothing was wrong. But I could not help remembering how dangerous this area could get. As I ate it came back to me how, the morning after Joanne and I had moved in, we found a dried-up puddle of blood on the pavement outside our door. Later that day a neighbour told us what had happened. While we were sleeping, someone had hacked his wife's arm off with a machete.

But we'd no money to live anywhere better. Leaving the moon had consumed most of our savings. We could only afford the Notting Hill flat because Joanne's parents helped us out, and that only with difficulty ...

I remembered I hadn't called them. At the same moment, I realised the telephony package at the flat wouldn't work. The lines had been disconnected long ago. The waiter came over to gather my plates and I asked if there was a phone I could use. He gave me an odd look: these days, to be without a mobile phone was next to being vagrant. But there was a wall-unit downstairs, he told me; voice-only, and only if I had a smartcard.

I descended a narrow wooden staircase to the toilets. The telephone was mounted on the wall between the doors, so every time anyone went to relieve themselves I had to perform a shuffling dance to give them room. I pushed my smartcard into the slot at the top of the machine and read off the balance. In the Principality there was no 'international monitor' to screen my call to Lyons, but there was a delay while the line was rerouted to a mobile somewhere. I winced as the units spun.

'Ines.'

'It was Joanne's kid sister.

'Ines. It's Christopher.'

There was a puzzled pause. 'Christopher. Where on earth are you?'

'London.'

'Mum and Dad have been calling Leeds for hours.'

'I'm in London still,' I told her. 'The police asked me to hang on here a few days.'

'Are you in trouble?'

I smiled to myself. Ines: always one for a good conspiracy. 'Of course not.'

'What have they told you?'

'You know about Joanne?'

'Some.'

'I had to identify her yesterday.'

There was a long pause. I didn't like to think how she was taking all this. 'Christopher, for God's sake, where have you been all this time?'

'Leeds,' I said.

'Why didn't you keep in touch?'

'I guess I felt awkward,' I said. 'Things went so badly with Joanne. I wasn't much help to her.'

'I missed you like crazy.'

'I'm sorry,' I said. 'Thanks for nothing.'

'What did they tell you?'

'They said her death was suspicious. What a horrible thing to say. Like they think she's pretending or something.'

'How are the folks?'

'Angry. Oh, it's not just you. They're *always* angry. It's been difficult here. Joanne never called them. They've been fearing the worst for months.'

'About what?'

'They figured Joanne was mixed up in something.'

'What sort of thing?'

'Hell, anything.'

I couldn't help but smile. 'They always did think that.'

'That's my point. And now they're strutting around like they've been proved right.'

'I'm sure that's not what they think,' I said, but my heart sank, because I knew what they were like.

'Have you got a number?' she asked.

'No. The lines are dead at the flat and I don't think I can afford the reconnection fee.'

'Oh Chris you have to! Look, I can wire you some cash if you're short—'

'Don't you dare,' I said. I stared helplessly at the phone's LCD display, the spinning, dwindling figures. 'Let me get off now and I should have enough to get it sorted out. I get my disability cheque on Friday.'

'Don't disappear on me again, Chris.'

'I won't,' I promised her, winding up the call.

'Chris,' she said.

'What?'

'Are you sure you're not in trouble?'

'Of course I'm not. Why?'

'Joanne called me, once or twice. Since you separated. She said you and she were involved in something.'

'Stop,' I snapped. 'What phone are you using?'

'Oh come on, Chris, I'm not totally stupid,' she said.

'Well?'

'It's my boyfriend's mobile.'

I felt a pang of absurd jealousy. 'Okay.'

'Well? What happened?'

I thought about it. I didn't know. I said, 'We weren't involved in anything. At least, not together. I take treatments for epistemic appetite imbalance.'

'Doing that's illegal?'

'The drugs are. They turn the plugs back on. And the man who runs the clinic also pedals pirated accessories.'

'But Joanne had EAI too.'

'Yes,' I said.

'Well?'

'I don't know what she was doing.'

'You can—'

'I said I don't know. I never knew.' I felt the way I'd felt with Rence: that I'd failed Joanne somehow. 'She never told me,' I said.

I waited with my hands clenched for Ines to start picking me apart. But all she said was, 'When you left for Leeds, she got me to send her money.'

'And did you?'

'Of course. In return for knowing where she was. I knew where she moved to once she left your flat. She said never to give the address to anybody. Not my parents. Not you. And then yesterday the police called and they asked me if I knew where she was living.'

'Did you tell them?'

'Mum and Dad were with me. I didn't want them to know I'd spoken to Joanne in secret, so I didn't say.'

'Give me the address. I'll pass it on.'

'Will you?'

'Sure.'

She gave me the address of a flat in Soho. I scribbled it on the back of a receipt. 'Chris?'

'Yeah?'

'It's a terrible thing.' I caught the trace of a sob in her voice. She was trying to hold it in for me.

I wondered how long she'd been crying.

# 8

Afterwards I rang the number Rence had given me. But nobody seemed to know where to send the call. It was so confusing, I wondered for a dizzy moment whether I was hallucinating again. In the end they started playing 'Tie a Yellow Ribbon' at me and I replaced the receiver. I could always try again later.

As I walked home, something Ines said to me began to spin around in my head.

*You and she were involved in something.* What had she meant? On our return to Earth Joanne and I had disagreed so radically, had fallen apart so catastrophically, that we'd hardly been 'involved' at all.

I knew that Joanne had looked for something to soothe her EAI. Obviously: hadn't we all? But she'd never have chosen the sort of treatments I'd picked. She hated them; hated me for subjecting myself to them. 'It's like living with a corpse,' she screamed at me once. But I was blind and muffled, and until I touched her face I didn't realise she was crying.

I stopped and looked at the address again. It wasn't a part of town I knew well. I wondered what had drawn her to it. I slipped the paper back into my pocket. I noticed I'd overshot my turning; I was halfway to Notting Hill Gate. I made to go back but the thought of confronting the flat made me hesitate. What was I going back there for? What was there for me? Creaking floorboards, dripping taps, shouts from the street—

I decided to hand Joanne's address to Rence in person. If he wasn't around I could leave it at the desk. At least I would get to talk to someone, if only the receptionist. I walked as far as the main street and boarded an east-bound tram.

I got off the tram at Victoria Gate and entered Hyde Park through a wooden kissing gate. Belgrave Square lay to the south of the park, and it was quicker for me to cross it on foot than go to the bother of changing lines.

A metalled path contained by chicken wire fences ran beside the Serpentine. The fences were grown over with brambles and dog rose. Beyond the path, rising gently from the water, lay allotments: a furious cat's cradle of pasted and raked surfaces sprouting artichokes and gooseberries and stunted fruit trees. Facades of netting and bamboo and stretches of tilled earth crisscrossed each other, their perspectives flattened by the smoky autumn light.

The path grew narrow and muddy, thick with nettles and dead grass. To my right the lake reflected the colourless sky in

51

a white yawn. There was a restaurant on the other side of the water, and a shady terrace. There was even a bridge that might have led me there; but it had fallen in long ago. Boys dived from its concrete stubs and climbed back up canting slabs of tarmac, shivering and flapping their arms. Little rowboats – hired from a kiosk near the restaurant – gave the submerged wreckage a wide berth. I walked up the stump of the bridge to where the concrete had sheered off. Blocks of it hung from bent and rusted iron rods, the way leaf-litter clings to a spider's web. The water below was stagnant, covered with a hectic green growth: in the shady mud beneath the pile, a mass of pink trumpet-shaped flowers threw off a strange, unseasonal scent. I paused a moment, studying their long serrated, simple leaves, but I did not recognise them.

A few yards further on the tarmac path reasserted itself, leading me straight to Hyde Park Corner. From here, Joanne's flat wasn't much further to walk than Police headquarters. I looked at my watch. It was 10:45. Rence needed the address. I looked for a telephone kiosk. But this was London, not Yorkshire, and public booths were unnecessary; nearly everybody had a phone of their own.

The Police building then: I wondered how to cross the many conflicting lanes of traffic. I studied an underpass map. There was no direct route. The quickest way across led me out of my way at first, on to Piccadilly – and towards Joanne's flat.

I entered the warren of underpasses and came up in the middle of a line of tram stops. There were dozens of trams and all of them went at least as far as Piccadilly Circus. On an impulse, I boarded the first one I came to. We pulled out into the traffic. There were bound to be phones near the Circus. I'd call Rence from there.

But there weren't. And I was so close to Joanne's flat now, visiting it wouldn't take more than ten minutes.

I walked up Shaftesbury Avenue, between ruins so overgrown, they seemed ancient and mysterious, benevolent as the sleep-drugged castles of a fairy tale. And when I turned off Shaftesbury Avenue into Windmill Street, it was as though

I'd somehow crossed back into Yorkshire: the cobbled, horse-drawn idylls of Settle or Penistone. The lane, dark with ivy, rambler roses and wisteria, was treacherous underfoot. I picked my way carefully through a darkness lidded by matted clouds of raspberry and bramble.

I turned right, dog-legging east down Brewer Street and Bridle Lane. Joanne's fortress-like condominium overhung Beak Street, bristling with derelict antennae and CCTV cameras like the gateway to a Lilliputian police state. Beyond it, however, lay only more of the same: defunct, dog-rose-strangled industrial buildings subdivided into garrets and studios; cafes for anarchists; cafes for drag artists; cafes for prostitutes and students and failed poets.

There was a keypad and a camera on the wall beside the entrance. I pressed the Trades button on the off chance, but it didn't release the lock. Besides, I hadn't the time to hang around. I looked at my watch.

It was noon. I gave a guilty start, seeing how late it was. I waited a moment by the door, thinking now that I'd pressed a button, I should wait in case someone showed. A steady throbbing penetrated my forehead, too low and soft to be a sound. I guessed it must be a generator beneath the building. The sensation reminded me unpleasantly of my illness. I stood away from the door.

I was thirsty. There was a newsagent's built into the ground floor of the block. A sheet of paper taped to the door bore a legend in magic marker: 'No DOGS In This Shop'. A plea, I wondered? A boast? I went in and bought a can of water. I walked past the lobby and glanced in again. There was still no one about.

I looked at my watch. 12:45. There was no point hanging on longer. I'd finish my water and leave.

There were roadworks opposite the entrance. A stack of yellow plastic pipes, held together in a frame of wooden batons, took up most of the pavement. I drained the can and sat on the pipes, watching the entrance. It wasn't much past 1.00 but the whole area seemed deserted.

About twenty minutes later a woman carrying an empty shopping bag opened the front door. I hurried across the road. As she stepped into the street I slipped in behind her, grabbed the door before it shut and went inside.

The vestibule, lit by a handful of bare forty-watt bulbs, was tiled with grey flecked linoleum. The lift was out of order. I climbed two flights of stairs and pushed open the fire door. The hallway echoed oddly to my footsteps.

Number 21. A small and withered yucca leaned drunkenly out of a plastic pot on bricks by the door.

I knocked. There was no reply. I glanced around, then knelt and felt under the plant-pot, between the bricks. My fingers found the plastic oblong, and I sighed: I knew so much about her. What she ate and what she liked. What she had no time for, and all the silly things that made her cry. How to please her, to excite her; how to lose her sympathy, and get it back again. Time had gone by – a year – since I'd lived with her. Longer, since we were happy. Yet I'd held on to all this knowledge. All this wisdom. Why? Had I thought secretly – unconsciously, even – that I might get her back? Was I that much of a fantasist?

The key was dusty and scratched and it took three swipes to unlock the door. As I pushed it open, something inside rustled, like dead leaves in a draught. A couple of feet back from the door, a screen made from black plastic bin-liners, stuck together with brown parcel tape, hung from the ceiling, blocking my view. I pushed through it. A few feet further on there was another screen. The bin-liners formed a cell. A bare bulb beyond the further screen burned brownly through the thin plastic, filling the enclosure with light the colour of old blood.

There were footsteps behind me. I turned. A shadow appeared behind the vestibule fire door. I swung the front door quickly shut behind me, and waited. More footsteps; the click and bleep of another door opening; the snap of the latch; silence.

I turned around, facing into the hall.

No sounds came from the rooms beyond. But I could feel a presence. A tension in the air, like the high-pitched whistle of a cathode ray tube.

The whole flat had been partitioned. Black plastic screens divided each room into a series of alcoves. Wires trailed over the floor, like strings spooled out through a tawdry maze by nervous explorers. At the end of the hall, the living room gave off a heady, solvent heat, and the bin-liner screens swayed to and fro in a strong current of toasted air. The room gave off a confused glow: bright splashes of colour against a ground of static and video blue.

I edged my way in.

Every cell had its machines. Old-fashioned terminals, toy computers, portables, Watchmen. Every video display was tuned to a different channel. There were programmes about nature. About life on the Moon. Educational programmes about biology and earth sciences. Ante-natal videos. Land-sat footage. TV phosphorescence lit the rooms from below, turning the makeshift plastic curtains into tongues of grey fire.

The cells differed subtly in size and shape; each was the site of some unique ritual. I entered one and kicked over a bottle of red wine. The stench of vinegar rose in the air.

A pile of empty bottles hid the picture playing on a large flat-screen display. I think it was tuned to a nature programme. Something about soldier ants. Bright primary colours leapt from the screen through the distorting bottles, losing their qualities the deeper they went, becoming bit by bit the same greens and browns as the bottles themselves.

The next cell had a cotton pallet. There was a sheet screwed up into a ball at one end, a foam pillow without a cover at the other. About twenty Watchmen were lined up along the side of the pallet, each plugged into its own transformer. The air here was scorching, and so dry I could hardly breathe. Each screen was running a different program. Self-evolving animated forms bloomed and swirled: brave stirrings of virtual life.

I couldn't make sense of what I was seeing. My head pounded. The toasted air crackled in my throat.

With these screens, had Joanne somehow tried to simulate her lunar state of mind? I looked around me, seeing the place with new eyes. If she had meant it to echo the multisensate, endlessly fertile mind-state we had shared on the moon, then she'd failed. This was nothing but a cheap and cruel parody.

I crossed from one cell to another, hunting for some sign of the woman I knew. But there was nothing of her here. No books, no plants, no trinkets. Where were her clothes?

The flat had absorbed her.

I went into the bathroom. The air smelled strongly of bleach and air freshener. The walls were dark blue. There were dribbles and smears everywhere, as though the paint had been applied with a rag. The bath surround was piled with plastic sandwich and doughnut cartons.

There was a cup full of mould on the cistern and a condom stuck to the side of the toilet pan. I opened the bathroom cabinet. It was crammed with make-up. It fell out onto me: bottles, pads, compacts, brushes, liners, pencils. I gathered them up, pushed them back into the cabinet and shut the door on them.

There was nothing here I recognised: no trace of the woman I loved. This wasn't a home, it was a lair. There was something primal about it; something childish and undeveloped.

I bent down, picked up a compact I'd missed, opened the bathroom cabinet again, threw it in and closed the door. Something caught my eye.

I opened the cabinet a third time, reached in, and pulled out a plasticated card. Within the blister wrapping lay three hypodermic syringes, each containing about 10 CCs of ruby-red liquid. Along each barrel there was a word: JEWEL.

I swept the makeup out of the cabinet and found four loose syringes behind a row of brightly coloured nail varnishes. I examined the barrels. JEWEL: no other marking. They came with needles ready-attached. Around each guard cap was a plastic sheath that read 'Sterile Until Broken'.

I had no idea what they were.

I pocketed the loose barrels and put the blister pack back in the cabinet. I stuffed the make-up over it and shut the door.

The kitchen was nothing more than a waste heap. Chip papers translucent with fat and Styrofoam cartons crusted with shreds of brown lettuce lay over the floor.

Near the door there was a red plastic bin. I took off the lid. A heady, gorgeous scent enveloped me. Cinnamon, oranges. Inside the bin were rags, spotted with brownish blood and slimed with a clear lubricant. I dug out a cleanish rag, wrapped it round the loose hypodermics and jammed the bundle into the breast pocket of my T-shirt.

There was no liner in the bin, and strange fern-like designs had etched away at the plastic, leaving a golden trace. The gold – it looked like spray paint – had dribbled down the outside of the bin and formed little puddles near my feet. I took hold of the bin, meaning to upturn its contents onto the floor, but it wouldn't budge.

The bin was rooted to the floor.

I emptied it out by hand.

At the bottom I found another syringe. The barrel was empty, and the spike was flecked with blood.

Kicking aside cartons and papers, I crossed quickly to the sink unit. There was some liquid scourer in the cupboard beneath the sink and I rubbed a palm-full of the stuff into my hands, then rinsed them off under the hot tap.

The bedroom was no different to the living room. All the natural arrangements of a home, all its usual uses, were done away with here. I came to an enclave larger than the rest, the floor piled with quilts and blankets. There was another TV, tuned to static, in front of the makeshift bed. Behind it there was a pile of clothing. I toed through it, and came upon a pair of man's underpants. In the blue static light, the quilts were spotted with dark stains. Wine, or blood? I couldn't tell.

I sank onto the bed and stared sightlessly at the flickering sheets.

This isn't a home, it's a hollow, I thought. A place to sicken in.

I was crying again. Whispering to whatever shred of her spirit still lingered here. I crossed to the window and parted the curtains. The mass of roofs below me seemed made up entirely of truncated shapes, roofs divided at the apex, bare eaveless walls, unfinished ornaments. Looking at them was like looking through a kaleidoscope: the whole city seemed fractured and disordered. *I would have built you palaces!*

Behind me, the front door clicked and swung open.

# 9

Heavy footfalls sounded on the thin carpet. Someone had entered the apartment.

I froze. My heart hammered in my head. I forgot to breathe. I was standing at the window. Right in front of it. I was framed in its light.

I ducked down behind the bed. A figure passed by the bedroom doorway. I glimpsed men's shoes. The soles were heavy, orthopaedic maybe.

The footsteps receded towards the living room. I heard the rustle of the plastic screens as the man edged from one dismal cell to another. I got to my feet and made slowly for the hall. I could hear the pile of the bedroom carpet, crushing under my shoes. I could hear the blood in my face. The air seemed to sing. I got to the door and glanced out. A black plastic sheet shivered and spasmed in an updraft of machine-heated air, a foot or two from my face: I couldn't see beyond it. I heard movement in the living room. The clatter of toppled machinery. I measured the distance to the front door. The treatments had left me unsteady on my feet: I couldn't just rush the door and hope to outrun whoever had broken in. Footsteps approached me again. I leaned back into the bedroom. They turned away; I heard the tap and slide of shoe leather against linoleum. The man had entered the kitchen. Pans clattered to the floor. I stepped out into the hall and edged towards the front door. I turned the handle. The mechanism was deadlocked.

It beeped at me.

I tore at the handle.

I heard footsteps behind me.

I panicked, tugged uselessly at the lock.

I felt myself lifted into the air. My head collided with the door. I flailed my arms. Heavy hands turned me round. I struck out blindly. A meaty palm enveloped my face and drove my head into the door, all the way through the door, into a dark cold place I could not name.

I opened my eyes and lay still a long time. My head felt like its insides had been smoked dry. I sat up and my brain clanged against the walls of my skull like the clapper of a bell. I blinked, lids scraping and singing across my eyes like chalk on a blackboard.

I stood up. Something was missing. A weight. I felt in the pocket of my jacket. The hypos were missing.

*Jewel* ...

Dumbly, I looked around the floor. Of course they weren't there. But the rag was. I picked it up off the floor and absently, not thinking straight, I dabbed it to the back of my head.

It felt like I was pouring boiling water over my scalp. But when I whipped my hand away, and looked at the cloth, the only blood on it was dry and brown: Joanne's. Cold comfort: I wasn't bleeding.

I went into the bathroom. I shoved the cloth into my jacket pocket and squeezed water over the back of my head with a flannel. When I turned from the sink I saw that the cabinet door was open. There was make-up all over the floor. I toed through it, and I looked inside the cabinet. The blister pack was missing. Whoever it was had attacked me, he had taken all the hypos he could find.

It was about then that I noticed the smell. Something caramelised and sickly, like oranges thrown onto a bonfire. I remembered the bin in the kitchen. The empty barrel at the bottom of the trash. I stepped out into the hall.

From the kitchen there was a sound like a woman's sigh. For a heart-stopping second I thought it was Joanne.

Fire burst like dam-water from the kitchen. It spilled along the hall and rippled over the ceiling like a wave. I hadn't even time to close my eyes before it curled around my feet. It shot up me, wrapped me in its helix, made a torch of me – and vanished. Flames rolled off me and back along the floor into the kitchen with a motion so smooth, they might have been on wires. The pain came. I drew in breath to scream, and the caramelised smell stuck in my throat like phlegm. Glutinous spittle dribbled down my chin.

Smoke roiled out of the kitchen like stinking fingers. I got down on all fours and crawled down the hall towards the front door. A ball of black smoke rolled over me and stuck its molten shoots in my eyes. I gasped with the pain and something viscous and lethal coated my throat and lungs. I retched and gasped and retched again. My vision screwed itself into a ball, pinpoint small, and I felt myself losing consciousness. Some animal part of me took control and the next thing I knew I was in the lobby.

The explosion was so loud I didn't hear it. I felt myself jelly in the force of the blast, and it seemed once again that I was falling, through the floor, back into the welcoming darkness.

But something drew me back. That good fairy. That tormentor who wouldn't let me sleep. My senses came back to me in wave after wave of vomiting fits.

There was nobody on the landing. The door to Joanne's apartment had been blown off its hinges. I looked around the foyer for it and I couldn't see it anywhere. How can a door just vanish? Through the torn doorway I saw something shining. Flame or TV light? I couldn't tell. The air in the lobby was deteriorating fast. I edged away from the doorway, back towards the stairwell. I leaned against the wall and pushed myself onto my feet. A wall of smoke pulsed in and out of the door of Joanne's apartment like a diseased lung.

The sucking sound came back, much louder now. The air drew away from me. I took in a lungful of nothing. Decompression dug fingers behind my eyes and pulled. I leaned and fell against the fire door and it swung out beneath me.

The sucking stopped.

I crawled forward over the landing. The door closed on my ankles.

The lung exhaled. A white fist punched out the toughened glass in the fire door. A bit of the glass fell in my mouth. The door snapped back like the jaws of a mousetrap, cracking against the wall. The safety hinge snapped and twanged. Threads of flame glanced past me. I tried to stand. I felt a warmth around my ankles. I looked down. My feet were on fire. In a single, instinctive convulsion, I kicked off my trainers.

I must have been concussed because I didn't even try to leave the landing. I just leant there against the wall, rubbing my feet, checking for blisters, until at last the firemen came. I grinned at them, stupidly. They were masked. I couldn't see their faces. I wondered if they were imaginary. Like the girl in Long Lover.

Someone grabbed me by the collar of my jacket. I started laughing. He dragged me down the stairs. I tried to help him. I tried to find my feet, but my legs weren't working. He propelled me through the lobby, through the doorway, out into the street. Faces wobbled past me. Mouths moved silently. It was as though I was looking out through the glass side of an aquarium. I fell to my knees in the middle of the road and retched up greyish mucus. Gentler hands took hold of me and led me across the street to the stack of yellow plastic pipes. Someone coaxed me into a squatting position on the kerb and stuck my head between my legs. I sucked in air. My lungs were full of ice, spiked with grit. My teeth started chattering and I could feel cold blood running up the veins in my hands. There was something digging into my left thigh. I shifted about uncomfortably, and when that didn't help I edged a clumsy hand into my trouser pocket.

My fingertips met something hard. I hesitated, heart beating, then reached further in and, like a conjuror surprised by his own magic, I drew out four hypodermics. I stared at them. Their unbroken seals. JEWEL on each barrel. The barrels were unbroken; they must have been plastic.

Surprise robbed me of the urge to vomit. Numbly, I reached

into my jacket and drew out the blood-spattered cloth. Once again I wrapped it carefully round the hypodermics.

People were streaming out of the apartment block. Mothers and babies; old men, pushed from side to side by the press of excited, grinning children; a chinaman in a mandarin-collared pinstripe suit, hiding his face with his hand. Flames licked the sills of the apartment windows. It was raining soot: a thin particulate that tickled my scoured throat.

Sounds started edging back into my head. The murmurs of the crowd. Sirens—

A black Jaguar, blue lights flashing behind its radiator grille, turned the corner into Beak Street. I tightened the cloth round the hypos and pushed them deep inside one of the pipes. The car pulled to a stop behind the furthest fire tender. The windscreen reflected the dirty sky, hiding the driver from view. Then another tender eased past, its high sides shielding the Jaguar for a second, and I saw Rence talking into a portable phone.

He was looking straight at me.

# 2
# ANTS

# 10

The moon.
Thinking back to that time, I feel as though I am examining someone else's life entirely.

Like most people, I was drawn there by the advertisements. These appeared in the sort of urbane style magazine you might find anywhere where there's money or the promise of it: in the lobby of a Vietnamese restaurant in Melbourne; folded back on itself underneath a copy of *Vogue* in an orthodontist's waiting room in Pnom Penh; or abandoned beneath the buffet table of a transcontinental train running between Moscow and Beijing.

The text of these advertisements combined offers of varied government employment with tourist-company hyperbole, as if to suggest that in a world already mapped, portioned out and colonised by artificial intelligences, you might yet stumble upon a lost city whose timid, butterfly-winged denizens would with their clumsy, complicated dances, impart to you the secrets of insect millennia.

Such promises, stripped of their sophisticated setting, were a rather puerile sort of wish-fulfilment. Most of us spent our time on the Moon convinced that, should the moon's foreignness become in any way uncomfortable or oppressive, it could somehow be dismissed: drowned in the smell of familiar fast food, or shattered by the latest Gamelan beat spilling from the door of a neon-lit bar.

Little reference was made to the machines they would put in our heads, perhaps because, when the adverts were drawn up, the machines did not yet exist.

All new forms of life develop quickly. Machines, because they can go back and correct their evolutionary mistakes, develop blindingly fast. Every year, machines more than double their cognitive complexity. When this process began, those adding machines and microchip toasters were so simple, their evolution was barely noticed. That, of course, is the beauty of geometric progression: blink once, and everything has changed in an instant.

When our machines overtook us, too complex and efficient for us to control, they did it so fast and so smoothly and so *usefully,* only a fool or a prophet would have dared complain.

After all, machines have done little more than digitise those parts of our lives that we've lost control of already. You don't need a machine to run an unpredictable stock market – or, for that matter, to orchestrate an unavoidable war. Machines just put a convenient box around the mathematics that were there causing the problem in the first place.

People – like the molecules of water swirling out of a tap – are a big-number problem, and taking away the calculator doesn't take away the maths.

For a while there, machines did actually give us more control. They were our way of grasping the big-number problems of our existence.

The trouble was, they proliferated so fast, they started generating big-number problems of their own. The first symptoms of this were suitably primitive: early networks, plagued by viruses. Simple forms of digital life, preying on the more complex forms, forcing them to develop sophisticated defences, or, more radically, to ingest and make use of their attackers' code.

The later symptoms were more complex. Programs, swimming around the early global networks, began to explore different evolutionary strategies. They fed off each other, developing and shattering alliances, in much the way proto-cellular organisms thrashed out the first, essential treaties that led to invertebrate life.

Only machines, of course, did it much, much faster.

Suddenly, with such advanced and constantly improving machines to hand, all sorts of projects became viable. All sorts of adventures beckoned.

The moon was one of them.

# 11

New senses take time to work properly – ask any baby – and I had been on the moon for nearly a month before I got the first, synaesthetic hints of them. First, as was usual, I became telepathic.

My first architectural assignment had come up in Eddington, on the farside, and I had decided to travel there overland. The journey took four days. There were six of us on that journey, including the capcom, rolling about in the pioneer-level discomfort of a twelve-wheeler portable transfer habitat.

I could have covered the journey in about an hour by dart. But I was going stir-crazy. The last thing I needed was to be buzzed seamlessly from one notional location to another in a windowless tin-can.

Since my arrival, extreme sunspot activity had kept us all underground. And even when it became safe to topside, there was nowhere for me to go. Everyone else headed to the airlocks, but that wasn't any use to me: I was months away from earning even the most junior of EVA licences.

At least, travelling by PTH, I could look out of the windows.

I was the baby of the party. The other passengers were veterans, here to take advantage of our leisurely schedule. Right now, I was alone with the capcom – a pre-Apolloco retiree who could remember the days of the government stations. The other passengers had EVA'd, walking out of sight behind a complex of scree slopes and partial structures marring the outskirts of Eddington.

'They found a bone near here,' he said.

'Yes?'

'At the edge of this sea.'

'Where?'

'Markov. Ten klicks out. Sixty west, twenty north. A human calcaneum.'

'What?'

'It's the bone in your heel.'

I watched his face, reflected in the port glass. It gave nothing away. I said, 'Maybe when the *Sally Ride*—'

Already he was shaking his head. 'No scorching,' he said. 'No flesh. No impact mark, either. Covered by dust.'

'They date it?' I asked, giving way to fancy.

He grunted. 'After how much solar rad?'

I shrugged, and turned back to the window.

Nothing obvious, like a skull, or a femur. A *calcaneum*. A nice touch, if you were inclined towards that kind of here-be-dragons bullshit.

But as a story it was an anachronism even before its teller opened his mouth. There would never be an audience for it. No generation of wide-eyed newcomers or frightened children to entrance, not this time. No sooner did the capcom and his kind make up their first crude mythologies of the place, than they were blown aside by the convenient social geometries of the cities, the bright certainties of evenings at the multiplex, the quartz-accurate rhythm of railways and radio schedules.

There would be no time, this time, for fireside stories; no time to shape, out of old men's malign leavings, a national identity. Not one generation would pass before the myth-free moon was all mapped, mined and mailed to abstraction.

There was something pitiable about the capcom and his prehistoric stories. 'And a skull atop the Montes Rook,' he said, to himself. Out the window I saw them emerge, one by one, stepping clumsily in heavy silver suits – the kind that let you EVA without prebreathes or equalisation.

There was no telling them apart of course – all you could do was count them back. Spill-cones towered above them, giant hills raised by mechanical termites. Hardened shelters, perhaps; or deep shafts for x-ray telescopes. Entrance points, maybe, for the Honeycomb – that vast catacomb, sphere within sphere, that would one day riddle the moon with subterranean settlers, even down to the mantle. Or big, simple mistakes, perhaps: the fist-sized robot workers, losing contact with the mother-swarm, erecting in their loneliness and loss a temple to themselves. It happened at the outskirts of most places, and it all got bulldozed away eventually.

Above and behind them, inseparable from their scaffolding, rose the latticed skeletons of shipbuilding yards. Slender metal probosci hung poised over their open roofs ready to pluck out the meat within. So, one day, they would. They were slingshots, built to toss prefabricated sections of spacecraft, not only out of the shipyards, but out of orbit entirely, hurling them – within a few tens of metres – to fabrication yards hanging in Lagrange orbits above the Earth.

Quite what the receiving yards did with all that momentum I wasn't sure. I was still finding it hard to operate low-gravity lavatories. Each day left me feeling that my learning curve was bending back over me like a breaker.

Finally, above and behind the shipyards, towered the walls of the Eddington crater. Railways swung like luminous ribbons along the crumbling, precipitate walls. Settlements were fantastical pinpricks of light, issuing from crude holes in the regolith. The sky glittered and swirled with scraps of silver as airborne construction robots – some no bigger than a fist – flocked and swooped over the city, hunting for something to repair.

The pressure in the cabin dropped suddenly, taking me by surprise. The EVA party had already returned.

To save resources, the PTH used the cabin atmosphere to pressurise the airlock. I held my nose and blew to get the hammering out of my ears. The hatch slid open and a scant, inrushing draught whispered through the cabin.

I left the observation bubble and jumped the stairs to the lobby. Louisa was already out, wiping down her neck and shoulders with a towel. I said hello and her schizophrenic-bright eyes skittered from one side of my face to the other. Warabe followed: a scholarship visitor barely out of his teens; he had the team's videocam slung over a bare shoulder.

'How was it?' I said, as eager as a puppy and about as subtle. Warabe paused to make small-talk while Louisa, self-absorbed as ever, headed for a needle shower in the rear nacelle.

Bradley Hight and Joanne Rynard were the last to enter. I couldn't decide whether they were an item or not. There was a constant, unspoken communication between them – although, right then, I had little idea how literally that metaphor could be realised.

Bradley shucked off his neoprene balaclava and for a moment his long blond hair fanned out like a sunburst.

Joanne patted his hair down and smiled at me. 'Did Willis tell you any good stories ?' The capcom must surely have been within earshot, but she didn't pay it any mind.

Bradley took Joanne's hand in his own and swung it forward and back, playfully. He was like a big kid.

I said, 'He remembers the government stations.'

Joanne shrugged and headed off to join Louisa in the shower. Bradley patted her bottom as she went.

There was an easy sexuality between these four. At first I put it down to the enforced intimacy of the PTH, but I didn't see the capcom wandering around in his underpants.

It was a peer-group thing: it wasn't extended to me, and if it had been, I don't like to think what sort of a fool I'd have made of myself. Louisa and Joanne had the power to provoke – Louisa, strangely absent, jerking her body this way and that in great sprawling gestures; Joanne with her intense silences and balletic self-importance. The men's childishness nettled me, though – Warabe with his preppy smile; Bradley with his surf-Nazi taste in T-shirts.

'What's Six point-three when it's at home?' I asked him over supper. Even Bradley had the decency to colour up about that one: a nasty lime-green sleeveless number, too tight across his overdeveloped chest to be a purchasing error.

'6.3kPa,' it read, in big bold white letters.

'It's the atmospheric pressure at which water evaporates at body temperature.' This from Louisa, without a trace of irony.

Bradley tried making light of it, but there was so much testosterone coming off him you could have bottled it and stuck it in beef cattle.

'What's your lowest?' I asked him. The lower the pressure in your suit, the more flexible your suit can be, the more you can do. Not that any suit will take you lower than twenty-four, so that was a particularly asinine slogan Bradley was wearing – like a crag climber sporting the words 'Volcano Interior' on his chalk bag.

'Twenty-five kPa,' Bradley said, on cue. 'Jesus, my back hurts.'

Whether that was to get Joanne a-rubbing or to make me feel bad, I wasn't sure.

It was because of me they'd had to wear such clumsy gear. I hadn't been through any kind of EVA training yet, so the PTH was being kept at normal pressure. Which meant that Hight and his friends didn't have the chance to depressurise sufficiently to wear lightweight suits for their moonwalks. Not unless they wanted to spend their whole trip in the airlock pre-breathing pure oxygen.

'What made you choose overland anyway?' Bradley said, not over-friendly.

I blanded him out with a smile.


I slept no more that night than I had slept on any night since arriving on the Moon. It went deeper than the fact of living on the PTH. I had no home yet, no stable life, no regular job; I was living on my nerves. Plus I didn't need so much sleep here anyway: weak gravity and no diurnal cycle saw to that.

And there were the dreams, of course. We were warned about the dreams.

A handful of accessories were already on-line inside my head. The grey clay draughting environment where I designed my buildings was already familiar to me. In an eyeblink, I could take myself there. And retrieving information from the digital realm of webs and data cores was a mere secade of the eyeballs away.

71

The more complex devices they'd stuffed in my skull – the new sensoria and mental gifts – were fitful, slow to stir; but they were there. Some of the simpler domestic electrical devices – lights, TV, microwave – were already responding, albeit fitfully, to my thoughts.

It was as though my mind, after a lifetime suspended in the tight, amniotic container of my skull, had found itself suddenly birthed and delivered, adult and entire, into a large, well-furnished, utterly alien room.

No, not a room. A mansion, with many floors, and many rooms, and many of them locked. By day my mind explored the rooms one by one, orderly and unafraid. And with each day, more doors would open to its touch, more lights respond to the flick of a switch. Aware of its guest, the mansion was coming alive.

At night, my mind lay curled up on itself, and listened. Listened to the creaking of distant stairs, the clanking of steam freshly raised in old pipes; twigs brushing against high windows. Keys jangling. Doors unlocking. Doors *opening*. Voices.

Sometimes I dreamed I was flying through my workspace, raising cities from the sterile grey. Road after road, underpass and flyover, alley and cul-de-sac, fleur-de-lis interchange, pedestrian walkway, corridor after corridor, door after door and every one of them locked, always locked. Locked so I couldn't pass through, couldn't lose myself, but could only fly on, creating the townscape before me, laying down my own track.

And it came to me then that I was no longer flying. I was running. I was running away. Running from the sounds behind me. The jangle of keys, the squeak of hinges. Fists beating on locked doors and the doors opening. *Voices ...*

I heard myself cry out, and woke, heart hammering.

I found myself swaddled in a soft, spongiform cradle.

I sat up. Plastic curtains rippled and creaked, bare inches in front of my face. Kevlar restraints eased me gently back into my cradle.

I remembered: the PTH. My last night on board, this – and at this rate no more restful than my first.

In the bottom left of my visual field the draughting suite icon – a daft plasticine man – waved and smiled.

I raised my eyebrows at him.

He stepped obediently forward, reached up to my eyeballs and tore aside the view as though it were a curtain.

I had expected to be confronted with a plastic rendition of my recent nightmare. But, as I hovered above my design suite, I saw with relief that the grey plane was without feature.

The suite was learning, finally, to ignore my dreams. I balled the grey plane and tossed it into the lower left corner of my visual field.

Regular vision returned, the sleeping cell rebuilding itself around me. Colour came last – the liquid blue of the nightlights out in the corridor.

I glanced at the straps and willed them to release me. They wound back into the spongy walls. I pushed the curtains aside. The plastic felt greasy on my palms.

Out in the corridor, behind other curtains, in cells full of blue light, the other sleepers turned and curled fitfully, like wasp larvae. I remembered the sight of glittering insects over Eddington; the way they swarmed. I wondered if any of them were human.

On my way to the head, I saw that one of the curtains was drawn back, and the sac within was empty.

The lavatory fan was too big and too noisy for a high pressure environment like this. The sound carried in the thick air like the backwash of a helicopter. God knows how the others slept, but they did. All except one: the sac nearest the head was still empty.

I pulled myself hand over hand into the observation cabin.

He was looking out the forward porthole, his bare foot resting on the chrome lip, his head and trunk hidden by the back of the capcom's chair.

I stepped up to him, murmuring some greeting.

Warabe Utenabe crossed his hands behind his head and looked at me. He was naked. In the green radar light, the tip of his erection glistened like the head of a finely turned chess piece.

He blinked at me. Something chittered behind my eyes. The cluttering diminished; in a few seconds it came back. The rhythm cycled over and over, like radio static, like waves.

'Warabe?'

A line of spittle slid from the corner of his mouth. It hung from his chin a moment, and when it fell, pooling in the hair around his nipple, a sharp localised pain raked my head. It felt like I'd been shot.

I went back to bed. I hesitated a second, before drawing the screens, watching the others. Behind their waxy curtains, it was impossible to make them out, or their movements, with any clarity.

They seemed to be pulsing.

In bed, I slipped off my pants, balled them up and stowed them in the locker above my head. There was ejaculate on my hands.

# 12

Amenities came raw in Eddington, unglossed and unvaried. Large, flat-roofed supermarkets dominated every street. Their glass frontages, obscured by crude handwritten adverts on fluorescent cards, reflected the facets of the Fuller domes in tones of acid green and migraine pink.

Between them, squeezed into the interstices of loading bays and tram platforms, a handful of family businesses dealt shoddily in the basic appetites. Organa Foods heated up ready meals in industrial-size microwave ovens for departing patrons of the Pussy Cat Erotic Bar; in Fat Larry's Adult Diner, squeezing between the plate glass and the wagon-wheel rood screen, permed waitresses twisted their stained white aprons around their fingers and stared, blank-eyed, at the vegetable stalls outside Natura Grains, waiting for something to happen.

Here, under the absent lunar sky, under the unyielding pressure of the Fuller domes, all fleshly pleasures wilted, requiring constant, ersatz stimulation.

'It's a dump,' I said, more surprised than disappointed.

'Even women visit the brothels here,' said Joanne: an irony I couldn't unpick.

We came to a church. It was made of boulders smoothed off by laser and set in thick slabs of mortar, like something a child makes out of beads and plasticine. It looked like a full-scale edition of those Wade models they sell in jeweller's shops in limited editions of a billion. Where the apse should have been, a fast food concession flooded the small cobbled square with neon: 'Pizzeria Aghar', in fly-killer blue.

'Hungry?' she asked me.

'Suddenly, no.'

She laughed. She said, 'I know a place.'

She came to Eddington every month or so to buy the latest gear for her work. Backstreet fabricators sold micromanipulators at sixty dollars a gramme, solar cells the size of a fly's wing, self-reproducing mouthparts that chewed regolith down to the atom, making metal and glass and helium 3.

She used the parts to construct her own builder robots, and bred them under strict quarantine in a licensed cleanlab many klicks from the Concessions. The structures her robots made had the simplicity and elegance of fractal sculptures: hornets' nests, spiders' webs, vegetable forms. She said one day they'd make cities, those insects of hers. I was new to it all: I didn't know whether to believe her.

She took me to a cellar bar where the waitresses wore clothes and the diners had smooth faces, their skin not yet ravaged by years of pure-oxygen breathes.

I said, 'It's not just the people here: this whole place looks old ahead of its time.'

I said, 'It's like a bomb wiped out the culture but left the people standing.'

She told me to order the borscht. It came in a small cauldron, hung on a metal tripod over a candle-flame. I ladled the meat and beetroot into her bowl.

I said, 'Where's Bradley?'

'Some nightclub somewhere.'

Are you meeting him later?'

'No,' she said. 'Why?'

I asked her about Warabe Utenabe. She told me he had a research farm in the valley north of her and spent his days in a 28kPa pressure suit, watching wheat seeds germinate at pressures so low, a human being exposed to them would slowly boil away. 'And he makes plants for Bradley,' she said. 'Strange new forms. Insectivorous grasses. Meat trees.

'VR add-ons,' she laughed, when I misunderstood. 'They're not *real*. Just conceptual designs. To go in Brad's theme park.'

Louisa Goggi and Bradley Hight were building a virtual playground for the Moon's post-human population to meet up and relax in. Bradley herded code: Louisa handled the information flows. 'They spend most of their time in the Mess together.'

It was the working title for the theme park. Mess, as in messroom. Mess, as a self-deprecatory joke.

'Is that cool with you?'

She didn't understand me.

'I mean, you don't mind?'

'Mind what?' she insisted, backing me into a corner. 'Them being together,' I said.

'We're all "together".' She looked at me. 'Why do you find that so troubling?'

I had had enough of being embarrassed. I was fed up with having their menage paraded in front of me. 'It seems infantile,' I said. 'Immature. I suppose I sound very old-fashioned,' I added, unable to resist a sneer.

She didn't talk to me much after that. She didn't seem

annoyed, especially. But I had broken something. A fragile trust: unimportant to her, but for me – new, and unused to things – valuable.

I thought about Toronto, the well-tended enclosure with its sterile stream and anti-climb trees, and the fastidious childhood I had run from, but which I would never outgrow.

The restaurant was full, the diners animated, but few words were spoken. I listened in. Since arriving, my hearing had become unnaturally acute. I had put it down to the slightly higher air pressure here. It seemed I could tune into any conversation I wanted – only I couldn't make sense of what I was hearing.

Behind me:

'No greater inconvenience than a thorough wetting.'

'You have been in there, haven't you?'

'You think our activities are unpremeditated?'

The table to its right:

'But you don't envy me.'

'I don't believe there is malice.'

'Too much of a bother.'

Ahead of us:

'Why yes.'

'Yes, she did.'

'She did.'

Suddenly, I couldn't work out which conversation was which. Disorientated, I turned, trying to follow each speaker by the movements of their lips. Whether it was a residue of gravity sickness or an imbalance of pressure in my ears I don't know, but suddenly nobody seemed to be sitting at quite the right angle to each other. People and furniture separated, like the overlapping eels of an animation, shifted out of true by an unseen hand.

'I'm falling,' I said.

'You're not falling,' she said.

'I'm falling!'

Her laughter was liquid. 'Not falling.' Her hand was hot against my hand, melting it, drawing it in. 'Quite the reverse,' she said.

*

She told me my accessories were coming on-line, that there was nothing to be afraid of. That I wouldn't be able to sleep.

'I'm exhausted,' I laughed.

'You won't sleep.'

'I'm dead on my feet!'

She knew a good hotel and took me there. Everywhere we walked we collided. Our walking was one long, soft collision.

The hotel foyer was full of nasty wrought-iron garden furniture. The ceiling, of backlit frosted glass panels, reminded me of a greenhouse. There was a turquoise awning over the reception desk.

Joanne got me booked into a single room on the floor below hers. I said goodnight.

She said, 'There's a sauna on my floor. If you want to go on talking, that's where I'll be.'

'Yeah, right,' I said, closing the door.

The fridge was full of Cold Duck beer. I fell across the bed and drank from the bottle, and reached out with my mind to turn on the TV.

'If you use plastic bags, then you need the super-sealer!'

I hadn't the psychic finesse to change channel and I couldn't be bothered to go pick up the remote, so I just lay there and let it wash over me.

'The super-sealer: an extraordinary sealing device!' It didn't know how to stop. I went to the bathroom and splashed cold water over my face. When I got back: 'Any plastic bag can be sealed with the super-sealer!'

I couldn't get her face out of my mind. When I closed my eyes, there it was. I drained the bottle and let it drop over the edge of the bed.

In a final bid for attention, the TV offered me two super-sealers for the price of one, 'One for the den and one for the kitchen!' It didn't end, just tailed off into a rambling monologue about garden centres. I couldn't work out if it was an advertisement or not. I turned it off.

The coffee maker made me a caffe latte that was okay until the final mouthful: all salt and detergent.

I could hear her now. I could hear the way she said things. I remembered, when I'd misheard her one time in the restaurant, 'I speak funny,' she said.

I laughed.

'No, really,' she said. 'I need my own interpreter.'

There were some shrink-wrapped sandwiches in the fridge behind the beer, but the only ones I fancied were egg and bacon, and the egg was full of lumps of dark, dried yolk.

I knew why I couldn't sleep, and it had nothing to do with the accessories in my head.

When we were walking to the hotel, I'd asked her where she came from, and she said, 'Imbrium.'

'No, I mean, where did you come from originally?'

In reply she just shrugged, and cupped her hands around an imaginary pregnancy.

I was awake, I was alive, and it had nothing to do with strange machines, or new powers.

I closed my eyes and gazed at her.

(Her laughter was liquid. 'Quite the reverse.')

I knew what it was.

Joanne was French. She'd spent most of her life in Paris. But her mother was Finnish, and every summer they went and stayed with her family.

'They all have these silverlog cabins in the Lake District, and when you're a kid it's a horror story. Two days to get there, a week to get the heating started, and then the relatives turn up with one box of vanilla ice cream and eat all your food.'

No one had used the sauna for hours, and the air was impossibly dry. But when she poured water on the coals, the tickle left my throat and the scent of pine resin filled the air.

She told me, the last time she visited Finland she was thirteen, and she'd been allowed to bring a friend along. 'All the grown-ups went off to meet Uncle Heikki one night and we got totally pissed. We were pouring vodka and Campari and creme de menthe on the coals and getting high. The next year the wood still smelled funny.'

'Do you still keep in touch with your mother's people?'

Only the week before she boarded the PTH, she had received an email telling her of her uncle Heikki's death.

He'd been out hunting reindeer, sharing a shooting platform high in the trees with a drinking companion of many years. They were crouching on the platform and they could hear the reindeer approaching. 'Heikki had a heart attack from the excitement.'

'Jesus.'

'Oh, no.' She put her hand on my shoulder. 'It's lovely.' She turned and ladled more water on the coals, and her free hand was pressed over her heart, to stop her towel slipping.

The gesture reminded me of the Italian paintings I'd once studied: that hand-on-heart gesture ran through everything like a musical phrase. A warm theme, capable of countless humane variations: shielding your modesty, or declaring an oath: swearing your loyalty, or your love.

'He died with the thunder of hooves in his ears.'

'I understand,' I said, because I did. Because there was a thundering in my ears, too.

I wanted to hold her. I wanted to hold my head against her breast in the night and hear her heart thunder steadily against her ribs.

I wanted to tell her everything. I wanted her to tell me everything.

Maybe that was what it took. Perhaps that was what the accessories in my head needed, and were waiting for: a sudden willingness to open up, and know. A sudden, shuddering thirst, to trigger the flood.

# 13

I have smelled sunsets, and felt the chatter of digger ants tickling my palm. I have tasted jazz, and it's as sweet as honey and tart as a lime. I have seen the rainbow flow of a woman's scent, and heard the soft, melancholy strains of her smile.

On the Moon – that dull ball of rock, four hundred thousand klicks away – the world spread out its wares for us. It opened for us, wanton and eager as a time-lapse rose.

On the Moon, we had many ways of seeing. One minute, we might use our artificial senses to survey the solar system from satellites and surveyor craft; the next minute, we'd be peering into the secrets of the Lunar regolith through the tiny faceted scanners of insectile builder-robots. We might even – with permission – watch the world a while through another's eyes.

Post-human, more than human, something else, we seemed unstoppable. When Apolloco's spin-doctors described us to Earthside investors they used comfort-words like 'efficiency', 'cost-benefit' and 'accountability'. But no one on the Moon believed a word of it.

We were no commercial concern. We weren't there to balance the books, or improve productivity. We were something more. An experiment perhaps. The bizarre and gothic product of Earth's largest sterile laboratory, the Moon.

Few of my memories of that time can be translated. Language communicates human ideas, human values – and we were not human.

I can describe, but it is like describing a dream. The images don't add up, because the feeling that wires those images together has come unravelled. What's left is a box of bits.

If you were blind, I might say: sight is like a symphony, only all the notes are playing at once, and wherever you turn your attention, a new harmony becomes dominant.

Once I could 'see' the tensile properties of things, it was

like seeing the rhythms within things, only outside time; as though each particle of the view contained within itself whole symphonies, themselves realisable at once, though different harmonies in them were realised in rhythm.

Rubbish. Nonsense. Try again.

Try telepathy, maybe. But that is even worse. A human being who can 'see' tensile stress is still human, more or less. But someone who can communicate without language isn't.

I was right about Joanne's ménage. It *was* infantile, from a strictly human point of view. Infantile, in the sense that it had more to do with curiosity than love. But curiosity, to a telepath, is the point. Telepath sex is a mutual exploration in a way that human sex, whatever the manuals say, is not. Yes, I slept with them.

I have wandered on millipede legs deep into the regolith through tunnels as narrow as a baby's ringer. I have held Joanne's head in my hands and watched her lips softly part as a new lover's fingers stroke her to orgasm. I have lain at the bottom of deep shafts and looked through x-ray eyes at the cosmos, hunting for extraterrestrial life. I have been seduced and petted by artificial intelligences. I have felt the great muscular ache and spiritual weariness of the flimsy lunar launchers as, day in, day out, they hurl material from the Moon's gravity well into space. I have tasted salt. I have eaten glass. I have flowed, and I have burned.

Now this is all I have: a language that refuses to admit the rightness of what I was.

Bradley Hight and Louisa Goggi kept fifty square miles of private country in their living room. To help them concentrate, and preserve their control, they had eschewed the usual mass-telepathic data stores and design engines, plugging themselves instead directly into an environment generator of their own design. The tank of blood-heat saline in which they worked, deprived of all sensory distraction, was so big, you had to squeeze against the glass to get through to the kitchen. Bradley handed the drinks through to me one by one, before squeezing through himself. 'Okay,' he said. 'Ready?'

Louisa and Bradley's VR theme-park was in beta-test, and they had invited Joanne, Warabe and I around to play in it. Here, in Hight-and-Goggi-World, the Moon's artificial intelligences and post-humans could meet on something like equal terms, talk in something approaching human speech, and enjoy what at a stretch were human comforts.

'It's not supposed to seem special in here.' That was how Louisa Goggi explained it to us. 'Comfortable, yes, but not special. The whole point of this place is it *normalises* our condition and our communications. Like a desktop on a computer screen normalises the programs inside.'

Curious, Joanne and Warabe and I blinked our way inside.

We pierced the place at its weakest point, descending from space of no mathematical value into the fractally uncertain upper atmosphere. Buffeted by strange mathematics, we struggled not to meld, to keep our homoncular integrity as we descended, angel-like, into Hight and Goggi's giant playtime world of thrilling textures and unreal joys.

It was sunny, as always. There were clouds – there were always clouds – though once you reached ground level they never obscured the sun: one of the place's many improvements on reality. Fish swam through the air, trailing the banners their sponsors had insisted upon: Sony, Brahma Cola, Subaru. Rocketships flew by, the unreal air bending and whooshing quadraphonically behind them.

The ground came in view. We had emerged in countryside: moods and sceneries abutted each other promiscuously. Snow-capped mountains rose out of barren red deserts as abruptly and cleanly as Ayers Rock. We swooped past the mountain's forest eyries. The slopes beneath us crawled with virtual prey: mountain lions, cougars, monkeys, giant birds. Half an unreal mile to the east lay precipitous and icy slopes. The first people came in view, skiing down bespoke contours at breakneck speed. I lost more height and scudded past the steepest slope. In the hyper-clarified air, I saw how the snow healed, the scars of countless skis vanishing as the surface reformed to ideal compactness.

Leaving the mountain behind, we tracked across meadows and heaths to a gentle, wide blue river. A sharp, inertia-less deceleration brought us hovering unseen over a bathing place. Youths of both sexes bathed naked in the river, laughing and splashing. Some of them were improvising a game of water polo, with goals on either bank. When, exhausted, they climbed out, the water ran like mercury from their honey-coloured bodies, leaving the flawless skin bone dry.

Content, we rose up into the air, and on, towards the first cross-hatchings of a vast metroplex. Carefully tended parks, orchards and vineyards stretched to the horizon. Ziggurats and pyramids squatted complacently in their own grounds. There were more rocketships here, flitting in and out like bees through the gaping, flashing portals of streamlined docking towers.

The people, we had been told, were there purely to make up the numbers, and act as a palliative to our relative aloneness on the Moon. They would, we had been promised, react as well as any VR doll. Responsive. Acquiescent. The Carioca look was everywhere – Louisa's influence, I guessed, her youth spent in Brazil. The men were short and swarthy. Among the women, pert, full breasts and generous backsides were the norm. They rode the smooth camber of the plasticated streets on silver bikes to assignations in the endless parks. Behind rhododendron screens they greeted Latin lovers, ate picnics of mango and passionfruit and soft cheeses, knocking it back laughingly with consequence-free, self-chilling champagne.

There were no actual children here in these endless gardens, well-coppiced estates and communal athletics grounds, but youth predominated, and pubertal forms were common. Bradley's contribution, I guessed, knowing – after so many telepathically-enhanced couplings – his desires.

And up again, and on.

Downtown rose on the horizon, all glassy domes and mirrored obelisks. The streets, which up till now had followed an

Angelino grid pattern, gave way to a more complicated math: an Escher's knot of hilltop lanes and public stairs around a fractal rose of waterways and fishing harbours.

Here more northern dreams began, and many women boasted skins of Pre-Raphaelite cream, their teenage breasts pushed up and out by cups of electroplated chrome; silver sheath dresses ended just above the knee. Their men, older on the whole, had the rugged outdoors look to which Hight pretended in life. (Not that you needed telepathy to realise that; you just had to read his T-shirts.) With thick mountaineers' fingers they brushed their ponytailed hair off the collars of their soft black jackets and walked along nonchalantly, weathered hands tucked into the front pockets of their crease-free Armani jeans.

Joanne and I left Warabe contemplating the maze of stairs and wandered round the little pleasure harbour, all gift shops, yachts and thirtysomething bars. Shoppers flickered in and out of them insect-quick. Time was being distorted round the shops' entrances, so the trade might be more comfortably accommodated. One shop was so busy, its customers were a grey blur, a fuzzy grey semi-transparent river of people shunted by the operating system into narrower and narrower quanta of time. 'Frills,' it said, over the door. 'Importers of *Objets d'Art* and Authentic Interiors from the Orient.' The window was crammed with cushions, batik dresses and Indian silver jewellery, lovingly simulated from copies of copies of copies of some antique traveller's idea of ethnic design.

And for those of us still conscious of their virtual nature – newcomers and the morally unsure – the Shark Bite Surf and Snow Centre next door offered a less problematic selection of 'authentic' goods. I studied the window display, reading off the labels and designer names. Sunglasses by Bolle, Killer-Loop, and Dragon; Standard Deluxe T-shirts; wetsuits sporting dayglo legends Quiksilver, Bodyglove and Ripcurl. In a world that's faked, I figured, brandnames – being without substance – alone remain authentic. Joanne took me by the hand. 'I've had enough,' she said.

'And me.'

'Come home with me,' she said.

I turned.

Her body had gone flat. It was two-dimensional: a window on another place entirely. A dark interior. She took me by the arms. Her hands had no dimension, and it dizzied me to watch them draw me in.

I stepped inside her.

I found myself in a flagstoned hall. Architraves of simple dressed stone supported a high roof decorated with polished plaster. There were no windows: balconies stood open around the room, and the night air – summery, scented with camellias – stirred the linen curtains gently, like the movements of a woman. Wrought-iron candelabra filled the room with hesitant light, as though the gloom were something solid to be nudged through.

There was little furniture. A single chair. A day bed. One glass upon the table, the bottle open beside it. This was Joanne's space – so private, none of us had had any idea of it. A place for her to be truly herself.

And now, I was here. Was I the first? Did it matter?

'Of course you're the first.' Joanne walked into the light, picked up the glass and poured. As she raised the glass, its twin emerged from behind it: VR sleight-of-hand.

'I thought we were going back to the hotel,' I said. My voice carried naturally in the space, as though we were on Earth. Gravity, too, appeared to be Earth-normal, though I felt none of the exhaustion I would have felt had the gravity been real.

'No, silly. Home.'

The wine was rich and chewy and tasted faintly of liquorice.

She crossed to the day bed, cast away on an island of candle-light, and beckoned me to join her. She was wearing a black dress, low in the back and long, reaching almost to her ankles. Heavy silver earrings – strange, seaweedy forms – tangled them-selves in her hair. 'What did you think of it?'

'The theme park?'

'They don't like you calling it that.'

'I know.' I swirled the wine around my glass, raised it to my nose and breathed. 'They're not architects.'

'No.'

'And isn't there something contradictory about it? Why normalise what we are? I thought we were supposed to be different.'

'You felt it too, then.' She set her glass on the stone floor and lay back on the day bed. The black velvet shaped itself to her like a pelt.

'Felt what?'

'The fear. The escapist's fear of the big nasty real world.'

Was this why she had brought me here, to her own VR realm? To criticise our friends? No: outside this space, her thoughts would not be hidden from them. They'd already be known.

I said, 'We're compromised ourselves, remember?' I cast a hand around the room – her own escapist space.

'It's crass,' she said, ignoring my little ironies. 'Clouds but no shadows. Why does that appeal? Because when we were human, the clouds dulled our view. Water that dries instantly. Why? Because when we were human, water got in the way. But we're *not* human!' She stood up, agitated by her own argument. 'We have the chance to realign ourselves with the world. A real chance – there hasn't been an opportunity like this since the invention of tools, or the first hootings of language. We can make everything different, *and* keep it real. But what are we doing instead? We're just pandering to our old limitations!'

'Perhaps we have to stay a little bit human,' I said, not understanding her fury.

'Why?'

'Perhaps.'

'For crying out loud, Chris, why—' She stopped herself. 'Say it.'

'Why do you have to be so bloody mild?'

I had no answer for her. Perhaps she didn't need one. I drank off the rest of the wine and went to the window. There was nothing to see.

I heard her footsteps behind me. 'I'm sorry,' she said.

'There's nothing to be sorry for,' I said, but I couldn't help letting my resentment show just a little: 'I just have no objections to being human.'

'Is it human to be cosseted the way their park cossets us?'

'No,' I said. 'There we agree.'

I felt her hand on my back. I felt it slide around me. I leaned back into her arm. I could smell her. Her smell: unedited, unimproved. Unimprovable.

'I want to show you something,' she said, and cast her hand over the void.

Abruptly, as though a switch had been thrown (which it had) there was a world beyond the room. We were perched, I saw now, on the edge of a crater. Below us, the. fractured walls descended about six hundred metres to the sharply cleft valley floor. Vertiginously deep valleys, parallel with the crater wall, confused its already complex geography. It was so wide, its far side was hidden by the line of the horizon.

'Arzachel,' she said, naming one of the more prominent features of the near side.

'It's beautiful,' I said, trembling. Afraid to fall.

'Watch.'

From out the sloping, broken, mountainous terrain, a maze of stairs and passages emerged. Tall, schematic towers rose up through the mighty cracks in the crater floor. Elevated tramways and fistulae of towns and public parks consumed the crater walls. False perspectives at once filled up and made mysterious the blank and savage space the ancient meteor had left.

'This,' she said, 'is what I want.'

I stared and stared.

'This is what I want my builder ants to build. The first real city on the Moon.'

I could not deny it.

It was not fantastical: the world, after all, has its physical limits. But her city of Arzachel was a varied place, a place that might sustain a dream or two. Its vistas were never as extreme as they appeared, but duped the eye superbly. Its parks and gardens – dusty scratchings merely, at this early stage – folded their scanty space up in themselves like mazes. Even in their sketched-out state, they lent the city depth and mystery. 'Build something,' she said.

I knew that to rush anything solid into her creation would be bathetic. A bauble; worse, an intrusion. I needed, more than a building, a piece of language – something to show her I understood. I turned back into the room, called up my draughting suite, measured and mixed, blinked my way out again and pasted what I had made into her room.

Over the cold grey flagstones the surface raced, grey-white and crumbled. It inched in under our feet. We tottered. It reached the edge of the balcony, and stopped, flaking off, an age-softened surface.

Joanne let go of me and took a few tentative steps. She bent down and put her hand to it.

'It's warm!'

I returned her smile.

'It's beautiful,' she said.

'It's real. I mean, I've copied a real flooring.'

'What is it?'

'*Impasto di gesso.* Marble dust and plaster.' It swallowed the candlelight and re-emitted it in milky pools.

I laid my palm on her back. I could feel the electricity thrilling through her spine.

Not a new sense, this. A very old one. 'I love you,' I said.

# 14

Take a PET scan of a person's brain, and you will see how neural patterns eddy and twist across the cerebrum like the weather-patterns on a TV map. And it may occur to you, quite naturally – as a revelation, or maybe as just an idle metaphor – that weather and thinking are the same thing.

But are you likely, after that experience, to go out and worship the weather? Not especially. The reason you don't, is you can be pretty certain that the weather doesn't reason. Or – let's be precise here – that even if it did reason (how would you know one way or the other?), *there's nowhere for that reasoning to go.* Weather is amorphous: it can't do anything but be. Thought, without a thinker, can't do anything but think.

Think about money. Same thing. We live our entire lives according to economic rules; we depend upon the smooth running of the economic system. When it glitches, people starve, commit crimes, go mad, die. No one but the most egomaniacal of despots could ever claim to 'control' money, any more than a helmsman on board ship 'controls' the weather through which the ship sails.

But then again, nobody – except in the most facetious sense – worships share price fluctuations.

At least, not until recently.

A hundred years ago, we'd have confidently said, money is like the weather. Unpredictable. Complex. A big-number problem. And it was because money behaved like the weather – fickle; even dangerous at times – that we built machines to try and control it.

*Machines.*

Machines that every year, get twice as complicated as they were the year before. Machines that by 1980 could compute, by 1990 could mentate, by 2010 could be said to be conscious, and today are considered capable of *intention.*

Once money was like the weather: without form or boundary and so, senseless of self. What we did when we mechanised our stockmarkets was put all that messy, unpredictable money in a box – a box that was designed to order, and compute, and mentate, and intend; to evolve.

We had meant to control money. Instead, we gave it self-control.

Suddenly, money isn't like the weather any more. It has boundaries. It has form. It has a sense of who it is.

It was in my sixth year on the Moon – the fifth year of my marriage to Joanne Rynard – that money started spending people. Joanne and I didn't know it at the time, but we were in at the very start of it.

Over the years we had lost touch with our friends Bradley Hight, Louisa Goggi and Warabe Utenabe. Shortly before they returned to Earth, they looked us up, and we went out to dinner. Jim Durrell was there, too – a good friend of mine, by this time, and a regular EVA partner.

Warabe told us how Loewy, a small Swiss merchant bank, had head-hunted them for its financial futures operation. We were pleased for them. They were so much looking forward to going home.

They had not, in the end, taken to life on the Moon. They had spent most of their time refining their theme park, and had engaged little with the real construction on which the rest of us were engaged. The rumour went Warabe had actually been asked to resign his post at the agricultural research station because he'd been spending so much of his time designing virtual ecologies for Bradley and Louisa.

Jim Durrell engaged Bradley in a heated debate about the advantages of using helium as a diluent in EVA breathing mixture, and generally managed to field the worst of our arrogance, but I guess Joanne and I were rather patronising. Joanne's microrobots were even as we spoke constructing her dream city of Arzachel – now our joint project – and it was hard for us to take seriously the idea of three post-humans going to work for a bank.

Joanne's minute robots, barely bigger than the termites they distantly resembled, were breeding and spreading across the whole Moon. There were billions of them; great swarms of artificial living things. They were tireless, unstoppable, and endlessly fertile. They ate constantly, chewing down the iron-rich regolith covering the lunar surface, processing, refining and excreting. Every few weeks each inch-long robot gave birth to a perfect copy of itself. The robot population more than doubled every month. They were our tools, our billion tiny hands; with them, we were going to transform Earth's desolate, pitted satellite, bringing it to life at last.

Much of the logistics of the construction effort was being processed telepathically by the preconscious structures of our brains. Joanne was having to take headache pills because of the number of new programs being pumped back and forth every second through her skull.

That evening, it seemed to us that we were the real pioneers; Utenabe, Hight and Goggi merely our bourgeois hangers-on.

It didn't take them long to prove us wrong.

Once the three had readjusted to Earth's gravity, Loewy flew them Business Class to Singapore and put them up at a luxury apartment block overlooking the river. Early each morning they swam together in the pool behind the Anguilla View. Waiters in starched white shirts served them breakfast at the water's edge. Star-fruit, mango, pineapple, gallon jugs of blood-orange over cracked ice. By day they cruised the jewellery stores and couturiers of Boat Quay. By night they danced to old-time jazz at Harry's. At midnight they sat under the umbrellas outside Lucky Leeson's, drinking Anchor beer and vodka shots. Below them on the river the yachts and motor boats of the new rich slipped by. They lit cigarettes from the table candle, and watched as the sharp prows of the yachts peeled the black water. When they turned and looked at each other, their eyes filled with mellow orange light.

Loewy hired local contractors to build them a workplace. Scuba experts, crisis-room nurses, systems analysts and psychologists worked together round the clock to complete the tanks by Loewy's three-week deadline. The bespoke life-supports came from specialist laboratories in the Minas Gerais region of Brazil; they were up and running within the day. But the neural feeds were Cantonese, and kept drifting off specification.

By the time Loewy's technicians resolved the problem it was late June, close on the rainy season. Outdoors it was thirty-six degrees in the shade and humidity was ninety-three per cent.

Those tanks of blood-heat saline, dimly lit by cool blue light, seemed heaven-sent to the three recruits. At the end of the first day's trading they cleared sixty-eight billion US dollars.

Back then, SIMEX – the Singapore exchange – was no different to any other big market. At its core sat a military-grade virtual environment in which corporate artificial intelligence dealt and counter-dealt at a speed no physical system could match. Artificial intelligence had been smoothly globalising financial risk for about fifteen years. Young companies found it hard to get an edge on the market.

But Loewy had figured out a way to outsmart their competitors. They would plug things into the global financial networks – things several orders of magnitude brighter than anything their rivals had yet developed. Things, moreover, that would cost them nothing at all to develop.

Human brains.

Afterwards, the press decided that Hight, Goggi and Utenabe must have had the whole thing planned out, even before they left the Moon. I don't believe that. I think Loewy rushed things; plugged them into an unsuitable system and rushed the psychiatrics.

The press called it Narnia; I don't think Hight, Utenabe or Goggi ever had a name for it. It's possible they were never entirely conscious of it. We'll never know, because when they pulled them out of the tanks for good, six months later, Louisa and Warabe went catatonic.

Bradley escaped custody by blinding his guards with the business end of a disposable biro. He was found, six weeks later, hanging by his neck from an I-beam in a defunct London Underground maintenance tunnel.

Narnia is an island two hundred miles long, south east of Hong Kong. Its main exports are hardwoods and wildlife, much of it unique to the island. Many of its plants have rare medical properties, unexploited by Western science. Large reserves of natural gas lie off its northern shore. But these are untapped, and the country derives most of its GNP from tourism. It is popular with families, with the yachting classes of Kowloon, the New Territories and Macau. It imports most of its highly trained, disciplined, and well-motivated workforce from China. It is unique in the region for its diamond-producing geology.

When this unknown, untapped new country fell in their laps, the AIs of Loewy's competitors, knowing no better, could not believe their luck. It wasn't their fault. They were financial engines. They had no need of maps. They had no real grasp of the world they governed. As far as they knew – as far as they *could* know – Christmas had come early. Santa had slid down the cyberspace chimney and left them a shiny new country, wrapped up in pink ribbon. They squabbled desperately with each other, like children with a new box of chocolates, each determined to get first bite of this rich and underdeveloped new market. Soon, every major financial institution in the world was unwittingly tending investments in ... Narnia.

Narnia acquired bridges and dams. It signed arms sales agreements. It leased mineral and mining rights. Trillions of dollars worldwide poured into Narnia.

But Narnia is on no map. No one has, or ever can, set foot there. If it can be said to exist at all, then it did so only briefly; in Loewy's corporate imagination.

When the truth dawned, six months later, the financial balance of the world collapsed. Political firestorms swept the developed nations of the Earth. Europe in particular suffered a period of sudden and revolutionary change. In Britain, re-surgent nationalism triggered a second civil war. Royalists took control of London, declared their independence and seceded from the European Union. Their bitter border war with the Federal Republic of England ran for just over a year. The route of the old M25 orbital motorway was mulched with the bones of the war dead.

I remember sitting with Joanne in our Sea of Serenity apartment, watching Michael Portillo's bones being consecrated during a state service in Westminster Abbey. Nearby mortar-fire drowned out much of the service. The Bishop of London kept having to prop up the idiot Prince Regent on his throne. Afterwards he threw his mitre at a photographer. Joanne said to me, 'No way are we ever going back to Earth.'

'You know what lunar gravity will do to our kids,' I said. 'They'll end up eight foot tall.'

'I don't care. If we have children we're having them here.'

You see, we thought we were free to do as we wanted. We thought nothing had changed.

But we were wrong.

# 15

Suddenly – overnight, in fact – money left the Moon. Share prices tumbled. Investors withdrew. To the people back home, our whole grand project suddenly seemed baroque and unnecessary.

Downsizing began immediately, as we fought to maintain our presence there. Plans for the Honeycomb — that grandiose vision of a Moon riddled with hives of living habitats – were soon shelved. Soon, even the surface biomes were being shut down. New endeavours, like Arzachel, were stillborn. Only half complete, they were eyesores to some, pathetic monuments to others; follies, either way.

Making a personal, photographic record of Arzachel was my idea. Joanne, dispirited almost to breaking point, tagged along only reluctantly. She disliked my enjoyment of the ruins. To her they spelled only defeat. She said to me once, 'It's a failure of will. All this bag-packing crap. All this balance-sheet bullshit.'

And I'd replied, 'We can only do what we can afford to do. Just because of what we are, it doesn't make us immune to economics.'

'Well it should,' she said.

She was right, of course; only back then I, like most people, couldn't see it.

'Come on, love,' I said. 'Smile!'

She turned her back, spoiling another photograph.

'Five hundred dollars,' I sighed.

'Use a real camera then, for Christ's sakes.'

Film cameras were rare on the Moon: I'd had to ship spares and special developing equipment from Earth, and it had cost me a fortune. But I disliked the cheaper, digital cameras. Joanne thought I was being pretentious, but that wasn't it at all.

I worked so much in the virtual, as architects have always done (we have always built our talents and careers as much on paper buildings as on completed structures) and so I had learned to treasure whatever few traces my work left behind. Notebooks, scribbles, drawings, the grain of charcoal on paper, the cupboards chock-full of tattered portfolios. The photographs were part of the same desire. They were something solid, something I could leave behind. Something to stand in for me, when death finally caught up with me.

Old-fashioned thinking, I admit, for a metal-head.

I steadied myself against a rocky outcrop – an eruption of regolith as jagged and repetitive as a spine – and patched my visual cortex into the viewfinder of my camera.

My depth sense collapsed, as the camera's single wide-angle lens hijacked my sense of sight. I watched through the camera as Joanne picked her way like an absurd orange bird across the frame. She turned to face me, her face dimly visible through the helmet of her suit. Behind her rose the great, melted-looking domes and arches of Arzachel, our grandest and most personal work. I tapped my teeth with my tongue, and the shutter clicked.

I walked over to her – if 'walking' could describe such an absurd, bouncing low-gravity dance (but we'd been so long on the Moon, many of our words and ideas had taken on eccentric, shifted meanings). I still could not see properly through the solarising faceplate of her helmet. I thought to patch in to her helmet camera – but at the last second I stopped myself.

We'd been advised to relearn the old limits of our human selves. That way – Jim Durrell had explained – we would limit the trauma of our stripping, when we returned to Earth. We had all accepted that life back on Earth would be no cakewalk. Hight, Utenabe and Goggi had poisoned the waterhole for the rest of us. People were going to treat us with suspicion. But no one dreamed for a second that the Court of Human Rights in The Hague would really do what it threatened, and confiscate our powers.

But they did: as one by one we left the Moon, doctors stripped our heads of the rare devices Apolloco had put there.

We tried telling them. We tried explaining that, having lived so long with these rare senses, losing them was like being blinded. But no one understood, or maybe wanted to.

'It's a passing panic,' Jim Durrell promised me, as he climbed out of his EVA suit. We had been climbing the Montes Rook. There were no skulls, anywhere. So we could wear the lightest suits and avoid any risk of pressure sickness, we'd been using helium diluent in our breathing mixture, both in our suits and on board the PTH. To any normal person, our conversation would have sounded absurd – Pinky and Perky debating the niceties of lunar politics in an earnest falsetto – but the machines in our heads made us comprehensible to each other.

'And when you look at the scale of the depression back home,' Durrell went on, 'it's hardly surprising people want something done, however irrational it is.' He struggled with a boot zipper. I helped him free it and asked him what his plans were.

'Apolloco are calling in as many of the original surgeons as they can find, to remove our accessories.' He shrugged. 'I guess I'll be heading down-well with you.'

I was so angry, I didn't even wait for him before leaving the lock. By the time he caught up with me I'd already taken my shower. I said, 'I don't see how you can be so bloody relaxed about it all.'

'Chris, you forget. History's on our side.'

'Excuse me, but I think the consolations of philosophy will pall rather when I'm being strapped to an operating table.'

'History's on our side, and so are our machines. We'll be back here one day, more radically changed than you know.'

'Really.'

'Think about it.' (Louie Huichang used to smile exactly the same patronising kind of smile, back in Kokanee, whenever he started on about Bauhaus textiles. Like he owned all rights to the subject.) 'When Europe discovered America, it needed to send settlers to the new-found land to develop it. With the Moon, it's different. We have machines, now, that can do everything we can do, only safer and faster. They can develop the Moon perfectly well without our interference. We're the first settlers in human history who didn't have to be here!'

I couldn't follow him. All he seemed to be doing was broadcasting bad news with a stupid grin on his face. I wondered then whether his disjointed manner wasn't a symptom of something. A sense of professional failure, or moral confusion. He, of all people, should have understood the human cost of making post-humans mere people again; yet here he was, ready to go home and join in the butchery – stripping us back to our human stumps.

He continued: 'The reason we're having to go home is because we're not changed *enough*. We're still too human for the AIs here to deal with. As far as they're concerned, we're just so much dead weight—'

'We are leaving,' I interrupted sharply, 'because we can't afford to stay. Not because some tin can with an attitude problem is asking us to leave.'

Durrell's smile was mischievous and infuriating. 'And the difference is—?'

I velcroed my coveralls shut and pulled my way up onto the observation deck. 'You're talking in riddles,' I said: the middle-class way of telling someone to fuck off.

'Look.' He followed me in. 'True, there's been no battle. No robot rebellion. No bloody, oily confrontation. The logic of our going home is there for anyone to read, in the balance sheets and business plans of a thousand government departments. But you've got to ask youself – who's running the economy so that we're not getting a look-in here?'

'Nobody runs the economy.'

'Really?' He strapped himself into his seat and consulted the navcomp. He had me hooked, and he knew it.

Finally, I gave in: 'You really believe the AIs are locking us out of the Moon?'

'Yes,' he said.

'So where's your good news? Why are you so bloody happy?'

He tapped the side of his head. '*Intelligence.* We're intelligent and now, at last, so are our machines. The better we get at talking to each other, the more likely it is we'll both get what we want. This setback – it isn't anything new. Think how as a kid you were imprisoned by busy roads and speeding traffic, all because the oil economy told you your life had to be that way. It's the same now. Economically, putting people into space is madness. A complete waste of time. We're imprisoned on Earth now as surely as we were imprisoned when we were kids. Only this time, this is what is different: *now we can reason with the car.* Now AIs run the economy, we can *persuade* ourselves back into space!'

'Joanne talks to AIs all the time,' I said. 'Not once have they ever turned around in the middle of a planning meeting and started talking politics.'

'That's her experience,' Durrell conceded. Then: 'I think if the doctors ever get Louisa and Warabe talking again, they might tell us a different story. Don't you?'

I folded my arms. 'They were friends of mine,' I said.

'I know.'

'Lovers.'

'I didn't mean—'

'Not counters in some bloody intellectual game.' Durrell, at last getting the measure of my anger, drove on in silence.

'Did you get the shot?' Joanne asked, over the radio.

I gave her the thumbs up. I glanced down at the camera. It

was rewinding. 'That's it,' I said, stowing the camera in its bag.

'I want to go see the suburbs,' Joanne said. So we boarded the rover and in a few shaken, trembling minutes we arrived at the outskirts of Arzachel City.

We'd come as part of a survey team to study the outermost features of the conurbation. Here Joanne's ant-like micro-robots, dimly aware that they had reached a preset barrier, had lost their will to live. Joanne had wired a deathwish into them, so that they would not overrun the city limits. Builders to the last, the swarms had made their last stand here, making solid their crisis and defeat in slipshod, misproportioned structures.

'Jesus,' Joanne said, 'what a mess.'

Stumbling and demented, the robots no longer had the wit for complex thoroughfares or well-proportioned parks. Instead they had scratched out in the dust their most basic algorithms. Life's pathetic signature. Ferny growths and spiral shells. Shapes so simple, even nature had outgrown them.

Such features were common to the outskirts of all robot-created conurbations. Until recently, neither I nor anyone else had taken much note of them, considering the spiralled road-beds and fernlike foundation patterns nothing more than the death-scrawl of defunct machinery. Come settlement, they and all the other occasional errors and follies of the robot workers would be bulldozed away.

So, in the name of civic ease, Arzachel would have lost its allure. It is the fate of all urban architecture.

But the moon did not progress, and by our failure, some-thing beautiful has been saved. A timeless construct. A brave folly. At last the moon has its ancient place, its citadel thrown up for their red-haired queen by digger ants.

Today I am glad that Arzachel will retain forever these relics and rough edges. Bearing the spoor of its dying builders, Arzachel – our lifeless monument – admits its debt to life.

# 16

Apolloco had meant us to become something – but what? What were they after? The next step in human evolution? The first supermen?

Instead, we birthed something they'd not expected and could not control. Intelligent artificial life: a network of computers and sensors that was now a separate entity, intelligent and self-determining. The sole inhabitant and governor of the moon.

It had cast us off, as easily and steadily as a fish sheds scales. Now it hung there in the night sky, silent and puzzling. No risk to us, but no friend, either. The man in the moon we'd always dreamed of, and made by us from our dreams.

So, Joanne and I settled in London and tried to be human again. No one really understood how hard that would be for us, least of all Apolloco's doctors. International law said we couldn't plug in any more, in case we took over the Earth's own AIs. Networks control so many human affairs, from trade to travel to tv, and they had bizarre visions of us cybersurfing the world like angels of death, triggering Armageddon wherever we went: controlling in real-time the trajectory of a spy satellite; inflating the price of wetware on the Nippon Exchange; triggering early-warning SCUDS on the Iran-Iraq border.

All we actually wanted was to get our senses back.

First, we tried Ballantyne.

He'd been recommended by Philip Lee – the lawyer we had used for the purchase of the flat. (Not many months later, Lee would represent me during the divorce proceedings.)

The heart Lee was born with was all fucked up with nicotine and sulphate abuse. The year before, he told me, he had had a series of minor attacks. A client had put him onto Ballantyne and Ballantyne had arranged for a transplant.

'He trades organs?'

Lee laughed at that. We were talking by wire, and as he leaned back the top of his head disappeared out of shot, leaving only a jaw, stubby grey teeth, a neck, like something by Francis Bacon. 'Grows them,' he corrected, swimming back into shot. 'Transgenic pigs. He has a farm in Cubitt Town.'

'Legal?'

'As good as.'

'Reliable?'

Lee beat his chest.

'So what's he doing treating metal-heads?'

'He's ex-army. Intelligence, apparently. Selling booby-trapped accessories to Russian metal-heads to fuck up their Karelian campaign.'

'You fill me with confidence.'

'Thing is,' said Lee, 'he's engineered himself a regular supply of ResponsIV through his old service buddies.'

ResponsIV gets the brain and Apolloco's plugs talking to each other. Lee surely knew I'd be familiar with it, and what it could do for me. He gave me the spiel anyway. 'Ballantyne runs a clinic,' he said. 'It's buried away on the wrong side of the river. You want to meet some satisfied customers?'

I told him to set things up, and that weekend Joanne and I went round to see what sort of operation Ballantyne had going. We were picked up from the flat and driven to the clinic in the back of an opaque-windowed ambulance. We had no idea where we were going. The journey was long, and spooked Joanne badly. 'The place is secret,' I reminded her. 'What would you rather? Be blindfolded?'

I was only making it worse for her. Finally I got wise and shut up.

The clinic itself was gashed together inside a derelict nineteenth-century hospital. It took up only a handful of the relic's endless corridors and dim, echoic wards. We weren't allowed to see much, but what we saw reminded Joanne, she said afterwards, of field hospitals she'd seen in war movies.

But it was the patients that scared her most. Some of them

had descended deep into catatonia. They were the very worst cases, but even the most recovered were exhibiting some symptoms: aphasia, anarthria, apraxia, dysarthria, dysphasia, dyspraxia, homonymous hemianopia.

I don't think Joanne wanted to face what EAI did to her. She didn't want to admit that it made her like this from time to time. She even denied I was ever like this. But I knew that wasn't true. When EAI struck me full-on, I was quite as bad as anyone in that recovery ward.

'ResponsIV is our drug of choice. ResponsIV reactivates the interfaces in your skull,' said Ballantyne. 'Simply, it reminds the brain that it's supposed to respond to the world outside.'

The walls of the corridors had been slapped over with happy, orange, you're-not-really-in-hospital gloss paint. It had bubbled up in patches and when I ran my hand over it it crackled to pieces revealing cream tiles. Red linoleum flooring had split along the edges of creaking floorboards. The submarine-like plumbing rattled and racked as though it had contracted a respiratory disease. That and Ballantyne's Barnum & Bailey School of Medicine patter had Joanne practically clawing at the windows to be rid of the place.

I was impressed. I liked the dedicated manner of the nurses, the cleanliness of the floors and the bed linen, the orderly, efficient flavour of the tour. More to the point, I was ready to accept the realities of my illness – the aphasia, the apraxia, the occasional loss of the swallowing reflex, and all the rest that EAI brought on. (Joanne said I was too ready, that I admitted defeat too easily.)

When we got home, that same night Joanne went out to a metal-head's pub in Bow. I knew what she was doing. I knew the risks she was taking. But we'd been through the arguments together so many times, I no longer had the energy to stop her.

Instead, while Joanne was running the gamut of the accessory pirates, I sat at the living-room table, sticking ResponsIV up my vein.

ResponsIV is the drug post-humans use to access their

strangeness. It on-lines their new senses; it wakens their strange spiritual powers. Once you're stripped – once you're made human again – taking ResponsIV shouldn't make any difference. But it does. For a few heartbreaking seconds after you inject it, it feels like everything is back. All the things Apolloco put in your head. All those strange post-human toys.

For a second, my skull bloomed. For a moment, my mind spilled open. Erupted. Folded back on itself. Tremors bloomed under my feet. Electricity stuffed itself in my ears. The bruised rhythm of the fluorescent light in the kitchen; the fierce whine of heating elements under the living-room floor; the microvoltages of telephones and fax machines in neighbouring apartments.

Then the feeling fades, the way everything does. Nothing really happens. No grace is bestowed. There are no such things as fairies. Like memory itself, it's all a trick. A trace. A killing echo. The itch of an amputated limb ...

Joanne came home about midnight, unscathed. When I asked her what had happened she just said that she'd passed the word around.

Two weeks later she handed me an envelope containing two first-class air tickets to Monaco. I asked her where she got them from. She tapped the side of her nose and grinned.

# 17

Her contact, Pete O'Connor, was Irish-American. The way he dressed and the way he moved and even the rhythms of his speech craved Ballymena.

His BMW 8-series was waiting for us at the airport.

He drove us to a steak house and ate most of a cow like it was a theatrical performance. Then he took us to our hotel. He had us up drinking at the bar until 4 a.m. by which time Joanne was deliciously drunk. It was obvious he lusted after her. He could hardly take his eyes off the hem of her skirt. But as soon as he realised I had seen, his manner changed completely. He grew less chatty, more witty; less crude, more urbane. He had a way of raising subjects so that it took both of us to answer him. He became, in short, the perfect gentleman.

The mask cracked only once. When Joanne headed for the bathroom, he followed her with his eyes, taking the measure of her Monroesque cantilevered walk. I wondered if he'd guessed the secret – that her left leg was very slightly shorter than her right. When she was gone he turned back to me and caught my eye. He wasn't embarrassed. He just grinned. And whether it was the alcohol, or something candid in his eyes, I don't know; but I found myself simply grinning back at him, unthreatened and unoffended.

Joanne returned, and when she saw us, her eyes filled with humorous knowledge. 'I see you two have bonded, then,' she said.

O'Connor looked at me with astonishment that was only half a put-on. 'She ever cut herself, Miss Sharp here?'

'Her party clothes are ribbons by the evening's end.'

And with that thought,' he said, smiling, and clambered carefully out of his chair. He couldn't have really been drunk – not with his genes – but he was certainly acting the part. 'Come round about eleven. I'm in the pile opposite, Forte Imperial I think it's called, but who the fuck knows or cares?'

We shook hands with him, and when he was gone we went up to our room.

We made love all night. I don't think we slept more than an hour. We came and came. She felt hot and tight against me, and the muscles in her stomach were hard under my hands. We stopped, eventually, and dawn came up, and the first, nauseous feathers of hangover started flapping around our heads. We lay shaking under the sheets, drinking orange juice and medicinal vodka out of the minibar. When we touched, a current ran through us. In the grey light, her skin glowed with static, and

105

when she smiled and ran her fingers through my hair I felt something drop inside me.

Crossing the road to O'Connor's hotel was a nightmare. Everything was an effort. Every sound grated. Joanne, who never liked admitting a hangover, was hiding her sunken eyes behind wrapshades. It was dark in the lobby and she kept tripping on the edges of expensive rugs.

'Room four-oh-six, if you'd like to go up.' The clerk pointed to the lifts.

'It's open,' O'Connor shouted when we knocked at his door.

He was sprawled out in a wicker chair by open French windows, trying to cool off. He looked like he'd just run a couple of miles. His face was red. His loud Hawaiian shirt was sticking to his stomach. A gold crucifix hung from a fine chain round his neck. There was a liquor stain on his cream chinos. 'Want a drink?'

Joanne grimaced and shook her head. The steel blue lenses of her wrapshades reflected the room in steely blues and greys.

'Take a seat.'

Joanne reached into her handbag and drew out a soft-pack of Gauloises Lights. O'Connor took an ashtray from the folding table by the window and placed it on the arm of her chair. She blew the first lungful of smoke towards his face with a delicious arrogance.

O'Connor crossed to the bar. 'Hope you don't mind.' He pulled the stopper from a half-empty bottle of Jack Daniels. The wet pop of the cork must have been audible in the bathroom, because the door opened and a blonde girl in a towel leaned out. 'Pete …'

'Hurry up, hon,' O'Connor said.

Joanne shot me a glance.

'Just a small one,' the girl begged. She couldn't yet be twenty.

He splashed a little JD into a highball glass and threw in a handful of ice grains.

'My love.' She leaned into the room, her free hand holding the towel in place. There was a hickey on the back of her shoulder.

She downed the liquor in one, screwed her eyes tight shut a second, then opened them wide. She looked just like Bambi. She stared from Joanne to me and back again like we'd just materialised in the room. 'Oh,' she said. She smiled vacantly. 'Hi.'

'Deena, go get dressed for God's sake, you're embarrassing my friends.'

She shot him a puzzled glance, like he was the weird one, and went back into the bathroom. She swung the door to, but it didn't close properly.

'I represent an agency,' O'Connor began.

She crossed to the sink and I saw her towel fall. Her thigh edged enticingly in and out of view as she bent to wash.

'We head-hunt for big corporations. We find clients for the sort of organisations that don't have to take local regulations too seriously.'

I tore my gaze from the bathroom door. 'The ban on metal-heads using their plugs is worldwide,' I said.

O'Connor smiled. 'Like I said,' he drawled, 'local regulations.'

Did he mean the Earth itself was a mere 'locale' to his people? Multinationals with serious off-world infrastructure were few. In fact, I could think of only one. 'You mean Apolloco secretly hires its own people back again?'

O'Connor laughed. 'You have a twisted mind, Chris. No, they don't!' But the idea pleased some paranoid part of him. 'Leastways,' he mused, 'not that I know of. They're too far up The Hague's ass to pull a stunt like that. No—' He shook himself free of the thought I'd planted in him. 'The names of the companies we represent don't matter. You may as well know now you'll never get to know who's the end beneficiary of your work. Does that bother you?'

'Yes,' said Joanne, stubbing out her cigarette, 'but going blind every quarter bothers me more.'

'Quite.' O'Connor looked at me, like he was waiting for my agreement.

'Go on,' I said, non-committal. Just then the bathroom door opened and the girl came out, dressed in blue Atelier Versace jeans and a silk halter-top the colour of burnished copper.

'So long, big man,' she said. She bent and kissed him on the cheek.

'Get out of here.' O'Connor slapped her on the bottom as she turned.

She shot him a come-on glance as she crossed to the door. 'Have a wild time, y'all.' The door closed with a bang.

O'Connor turned back to me, unbothered by the interruption. 'Our clients develop AIs. A perfectly legal business, that. They make corporate machines. Even trading machines.' He grinned. 'Bit of a hot potato, that one. Remember Narnia?'

'So why the need for post-humans?' Joanne's voice was cool, her suspicion smooth in her throat. She was enjoying herself. O'Connor's sass was rubbing off on her.

'Simple,' O'Connor said. 'Speed. They want to beat the competition. Develop new product faster than anyone else on the block. I don't need to tell you where you come in on that.'

No, he didn't. We knew all about how fast new machines, new buildings, whole new industries and conurbations grew, when our post-human talents were wired to mechanical flesh. The moon, strangely changed, strangely alive, was testament to our rare power.

'Basically you're R&D 'ware. Blue Sky project personnel.' He'd practised that one, clearly. In front of the mirror this morning, maybe. He knew how to make what he was selling sound sexy, whatever it was. 'You're the link between the humans who run these companies and the AIs who'll be running them in the future. A corporate interface.'

I had to admit it, he was good.

'How much?' said Joanne, throwing him off his beat.

'How—?'

'How much? Cut to it.'

O'Connor laughed. 'Hell, okay, don't bust my balls. How much? I don't know. I'm not the one to set the price. If you're interested in the principle of the thing, I'll speak to my contact, then we see what's to be done. It takes time. Wheels within wheels.'

'Trouble is,' said Joanne, 'we don't have time.'

*I realise—'*

'There's others,' she said. But she was pushing too hard. O'Connor glanced at me, to gauge my reaction. Maybe he saw doubt written there; either way, he didn't buy her bluff.

'You push a little hard, Mrs Yale,' he said. 'That's not a problem. In fact I respect it. But there is no one else, is there?'

Joanne didn't react. O'Connor smiled gently. 'You see, we put the word around. Until you and me shake on a deal, or go our separate ways, all other dealers will stay away from you.'

'You don't have that much punch,' I said. I wasn't quite sure what I meant but it sounded good.

'It's not a question of punch,' O'Connor explained patiently. 'It's simply a buyer's market. You want to approach someone else, that's fine by us. But while we're interested in you the others'll simply approach other post-humans.'

'Not all of them have our skills.'

'No,' O'Connor agreed. 'They have others.'

O'Connor held all the cards. It was foolish of us to have supposed otherwise. But he was anxious not to rub it in. He dug his hand down the side of the chair cushion and pulled out a packet of cigars. He set about the long and pointlessly elaborate business of lighting one up. 'I'm sure we can work something out,' he said. 'I'll speak to Mr Savvides tonight.'

'Your contact?'

'That's right.' He drew in a lungful of smoke and blew it out through his nose. 'Don't book any opera tickets this week. Things could be moving by Thursday.'

'Do we meet your contact?'

'Oh yeah.' O'Connor gestured grandiloquently with his cigar. 'You'll get to see Savvides. You'll like him.' He spat a grain of tobacco onto the carpet. 'Balls like pomegranates.'

# 18

Early Thursday morning, someone pushed an unstamped letter through our letterbox. In it were two business-class air tickets to Porto.

Joanne squinted at them. '*Business* class?'

'Maybe they don't have first class to Porto.'

'Maybe they guess we're cheap.'

I thought she was joking at first but after a bit I saw she was upset. So I rang the airline and sure enough, business class was as good as you got, and after that Joanne's mood improved.

'You're going to become appalling,' I said.

She slipped on the jacket of the new suit she'd just bought. Something with razor lapels to impress Mr Savvides. She turned to me, pouting, the wasp waist of her jacket bright with pseudo-military gold piping. 'You bet.'

'Any more of this you'll be chewing gum and drinking grain alcohol by the bottle.'

'Sit on the edge of the bed.'

'Aw, boss, not again.'

'Do it, punk.'

She studied her nails. They were long, and bright red. She never used to bother with them. 'Lie back,' she said.

'If you say so, Madam.'

Grinning – she could never play-act for long – she hitched up her skirt.

Sun through tinted windows flooded the baggage reclaim hall with bluish light. I caught my bag as it passed but missed Joanne's suitcase. She snapped it up. An Italian businessman stared frankly at her tensed calves as he waited in the line. She smoothed out her pencil-line skirt with her palms and grinned at me. She was on a high. It had all become some sort of strange, sexual game with her: the air tickets, the cars, the strange, ugly men with their cavalier manners and sharp, even teeth. I didn't want her to see how nervous I was, so I grinned back. She swung the case over her shoulder and walked round the loop of the conveyor towards me. 'Put your glasses on,' she said.

'We're indoors.'

'It makes you look cool.'

I felt for them: they weren't in my top pocket.

She tutted and picked them off my forehead. 'There.' She slid them over my eyes. The room sank into green gloom, as though an ocean had overwhelmed us. Joanne's skin was as smooth and cream and flawless as a car body. Her lipsticked mouth was purple like a wound. I wanted to kiss her.

'Let's go, tiger.'

We passed through customs and looked around for O'Connor. He wasn't by the rail.

'He'll be waiting in a bar someplace,' I whispered to her as we edged through the tourist crowd towards the phones. 'Watching us in a security mirror. Maker's Mark bourbon at his elbow.'

But no one showed.

'Fuck it,' Joanne said, 'we're grown-ups, let's get a cab.'

We hailed three before we found a driver who knew Savvides's address, and he looked at us like we were mad. We hardly touched Porto, and skirted the city's breeze-block suburbs on a ring road towards the hills to the north. Every slope here was terraced. Not an inch of ground was wasted. It was a poor country, and every trifling ledge and patch of soil was turned to account. Anywhere else, terraces like that would be used for vines. Here, they were sown with staple crops: cabbages, lettuce, potatoes. Artichoke bulbs on bizarre, leafless stems wobbled in the wind.

We left the orbital and the road rose and rose, into dry land and scree slopes. The scene was lunar in its desolation. There were no real landmarks, just vista after vista of thorn and shattered rock. Savvides's estate, when we came to it at last, looked as if it had dropped out of the sky. The white-painted wrought-iron gates were spotless. Beyond it, everything was bright and wet, as though someone had sprayed lacquer over everything. The huge pink confection of a house looked as unreal as a matte painting. The entrance phone was a brass antique parody in a white-painted box: the ear piece hung from a hook on the speaker. 'Chris and Joanne Yale,' I said. Behind me, the taxi driver reversed out of the drive in a squeal of tyres.

The iron gates swung open.

The raked gravel drive stretched before us, as winding and unreal as the Yellow Brick Road, past fountains and carefully topiaried shrubs. A distant, hurrying figure broke the fairy-tale illusion: O'Connor, his whisky belly bouncing uncomfortably against his trouser belt, raised his hand in welcome.

He was very apologetic. All hell's been happening here,' he said. 'First this Korean party didn't show, then the fucking electricity went out. Thank God you're here.' He said it as though our arrival would cure all household ills. It put Joanne at ease immediately. I envied him his strange, crude charm.

'Tony's on the court, come over.'

Tony Savvides was playing tennis against a serving machine. I'd never seen one in the flesh before. It looked like a piece of artillery.

Savvides was a small man with a shaved head. His scalp was as blunt and grey as a bullet. He moved across the court on the balls of his feet, but his trunk was as solid as a pit-bull's; there was no elasticity to his upper body at all. His Coq Sportif T-shirt was damp at the neck and at the small of his back. His shorts were brief, and when he turned I was startled by the bulge at his crotch.

We watched, and watched, waiting patiently for the ball reservoir to run out.

'These your friends?' said Savvides, when he was done.

'That's right, Tony.'

'Let's go sit by the pool.' He rubbed a towel back and forth across his neck as though he were trying to rub off his tan. 'This place is too fucking hot. Pete, fix us all the usual.' He smiled at us with his mouth: his eyes were dead and sunken, like a nerve had been cut. 'This stuff you've got to try.'

Three of Tony Savvides's men were swimming lengths against each other. There was a mosaic design at the bottom of the pool, but they were making too many waves for me to work it out. Two young blondes lay sprawled on a couple of sun-chairs they had pulled next to each other. They were pointing things out to each other in a copy of *Vogue*.

I glanced towards the house. It was painted pink and white, like a christening cake, and looked about as insubstantial. O'Connor was barely halfway to the door. Savvides had us to himself.

'You know,' he said, 'I never understood why you guys went there in the first place.'

'Where?'

'The moon, where else?'

Neither of us could think of anything to say.

'No grass, no trees, no skies.'

'There would have been,' I said.

'So what?' Savvides's tone was sharp. I'd misunderstood. He wasn't interested in conversation. 'All this extrasensory crap – so what? What's wrong with eyes, with skin?' His gaze slid fondly to the girls. They weren't reading any more. One of them was holding a mirror flat under the other girl's face while she powdered her nose from the inside. 'Seems to me,' he said, 'you guys had too much appetite. You couldn't see the good in what you had. An earth. Five senses. Youth.'

'Maybe,' said Joanne, neutrally.

'Damn right,' he said. 'That's the trouble with the world today. Everybody's too damn greedy.' His laugh was like a cat having its guts pulled out through its nose. 'Right?'

I tried to smile.

'You ever been to Azerbaijan?' Joanne and I looked at each other. 'Well?'

'No,' I said. 'No, we haven't been there.'

'Damn good accessories out of Azerbaijan,' he said. 'Best in the business. AI 'ware. Biomechanical systems, data storage gear made of DNA. Fuck, you must know all this.'

'On the moon we used Taiwanese product,' Joanne said. 'It's better quality.'

'But expensive.'

'That wasn't a consideration.' She was putting him down. She wanted him to know we were slumming it, being here. O'Connor had found her attitude touching. I didn't like to think what Savvides made of it.

'I need a couple of friends to take a present from Azerbaijan to an acquaintance of mine in Madagascar.'

''Ware?'

'Of sorts.'

'And once we're there?' I asked.

'We'll see.'

I said, 'This isn't quite what we were expecting, Mr Savvides.'

'Tony.'

'Tony.'

'Here we go.' O'Connor set down a silver tray loaded with highball glasses, a steel bucket of chipped ice and a bottle of white port. He had a boy with him. He was maybe twelve years old, and his face was pasty and swollen like a balloon. He was fat. He waddled round the pool edge like a penguin towards the girls.

'Tony was telling us he wants us to run 'ware through the EU customs barricade,' Joanne told O'Connor. 'You know, the way teenage girls carry drugs inside themselves? Not quite what we had in mind.'

O'Connor shot me a glance, like I should control her tongue. Like I could.

As the boy neared the girls he broke into a run. The one holding the compact snapped it shut and palmed it safely against her breast. The boy kicked her sunbed, trying to spill her stash, and waddled off again, laughing.

'Terri,' Savvides shouted. 'Put that shit away when my kid's around.'

'Yes, Tony,' said the girls together. Maybe they were both called Terri. It was that sort of a place.

The boy ran round the pool and drew to a halt beside

Savvides, gasping, his hands on his knees as he struggled for breath.

'Come sit down with us,' said Savvides.

The boy glanced at the tray. 'Is there any cherry Coke?'

'You get the boy a Coke?'

'No, Tony,' said O'Connor, 'I didn't know he was coming.'

Savvides sighed and patted the seat of the sun-lounger next to him. 'Sit down, Ray, 'fore you fall down.'

Once Ray was settled Savvides turned his attention back to O'Connor. 'Yeah,' he said, picking up the thread of the conversation, 'what did you promise these good people? The lady seems all upset.'

'I said you'd know what's around,' said O'Connor.

'That's right,' said Savvides, with satisfaction, as though O'Connor had correctly recited a catechism. 'I know what's available, what needs doing – and what needs doing at the moment is a run to Madagascar.'

'Which will get us what?' said Joanne. She looked hot in her black dress, and out of place. She kicked off her shoes and there was a hole in the toe of her left stocking. She didn't look svelte any more, not a bit the magazine seductress she'd been at the airport. I caught O'Connor watching her. I think he felt sorry for her.

'The money's not a problem,' said Savvides. I wondered how much of our conversation the boy, Ray, was picking up. But he didn't seem to be taking any notice. On the opposite side of the pool, one of the girls was rubbing lotion into the other's back. He wasn't taking any notice of that, either. He was watching the men, swimming back and forth. He squinted into the light, his eyes screwed up into folds of pale fat, as his dad's soldiers peeled powerfully through the turquoise water.

'We have illnesses to support,' said Joanne. 'Any delay is a problem.'

'You'll get to wear the accessories on the flight,' said Savvides. And if that's not enough – if you want to deliver late – well, we can arrange that. We'll give you a week by the beach if you like, before we take delivery. There's no hurry.'

'How do we get through customs?' I said. 'Wear hats?'

'The gear fits inside your skull. Our medical team in Azerbaijan can perform the operation while you're on your way to the airport. Twenty minutes tops, and you won't even need a general anaesthetic'

I stared at him in horror. Incredibly, Joanne seemed to buy the deal. And what does it do? What do we get to see when the stuff's inside us?'

'It's a government special services package. Airwaves monitor.'

'You mean it's a radio.'

'I mean—'

'This is shit,' Joanne said, losing it suddenly.

White port dribbled from the edge of O'Connor's glass onto his T-shirt.

'Fourteen thousand New ECUs is not shit,' said Savvides, tightly.

'Even in roubles it's not what we want.'

'You'll do as Dad tells you and like it,' said the boy.

Joanne and I stared at him. We couldn't have been more surprised if a piece of garden furniture had spoken. He hadn't once looked at us, or taken any interest. He still didn't take his eyes off the swimmers. His breathing was laboured. A line of belly showed between his shirt and his trunks; smooth and white with a sheen like lard.

'You don't get out much,' Joanne said to him. 'Do you?'

Savvides's mouth compressed into a grim line. His lips went colourless, like scar tissue.

'Fuck you,' said the boy, idly.

Savvides looked from the boy to Joanne, to see if she would say something else – compound her mistake.

Instead she reached into her purse and drew out a cigarette.

'You should know I don't let people smoke around my boy.'

She looked at the boy. She looked at Savvides. 'Fuck you,' she said.

Savvides leaned forward, plucked the white cylinder from her lips and flicked it into the pool.

Joanne stared at the water: her eyes were blind with reflected light.

'Hey, what is this?' said Savvides, lightly. 'We were getting on fine. This is just a crossed wire. Let's not fuck up the day. Ray, go on inside to your ma. You look broiled to shit.'

'I'm okay.'

'Go get yourself a cherry Coke.'

'Let Pete get it.'

'Go on now.'

Ray let a second go by, then flung himself out of the seat and stormed off back to the house. The tantrum would have been impressive, had he not had to fight so hard to get upright.

'And you,' Savvides said lightly to Joanne, 'should keep a civil tongue.' He turned to me. 'She talks to you like this?'

'I'll answer for myself,' said Joanne, taking out another cigarette. Savvides sighed. He looked at me and waved his hand at my wife, like he was demonstrating something. She blew the smoke away from him, over the water.

'So is someone going to tell me what the problem is here?'

'It's my fault, Tony,' said O'Connor, pouring oil on the waters. 'I told them there's R and D work going down. I guess I raised their expectations.'

'So there is,' said Savvides. 'R and D work's most of what we do. Pete wasn't bulling you. But we all pull our weight, you understand, you two? We need a couple of people with Apolloco-shaped holes in their heads to carry these accessories out to Madagascar, just as much as we need people to map and diagnose it once we get it there.' He stood up and paced back and forth in front of the pool, like a lecturer struggling to explain a difficult concept. 'You're not the only post-humans we work with. There are people have been working for us for months. People who walk around all day every day with our accessories in their heads. Because we trust them. Because we value their input. You don't make trust in a day. If you two want the easy, safe, rewarding jobs, first you've got to show me some commitment. Same as the people did who came before you. This is a good deal I'm offering you. I'm even giving you

a week's holiday with this valuable package in your heads—'
He hesitated; double-took, like something had just dawned on
him. 'Wait – you think Madagascar's going to cost you somehow? You think your hard-earned cash is going to have to go on
hotel rooms, on food and wine? Forget it. The expenses are on
us. It's a junket. Don't piss on it.'

It was quite a performance. I wondered how much strength
of will it took for him not to simply tell his swimming buddies
to kick the shit out of us.

I stood up. Joanne joined me and took my arm. 'Thanks,'
I said, 'and we're sorry for the crossed wire earlier. But no
thanks.'

I don't think he was surprised. 'You mind telling me why?'

'I wondered why you let your boy hear what you were offering us,' I said. 'Well, now I know. If kid's stuff is all you've got
for us, then our answer's no.' Joanne's grip on my arm tightened. Whether to stop me or to encourage me, I couldn't tell.

'Okay,' said Savvides, evenly. 'Who needs you?' He laughed.
'You've had one little junket on me already, coming here. If you
don't want more, why are you still here?' He stood up. 'Seems
to me,' he said, 'you just came to breathe my air.' There was no
warmth in his wide, white smile.

'I'll see you guys out,' said O'Connor. He wasn't happy; not
at all. I wondered how much trouble he'd be in when we were
gone, bringing punks into Tony's beautiful home.

'Have a good flight home,' Savvides called after us. Maybe
we'd got under his skin after all. 'Mind you don't choke on the
complimentary fucking champagne.'

O'Connor walked us as far as the gate. 'For pity's sake,' he
complained under his breath, like Savvides could hear us even
at this distance, 'did you have to break his balls?'

'You were right,' I said, 'they're too big for one man.'

O'Connor looked at me like I'd broken wind. 'Okay,' he
sighed, 'big joke.'

'If he has any real work, let us know,' Joanne said.

O'Connor looked at her. There was pity in his eyes. 'Start
walking,' he said. 'I'll phone you a cab. It'll meet you on the

road.' He turned his back on us, and went back inside. To what, I wondered? To serving drinks for Savvides and his boy? Some goodfella.

We walked down the road in the dust and the blistering heat, in inappropriate clothes and with stupid grins on our faces. It had been an adventure. 'I can't believe you said those things to him,' I said, and Joanne said, 'He was full of wind. It was a waste of time coming here.'

'Yeah,' I said, 'something better will turn up.' At the time I believed it, almost – so I wondered why I had such a bad taste in my mouth.

From the valley floor we heard a car, labouring through the gears, approaching us. We exchanged a look – and then I knew what was wrong. Joanne was feeling it too – it was fear.

That was why we had pissed off Savvides. That was the real force driving our big talk and bullish gestures: fear. And Savvides, being Savvides, would have known that. We hadn't riled him. We weren't important enough to rile him. We had simply made fools of ourselves. And why? Because what Savvides had offered us – what he represented even – had scared us. Smuggling 'ware across national boundaries carries a mandatory life sentence in most countries. That's aside from any psychiatric or forensic damage The Hague does to you. More than one 'ware-runner had come into court brain-damaged thanks to police due process. We weren't ready to take those risks yet. We weren't desperate enough.

The taxi appeared. It was just a taxi. No hit men in Armani suits and wraparound shades. Just a shrivelled little woman in an antique Fiat Punto who talked all the way to the airport in a language we could not understand.

They served us champagne on the flight home. We weren't smiling any more. We felt ashamed, and did not look at each other. I remember thinking, no way would we ever be desperate enough to work for frightening, comic-book figures like Tony Savvides.

\*

Now, two years on, I wasn't so sure.

Yes, I'd found my niche with Ballantyne, content with the half-life his treatments gave me.

But Joanne – what had Joanne done? Had she become desperate enough at last? Had she found herself another O'Connor?

# 3
# AFTER LIFE

3

AFTER LIFE

# 19

'Where are we going?' I said. 'I thought we were going to police headquarters.' But nothing I said made any difference.

My arrest – if arrest it was – should not have surprised me. In some countries, this sort of thing happens every day. Because of what I had been, suspicion followed me around everywhere like an unpleasant and intimate smell.

I had the seat to myself, and they hadn't cuffed me. But they didn't need to: the rear doors had no handles. Both policemen sat in front, separated from me by a wire mesh. I studied the backs of their heads. The driver's neck was raw red, as though he had scraped it smooth that morning with a cut-throat razor. But he was so young: had he even begun shaving?

It was late afternoon. The light over London had a delicate, fiery tint; air pollution in league with autumn. We drove through Whitehall and passed the grassed-over ruins of the Houses of Parliament. A low fence surrounded the site, and kiosks sold tickets to tourists who had come to walk around the ruins. An open-air service was under way in the shell of Westminster Abbey. Camera flashlights bounced off the shattered walls like a memory of mortar fire.

'Are you going to tell me where we're going?'

We continued down Millbank to the edge of the river and crossed at Lambeth Bridge. Downstream, the shattered remains of Westminster Bridge stuck up out of the churning water like accusing fingers, made bloody by the fading light. We crossed the river and turned east along the Embankment.

'You can tell me.'

But I frightened them; they said nothing. One look at my head, and the plugs installed there, had been enough to intimidate them. They were young, unfinished, and afraid of me – and they had guns.

Now we were on the South Bank it wasn't hard to guess our destination. Sure enough, a couple of minutes later the soft, adobe lines of Apolloco's incinerator tower rose above the tattoo parlours and taxi offices of Wandsworth.

We descended a narrow feed-road into the hospital's underground carpark. The enclosed space made the driver even more nervous. He flung our car around the ramps and narrow passages as though dodging an invisible pursuer. His eyes flicked compulsively back and forth between the windscreen and the rear-view mirror.

He seemed surer of his territory once he was out of the car. 'Please step outside,' he said.

I retrieved my socks from the footwell and began straightening them out.

'Mr Yale—'

'One second.'

'Step out, Mr Yale.'

'I need my socks.'

'Please step outside now.'

I shoved my socks in my jacket pocket and climbed out of the car. 'I only wanted to put my socks on.' The concrete was icy against my bare feet.

They grabbed me under the arms and frog-marched me into the lift. We rode up to the lobby. From there they led me down a corridor I didn't recognise. Their grip on my arms was fierce. They were practically carrying me. I paddled my feet, searching for the floor. 'I can walk!' I said. The tiles were cool and tacky on my toes. 'I can walk!' I kept saying, but they didn't take any notice. A young Indian intern ran up the corridor and fell into step with us. He typed something into his clipboard: 'Christopher Yale?'

'Yes,' I said.

'Yes,' said the man on my left arm. 'Has he been here before?'

'Sure,' the policeman said, 'take a look at his head.' The intern peered at the scars on my scalp. 'Yes I see.'

'One of yours.'

'Really?'

'The moon, so he says.'

'We have a scanner ready,' the intern said.

'Rence wanted us to use the secure room.'

'Our database is off-line. He'll have to re-register.' The intern glanced me over. 'Where are his shoes?'

'He didn't have any shoes.'

'No shoes ?' He peered into my face. 'You have to wear shoes, Mr Yale,' he said, clearly, as to a child.

'I kicked them off. They were on fire.'

'You should have some shoes.' He typed something.

Maybe he didn't believe me. Maybe he thought I was fantasizing. I wanted to explain: they really were on fire. I was in a fire. Can't you smell it on my clothes? I knew for certain the intern had got the wrong impression of me. If I could only set the record straight about my shoes, then maybe he would delete whatever he had typed ...

I was thinking exactly the way they wanted me to think.

'Has there been any change in your general health within the past year?'

'No,' I said. I wondered how many more lies I'd have to let slip.

'Are you under the care of a doctor or clinic?'

'No.' (There went another one.)

We got into a lift. It went down. This part of the hospital was a mystery to me.

'Have you had any serious illnesses or operations?'

The lift fell and kept falling. How many basements were there?

'Do you have or have you ever had rheumatic fever?'

'No.'

'Congenital heart disease?'

'No.'

Angina or stroke?'

The doors opened. The corridor was blistering white. Tiles covered the walls, floor and ceiling. Orderlies in loose white shifts flitted in and out of the corridor, bureaucratic angels in an hygienist's heaven. 'Epilepsy or fainting spells?'

'No.'

'Diabetes?'

We stopped at a pressurised door.

The HazNano warning sign,

stood out bright orange against the beige plastic, like some outlandish artificial growth come to over-run the hospital.

The officers let me go. The intern gazed cow-eyed into a smoked glass plate. The door recognised his retinal ID and trundled open. A cool draught feathered my hair. The air smelled of a dentist's waiting room.

'This way, Mr Yale.'

I stepped in. The room was the size of a toilet cubicle. 'Do you have a cardiac pacemaker or other cybernetic prosthesis?'

'No.'

'Do you get short of breath when you lie down?'

'Depends who I'm with.'

The inner door cycled open on a cavernous round hall. The walls were soft and felty and uneven. Lint hung in irregular folds over them like the gills of a tree fungus. White gluey patches clung unevenly to the lint, as though some bizarre machine had gone round gobbing white paint randomly round the room.

I stepped inside. The floor was concrete painted with a wear-resistant lacquer. It was bitterly cold against my feet.

The ceiling was concrete, sprayed white. Fluorescent lights hung in a circle around the room. Their objective light robbed the room's few objects – a dentist's trolley, a plastic changing screen on castors, an x-ray camera on a heavy tripod – of their expected shadows.

'Have you ever taken addictive drugs?'

'No.'

'Anticoagulants?'

'No'

In the centre of the circle of lights the even whiteness of the ceiling gave way to a rough area of charred and bubbled paint. Under the charred area sat a dentist's chair, all vinyl and steel. Kevlar straps hung off it in long, untidy loops. The headrest had built-in clamps and straps for immobilising the sitter's neck and jaw.

'What is this? Is this a scanner?'

'Do you bruise easily?'

'No. Do you?'

'Do you take an oral contraceptive or other hormonal therapy?'

'What is this?'

The young doctor switched off the clipboard and tucked it under his arm. 'Please undress,' he said. He pointed to the changing screen.

I couldn't take my eyes off the chair – the straps.

'Over there, Mr Yale, hurry along.'

'If this is a scanner I don't need the straps,' I said.

'Mr Yale?'

'I don't need the straps. I know how to keep still.' He considered me doubtfully. 'I'll still need to bolt your head to the chair.'

'I know that.'

'Please undress.'

I looked doubtfully at the screen. 'Why do I have to undress?'

'Certain fibre types affect the scan.'

I took my first, uncertain step towards the screen. 'I didn't know that.'

'Ah,' said the intern, as if this proved some obscure point.

Behind the screen, I fumbled out of my jacket and shirt. There was a metal chair to drape my clothes on. I shed my underpants and stepped from behind the screen.

The intern was arranging instruments on the dentist's trolley. I crossed to the chair. The air in the room was still, the temperature exact. I hardly felt naked at all. Only my feet, sore and scratched, smarted against the freezing floor. I was nearly at the chair when the intern turned round and gave me a brief, chill glance. 'There's a gown,' he said, 'hanging on the back of the screen.' He said it without emphasis, as if my exposing myself to him was the sort of mistake he'd expected from me.

I retreated, blushing. I looked for the shift. It was the same translucent plastic as the screen, which was why I'd not seen it. I slipped the shift over my head. It was stiff and cold and it reminded me of body bags I'd seen on TV. I straightened it over my knees and stepped out again. The material crackled and bent absurdly as I crossed to the chair.

The intern wheeled the trolley over to the chair. He snapped on a pair of latex gloves. 'Take a seat, please,' he said again, loud and distinct, as though I were hard of hearing.

'I want to see Durrell.' I wished my voice were steadier.

'I beg your pardon?'

'Mr Durrell. Jim Durrell. He was my surgeon when I returned from the moon.'

'I'm afraid Mr Durrell isn't available. Sit down, please.'

'Where is he?'

'Mr Durrell? Right now he'll be in surgery, at our Wapping site. Now will you please sit down?'

I sat. I felt like a scrap of waste meat amid all this steel and glass.

'This is an MRI scanner,' the young man told me, rewarding me for my good behaviour. I read his name off his badge: Nouronihar. What kind of name was that? 'We believe you may have exposed yourself to compromising technology.' He tore a swab from its wrapper. 'Roll up your left sleeve, please.'

'What is this?'

'Just a blood sample.'

The treatments Ballantyne had given me might still be traceable. I wondered if I should say something about them; whether it would go better for me if I did.

'Mr Yale?'

Wearily, I did as he said.

Nouronihar slid the needle painfully into my vein. 'This won't take a second.'

When it was over, Nouronihar told me to sit back in the chair. He fixed the brace round my forehead and tightened a kevlar band under my jaw. When my head was secure, Nouronihar began tightening a strap around my waist. I grunted and kicked my feet.

Nouronihar leaned vaguely into my field of view. 'Mr Yale?'

I grunted. What else could I do? The band round my jaw was so tight I couldn't even grate my teeth.

'Are you sure you can sit still enough for this?'

I gave him a thumbs-up.

'Hm?'

I grunted a third time. It was all I could do.

Nouronihar peered at me, dubiously, as though he expected some more positive answer. 'Well, we can give it a try,' he said. 'Keep as still as you can.' I heard the door cycle shut.

I was alone.


It was a subtle sort of rape: no blades, no probes, no forced distension of the orifices. No tang of blood, no drill to leave a brassy taste in my mouth. No motion of machinery. No electric hum.

Thirty seconds passed.

The rapist was a very thorough robot. It mapped every nerve, gauged the barometric pressure of every millilitre of my cerebrospinal fluid. With nuclear-magnetic fingers it traced the etched surface of my bones and searched each nick and score and working surface for illicit meaning. It read my sperm, playing the double-helix of my genome like an accordion, and looked to see what illicit thing might have dropped from between the diribonucleic folds. It watched my thoughts spill and spiral across my cerebral cortex. It followed them, scrolling through the magnitudes, in and in and in, so that nothing remained unpenetrated.

It left me whole – and it left me with nothing.

*

Nouronihar came in again. He unclipped the band round my jaw. I chewed the air, trying to get the feeling back into my mouth.

Nouronihar gripped the wheel that adjusted the clamp round my head and turned it – the wrong way. My skull flexed. A sickening pressure flooded my eyes. I cried out. Nouronihar tutted and turned the wheel the other way, releasing me. 'If you would like to get dressed again now, Mr Yale.'

I creaked and crumpled my way back to the screen. The plasticated shift was sticky with my sweat and as heavy as tarpaulin. I wrestled free of it.

The door to the room cycled open. Footsteps approached the screen. I threw on my shirt and grabbed my underpants from the chair.

Nouronihar bent his head round the screen and blinked at me. 'Mr Yale? This is Mr Ballantyne.'

George Ballantyne stepped into view. Hearty, red-cheeked, arms akimbo like a greetings-card Father Christmas, he blocked Nouronihar out completely.

'Mr Ballantyne is from the police! He will explain any further procedures.' With this the intern hurried to the door. His footsteps were as quick and light as a bird's. The door cycled again.

Ballantyne chuckled. 'I made him nervous, don't you think?'

'Get out of here.' I wouldn't meet his eye.

Ballantyne tutted.

'George, I'm dressing, get lost!'

'Seen it all before, lad,' he sniffed.

'Will you please—'

'Wiped your bottom more than once, I have.'

'Christ,' I muttered, tugging my trousers on. 'What the fuck are you doing here?'

'Rence needed someone to ferry you to headquarters for questioning.'

'*Rence?* You work for Rence?'

'I'm a policeman, remember?'

'But he's working for The Hague!'

Ballantyne's grin was as sudden as though someone had

thrown a switch inside him. 'Special technologies division,' he reminded me, savouring each syllable as though it were a coin.

'Jesus Christ, George, you like living dangerously.'

'Can you think of a better way I can keep the Filth away from the clinic?'

I shoved my shirt-tails into the waistband of my trousers and stomped towards the door.

'Where are your shoes?'

'I haven't any shoes.'

'Where are they?'

'I haven't got any.' I examined the door. It was like the door of the police car: no handle. How did it open?

'Well,' said George, 'I suppose it doesn't matter.'

'Of course it fucking matters. I want some shoes. I want something to put on my feet!'

'Come on, then,' said Ballantyne, easily. 'We'll find somebody.' He looked into a smoked glass plate and the door cycled open. If your retinal records weren't on the hospital computer, you couldn't get in or out.

I gave the room a farewell glance. The soft walls, the burned ceiling. Ballantyne followed my gaze. 'The doctor not tell you?'

'Tell me what?'

'The last man Rence sent in here had a head full of pirated accessories. When they scanned him his head exploded.'

# 20

Ballantyne led me through the hospital lobby. My toes hurt. The slippers the hospital had found for me were too small.

Ballantyne looked sideways at me. 'So what were you doing in Soho?'

'It was Joanne's flat.'

'How do you know?'

'Her sister told me. Joanne told her to keep it a secret.'

'How come she didn't tell Rence?'

'I was going to.'

'Well?'

'I forgot.'

'So how come Rence turned up at the fire?'

'You know about that?'

Ballantyne's laugh was humourless, full of tension. 'One moment we were scanning next month's budget projections, next he gets this phone call and he's waddling down the corridor screaming for back-up and a fast car.'

I thought about it. I was still concussed: nothing made any sense. 'I guess someone followed me,' I said.

'You saw someone?'

I thought about the man in the flat. The missing Jewel. The hypos, stripped from me, and then replaced. 'No,' I said. 'I saw no one.'

Ballantyne walked beside me in silence for a while. Then he said, 'This could be bad, Chris. It means Rence knew about the flat all along.'

'Looks like it, doesn't it? Since they just put me through the scanner.'

'Oh, that. That's just intimidation. Forget about it. But if Rence knew about the flat and didn't tell me, then he's playing some game I know nothing about.'

I wondered why I was supposed to care about that.

We entered the lobby. Low sunlight fluoresced against the dirty glass. I rubbed my eyes. My head throbbed. Ballantyne was pulling his usual trick: drawing me into one of his paranoid conspiracies. As if I wasn't in enough trouble. He said, 'When you were in the flat – I suppose you were touching everything?' His sense of assumed authority was strong.

'I suppose.'

'What did you touch?'

'The door handles.'

'Yes?'

'A bathroom cabinet. A few sheets.'

132

'Anything else?'

'Some kitchen stuff. A bit of clothing.'

Ballantyne sighed. 'You know,' he began, awkwardly, as if explaining a point of social etiquette, 'you're going to have to tell Rence you were there.'

It was a strange thing for him to say. 'Of course I'm going to tell him,' I said.

'I'll be sitting in on the interview,' Ballantyne said. He was trying to chivvy me; to appear in control. 'There's nothing to worry about, sonnie.' He was playing the Scotsman again. The comical highland uncle. 'We have to stick together.'

'Really.'

We walked side by side to the doors. I stepped on the pressure mat and the door slid open. I offered Ballantyne the exit: 'Lead on, Macduff,' I sneered.

Ballantyne shot me a warm, avuncular smile, pleased that I was entering into the spirit of things.

I watched him out of the door and followed him down the steps. It was so strange, him being here. As though one part of my life had erupted in another, quite separate part.

It was then I noticed his shoes.

George drove us into a back alley behind Waterloo East station and pulled to a stop. Out of the glove compartment he drew out a plasticated card of hypodermics. For a heart-stopping moment I thought they were Jewel. But the barrels were full of a colourless liquid. ResponsIV. The illegal, sense-saving concoction he fed his patients at the clinic.

'You never had your booster shot,' he said. It was true. I watched his thick, muscular fingers tear a hypo from the pack. 'Come on, lad,' he said.

His thumb trembled on the trigger of the hypo.

'Your arm, lad.'

A second passed.

'What is it?'

I couldn't speak.

He turned the hypo over in his fingers and handed it to me. 'Well,' he said calmly, 'do it yourself.'

I took the hypo from him. I checked the seal. The Apolloco stamp. It seemed okay. I put it in my jacket pocket.

'What are you doing?'

'I think I'll save it till after Rence's little chat.'

He bit his lip, annoyed with me. 'Then give it back to me,' he said. Annoyance cut through his lilting, *faux*-Dumfries accent.

'No way.'

'I'll give it back to you later.'

'Uh-uh.'

'You're not walking into Hanover headquarters with twenty CCs of ResponsIV in your pocket!'

'Watch me,' I said.

Ballantyne let it go. 'As you like,' he said. He turned the key in the ignition and pulled away from the kerb. 'Just don't drop the fucker on Rence's carpet.'

He drove us in silence over Waterloo Bridge and onto the bulldozed and unmetalled throughway that was the new Strand. I watched him out the corner of my eye, wondering why he had allowed me this paltry victory. The hypo was glass; it was heavy. It tugged oddly at my jacket when I adjusted my seat belt.

I said, 'Why was Rence having me followed?'

Ballantyne's grip on the wheel tightened.

'Do you know?'

A discoloured patch appeared along his cheek-bone. 'I don't know,' he said, 'but I can guess.'

'Well?'

'Joanne's head injury has got Rence thinking about pirate-ware. This morning Forensics phoned through a new set of lab tests. Something showed up. Whatever it is, it's got Rence running round like a chicken with its throat cut. I walked into his office this morning to talk about overtime cuts and new bonus schemes, and he was on the phone to Amsterdam sorting customs clearance for a Hague away team. The Hague in *London?* The Prince Regent himself must have crayonned his X to let them in.'

I stared sightlessly at the muddy wasteland of the Strand, the gravel isthmuses, the spinning wheels of the bikes and pushcarts churning up the ruined earth. 'Because of Joanne?' I said.

Ballantyne grunted. 'I hope not, laddie. I hope I'm wrong. Because if The Hague's taking an interest in this case then we're both in the shitter.'

'Where are your shoes?' said Rence, staring at my slippered feet.

'It doesn't bloody matter,' I said, 'I don't give a flying fuck about my shoes.' I kicked my slippers off and wiggled my aching toes.

Rence flinched and sat back in his seat. His face was a mask of distaste, like I'd just mooned him. 'Ballantyne?'

'They were all the hospital could find,' said Ballantyne. He shot the slippers a speculative glance. 'I think they're a bit tight for him.'

I swallowed down a growing hysteria. 'Can we please—?'

'What were you doing there, Mr Yale?' Rence fixed me with his steady green gaze.

'I wanted to see where she lived,' I said. I couldn't meet his eyes. 'I wanted to see for myself.' Beside him, Ballantyne gave me a careful, almost imperceptible nod of approval.

I wished I'd kept my slippers on. I felt naked.

'How do you know it was Joanne's flat?'

'Her sister told me. Ines. Joanne told her never to tell anyone. She was nervous.'

Rence said nothing.

'It wasn't her fault,' I said.

Rence wasn't impressed. His eyes were steady green lights, shining with secrets.

We were sitting in a small, beige papered interrogation room. A formica table separated us. Two microphones bloomed from a small, regular hole in its centre. Rence had a digital notepad in front of him. He turned a black plastic stylus over and over around his fingers as though he were practising a magic trick.

'Where did you sleep last night?'

'At my flat.'

'When did you leave?'

It went on like this for maybe twenty minutes. He was wearing me down, going over the same things constantly. He was trying to catch me out. Ballantyne said nothing, but watched me closely.

'What time did you say you got to the flat?'

'One-fifteen.'

'And what time did the fire start?'

'Maybe an hour later. I don't know.'

'How come?'

'I told you. I fell asleep.'

'What woke you?'

'The smoke.'

'You were lucky.'

I stared at him. Ballantyne stared at me. 'I've told you,' I said. 'The place was full of electrical gear. I must have kicked something. The place was a tinderbox.'

Rence didn't even blink. There were dirty bristle lines in the creases around his mouth. His thick, colourless fingernails were ragged, as though he'd crawled out from under the earth. All right,' he said. He stood up, came round the table, leaned over and stuck his face into mine. He smelled of French cigarettes and bad coffee and earth.

I leaned back. The chair tilted under me. 'Let me tell you what's going to happen. A team from The Hague arrives tomorrow morning. We're going to bus them over to the Apolloco hospital in Waterloo. Apolloco is going to loan them whatever equipment they ask for, all the very latest gear. Scanners you never dreamed of. Then we're going to drive them to the flat. And we're not letting them out of the building until they find out how and why you set the place alight. A fingerprint. A particle of skin. A hair. A footprint. A pheromonic trace. A fart. The *echo* of a fart. And when they do, which they will, I'm going to serve you up to them on a platter. Do you understand?'

'I didn't—'

'Do you understand?'

'I told you—'

'Have you heard me?'

'Yes,' I said.

'Have you heard me?'

'I've heard you.'

He marched to the door. 'Get him out of here,' he said, without turning round. 'Inspector?'

He turned to me, slowly.

I said, 'Joanne's head wound. How did it happen? Did something go into her skull? Or did something come out?'

Rence stared at me with contempt. 'Don't leave town,' he said. He slammed the door behind him.

Ballantyne leaned into the microphone. His voice was subdued. 'Interview concluded—' he glanced at his watch. 'Twenty-eighteen.' He hit a button under the microphone and ran his hands through what remained of his hair. 'Jesus, what was all that about?'

I shrugged. 'I was thinking about the burn-mark on the scanning-room ceiling.'

'Now he thinks you're playing with him.'

'He thinks that anyway.'

'And you want to encourage him?' He stood up. 'Come on, I'd better get you out of here.'

'The more he thinks I know, the more he'll let slip.'

Ballantyne raised his eyes up to heaven. 'Now for God's sake, don't talk to me. We're not supposed to know each other, remember?'

We walked in silence through the lobby. At the doors he stopped me. He glanced around. There was nobody at the desk. Two civilians sat on green plastic chairs nearby, but they weren't taking any notice of us. It was his chance to give me the usual parting homily. 'Go home, Chris. Get some sleep. We can't afford any more trouble. You heard what he said about The Hague. Let it go.'

'Sure,' I said.

I said, 'It was frostbite, wasn't it?'

'What?'

'In the Karelian campaign. It was frostbite ate your toes.'

He glanced down reflexively at his feet. His heavy shoes.

I walked off. I wasn't in the mood for his excuses. As I turned the corner I glanced back at him. He was still standing at the open door, as I knew he would be. His face was sharply lit by lobby light, his mouth a black O of dismay.

# 21

I hobbled over to Knightsbridge, past the mortar-blasted shell of the disused subway station, and walked along Kensington Gore. Rence's interrogation had wound me up, and if I didn't walk the mood off I'd never sleep, exhausted though I was. I was halfway along Kensington Road, watching the mounted police practice their night-riding on the sandy road beyond the highway, when a black car pulled up at the kerb. The door swung open. I imagined Hague agents, doors without handles, subtle forensic penetrations ...

'Christopher!'

It took me a moment to recognise him. 'Jim.'

Jim Durrell grinned at me. His teeth were long and greenish in the streetlight. That and his face, which had softened since I last saw him, gave him the look of a cadaver. 'What happened to your shoes?'

'Nice car,' I said. Its glossy bodywork reflected the lights of the hotel opposite like an insect carapace.

'Well come on then!'

It hung low on its suspension like a racer and I had to crouch to get in. There were so many lights flashing on the dashboard, it looked more like a plane than a car.

'I only got back this afternoon,' he said. 'I only just heard.' I couldn't meet his eyes. He'd known Joanne before I had. 'I'm so sorry, Chris.'

'Thanks.'

'Listen.' He hit the brakes needlessly hard, and the seatbelt dug the ResponsIV barrel into my chest so hard I thought it was going to break. 'Let's not go back to your place. Let's go get a drink.'

I shrugged.

'Yes?'

'Okay.'

'Okay then.' He swung the car around. 'I tried phoning you but your terminal was out of order.'

'I'm getting it reconnected.'

'So I figured I'd drive round and see if you were in. For fuck's sake, Chris, what's going on? I come into the hospital this afternoon to a message from some intern that the police are scanning you in the high-security wing. An hour later Gerald Rence is wanting to know how I know you.'

'*Gerald*?'

'Yeah.' Durrell grinned again. His cheeks were soft and toneless. Tendons like wires pulled them into loose sacs beneath his cheekbones. The sight stirred an early memory: clowns' heads, hanging from trees. 'Gerald. His great and shameful secret.'

'You know him?'

'He's seconded to the The Hague. He called me home a few days early to help dress an investigative team with fancy forensics gear.' He glanced at me. 'You okay?'

'I didn't think you'd know him.'

'Are you kidding? The Hague say jump, we Apolloco boys ask how far.'

I let conversation slide a minute and rested my head against the soft grey velveteen of the headrest. I could still feel the place where Ballantyne had pushed my head into the door, and my nose felt as though someone had stuffed it with pine needles. Whenever I forgot and scratched it, a red-hot needle shot through my right eye.

I kicked off my slippers, but at the same time I had to fold my arms against the car's febrile air-conditioning. Durrell was born in the outback of Australia and never felt the cold;

139

I'd spent my student years in an artistic commune up in the Rockies and wore cardigans in the middle of June.

This was the first private car I'd ridden in since moving to the Republic. Since the global oil drain had begun to bite, private transport was becoming more and more the luxury of the governing class. But Durrell hadn't taken enough care of it to make it the status symbol it could have been. The upholstery smelled of trainers, and there were sweet-wrappers in the foot-well: unmistakable traces of unglamorous family outings and routine school pick-ups.

I said, 'Did you say you'd been away?'

'Constanta, with the kids. We got back this afternoon. It was okay.'

'Diane?'

'She stayed home. She's well.'

'And the kids?'

'Tummy trouble, as usual. God knows what crap the Soviets poured into the sea there. I swear it glows in the dark. Laterna?'

'What?' It took me a second to remember the name of the bar. 'Yes, sure. Old times.'

'That's right.' I could tell he was looking beyond the road to some private space. He had remembered something that troubled him. 'Are you sure?'

Joanne and I used to drink there with him on our return from the moon. That was before he met Diane. The three blind mice, we called ourselves. But the joke soon wore thin, as the EAI set in, and the reality of our blindness began to bite.

I said, 'It's fine.'

The Laterna lay east of St Martin's Lane, a short walk from the markets and sideshows of Covent Garden. It belonged to a Russian immigrant family and they had modelled it on some blousy racial memory of the drinking houses in old St Petersburg. Drinks were served in the hall, which was divided down the middle by a long, hardwood bar. Leading off the hall were about half a dozen rooms, crammed with sideboards and easy chairs and ornate oval mirrors.

A large dining table covered with a hand-embroidered lace tablecloth dominated the room we used to drink in. Couples and groups who took up the empty chairs there soon found themselves sharing their conversation with everyone else round the table. This time, though, we went into the largest room, since it offered the best privacy. Frosted glass panels in hardwood frames divided the space into snugs. Flower arrangements with blackbirds' eggs in them decorated each table. We took seats in the corner of the room, by a window with stained glass panels round the central pane. Motes of coloured light wandered back and forth across the tablecloth.

'What are you drinking?'

I asked for a tea. It came sweetened with honey in a pewter-handled glass. Jim brought back a beer and a small liqueur glass of salmiakki vodka, a black, glutinous liquorice concoction he'd discovered in Helsinki during some conference or other. 'So.' His smile was guarded and uncertain: two years and a death divided us. He let the smile dissolve, and his face became unreadable. 'I'm so sorry,' he said. 'She was a wonderful woman.'

Durrell had let himself spread markedly in the two years since I'd last seen him. His hair was thick and carefully waved; unless you ran your fingers through it, you'd never know he'd had the plugs installed. His suit was precisely the suit you'd expect a London professional to wear. Durrell had gone native, and his appearance was impressive and disconcerting. Most post-humans never really caught up with the manners and style of the homeworld. Some, like me, had never really tried.

I lifted my glass. 'To Joanne,' I said, softly, meaning to break the tension between us; to show that it was all right to talk about what had happened. But it wasn't all right, and he could see it in my eyes.

The other parts of my face, of course, had additional stories to tell. 'Fuck, Christopher, what happened to your nose?'

'I got caught in a house fire,' I said. 'A door banged into me.' I told him what I'd told the police. I didn't tell him about Ines, or who the flat belonged to, or about Ballantyne. I told myself

I was protecting him from what he didn't need to know. The truth was, his mentioning Rence had rattled me.

'So why did they scan you in the high security wing?'

I shrugged.

Durrell watched me closely. 'There's more to it, isn't there?'

'I guess.'

'You want to tell me?' Durrell's fat, slack face didn't carry concern well. He looked like a deflated cherub. His skin had a grey, dusty appearance: too many hours spent in the air-conditioned corridors of the Apolloco hospital.

I shook my head. 'Not here.'

One night after our return to Earth, Durrell and I had come to a drunken, late-night understanding. We both knew how likely it was that one or other of us would turn to pirated accessories to ease his epistemic hunger, and we'd agreed to watch each other's backs. It hadn't been necessary, as things turned out. I'd found treatments that, while themselves illegal, didn't involve me in any active piracy. And Durrell—

Well, what about Durrell? He'd always given me the impression he was one of the lucky ones – one of the very few whom EAI didn't altogether incapacitate. But for all I knew he might be one of Ballantyne's patients himself.

Within reason, our understanding meant we could be open with each other. But I'd never even told him about Ballantyne's clinic, and there were better places to spring those kinds of revelations than the middle of a public bar.

I leaned back until my chair knocked against the wooden dado.

'Do you know what happened to her?'

'No,' I said. 'Some kind of trauma. A head wound. Beyond that they're not saying. Rence is feeding me riddles and I think it's to cover the fact he doesn't know anything himself. Is he always so unpredictable?'

'Unpredictable how?'

'First time I saw him butter wouldn't melt in his mouth. Today he came close to shoving his fist down my throat.'

Durrell picked at the label on his beer bottle. The cooler sweat had loosened the glue and the paper bunched up easily under his thumb. 'He's always seemed fairly steady to me,' he said.

'I guess he wanted to make an impression.'

'Maybe The Hague's visit's making him nervous.'

'You know why they're here?' I asked.

'No.' He looked at me. 'Do you?'

'No.' But all the things I wasn't telling him were making paranoid patterns in my head. Rence's riddles, the flat, Ballantyne's arson – I had to share these things with someone. I said, 'It's Joanne, isn't it? Joanne's the reason The Hague are on their way here.'

The idea seemed to stagger him. 'Is it?'

My tea had gone cold. 'Let's get out of here.'

'Already?'

'I want to show you something.'

The air outside was cold and dry and metallic-smelling. Beak Street was only ten minutes away, but Durrell still wanted to drive there. I insisted we walk. It didn't occur to me until we were halfway down Old Compton Street that he was afraid. With his expensive car and his apartment in Stratford Tower, he felt alien and foolish on these poor and broken pavements. A gang of students burst from the door of a jazz bar, jostling Durrell into the road. He elbowed through them and hurried back to my side like a nervous foal. His uneasiness was strange; he looked so ordinary. I was the conspicuous one: too thin, too tall, too pale.

Underneath the crisp savour of the season, there was another smell – the sickly sweetness of gasohol from the buses running back and forth along Shaftesbury Avenue. As we neared Beak Street, I noticed another smell: the burnt-spice stench of the gutted apartment. We turned the corner and the block came into view.

'Is that it?'

I nodded. There were only a couple of streetlights working,

and the damaged flat looked little different from the others. Maybe there were tongues of soot above the windows – but they could just as easily have been a trick of the light. Glare from the brightly-lit foyer left afterimages trembling behind my eyes.

'Wait here,' I said.

'What are you going to do?'

'Don't worry, I'm not going inside.'

'I'll come with you.'

'No. There may be police on the street.'

Durrell rolled his eyes, exasperated. I walked down the pavement opposite Joanne's block. The yellow pipes stacked at the side of the road were sweaty with condensation. I glanced round: the street appeared deserted. I remembered the CCTV cameras mounted above the foyer entrance; but it was too late to worry about them. I knelt down and looked inside the pipes. But the light was too poor to penetrate inside them. I reached blindly in and touched the damp, crusted cloth. Repressing a shudder, I drew the bundle out and unwrapped it. In the harsh yellow light from the lobby, the bloody stains were black as ink. I took a hypodermic from the bundle, wrapped it up again and slipped it into my jacket pocket. I walked back to Durrell, found a doorway and stepped into the shadows. 'Come here.'

'For fuck's sake, Chris.'

'Here.'

Reluctantly, he stepped into the doorway with me. I handed him the hypodermic. He stared at it, bemused.

'I found it in her apartment.' I told him about Ines's phone call. About Joanne's apartment, and finding the hypodermics there.

'And the fire?'

'There was so much electrical stuff running – maybe I kicked a wire. Maybe there was a short. The place was a tinderbox.' There was no point yet telling him what really happened.

Durrell stepped out of the shadows and angled the barrel into the light. 'What is it?'

'Have you heard of it?'

He shook his head. 'Could be a vitamin shot, I suppose. With a name like that it could be something cosmetic. Antioxidants. Melatonin?'

'You tell me.'

'What do the police say?'

'I haven't told the police.'

Durrell tapped the hypo thoughtfully against his palm. 'What do you think will happen when Rence finds out you've been holding things back from him?'

'I don't know,' I said.

He handed the hypo back to me.

I didn't take it. 'Can you find out what it is?'

'Me?'

'I don't know who else to ask.'

He took it back. He held it gingerly, like it might bite him. His expression was eloquent. 'Thanks a million,' he said

# 22

We eventually found a cafe Durrell dared to enter. Living in homogenised splendour near the top of Stratford Tower had given him a terror of anything 'too local'.

'Look,' I said, losing patience, 'if we don't find somewhere soon my toes are going to drop off.'

We sat at a table in the back, where people wouldn't overhear us, and I could warm my bare feet surreptitiously against the radiator. Durrell ordered a double cappuccino.

For the second time that evening, I wondered how Durrell handled his EAI. He never seemed in less than perfect control of his senses. He was constantly finding things to interest him, to smile about. He noticed the large, horizontal crack running along the wall beside us and turned in his seat, following it to the door.

Here and there along its length, patches of plaster had been hacked off the walls revealing friable, poorly-fired brick. The transoms above the doors were stripped back to the plaster-board wattling. A sheet of rusted corrugated iron hung from the ceiling, hiding the lightbulbs. Light bounced back over the ceiling, and poured from rusted spots in the iron sheet. The floorboards were loose and the table trembled whenever anyone walked past. The ambience was in-keeping with the area, in a perverse way. The distressed vibe reflected the war-damaged street outside.

I said, 'Do you think Jewel could be some sort of treatment for EAI?'

Durrell used his spoon to scrape froth from the edge of his cup. 'What makes you think that?'

'What else is it likely to be? She must have been taking something for her EAI. What do you suppose she was on? Codeine?'

'I thought she was plugging into pirateware.'

I shook my head, not wanting to remember how likely that was; how keen she'd been at one time to try it. 'You know Joanne,' I said. 'She liked handling things her way.'

'Nobody can do that,' he said. 'Not with EAI.' A significant admission, that, coming from the man who spent his professional life handing out aspirin to redundant metal-heads.

'So can you help me? Can you find out what Jewel's for?'

'I can ask people if they recognise the name. But if The Hague's setting up camp at the hospital I can hardly go waving the thing around.'

'I'm not asking you to take risks.'

'You're coming bloody close.'


It was past midnight when we left the cafe and walked back to Durrell's car. For the past hour Durrell had been knocking back coffees, trying to wake himself up for the drive home, and the caffeine rush had made him fractious. To make up for his changed mood he insisted on driving me home.

'It's miles out of your way,' I protested.

'Fuck's sake, Chris, get in!' He swung into Bayswater Road on a fluid line between cyclos and bicycle rickshaws. 'I'm speaking to Rence tomorrow,' he said. 'I'll see what I can find out about this Hague mob.'

'Thank you.'

'But I still don't see why they'd have anything to do with Joanne.'

'Nobody's telling me anything. It's making me paranoid.'

A tram slid into the lane ahead of us and everything started to snarl. Bikes and motorcycles began jockeying, crisscrossing in front of us in crazy, feral patterns.

'You know what the Met are like with metal-heads,' said Durrell. 'You could die of pneumonia in this town and they'd suspect some techno-conspiracy.'

'She died of a head wound,' I reminded him. There was something about Jim Durrell I didn't remember from before; something flippant. Perhaps stripping post-humans at Apolloco's hospital had inured him to the tragedies that so often followed upon their return to Earth. Perhaps he had heard too many sad stories. Whatever the reason, his sympathy wore off too easily. There was an underlying callousness about him: I didn't like it.

We swung a right into Pembridge Road, leaving the lighted part of town behind. Durrell drove cautiously. He was uneasy, rolling his lovely street-missile through these unpredictable streets. But it was a point of honour with him to deliver me safely home. We got as far as Lonsdale Road, and he was still insisting on driving me up to my door.

'The mews is too narrow,' I told him, tugging at the passenger door. It was locked. The car was still moving. 'Set me down here Jim, it's fine.'

'Are you sure?'

I felt a sudden, unbidden contempt for him. Fear of the poor parts of London was something Durrell could afford. Durrell, with his new wife and his adoptive family and his suite perched half a kilometre above the cooking-fires and open sewage channels of the city. 'You know,' I said, 'it's not that bad round here.'

Durrell stopped the car. 'Sorry,' he said, not quite meeting my eye. Our circumstances were so different now. We had grown apart. I got out the car and leaned back in to shake his hand.

'Take care, Chris,' he said.

'You too. Kiss the kids.'

I unlocked the front door and climbed the stairs up to the apartment. The place seemed untouched. I palmed the plastic curtain aside and entered the bedsitting room. The blankets were heaped and twisted as I'd left them. There was nothing out of place.

It didn't make sense. Why would the police have put me through the humiliation of a scan if they weren't going to search my apartment? But they had searched these rooms once before, and they were tidy then, too: there had been no sign of an intrusion.

Perhaps they didn't need to turn places over any more. Maybe they used some bizarre scanner, mapping the molecular structure of dirty washing and toenail clippings and old newspapers, sniffing for controlled substances and contraband wetware. I remembered Rence's threats. Tomorrow a team from The Hague, armed with Apolloco's rare hardware, would be hunting through Joanne's burnt-out rooms, molecule by molecule, looking for something to incriminate me.

I prised my feet out of the slippers and sat on the edge of the bed. A wave of vertigo washed through me. I had to grab the sheets to steady myself. I put my head between my knees. It didn't help. My eyes swam with exhaustion.

I lay down and turned on my side, but I was too tired to sleep. Too much was happening; I couldn't deal with it all. Bits of the day kept slopping out, running behind my eyes, forcing me to relive them. Rence's face, an inch away from mine; black smoke pulsing at the door like a lung; Ballantyne's fist. The scanning-chair clamp tightening around my head; the broken plaster of the cafe walls ... Images clattered epileptically through my head. I opened my eyes and stared cross-eyed at the rumpled cotton duvet cover. The threads and pilling on the cover seemed gigantic, a forest of frightening alien forms. I had my ear pressed to the sheet and I could hear my heart beating out its wet, obscene tattoo. I shifted on the bed again and something dug into my hip.

Muscle by aching muscle I somehow got back on my feet. I pulled the bundle of Jewel hypodermics from my jacket pocket.

I drew the heavy curtains, tugging them along the stubborn runner, then sat at the table and unwrapped the cloth. It was dirtier than I remembered. Queasiness washed over me as I traced the dark spatterings of Joanne's veinous blood, the tacky, yellowish crusts of dried lubricant. I picked up a hypodermic and turned it over and over in my hands. There was something special about it. Something about the way the liquid inside it caught the light.

It looked as though there were specks of gold suspended in the red, but when I looked closely, there weren't.

I wondered where to stash my horde.

I went into the kitchen and opened the fridge. There were plenty of free shelves in the door but the idea of them sitting there in the butter dish was repellent. I opened the cupboard above the sink. The inside smelled of stale cumin. Spilled pulses lined the shelves. I shut the door and went back into the bed-sitting room.

I went to the bookshelves by the bed and took a *papier mâdché* bowl from the top shelf and dropped the bundle inside. A minute later I took the bowl down again and tipped the bundle out into my hand: not there ...

I knelt before the dresser, pulled out the bottom drawer, and untucked the tissue paper from round Joanne's wedding dress. I slipped the hypodermics from the cloth and laid them in a row upon the dress. I folded the silk back on itself, rearranged the tissue paper, and closed the drawer.

Which left me with the cloth.

It was too grotesque to treasure, but I couldn't bring myself to throw it away. I crossed and recrossed the flat, growing more and more anxious, until, exasperated with myself, I balled it up and threw it into the cupboard under the sink.

I went into the bathroom, looking for something to send me to sleep, but there weren't even any aspirins. Then I remembered the ResponsIV hypo Ballantyne had given me. It was still in my jacket pocket: it had been sitting there so long, I'd ceased to notice it. I thought, I'm a walking bloody pharmacy today. I went back to the bedsitting room and sat at the table. I was tired, and my hands were shaking. On my third try I hit the vein.

# 23

Joanne's burial plot, tiny and undistinguished, lay right up against the edge of the cemetery, in the shadow of a wall topped with barbed wire and sickly acacia.

Three weeks had passed since I'd run into trouble with Rence, and the weather had turned in that short time to a dank and dismal autumn. It had rained earlier that morning: the grass around the hole was thick and wet. The damp was seeping into, my shoe along a split in the sole. My sock was drenched and it had rucked up painfully around my toes. I shuffled uncomfortably.

The cemetery was old and heavily-wooded. Mausoleums lay derelict and mysterious in nests of hawthorn. Obelisks raised modernist fingers into the pale green canopy. Here and there, leaning drunkenly from mossy plinths, stone angels were looking in every direction but mine, as though preoccupied with their own difficulties, pushed year by year out of the earth like milk teeth by the strong roots of trees.

Rence was there, immaculate, giving the lie to the cliche of the ill-dressed copper. Durrell, in a tie too loud for the occasion, looked no different to when he was consulting at the hospital. Joanne's parents and Ines, who had arrived by train only that morning, had manoeuvred themselves to the other side of the tiny grave, opposing me across the ruin of their daughter. Marie Rynard had taken her surviving daughter's arm under her own and was gripping it tight; a hungry, possessive gesture.

'... dust.'

The men from the funeral parlour lowered the coffin into the cramped hole. I was surprised by a feeling of relief. It was over at last. All my useless pity.

Marie Rynard sobbed into a handkerchief. A thickset woman, she was an unlikely mother for such elfin daughters. Her husband, Paul – they might have been brother and sister, they resembled each other so closely – stood motionless, his arms by his sides. Tears rolled unchecked down his cheeks. For them Joanne's death was sudden. A catastrophic blow.

I caught Ines's eye. Ines was different. Her face was dry and – like mine, I imagined – ashen. She had been intimate with Joanne's disintegration ever since her return to Earth. Unlike her parents, she had known for a long time something like this would happen.

It was a large cemetery, though the obscuring trees and undergrowth stopped up any vistas. The hill on which it was sited was steep: once or twice a jogger ran past; an elderly couple with a dog; schoolboys in uniform. The boys had avoided the gravel path entirely, following a muddy shortcut between stands of larch and broken, overgrown gravestones. They hesitated when they came upon the funeral party, painfully reminded that they were walking on the dead.

Behind them, circling around us, I saw a sickly looking man of indeterminate age. His ginger hair lay plastered over his scalp like a stain. He walked with deliberate, pugnacious strides, as if stamping something out. He didn't seem to be going anywhere in particular. There was something strange about him – theatrical.

I forced myself to look away. I didn't want him in my head when I looked back on that day.

The end of the service caught me unawares. The first I knew of it, Paul Rynard had drawn me off, away from the gaping socket. The old man's grip on my arm was firm but jerky; he was fighting off tremors. I went with him down the gravel path, not knowing what to expect. Was the shuddering a sign of infirmity or strong emotion? Was it commiseration the old man wanted, or confrontation? Ahead of us, the red-haired man dodged across the path. He was going round in a circle, moving from tree to tree in what appeared to be an agony of indecision.

Paul Rynard stopped abruptly in the middle of the path: a stout, weathered man, the years had stretched and softened him. 'Who did this, Christopher?'

'I don't know,' I said.

The old man shook. 'Who did this to her?' For the first time I detected, behind the apathetic wetness of the old man's eyes, the traces of authority. But the flesh was old and soft, and when his wife came up and laid a hand on his arm, he looked only more grey, more pliant, more defeated.

Marie led her husband off without a word. She blames me, I thought. They both do. Angered, I did not follow them.

The red-haired man leaned out from behind an obelisk, saw me staring, dodged back again. I walked down the path towards him. I was angry. I don't know what I was planning to do. Get the measure of him, I suppose. Normalise him. Make him forgettable. Stamp him out.

'Chris!' Ines ran up and embraced me, hard. She was shivering.

I stopped. I peeled her gently from me. She was still the thin, hot girl I remembered: she moved her gawky limbs with sharp precise movements, as though there were electrified wires running under her skin.

Her eyes were full of confusion and hurt. I didn't know what to say. I felt unmanned. 'You know—' I held her gently against me. '—your dad just asked me who killed her. Like I should know.'

'Oh,' she said, letting me go, 'ignore him. The old fool.'

I wanted to say something helpful. Something to comfort her. But everything that came to mind was selfish. 'The police are investigating this,' I said. 'Why doesn't he talk to them?'

'He's off in a world of his own. They both are.'

We watched as Marie led her husband back to the miserable hole. The couple stood at the grave's edge and turned to survey the rank plots and broken stones; Paul held his head high on his wattled neck. There was something ostentatious about the picture they made: stony, motionless as catafalques. 'What's it been like at home?' I asked her.

'Miserable as hell. I've stayed away as much as I could.'

I remembered her boyfriend, and felt empty. I had the sudden, bizarre urge to tell her off for abandoning her parents. Instead I said, 'They think I should have stayed with Joanne.'

'And should you?'

'She wouldn't have let me.' I glanced around idly, but the red-haired man had gone again. 'Who are you looking for?'

'No one.'

'Who was the man in the grey suit?'

'Rence. He's a detective inspector.'

'He keeps himself to himself.'

'I'm under suspicion. He's only here to make sure I don't run off with the body.'

'Chris!'

'Sorry.' A sudden movement distracted me: the red-haired man again, moving slowly from stone to stone, towards the grave.

'God, what an ugly thing to say.'

'I'm sorry, Ines. Look—' I took her by the shoulders and fixed her with a confident smile. 'Go on back to the car. I'll meet you at the hotel.'

'I thought you were coming with us.'

'I'll be there. I'll take a ride with Jim Durrell or someone if you want to go on without me.'

'Of course we don't.'

'Wait for me, then. I'll only be a minute.'

Ines looked puzzled, but she didn't say anything. When she was gone I looked round for the red-haired man. The intruder with his stupid, striking walk. He had vanished again.

I followed the gravel path back towards the burial plot – deserted now – and found a muddy track no wider than my palm. I followed it between the trees and broken stones. I came upon him suddenly. He was sitting with his back to a large, unadorned sarcophagus, covering his face with his hands. He was wearing a white button-down shirt and a pair of blue jogging pants. His shoes were encrusted with mud. He had the pale, anaemic bird-boned look of a fashion model, or a lunar returnee. 'Hello,' I said.

The man twisted suddenly and painfully towards me. He was as gangly as a boy. But his face was blotched and dry and there were marks like liver spots on his brow and his cheeks. I kept walking towards him, willing him to be normal. Just an ordinary man. But the closer I got the harder my heart beat. His face had the cured, drawn quality of a heraldic figure: the joker in the card deck. He leapt up.

'I'm sorry—' I said. God knows why. Before I could say anything else, he scampered off between the trees.

'No, look,' I shouted after him. But he only sped up. He hit a wood-chip path and turned down it, skidding slightly, and disappeared into the narrow gap between brick mausoleums.

I traipsed back down the hill. That strange, inept intruder on my grief was going to be with me forever now. Memories of his face beat themselves against the walls of my skull like bluebottles trapped in a glasshouse. And my broken shoe had come apart completely. The sole flapped ridiculously, scooping peas of wet gravel up under my foot.

In the end only Ines had waited for me. I met her at the main gates. 'You should have gone on,' I said.

'Oh, stop being so bloody self-effacing,' she said angrily.

We walked towards the main road. Ines spotted a cafe on a nearby side street and wanted to go in.

There was an espresso machine, and a glass cabinet for cakes – almost empty – and a melamine shelf running along the left hand wall. The wall was tiled with mirror glass. We pulled a couple of stools together near the door and kept catching each other's eye in the reflections.

I asked her, 'When did you last speak to Joanne?'

'It must have been July,' she said.

'Before her birthday? Or after it?'

'A few days before. It's how I remember,' she said.

'How did she sound?'

'Together. But she wouldn't tell me what was going on with her.'

'What did she say?'

'That things were normal.'

'Normal how?'

'I don't know, Chris.'

'You must—'

'*Chris.*'

I bit my lip. 'Sorry,' I said.

She shrugged.

Her birthday. July nine. Three months later, she was dead. Three months unaccounted for. Unless The Hague could recover something from the burned-out flat.

'Ines,' I said, coming to a decision.

'What?'

'She was plugging into something.' I had to tell someone. I had to confide, and Ines – I knew, from the way she had kept Joanne's address a secret – was young enough and romantic enough to take my confidences seriously. 'Did you know this?' I asked her. 'That she was plugging into pirated gear?'

'No. What sort?'

'I don't think anybody knows. I guess it gave her access to an AI somewhere. A satellite network maybe. That would be the closest thing to what we had on the Moon.'

'But what would be the point of that?'

'Just that – to have another set of eyes again. Escape the boundaries of her skull—' I stopped, self-conscious. It was hard, explaining to someone the strange senses of the cybernetic realm. Every time I tried I found myself drifting off into bad poetry.

'I didn't know she was doing that,' said Ines. 'She never said.'

'I'm not supposed to know either.'

'I won't say anything.'

She had forgotten her earlier frustration with me. She was leaning towards me in her seat now, watching me intently.

155

This, I realised, was what I could give her; this was what she wanted from me.

She wanted a riddle. Something answerable. Any mystery, however petty, so long as it buffered her from the yawning senselessness of her sister's death.

# 24

The next day I rode a tram east. We pulled into the Docklands terminus on an erratic, rattling course between the muslim missions of Blackwall. The terminal building was dark and echoic, like a gigantic tin barrel beaten roughly into shape. I crossed the maze of bays and pavements to the main road. I cowered under a shop awning and peered through the downpour for a cab. But none came, and finally I settled for a cyclo to take me round the Isle of Dogs.

The driver was a skinny twelve-year-old in red cut-off jeans and a combat jacket buttoned up tight under his chin. He grinned incessantly: I couldn't tell if he had understood the directions. He revved the little moped rickshaw pointlessly, filling the air with the candy smell of gasohol, and thumbed it into gear. We careered down muddy tracks between the farms and smallholdings of Cubitt Town.

Finding out where Ballantyne lived had meant a call to Philip Lee, my old solicitor. I timed my call badly, scant hours after Rence had released Joanne Rynard's name to the newshounds. Lee, who fixed on the trivia of local feeds and Mondo stations, was already up to speed. 'How come you didn't ring and tell me?' he said.

Why hadn't I shared my ex-wife's death with him? Because it wasn't any of his bloody business. Ever since Lee arranged my divorce he'd had this idea we were pals. He acted the part well.

Sometimes he almost had me forgetting that it was all a bluff: that we had no ties.

He asked me if I needed representation with the police. I did, and I should have arranged it much earlier, but I lied and said I was fine. Lee was the last person I wanted, with The Hague on their way into town.

'I missed the funeral,' he complained. I waited patiently for him to run out of spiel. There was something painfully autistic about his attempts at commiseration: 'I'll lay some flowers tomorrow,' he said, in a businesslike way.

'Yeah,' I said, 'thanks.' Finally I got him to listen to what I wanted from him.

Lee was hazy about Ballantyne's address, but there are only so many farms on the Isle of Dogs, and fewer piggeries.

The rain eased as we rode, and I drew aside the plastic rain-shield. Peeling wooden houses with slanting tin roofs stood on stilts above the Thames's shingle banks. Gulls picked at piles of refuse. Open gutters emptied a viscous orange scum into the gelid black water of the river.

The cyclo dropped me off at the foot of Mudchute Farm. I scuffed my way through the mud and slush up to the gate.

There was little to see at this time of the year: bales of winter feed under tarpaulins weighed down with old tyres; equipment of uncertain use, apparently abandoned.

The farmhouse itself was bland and modern. It was surrounded by straggling flower borders and dead vegetable beds. I knocked on the door. I was about to knock a second time when it cracked open. I glimpsed, in the gloom of the unlit hall, a small, delicately-featured Asian girl. 'Yes?' she said.

'I'm here to see George Ballantyne.'

The girl edged the door back so there was barely an inch gap. 'He's not here at the moment.'

I put my hand on the door, holding it where it was. We watched each other, stalemated. 'Please,' I said. 'I'll wait.' I let the door go.

'Can you tell me what it's about?'

'It's a personal matter.'

The girl opened up the door to see me better. I saw that she was not young: her height and the smallness of her features had deceived me. She wore an ankle length beige sheath dress. Her hair was long and gently waved. She wore no make-up, and there were dark circles under her eyes. She looked anxious, and defeated. 'I know you,' I said.

She blinked at me. 'I beg your pardon?'

*Never say you don't believe in fairies ...*

'Mr Yale, isn't it?'

'You visited me. In Yorkshire: you looked after me.'

The woman opened the door wide. Her tone was friendly but businesslike: 'If this is about your treatments you'd be better off ringing the clinic'

So she knew about the clinic.

'It's not about my treatments.'

'I don't know how long he'll be—'

I just stood there, smiling reassuringly, letting my height and the distinctness of my grey eyes stand in for an assertiveness I did not really feel.

The woman sighed. 'You'd better come in.'


Inside, I found myself in a cityfolks' illusion of a country cottage. The hall sideboard was cluttered with porcelain figurines and on the busily papered walls there were sepia-tinted photographs of the Mudchute site through the centuries.

She led me into a living room cluttered with embroidered cushions, antique chairs and lace samplers: 'Make yourself at home,' she said. 'Do you want some wine?'

I looked around for somewhere to sit, but the neatness of everything, the sheen of polished wood and the starched whiteness of the antimacassars, intimidated me. 'No thanks,' I said.

'Coffee? Tea?'

'Just water.'

'Fizzy?'

'Sure.'

She was wearing heels. They clicked lightly on the terracotta tiles of the kitchen. I was still looking for a seat I dared sit in. It was all too perfect to be welcoming.

She waved me into a seat and sat down opposite me. Between us there was a coffee table piled high with country-living magazines. She set down the bottles and the glasses she had brought from the kitchen. 'My name's Shazia,' she said, spearing a pump-action corkscrew into a '98 Devon Sauvignon.

'Christopher,' I said, helping myself to carbonated water (from the White Peak, I read off the label).

We drank in silence.

She said, 'I hope the weather didn't make your journey too difficult.' Her bland smile confused me. I looked away, searching for signs of life. There was nothing out of place. Even the magazines were stacked with regimental smartness.

'I should thank you for looking after me,' I said. 'In Yorkshire, I mean.'

'Thank George,' she replied, simply. 'It was him sent me to you.'

She was lying. Or Ballantyne had lied, the day he came to see me in Long Lover – but why?

I said, 'Do you do a lot of work for the clinic?'

She sat back in her seat. 'I'm not heavily involved,' she said, quickly distancing herself. I wondered who she was.

'You work at the farm here?' I asked, fishing for clues.

A half-smile formed at the corners of her mouth. It was a bitter little expression, gone before it flowered. 'I help out where I can.'

'Right,' I said, nodding like an idiot. And when the silence dragged: 'You must be quite a help to him.'

'I hope so. I'm his wife.'

I stared at her. 'I'm sorry,' I said, belatedly, 'I–'

Shazia waved me silent. She knew what I was going to say. 'Are you sure you don't want some of this?' She gestured with the bottle. She was already on her second glass.

'No, thanks.' I knew I ought to drop the subject, but I couldn't. 'George never mentioned–'

'Is this about Joanne?' said Shazia.

I didn't know what to say.

'I'm sorry,' she said, staring into her half-empty glass. 'I heard what happened.'

I wondered how much she knew.

'George tells me you lived on the moon.'

I couldn't face the thought of all that. 'We separated a couple of years ago,' I said, changing the subject.

'Will you excuse me a moment?' Her careful, precise speech made her sound drunker than she was. I watched her out of the room and up the stairs.

I watched her all the way up, watched as the black smoke-curls of her hair melted and spread into the darkness of the stairwell. I stared into the darkness. Heard the click of her heels on bare floorboards, the hiss of her pantyhose. When she was gone, I wandered round the room. I examined the ornaments – a few Goss, one Wedgewood – putting each object back in its appointed place with nervous hands. It was more a museum than a house. A sterile magazine-dream of country living.

Upstairs, I heard a cistern flush. I waited for Shazia to come back downstairs, but nothing happened.

I came to a door, a few inches ajar. I palmed the door open and looked inside.

It was a chapel. A shrine to all things lunar.

Prints of cities covered the walls: Humboldt, Heaviside, Riccioli, Byrd; even Arzachel. The ceiling was black, dotted all over with paint-spatter stars, and in the corner by the window there was an inflatable lampshade of the Earth seen from space. The carpet was moondust grey.

Mementoes and souvenirs cluttered every surface. Mission patches, pens and mugs, figurines and children's toys, models of lunar rovers and plastic dolls in evac suits. A souvenir mirror from Le Verrier. Tools and trinkets from outbound expeditions. Signed photographs of early settlers.

Everything here was lunatic.

A *faux-moon*, a plastic moon, a moon of would-bes, fanatics and dreamers. A moon of failures and sad stay-at-homes. 'Quite a display,' said Shazia.

I backed out of the room. 'Isn't it?' she said. 'I'm sorry.'

'Something of a den,' she added. She sat down again. She had changed out of her dress into work gear. Her hip-bones jutted out sharply against her jeans. A cotton twill shirt played down her generous breasts. She was a picture: a cityfolk's dream of a country wife. Her hand gravitated towards the wine bottle. 'He wanted so much to go to the moon. Well, you can see—'

I wondered what she was trying to tell me. I said, 'I never realised he was so interested in all of that.'

'When he was in the army, every year he would put in for the moon.'

'Really?'

'He failed the medical,' she said.

I thought about it. 'His feet,' I said. 'Of course—'

'Not his feet!'

'Oh.'

'During the Karelian campaign, the army junked their front-line forces with organo-phosphates.' Her eyes glazed over, assaulted by memories. 'He was never right after that,' she said, in a little voice.

'But he seems so—' I searched for a neutral word.

'He's got chronic multiple myeloma. The operations you went through—' She tapped the side of her skull. The plugs behind my ear itched. 'The operations that made you post-human – they'd have killed him.'

'I had no idea,' I said.

'The army tried putting a plug in his head once. It caused a massive immune response. Meningitis. Brain damage. You know he had a stroke?'

'He never said.'

'Well, why would he?' And then she said something so strange, it didn't really register at the time. Only much later, when the investigation was all over and I'd returned home to Leeds, would I understand its significance.

'He's trapped inside his skull,' she said.

I thought of Ballantyne, and his clinic. For someone

disappointed as Ballantyne had been, running such a place was a strange thing to do. Had his patients' specialness chafed him? Had he spent his days dreaming of the rare senses they had once possessed – senses he himself would never know?

I thought of Ballantyne's rumbustious bullying, his avuncular, overbearing bedside manner. Were they the symptoms of a well-hidden jealousy?

'George tells me he's working for the police,' I said.

'Probably,' she said, as though this were only one of Ballantyne's many pecadilloes. You could feel the resentment there, at the back of everything she said. We talked about nothing for a while, that bottled-up rancour swelling up inside her with each passing minute. Her gestures were full of tiny, neurotic rebellions. She put the wineglass back on the table and missed the coaster, and when she picked the glass up again there was a water-mark on the varnish. Once she reached out, for no reason at all, and pushed a pile of magazines out of true.

'How did you meet him?' I asked her, to see what would happen.

She said, 'I studied agriculture at college. I came to London for the farming experience. I went to work on the Isle of Dogs; one of the organic smallholdings by the Thames.'

'And George?'

But Shazia was telling her story at her own speed. 'What's the point of organic farming in an artificial world? We'd have these long debates, and we'd talk about "saving the environment". And afterwards we'd go outside and across the road from us there was sugar cane growing by the Thames, and a fishmonger's stall selling squid by the metre, salmon by the pint, and in the offices across the river there were accountants floating in saline baths with their heads stuffed full of wire, using cyberspace just to balance the company's books. I thought, who are we kidding? We either reject everything artificial, or we don't reject anything at all. Then I met George.' She refilled her glass.

She was drinking at a prodigious rate. I slugged back the rest of my water. Shazia's hand was unsteady as she poured me a second glass. When she leaned forward, I saw that her eyes were bloodshot.

'I first visited George to complain about his sprays. Mudchute Farm overlooks the smallholding where I worked. His toxins were leaching into our soil.'

'You were fraternising with the enemy, then.'

'Yes.' She looked straight at me. 'Yes. That's what made it so exciting.'

I said nothing.

She drained her glass and stood up. There was a hostile edge to her voice now: 'He'd just set up his transgenics operation. You know, the pigs with human hearts? The way he saw it, it wasn't a question of whether something was "made" or "natural". Either way, it was an artefact. Something designed. He had so much energy. So much enthusiasm for the idea.' She drained her glass and stood up too fast. She wavered: for a second, I was afraid I'd have to catch her.

She said, 'I want to show you something.'

She led me round the house. It had stopped raining. From here there was a clear, impressive view of Canary Wharf and the grandiloquent towers of the city. I folded my arms against the cold. I should have put my jacket on.

But Shazia didn't seem to notice the cold. 'Does it ever seem to you,' she said, 'something big is about to happen? That we can't go on like this? Natural, artificial. Human, machine. That none of those things means what it used to mean and everything must change somehow.'

'We had that feeling on the Moon,' I said. 'Of course, it was different then. We felt like we were in control. We thought it was us making the changes.'

'You were going to make it wonderful.'

'Of course.'

Shazia stared across the river at the pyramids and obelisks surrounding the old Admiralty buildings. And here?' she said. 'Will it be wonderful here?' Her eyes were blind with icy late-afternoon light.

'For someone or something,' I replied, 'it's bound to be.'

Behind the house there was a piggery. It was a new building of steel and rough recycled bricks. The floors were rubberised. The pigs were in straw-lined cubicles behind plexiglass doors. Each cubicle had a light of the sort that is supposed to simulate daylight but somehow only bleaches the colour out of everything. Flat, slow harmonies trembled through the shit-scented air. Every pig was exactly alike.

'They're engineered,' said Shazia. 'Human livers, spleens, kidneys.' She made a sound, something like a laugh. 'You don't think he'd trade in anything *shoddy,* do you?'

I chewed the inside of my cheek. She was trying to distract me, by rubbishing her husband. I wanted more than that. I wanted her to tell me what she knew about Joanne – but for that, I'd have to earn her trust. I had to take things gently.

She said, 'Most of London's broken-hearted come to him.'

'There can't be many farms like this,' I said.

'Oh, it's not legal,' said Shazia, with studied carelessness. 'Decriminalised, George says.'

I couldn't imagine anyone wanting to have their organs replaced in a dodgy backwater like London.

'What's it like,' I asked her, 'doing this sort of work?'

'It's a living,' she replied, blandly. 'Nobody wants to die: it's a service.'

I decided to push it. 'But it's not what you started out to do, is it?'

She shrugged. 'I love my husband.'

I knew from her stance and the flatness of her voice, she meant something else. But I couldn't tell what.

'Still,' she sighed, when I did not reply, 'we just have to get on, feed these poor devils.'

I nodded; I'd been outmanoeuvred. She had got me out of the house, as though to tell me some secret, but the revelation when it came was a tawdry one. Now it would seem brutal if I stayed any longer.

'I'd better go,' I said, grimly amused at my own delicacy. So much for the hard-bitten private dick routine.

'I'll tell George you came.'

'Tell him to call me.'

'I will.'

I hesitated. 'You know,' I said, 'it's nice to meet you again – with my head screwed on, I mean.'

I had to pick up my jacket from the house. We walked back together. It was getting dark, and Shazia stumbled on a rut in the track. I caught her arm. Her hand tightened on my wrist. She didn't let go.

We got to the door and Shazia opened it. Too late, I saw that the light was already on. Ballantyne came bounding into the hall.

'Darling!' he said. Then he saw me.

# 25

Shazia froze where she stood. She leaned back, pressing her shoulder into my chest.

Ballantyne didn't miss a beat. 'Chris! Good to see you laddie, come in!'

'He's just arrived,' Shazia reported in a weak voice, stumbling into the hall.

'*Of course!*' Ballantyne bellowed, taking her into his arms. His good humour was flawless and terrible. He let his wife go and seized my hand. 'So good to see you, lad, I've been meaning to call you for weeks.'

Ballantyne's meaty hand propelled me along the hall and into the kitchen. The same hand that had shoved my head into a door. 'Come sit down. What a pleasure!'

In the kitchen, Shazia had the whisky bottle glugging over

a tumbler. Ballantyne pretended not to notice. She slugged it back.

'I put a roast in, sweet! God, it smells good.'

Shazia stood with her back to us, her shoulders knotted with tension. Ballantyne was bouncing bombastically around the kitchen, chattering about his precious roast. 'Come on,' Ballantyne enthused, 'let's make a proper meal for our guest!'

But it was Shazia who did all the work. The whisky had only made her more tense. She tried to peel a potato and it fell into the sink.

Ballantyne twisted his carnivorous lips into a girlish smile. He was determined to put the fear of God into his wife. Now and again, as she was moving from sink to cooker to counter, he reached for her hand, and then he would squeeze it: for me, a gesture of ownership; for Shazia – going by the look on her face – a private threat.

Still, she was doing a good job of resisting him. The way she looked off into some secret middle distance, the way, sometimes, she succeeded in steering away from him altogether, suggested that there was something ordinary about this game. An everyday hostility.

Shazia set the plates out. I looked deep into her face: her strong, wide, red mouth; her deep chocolate eyes; cheekbones so sharp they could cut you.

She brought the gravy boat to the table.

'Hope you like burgundy, Chris! God knows, Shazia does!'

Gravy spattered the clean white tablecloth. 'Oh blast.'

'I'll mop it up,' she muttered, already wringing a cloth out over the sink.

'We'll change it, dear,' Ballantyne said, and began gathering up the plates again.

'No, leave it!'

'Can't eat off this now, lassie.'

'It doesn't matter.'

'Take these.'

'Christ.'

Ballantyne rumpled the cloth up in his arms and threw it

into the washing machine. From a cupboard he pulled another cloth: blue and white, neatly ironed, starched.

Shazia pawed blindly for the wine and poured herself a glass.

'Now don't forget our guest.'

I helped her with the wine. 'And you?' I said, offering him the bottle.

His eyes glittered with suppressed amusement. 'Aye, thanks a lot,' he said, his mouth full. A crumb of meat stuck momentarily to his chin, then fell back on his plate.

He talked about the clinic.

He said, 'The hospital's so busy at the moment,' and, 'Those new dosages work a treat. Our patients are responding much better this month.' Reminding me of my dependency, the gift he bestowed at whim, and might yet withdraw, should I fail to come to heel.

When we were nearly done Shazia scraped her chair back and gathered the plates up with sudden, neurotic movements. Ballantyne hadn't finished eating but he didn't say anything. He let Shazia swipe the plate out from under his raised knife.

I said, 'Shazia tells me you sent her to look after me in Long Lover.'

Shazia closed her eyes and dropped the plates in the sink. The crash was tremendous.

'That's right,' said Ballantyne, not missing a beat. 'I don't know how I forgot.'

Shazia came back to the table. 'Yes,' said Ballantyne, 'she's quite the little angel, isn't she?' He leaned across as she was sitting down and gave her bottom a hard smack; he laughed.

Shazia didn't. I watched her as she ran up the stairs.

'I was waiting for you,' I said, my eyes still trained on the darkness: the shifting shadowland into which Ballantyne's wife, guts burning with whisky and wine and fear, had disappeared.

'I should have killed you when I had the chance,' said Ballantyne. 'What are you doing, coming here, you stupid prick? Don't you know you're under surveillance?'

I said, 'You knew about Joanne's flat all along.'

'Bollocks.'

'So your following me there was one big fucking coincidence, is that what you're trying to tell me?'

It was a sweet moment.

'Your fucking shoes,' I said.

He blinked at me.

'Your stupid fucking high heels.'

That hurt him. 'Chris,' he said, 'you cannae take the mickey about that—'

'I know it was you tried to kill me. You knew about Joanne's flat. How much else do you know? What are you protecting?'

Ballantyne rubbed his face with his hands. 'Oh stop it, Chris,' he said. 'You're losing the thread.'

'Am I.'

He folded his arms. 'Yes, okay, it was me followed you into the flat. Of course it was me. I'm a *policeman*. Who do you think Rence had following you?'

'He tell you to push my head through a door?'

He said nothing.

'Well, here I am,' I said. 'Try it, you piece of shit. Try it again.'

He shrugged.

'Well?'

'Time's gone by,' he said.

I looked at Ballantyne with new understanding. His sober eyes, the curious softness of his lips. His trembling hands. 'You saw something,' I said.

'That right?'

'You saw something in the flat that frightened you. That's why you burned it down.'

'I burned it down?'

Something snapped inside me. The next I knew he had my wrists in his hands. He was holding them away from his throat. It was easy for him to hold me back. He cocked his head to one side, puzzled; amused. Even his ridiculous comb-over was still in place.

I shook him off and turned away in disgust. He was stronger than me. There was no getting around it. If he wanted he could have snapped me like a twig.

I said, 'It was Jewel, wasn't it?'

'Jewel?'

'Stop dicking me around.'

'All I know is,' he sighed, 'when Joanne attended my clinic she was already dying.'

There was a lot of shouting. I don't remember much about that. Eventually, I started listening.

About a month before she died, Joanne turned up unannounced at Ballantyne's clinic. She'd been playing house with some accessory pirate Ballantyne knew from his military days – someone who'd first helped him find staff for the clinic. Ballantyne refused to tell me his name. He had told her enough about Ballantyne's business interests for her to be a threat to him.

'She didn't give me any choice,' he said. 'I had to take her in.'

'That or kill her,' I said.

'I hadn't need to kill her. I told you. She was dying. All I had to do was keep her in the clinic until it was over.'

To begin with, that was all he did. Just waited and watched while she grew weaker and weaker, more and more disorientated. What was wrong with her, she wouldn't say. Only that she had one or two weeks. Only that it didn't hurt.

'I couldn't take it,' he said. 'I couldn't stand it any more. She was refusing it all: everything we tried to do for her. Finally–' He clasped his hands together. It was a superb performance. 'I forced it on her,' he said.

Every test his staff could think of. Every scan. Every swab and stain. 'Nothing,' he sighed. 'We found nothing. The man she was living with, the man I knew – he'd disappeared. I sent Shazia up to Long Lover to see if you knew anything, but you were off with the fairies. While Shazia was away with you–' He met my eye. 'She died, Chris. I did my very best, I swear it. But she died, and now it's up to The Hague to work out why. Maybe she was running pirate accessories. Maybe they killed her. I don't know. That's why I didn't destroy the body. I need to know what happened to her, too. For the sake of the clinic and the people I'm looking after. Chris, are you listening? *I need to know too.'*

*'You just lie there,'* she'd *sobbed, helplessly.*

'It's *the treatments,'* I said.

'He's *turned you into a fucking worm.'*

'She wasn't one of your clients,' I said, willing the idea away.

'No? Who says?'

'If she was your patient—'

'Ask Shazia if you don't believe me. Christ, Yale, read the fucking writing on the wall, will you?'

'—then you'd know about the flat.'

He said, 'How would I know her address? She turned up on my doorstep, how many more times ? When I found you in the Beak Street flat I took a guess that it had something to do with her.'

'A lucky guess.'

He shrugged. 'Whatever.'

'And the fire?'

Ballantyne flung himself back in his chair. He looked tired suddenly, and old. 'What do you know about Jewel?'

'Nothing.'

'Pity. Neither do I. Which is precisely why I torched the place.'

'That doesn't add up.'

'Don't be a twat all your life, Chris. Do I have to spell it out? Joanne came to my clinic to die. I have no idea why or from what. But when they autopsied her, someone sure as hell found *something* — why else would Rence have got on the blower to The Hague? Now I'm sent by Rence to follow you, and what do you do? Go into a flat I've never seen before and stuff your pockets with a drug I've never heard of. All this while The Hague team are gathering round the Heathrow bloody baggage carousel! I have over seventy post-humans relying on me. I have a duty to protect my interests. I can't afford to have the police taking an interest in Joanne, or Jewel – whatever that is – or you.'

'You'd rather kill me. Is that it?'

'I left the fucking door open, laddie.' The Scots bullshit was back.

I said, 'You put the Jewel back in my pocket.'

'So?'

'You tried to frame me.'

His expression was profoundly bored. 'Christopher. You were the one who pocketed it in the first place.'

It was the first sensible thing he'd said. But I was far gone by then, and not in the mood to see sense. 'You know,' I said, 'I've still got it.'

Ballantyne stared at me.

'Jewel,' I said. 'I've still got it.'

'You must *want* to get caught,' he marvelled.

'Whether I get caught or not isn't the point,' I said. 'With or without you, I'm going to find out what it is.

# 26

At 1300 metres, Stratford Tower rose well into the cloud layer. It looked like something sprung from a jelly mould, then stuck all over with the tailfins of a 1950s T-bird. London had the Chinese to thank for such extreme monuments. After the civil war, clever money – Chinese money – had poured into the Principality, establishing within the ring of the old M25 an economic bulkhead from which the People's Republic might launch themselves at the rest of Britain. To the Chinese, coming late to everything, the chance of dominating Europe's least-developed market was a rare prize.

Whenever the idiot Prince Regent sneezed, Chinese management consultants wiped away the snot. China even bankrolled the government's move to the old Admiralty buildings at Greenwich. To the north: the great kilometre-high towers of

Stratford and Leyton stood sentinel over a new, deadly professional Chinatown of banks and big corporations.

Durrell and his family lived on the fifty-eighth floor. The next couple of Saturdays, I went round there to go swimming with them. His wife Rebecca had a boy of eight and a girl of ten from a previous marriage. Then there was Elizabeth, the latest of Durrell's post-human patients, who spent the weekends with them.

The first time, visiting them, I'd been impressed with the weekend arrangement. Durrell was good at personalising his relationships with his patients, treating their disorientation by human contact as much as by his regime of antipsychotics.

The second time, however, I noticed signs of strain; Rebecca in particular was treating their house-guest with increasing brittleness. And what had at first seemed seamless, now looked more and more like a clumsy botch: work and family in the same room, with all the attendant frictions.

My arrival was a cue for Rebecca to start rushing round after towels and bathing things, all the while chivvying the children to get ready. Emily was behaving badly today: she had decided I was an easy touch, and she was flirting outrageously. 'For heaven's sake!' Rebecca cried, shooing the girl out of the living room with little runs, flapping her arms like a crow. I smiled, thinking it was a game, but when Rebecca turned at the door, I saw it wasn't. 'For God's sake keep her out of here,' Rebecca snapped, giving the three of us – me, Jim, and Elizabeth – a look of blanket accusation.

Durrell's responses weren't helping. There was never a hint of conciliation from him; as if his wife were an anxious ward sister: difficult, but ultimately ignorable. With me, too, he was constantly shuffling his identities: at one moment a desolated friend; at another, a more or less distant colleague from our lunar days.

'You made a strange choice,' said Durrell, gnomically, once Rebecca had gone rushing off on some dismal errand or other. 'Moving to the Republic' And when I only shrugged: 'Leaving Joanne.'

So, I thought, he wants to play doctor, does he? 'She didn't want me,' I replied, hoping to embarrass him by a candid reply.

Elizabeth was sitting by the window, looking out. But whether she saw anything, it was hard to say. Her epistemic appetite was very low. Only the most brute stimuli excited her.

'You're convinced it was over between you when you left?'

'Yes,' I said. It seemed doubly wrong, somehow, to be conversing like this in front of Elizabeth. As though she was a dull child, a pet, or a piece of furniture.

After the evacuation of the Moon, Apolloco had retained a skeleton staff there, to assess the increasingly eccentric behaviour of the lunar AIs. While satellites and earth-bound telescopes were capable of recording the minutest change in the Moon's features, only eye-witnesses stood a chance of interpreting these changes. They came from the military, mostly: reconnaissance officers, like Elizabeth.

But now Apolloco had begun withdrawing even this skeleton crew. The AIs – aggressively prosecuting their own self-interest – had 'downsized' and 'rationalised' so much of the planet's life-support, not even these few remaining humans could sustain themselves.

Durrell considered my reply. 'I think it's important to hold on to that,' he said. 'That sense of closure.'

I stared at Durrell, losing track of his increasingly impertinent questions. 'You tell me not to feel guilty about leaving her,' I said, 'but clearly you think I am.'

'I just want you to think about it,' Durrell soothed. 'Think about what was your responsibility, and what was not.'

'You're counselling me.'

'I'm just—'

'Badly.'

Durrell laughed. 'I'm sorry.'

'I didn't come here for this.'

'Elizabeth?' Durrell said, fumbling for something that had caught in the lining of his trouser pocket.

Elizabeth turned at the sound of her name. Her face was a blank, paretic mask.

From his pocket, Durrell drew out a silver ball. He showed it to her. There was a tin bell inside it. It jangled. 'Here,' he said, 'take a look at this.'

Elizabeth swallowed, frowned, concentrated. She reached out.

Durrell pressed the ball into her palm.

I said, 'I remember that. The ball with the bell.' When Durrell had done stripping my skull, that ringing, shining thing had been my centre, a saving glimmer in a shrivelled world.

Durrell smiled one of his knowing, professional smiles. Dull anger filled me at the sight of it. I said, 'I didn't kill Joanne. Somebody else did. And moved the body.' But Dr Durrell was adept at avoiding confrontation. 'Are you comfortable there, Elizabeth dear?' he said. He leaned over and touched her shoulder.

She began swinging forward and back, striking the legs of her chair against the floor.

'She's getting impatient,' Durrell observed, objectively.

Joseph's sing-song echoed through the apartment. Durrell stood and stretched. 'Shall we go?'

Rebecca drove. She was not very good at it. She was nervous, and the controls seemed to fight free of her grasp. The transmission was manual and she jumped gears uncertainly, causing the car to lurch. She did not enjoy driving. I wondered why she bothered.

She seemed to be staking out her responsibilities wider and wider. She drove; she shopped; she kept house; she entertained, in a pleasureless fashion. She dominated the children totally. Jim didn't seem to mind. Perhaps he was glad to shed responsibilities, unwilling as he was to separate his home and working lives.

Certainly his rehabilitation schemes were intruding more and more into his private life; witness Elizabeth, pressed awkwardly between me and the children on the back seat.

The stomach-churning drive woke Elizabeth to her surroundings. She said the oddest things. 'That's no fucking hotel,' she said.

She thought she was still on the moon.

'Do you want to try the deep end this week, Elizabeth?'

'*That*'s no fucking hotel!'

And a minute later: 'It's some kind of –' She screwed her face up in disgust – 'ness!'

It was busy at the leisure centre. Rebecca swapped with Jim so he could do the parking.

'Most of everything is underground,' Elizabeth grumbled, scratching compulsively at her scalp, where the plugs had been.

Gently, Joseph pulled Elizabeth's hand away from her head. It was a thoughtful gesture. The children didn't seem to mind Elizabeth nearly as much as their mother did. 'Did you fight robots?' Joseph asked. Elizabeth awed him: a real soldier.

Elizabeth sniffed. 'Robots ?' She rarely answered a question directly, and then only to the children. 'Christ,' she sneered, 'you think that's all they are? Metal monsters? I've seen the AIs build in *skin* ...'

Markov, I remembered, going cold. That heel-bone ...

Rebecca fought free of her safety belt. 'Joseph,' she said, 'out the car!'

'*And. a skull atop the Montes Rook ...*'

'Great circuses of bone!'

Jim walked round the car to take care of his patient, but Rebecca snared him. Elizabeth worried her; she didn't want her near the children. She held her husband by the arm and spoke into his ear, soft and urgent.

Jim tossed his head angrily. There was no warmth there. He probably used the same gesture with his medical students.

'Come on,' I sighed. Gathering Elizabeth and the children, I led them into the leisure complex, away from the gathering row.


From the topmost diving platform, I discovered, it was possible to look down through the steeply pitched glass roof of the bathing house to the Fuller domes, clustered like the nodules of a nitrogen-fixing plant at the root of Leyton Spire.

The bathhouse itself was a brash affair; the flying buttresses

175

supporting the roof emerged cheekily from their thin marble cladding like iron thighs above a pale grey stocking, before disappearing up skirts of frosted copper. I stood a while, cataloguing and criticising this view with an architect's eye: if I did this long enough, the flutters left me, and I could take the dive. I was improving. I hadn't had to back out once today.

I toppled, fell, and entered the water straight enough. I swam the length under water and climbed out, savouring the healthy exhaustion of my limbs.

I found Jim Durrell at the bar sipping a red grapefruit juice. A sand-blasted glass screen divided the bar from the restaurant kitchen, polished here and there to allow tantalising glimpses of the activity within. Here, I remarked, was another architectural tease. It was repeated throughout the building, inside and out. Every surface was somehow incomplete, baiting the eye with hints of whatever lay beyond.

Layers within layers, striptease of stone and steel, resin erotica and peepshow glass: it reminded me of the moon. I wondered if that was the reason Durrell brought his patients here. Or was it simply a matter of convenience: a way he had of throwing work and family outings into the same fraying basket?

Nearby, Rebecca, Elizabeth and the children were playing in the children's pool. Flumes, fountains and a modest wave-machine lent gaiety to the tiled maze which, if it were drained, would resemble less a playground so much as the foundations of a demolished terrace.

'Elizabeth's regaining her independence,' Durrell remarked. 'She's testing herself, see? She's caught that ball three times in a row.'

I said nothing.

'There's real willpower with that one,' said Durrell, the self-satisfaction evident in his voice.

My answering smile was brittle. Determination, independence: Durrell spoke as though it was he who dispensed these gifts to his grateful patients. The truth was he gave nothing: he only took away.

A cry distracted us. Elizabeth climbed jerkily from the pool, clutching her head. 'She banged herself,' Rebecca called to Jim, angrily, as though it were his fault.

'She's all right!' Joseph shouted.

'We can all see that!' Emily snapped at him, imitating her mother.

'Out you get, you two.'

Elizabeth sat dejectedly on the pool-side, dangling her feet in the water. She was peering into the pool as though she had lost something.

'Liz! Come on!'

And then they were gone, leaving me alone with Durrell.

'You're a stupid bastard,' Durrell said. He said: 'I should have handed you to Rence the night you gave me that bloody hypo.'

'What happened?'

'I must have been mad.'

I ordered a mineral water. While I was waiting for Durrell to get to the point I let my gaze drift over the surface of the bar. It was made of a solid clear resin, swirled with pigments so that, staring into it, I lost myself momentarily in contemplation of ill-lit galaxies.

'If I get questioned by those bastards I'm giving you up, do you understand?'

I shrugged off the threat. Maybe my confrontation with Ballantyne had toughened me up. Maybe I was just tired. I said, 'What did you learn about Jewel?'

He drained the brownish slurry from his glass. 'It's hot,' he admitted.

'How hot?'

'Like The Hague's been crawling all over us like ants.' I watched as bubbles crawled up the sides of my glass. He said, 'I had to call in just about every favour I had, thanks to you.'

'I told you not to take risks.'

'How else was I supposed to find out what it was? You think I can just walk into any Apolloco lab when I please? You think I'd know which tests to conduct, even if I could?'

'What did you find out?'

'You've got a fucking nerve, Chris.'

'Well?'

'It could be Rowntrees jelly for all I know. The Hague impounded it the day after I booked it into analysis. God knows how they knew, but they knew. Thank God I was careful. They ran an audit trace you wouldn't believe, trying to find out which naive pillock dropped it in their laps.'

'I'm sorry.'

'Colour me pillock.'

'I understand what you're saying. I apologise.'

'Do you still have the other hypos?'

I nodded.

'Get rid of them.'

'You think I should hand them to Rence?'

Durrell stared at me. 'Christ,' he said, '*no!* Keep well out of it,' He shuddered. 'You show him you've a connection to Jewel, and The Hague'll be dicing your brain within the day.'

'What do you suggest?'

Durrell sucked his teeth. 'Come to the clinic,' he said. 'I'll box them Class A and have them incinerated.' I said,

'I want to know what it is.'

'Then let The Hague do their job. You're an architect, for fuck's sake. Leave the spook routine to the professionals.'

'And that's your last word, is it?'

'This is the last favour I'm doing for you,' he said. 'I must be an idiot to suggest even this.'

Not much of a favour, I thought – for him to destroy the only handle I had on my wife's death. And if The Hague were all over him, as he said, why did he want me to bring him even more of the stuff?

'It's not as if you can change what happened,' he said.

'I know that.'

'You're after the grail, Chris. I've seen it before, in the bereaved. You're not looking for reasons. You're looking for Truth. Truth in a syringe. Truth in a needle. Something you can hold. A talisman. It's not like that.' Absently, he drew a yin-yang sine-curve through the sweat-ring his glass had left on the bar. 'Truth doesn't stay still.'

'You know,' he said, when a moment's healing silence had passed, 'if you need treatment, I can always put you on one of my programs.'

I smiled a private smile. 'I thought you already had,' I said.

'Meaning?'

I gestured vaguely to the pool. 'I'm here, aren't I?'

# 27

That night as I was climbing the stairs up to my apartment, the terminal started ringing. I caught it just as the answering message kicked in. The screen blinked at me but no picture appeared.

'Hello?' I said.

There was a curious hum on the line, too ordered to be static. 'Hello?'

'Mr Yale?' A man's voice.

'Who's this?'

'Christopher Yale?' He must have been using some kind of scrambler. His voice came out pure and flat, like a synthesiser. 'You may remember me.'

'Send a picture.'

'There's no camera on my rig. My name's Peter O'Connor.'

I sank into the chair in front of the terminal. 'Yes,' I said, without feeling. 'Yes, I remember you.'

O'Connor must have plugged about a dozen anti-surveillance aplets into the line because his voice and the room tone yawed wildly about: now there was a hollow rumbling behind him, like he was speaking from the nave of a cathedral.

'I'm calling about your wife,' he said. 'I understand you have some questions about your wife.'

'You know her name,' I said.

'Yes.'

'Then fucking use it.'

'I'm sorry,' he said. I jumped: now it sounded like he was in the room with me.

'What do you want to tell me?'

'Not on the line.'

'Where?'

'Our mutual friend from Bangkok has the address.'

'We don't have a mutual friend,' I said. But he'd already cut the line.

Then it came to me. Bangkok. He meant my solicitor. He meant Philip Lee. Had Joanne told O'Connor about Lee? Or had O'Connor been doing his own homework?

The doorbell rang.

I rubbed my face with my hands.

It rang again.

I told myself it was only the Jehovah's Witnesses. That they would go away soon.

About twenty minutes later it rang again.

I went down and opened the door. It was Shazia Ballantyne.

She was standing there patiently, hands folded in front of her, self-conscious as a court witness. 'May I come in?'

I looked at her a long time, not knowing what to say.

'I thought I'd better come and see you,' she said stiffly.

Her clothes, too, were suitable for a courtroom: a beige wool suit and bottle-green high heels. She had dressed to impress, but the colours clashed. She had forgotten the rules; too many years playing *hausfrau* to George Ballantyne.

'Well?' she said.

I ran my fingers through my hair, and smarted as I touched the tender patch where her husband had run me into the door. 'Sure,' I said, off-balance. 'Sure. Come in.'

She stepped gingerly over the threshold. I led her up the stairs to the living room and sat her at the table. 'Would you like something to drink?'

'No, thanks.'

'A tea?'

'Only if you're making one.'

I filled the kettle. 'How are things with you?'

'I've left George,' she said.

I did my best not to let my excitement show. 'I'm sorry,' I lied, spooning Gunpowder tea into a brown earthenware pot.

She said nothing.

What happened?

'We argued. About my visiting you at Long Lover.'

'He didn't know, did he?'

'No.'

'Why did you visit me there?'

She said, 'Joanne asked me to.'

I stared at her. 'When was this?'

'Why did you tell him?'

'Were you there with my wife?'

'I didn't come here to be questioned, Mr Yale.'

The kettle clicked off. I used the excuse to turn away from her. I was so close. I willed myself to be calm. To take things slow. I poured boiling water onto the tea.

'I wanted to shake him,' I said. 'I wanted to see what he did. What I could get out of him.'

And you thought you'd use me as the lever.'

'I'm sorry,' I said. I loaded the tray and carried it to the table. 'I didn't start this.'

'Please—' She laid a hand on my wrist, then, after a second, she withdrew it again. 'I'm sorry.'

'What for?'

'Mr Yale—'

'Christopher.'

'Mr Yale, I came to tell you. George is closing the clinic'

It shouldn't have come as a surprise, but it did. I sank unsteadily into the seat opposite Shazia. 'I see.'

'I thought you ought to know. So you can make – other arrangements.'

*Other arrangements.* My skin tingled. There was a tiny window, a few months at best, between now and my next bout of EAI. Between now and then I would have to find alternatives. Join one of Jim Durrell's inadequate rehabilitation programmes.

Bus trips to Dartmoor. Strawberry teas. Flower arranging.

Or look for pirated accessories to fill the hollowness inside my skull.

'Mr Yale?'

I opened my eyes. 'It's all right.'

'He's afraid you were followed,' she said, 'the day you visited us. He thinks the police know about you and him.'

I thought about it. The reasoning was as thin as tissue. There had to be more to it.

I poured the tea straight out. I said nothing. I owed her nothing.

'You must realise how worried he was when you visited,' she said, defeated by my silence.

I handed her her cup. 'Not very strong,' I apologised, 'but if you leave it any longer it stews and you get a bitter aftertaste.'

'Christopher – please don't bland me out.' She tried to fix my gaze but I wouldn't let her; I looked away. 'Is that what I'm doing?'

'Yes. And I don't blame you.'

'Really?'

It would have to be pirate 'ware. Even with Rence and The Hague breathing down my neck, no way was I going to live the rest of my life as a cripple. Least of all under Jim Durrell's care: I thought about Elizabeth and I shuddered.

O'Connor: his turning up couldn't be a coincidence. Did he know about the clinic? Did he have work for me?

Shazia touched her lips gingerly to the edge of the cup and set it down again. 'George tried to kill you,' she said. 'Didn't he?' She might have been talking about a moment's misunderstanding at a cocktail party.

'I don't know,' I said. 'It was probably an accident.'

'He won't hesitate again if he thinks you'll damage him.'

'Are you threatening me?'

'Would you listen to me if I were?'

I shrugged. 'I think your husband knows more about my wife's death than he's letting on.'

Shazia's reply slid smoothly out: 'Oh Mr Yale,' she said, 'you must have realized by now: he *always* knows more than any-body else, about everything.' The irony in her voice could not disguise the fact the words had been rehearsed.

'You're a very loyal person, Shazia,' I said.

'Meaning you don't believe me.'

I shook my head. 'I don't believe *him*.'

'Getting him into trouble is not going to get you anywhere.'

I looked up from my tea, surprised. 'It brought you here. That's a start, surely?'

She said, 'You talk about searching for something, getting answers. You don't even know the questions. You don't even know what you want.'

'Yes I do,' I said: a blind denial.

'Really?'

'Yes!'

'Well,' she sighed, 'that's something.'

Her complacency snapped something inside me. 'Was it George?' I said. 'Was it him killed Joanne?'

She looked away from me. 'No,' she said. 'She was already dying when she came to the clinic'

'That's what George told me.'

'It's true,' she said, 'I know.'

'How do you know?' I said, knowing the answer already. Fighting it. Willing it away.

'I saw it.' She straightened herself in her seat and placed her hands in her lap, like a schoolgirl making confession: touching and useless. 'I was there,' she said.

'Tell me.'

She shook her head. 'There's nothing to tell,' she said. 'She came because she'd taken something. Something that was killing her—'

'Jewel?'

'I don't know. What's Jewel?'

'Go on.'

'She was too afraid to go to a legitimate doctor, so she rang the clinic. George tried to find out what was wrong with her. He tried to save her. But it was no use. Joanne wanted to see

183

you, before she died. George refused. He was worried about secrecy, as usual. George and I argued about it. I came to Long Lover to fetch you, but you were too ill.'

So. I stared into my tea cup. It was trembling. 'You were hardly ever conscious.'

'I get the picture,' I said.

I could have saved her. If I had only woken up. My mouth was full of phlegm. If I had only got up out of bed. If if if if if.

'Then what did you do?'

'I went back to the clinic,' she said. 'And she was dead.' She began to cry. 'That's all I know,' she said.

'Why didn't George destroy the body?'

'*What?*'

'Why didn't he destroy the body? He told me it was so the authorities could figure out what killed her. But so far he's done nothing but destroy their evidence.'

My callousness sobered her superbly. She was no longer crying. 'Maybe he should have destroyed her,' she said. 'He must have regretted it afterwards. Maybe he should have stabbed her with a scalpel the moment she stepped across our threshold. But he didn't. He tried to save her. He deserves your thanks, Mr Yale, not these horrible insinuations.'

She was lying, but I couldn't take any more. 'I think you'd better go,' I said.

She wiped her eyes dry with a tissue. 'Nothing I tell you will satisfy you,' she said, admitting defeat. 'I see that.'

I fetched her coat from the peg and held it open for her. She came up close to me, sliding her arms into the felt.

Then, for some reason, she lingered. Perhaps she was looking for a way to placate me. She noticed the photographs on the walls. Snapshots of the moon. 'Where's this?' she asked.

'Arzachel.'

She peered closer. I guessed that she was getting short-sighted. Too vain about her age to have the laser op, perhaps. 'It's incredible,' she said.

'Joanne built it. Or her machines did. That's her in the photograph.'

Shazia looked suddenly troubled. She reached up. Gingerly, she touched the glass with her fingertips.

'What is it?'

'I always wanted to go to the Moon,' she said.

'You and Ballantyne?'

'It was a dream we had.'

'You could have visited.',

'It wasn't George's way,' she said 'It's "Caesar or nothing" with him.'

'Shazia,' I said, with soft insistence, 'you haven't left him. You think you have, but you haven't. I wonder if you ever will.'

It was so inept a strike, Shazia didn't even get angry. 'I loved him, Mr Yale. That's all.' She straightened her coat. 'I'd better be going,' she said.

'Give me the address of the clinic'

'No.'

'If I can speak to George again—'

'No.'

I had nothing left. All I could do was plead with her. 'You know what the clinic means to me—'

'I know.'

'Without it I'm blind.'

'You and seventy-odd others. The only reason he closed down is because you're bringing the police down on him.'

'That isn't my intention.'

Her look was eloquent.

'Why should you disbelieve me?' I protested.

'Why shouldn't I?' she said.

'Because you "love George", I suppose.'

The blow was aimed true: 'You're not in a position to judge me, Mr Yale,' she said, bridling.

'It's a shame,' I said. Blanding her out a second time. 'I'd have liked to see my wife before she died.'

Shazia said, 'We haven't anything more to say to each other.'

I saw her down the stairs to the door.

In the porch light, I noticed the tired slackness of her eyes. 'It's happened before,' I said, gently, 'hasn't it?'

'What?'

'With Ballantyne. With your precious husband.'

'I don't know what you're talking about.'

'How many times have you told him you've had enough? How long does it last? Doesn't he get bored, you running off like that?'

'I know you're upset, Mr—'

'Call me Christopher.'

'Whatever.'

I remembered her hand on my brow in Long Lover. I remembered the way her hair weaved like smoke, like a hurricane of ink, as she ascended the stairs of her house in Mudchute.

I remembered the way Joanne's skull had been bashed in.

Was Shazia lying? Was she covering for George? Or were they both in the dark, victims of a wider conspiracy?

Shazia looked at me oddly. 'What?' she said.

Like her, I had nothing to say.

'What is it now?'

I stepped forward and gathered her up in my arms and I mashed my mouth against hers. Her lips were red and slack and cold. I squeezed the air out of her. Her arms hung limply by her sides. I closed my eyes. Nothing happened.

I let her go, amazed at myself.

'What was that supposed to mean?' she said.

'I don't know,' I said.

She searched my face for answers, and found nothing. She began to cry again.

'I'm sorry,' I said.

She just stood there, like she wanted the ground to open up beneath her.

I wanted to say to her, It's only hate. It's nothing to be afraid of. 'Goodbye,' I said. I waited by the door, watching her go.

She turned the corner, out of sight. But I could still hear her high heels, clicking on the cobbles of the mews.

# 28

Philip Lee was born into a wealthy Thai trading family. He'd come to London for adventure, thirsty for the gim-crack principality of countless crime shows, sci-fi thrillers and pornographic exposes. He was not the first son of a good family to lose his way and purpose in the nightclubs and brothels of Kensington and Clapham South. Years later, and after many fruitless attempts at reconciliation with his indifferent family, Philip Lee made London his home.

To make ends meet, he had learned to interpret his legal vocation widely. Much of his time he spent trailing errant husbands to whorehouses in Hammersmith and Chelsea. There was some contract work – chasing defaulters for nebulous credit companies – but it was, in his own words, 'mostly about fucking'.

The way I remembered it, those few nights Lee wasn't shadowing kerb-crawlers for embittered bitches in East Ham ('She's black, I can smell it on his shirts'), he would be lying awake in some basement room in Stepney, swigging bad cachaca and dreaming of home. Racecourses, sushi, fast cars: all for ever out of reach.

My first surprise came when I discovered that Lee had relocated to Westminster. The second came when I turned the street corner: the area looked half-way respectable.

I found it hard to imagine how the strange, disappointed man of my memory had turned things around for himself.

I buzzed the intercom.

'You're late!' Lee squawked, the cheap speaker flattening his voice. I pushed at the door. It opened grudgingly.

I entered Lee's office and stood there a moment, frankly astonished. I'd expected a converted bedsit, strewn with dirty laundry and yesterday's newspapers. This looked more like a photographer's studio.

Philip Lee, looking as he always did, seemed out of place in these tidy surroundings. He sat me down in an easy chair opposite his desk.

'Chris! At last!' Lee wasn't old, he had five years on me, but he had grown thin and ashen from spending daytimes indoors with the blinds pulled down. He wasn't much over five foot and, drying up, he had begun to resemble the malevolent dwarf of the fairy tale. For a brief, disturbing second, I imagined him with Rence. Two hobbits together, cackling in some basement as they counted out their horde of dragon's gold.

I sank back in the slick upholstery of Lee's chair, eyes slitted against the febrile autumn sunshine, flooding in through the north-facing lights. Near the back of the room, wire tines guarded a four-foot-wide light-well for the basement.

Lee said, 'I respect you for trying to find out about Joanne.' He came down to business very quickly. The human aspect of it embarrassed him: his detective activities were only ever a way of objectifying that which troubled and eluded him in his personal life.

'But?' I said.

Lee smiled wryly. 'Chris,' he soothed, 'think about the evidence. She *may* have killed herself.'

I didn't know what to say. It went beyond words. 'Phil,' I said, in a strangled voice, 'clearly you don't know what you're talking about.'

But there was no point being angry with Lee, any more than with a blind man who collides with you on the street. Lee lacked the human sense.

'The police haven't discounted suicide, have they?'

'What do you know about that?'

He smiled a complacent smile. 'I can be discreet,' he said.

I sat there, fuming. Of all the people to get involved, Lee was the last person I needed. 'Her head was stoved in,' I said. 'Her body was moved.'

'There were no signs of struggle.'

'So fucking what? Lee, I don't want to talk about this.'

'Granted,' said Lee, unembarrassed. 'But if you're right, what will you do?'

I looked at him blankly.

Lee said, 'Say you find your murderers. Most times it's not very hard, whatever the TV shows say. Then you'll be the same place she was. If you're right. At their mercy. Whoever they are.' He stood up suddenly, dusting off his hands, as though the conversation had soiled him somehow. '*They!* What the fuck are we talking about here?'

Lee had a point. What if I found them? I'd always supposed I'd always be several steps behind the police. That I'd simply be gathering the leavings of the official investigation.

But what if I got to the answers first? What if I found them? Unencumbered by the badge of authority, I could enter places and meet persons forever barred to the police.

But if I found my answers – if I found *them* – what would I do? Of what was I capable? I didn't know.

'Someone called Peter O'Connor was supposed to leave a message with you,' I said, cutting to the chase for both our sakes.

Lee threw up his hands. 'As you can see,' he said, gesturing like an inept conjurer at the papers messing up his desk.

'You must have it somewhere.'

'Sure,' said Lee, unhelpfully.

I stared him down.

Reluctantly, he began leafing through them. 'I know I had it here,' he muttered. 'Oh—' He drew out a sheet torn off a telephone pad. 'You're in luck.' He handed it over. On it, squared off with angry lines of felt tip, was the address of a pub in Hounslow. A date – the next day. And a time – 2 p.m. I pocketed the paper and stood up. 'Thanks for the help, Phil,' I said, making for the door.

'Whatever,' said Lee.

Then: 'Chris?'

I stopped by the door.

'I can't always be there for you, you know? If you get into trouble—'

189

I smiled, letting him off the hook, and closed the door.

O'Connor had picked a pub at the unfashionable western end of the River Crane, just south of Hounslow, where herons stalk desultorily around stacks of abandoned plastic pipes, and drowned bicycles fetch up against the piers of civil war munitions sheds. Not even the cyclo riders wanted to go there. So I was late.

I glanced into the pub and when I didn't see O'Connor I went out again into the car park. It was weedy with disuse. A low rail ran round the tarmac, and there was a boy watching me. He was sitting on the railing, swinging his feet. He was wearing a pair of black lycra long-johns and a thick cotton jumper of green and cream stripes. I went towards him. It was the red-headed apparition from Joanne's funeral. His postures and movements were adolescent. But his face, crazed with tiny wrinkles like orange peel, was an older man's. Since the funeral he had cut his hair back raggedly to the scalp.

'Peter?' I said, feeling foolish. Surely this wasn't him. Surely. They couldn't be the same—

'Knew you'd come,' O'Connor said, with bitter satisfaction, as though I were part of some dismal internal argument. O'Connor – of the 8-series BMW, the wrapshades, the glancing sexual encounters.

'Jesus Christ,' I said.

He was nothing like he had been. It was like looking at a skull and trying to work backwards to the face. He grinned. A white deposit lined the inside of his lips.

I couldn't watch him any more. I turned to face the pub. 'Shall we go in?' I said. I couldn't stop my-voice shaking.

O'Connor said nothing, and I didn't wait for a reply. He followed me eventually, scuffing his trainers through the grit.

The pub carpet was red. Padded vinyl stools, small round tables with cheap hardwood veneer, red plush banquette seating; there were photographs of boxers on the walls.

There was a middle-aged woman at the bar. Three men with

crew cuts sat in a circle around the table nearest the door. In the gloomiest corner a quadriplegic woman, strapped inside an industrial-looking wheelchair, she was drinking beer through a straw. There was a man with her, holding her glass, talking with her in whispers.

'Get me a lager, mate,' said O'Connor, needily. He dropped carelessly onto a soft bench, his back to a window of frosted, coloured glass.

I ordered a pint and a mineral water. The water came in a fist-sized plastic bottle; the label had faded to blue, it had been sitting there so long.

'You look like shit,' I said, taking a seat opposite. 'What the fuck ran you over?' I had been afraid, coming here. But the remains sitting opposite me provoked nothing but pity.

O'Connor wouldn't meet my eye. Sunlight poured in through the window, grazing his cropped head. There was an unevenness there. A lump formed in my throat as I realised what he was doing. He was tilting his head, very subtly, to show me. The weals were raised and pinkish: his openings recent and badly inflamed. 'Oh Jesus,' I sighed. 'Oh Pete, you idiot.'

'It's not what it looks like.'

'You stupid, stupid fuck.'

The sun went in, the weals disappeared, and O'Connor's face emerged out the glare. 'Who did that to you?' I said.

'I paid for it myself.'

I couldn't look at him. 'You had everything,' I said. 'Money, women.'

'I was sucking Tony's son's dick for a living and taking enough shit to drown twenty men.' He downed half a pint at one go. Were the marks on his hands liver spots? Or Karposi's sarcoma? 'So I got myself an edge.' He licked the thrush off his lips.

'What butcher did that? Where?'

'Madagascar.' He watched me. There was a hardness in him: a bitterness. He was amused at my squeamishness. 'You're as bad as she was,' he said.

'Who?'

His smile softened. 'Joanne,' he said, with unexpected gentle-ness.

The name hung over us like a soft ghost.

'You met her again?'

He cocked his head to one side, assessing me.

'What?'

'I guess you can take it.'

'What?'

'We were sleeping together,' he said.

I swallowed. The news was unexpected and savage in its way as Ballantyne's palm, ramming my head into the door. I tried to picture Pete O'Connor with Joanne. Next to my memories of him, this withered boy-man seemed watery and ill-drawn. And yet—

I remembered how O'Connor had run away from me at the cemetery. How he had stalked the edges of the funeral. How, afterwards, he had sat, curled up, among the graves. A hot bolt of pity shot through me. 'You and – you and Joanne.'

He didn't need to nod. Somehow, in my heart, I knew it was true.


Pete O'Connor and Joanne had never lost touch. O'Connor told me solemnly that they waited until a few months after the divorce before sleeping together. I guess he was trying to soften the blow. Actually, knowing about the affair came almost as a relief. Those thumby bruises on Joanne's thighs – they were nothing so alien and terrible, now I knew who'd put them there.

O'Connor kept urging Joanne towards pirate work. She never succumbed. When finally he found a way out of Savvides's employ, he moved to London and rented a flat in Beak Street, to be near her. Joanne went to see him most days, sometimes staying the night when I was safely out of my tree on ResponsIV.

He wanted her. He had wanted her from the moment he set eyes on her. He adored her. He moved to London so he could fuck her. For Joanne, though, it wasn't sex that drove her so much as need. ResponsIV had dulled me into uselessness. She needed a replacement: someone to hold her fracturing personality together.

Having her around can't have been any more easy for him than it had been for me. More than once he'd come in to find her beating her face bloody on his walls.

Seeing what he saw, what made him go to Madagascar? Maybe it was just the promise of money. Working with Savvides must surely have given him a taste for it, and pirate metal-heads stood to make a lot of money in the little time they were likely to remain alive.

What he told me was, he had wanted Joanne to go with him. He seemed sincerely to believe that pirated accessories were the answer for her. But what that explanation boiled down to was merely this: 'I'll plug in if you plug in' – hardly reason enough to get your head sawn open.

Besides, she never went with him. She stayed in London. In Beak Street.

I think I know why he went. He wanted to know her with new senses. I think he wanted to meld minds with her. To look at the world through her eyes. To achieve the level of union only post-humans achieve, through the rare machines in their skulls.

In other words, he was in love. Reason enough? I think so. I hated him for it. For the generosity of his heart.

'When I got back to her—' He stared into his empty glass.

'What?'

'I was too late.'

'What do you mean?'

'Get the fucking drinks in, would you, mate?'

She wasn't dying – not then. Quite the opposite. She was *better*. Excited. Distracted. She had no time for him.

'I thought she'd met someone.' O'Connor laughed at the memory: a bitter little sound. 'Love conquering all, even EAI. But it doesn't. Does it?'

Behind us at the bar, someone was tapping something over and over. A slow, penetrating rhythm.

'For God's sake,' I said, 'tell me it wasn't you bashed her head in.'

'Nobody bashed her head in.'

I desperately needed to concentrate. Think beyond the heartbeat pounding behind my eyes. But there was this sound, this regular knocking, going on behind me. I glanced round, irritated.

The woman at the bar was picking up her beer and setting it down again. She picked up the glass, it came to about an inch from her lips, and then she changed her mind and tapped it back on the bar. Changed her mind, and picked it up again. And set it down. 'Jesus,' I said, under my breath. I turned back to find O'Connor watching me, eyes brimming with pale distrust. O'Connor said, 'Has Rence put you up to anything?'

'No.' I raised my hands in an open gesture: look, no wires.

'I bet he did.'

'He didn't. Look—' I wondered if I should appeal to O'Connor's better nature. Assuming he still had one. Assuming he'd ever had one. 'I'm a suspect,' I said. 'I went to her flat before the police did and now I'm in the frame. I just want to know what happened to her.'

O'Connor hid behind his beer. 'Rence'll tell you eventually,' he said. He smiled an infantile smile: a child with a secret.

He was waiting for me to catch up. He knew I would. And eventually, I did.

'You're saying she took something, while she was away?'

'Maybe.'

'Maybe?'

He said, 'She left me. Finally. I moved out. I couldn't keep the flat on all by myself.'

'Where'd you go?'

'Your mate Ballantyne put me up.'

I practically choked on my water. '*Ballantyne?*'

'The contraband in my head was making me sick. He had a clinic. Where the fuck else was I supposed to go?' He grinned at the irony of it. 'Now, thanks to you, I'm in the gutter again, aren't I?'

'It's got nothing to do with me.'

'You're why Ballantyne closed down.'

194

'You may as well blame Joanne.'

'Well, let's face it, she was never much of a nurse, was she?'

I didn't want to talk about it.

'First she left you, then she left me.'

'We're not equivalent,' I spat.

'Whatever. Tell me, you get EAI, Chris, don't you?'

I nodded.

'Why? In your own words.'

It was an odd question. I thought about it. 'Because of what I was plugged into.'

'So the senses God gave you aren't good enough now, is that it?' He cast a lazy hand in a gesture that encompassed the bar, the canal, the old and weary world. 'How about this? After the Moon, and all they promised you – is this enough?'

I sensed I'd moved in a level. Not beyond the bullshit exactly, but into some intermediate place where at least the bullshit pointed somewhere. 'I get by,' I said.

'You get by,' O'Connor echoed. 'Well the fact is, Chris, Joanne didn't "get by". She couldn't, though God knows she tried.'

'Meaning what?'

'Meaning she was greedy,' O'Connor said.

It was impossible to guess at what he wanted. His behaviour, like his face, was neither infantile nor adult, but all stages mingled haphazardly. His motives seemed not to extend beyond cadging an endless stream of cheap lagers; they didn't even make him drunk.

I said, 'I want to know how she died. Can you tell me that? Have you anything to tell me about that?'

'I tried to stop her,' he offered.

'Tried to stop her doing what?'

'I didn't want her to do it,' said O'Connor. 'I loved her.'

'She didn't kill herself,' I said, doggedly. I tried not to remember the flat, the little bin-liner enclaves, the pallet, the soiled clothing. 'You're full of shit. She didn't kill herself.'

O'Connor shrugged helplessly. 'She said she wanted it,' he said.

I lost it again. It was getting to be a habit. I leaned over the table, took a fistful of O'Connor's jumper, and tugged him roughly towards me.

O'Connor clawed frantically at my fist. As he struggled, the sleeves of his jumper rode up. I glimpsed needle scars, chicken-tracking up his arms. Repulsed, I let go.

O'Connor fell back in the seat, loose-limbed, a discarded toy. 'It's what she wanted,' he sniffed, and rubbed his nose with the back of his hand. 'I'm like you, Chris. We both failed her. Neither of us was enough.'

'So how come, if we're so much alike,' I said, 'come her burial, I was by her graveside and you were hiding in the fuck-ing bushes?'

'For God's sake, Rence was there, remember? How could I show myself?'

I leaned back in my chair and looked away from him and tried to get the lid back on my frustration. .

The three men near the door were eating sandwiches. They groped for them. Hesitant fingers paddled the thick slices of white bread gingerly, like insect feelers. The man facing me sniffed loudly before biting off a mouthful. I looked away, faintly disgusted; then something – some piece of understand-ing – clicked into place. I looked again.

The three men – silent, seemingly unaware of each other, each looking into some landscape all his own -they were blind.

Three blind men, like the mice in the nursery rhyme.

Three blind men with shaven hair.

They were metal-heads.

Slow, fumbling, enfeebled. Post-humans: their epistemic appetites ripped out with all their gear.

I looked at the woman in the wheelchair, and the woman at the bar, picking up her drink, putting it down, picking it up, putting it down. I knew, now, what sort of place this was. What it was market for. I cast a quick glance at the blind men, the quadriplegic. 'This is a pirates' place. Why did you bring me here? I'm not part of this.'

The man feeding the cripple beer caught my eye. He smiled a friendly smile: the smile of a comrade.

'I don't want accessories, do you understand? I don't want to plug in. Is this why I'm here? Ballantyne told you I'd be desperate? An easy touch?'

The woman at the bar, distracted, fumbled her pint. The glass fell, rolled and smashed onto the floor behind the bar.

Nobody was serving.

Nobody came in.

O'Connor said, 'Why don't we stop fencing, Chris. For Joanne's sake.'

I stared at him. This animated corpse. This smiling thing. 'Don't you dare—'

'We both know you have Jewel,' he said.

It must have shown on my face. O'Connor smiled, seeing that he'd aimed a true blow.

Then I remembered. That night, leaving Ballantyne's house in a fit of righteous anger, I had told him. I'd actually told him. 'I've still got it,' I'd said.

And Ballantyne, being Ballantyne, hadn't wasted any time turning the information to his advantage.

'Let me have some,' he said. 'I don't want it all. Just a hypo. A shot. That's all it takes.'

'To do what?'

'It's a nanotech thing,' he replied, like it was no big deal, his telling me this. Like this wasn't the very information I'd been after. 'A biological wetware package. Machines so small you can inject them. New senses, new powers: they grow inside you. No need for surgery.'

I stared into my empty glass. It was impossible. And yet it explained everything.

'It's the next big thing, you know' he said, and smiled a death's-head smile.

# 29

The detective looks for a single cause. The detective hunts through the spreading World, dismissing the irrelevant, the ambiguous, the accidental, and searches instead for the one Answer.

The World, on the other hand, has no focus. From a single cause, it extemporises a complex creation, a live and changing mass, an endless spew of things. The World doesn't care for answers: only questions.

The detective's truth and the World's truth are different. Find one, you lose the other.

I hadn't been much of a detective. I hadn't had to be. Answers had been thrust at me – thanks to Jewel, the drug I'd acquired almost by accident.

But those answers only prompted further questions.

If Jewel was an injectable accessory, where did it come from? It was far in advance of any technology I'd ever heard of.

And if it was so rare, how had Joanne acquired it?

And how had it killed her? And why?

And why, given that she died, did O'Connor – his head already butchered by a black-market surgeon in Madagascar – want to shoot it into himself?

Why, come to that, had Ballantyne told O'Connor about my supply? If it was so valuable, wasn't it in Ballantyne's interest to steal it for himself – especially now he'd gone to ground and closed the clinic?

The trouble was, I wasn't really a detective. A detective looks for the solution to a single question. I, on the other hand, had gone looking for the truth. And as Durrell had warned me, the truth doesn't stay still.

I used the phone box in the, Japanese cafe on Portobello Road to ring Police headquarters. I gave a false name and asked for Ballantyne. I made up some story as a cover – I forget what. Eventually I was told he had gone on indefinite leave.

So he really had gone to ground—

I don't know why. Maybe I just wanted another punch-up. But I went round to Mudchute Farm again. From the outside, the brick house looked more like a hangar or a factory unit. No one answered the door. Inside, everything was in its place: ornaments, furniture, books. I waited and no one came. It was very quiet.

I walked round the back and into the piggery. It was silent. The air conditioning was off. So were the lights. The air smelled of rust – or blood. I looked through the plastic porthole into the first cubicle, the second, the third. I couldn't see anything. I opened the door of the third cubicle. Flies buzzed round my face. The cell was empty.

So were all the others.


O'Connor rang up, every couple of days. He wanted an answer from me. He wanted a hypo. Every time he called, he was a little less elliptical, a little less subtle. I hoped to God Rence wasn't tapping the line.

As for O'Connor, I didn't know what to say to him. I wasn't going to give him Jewel. For all I knew it had caused Joanne's death. God knows what it would do, let loose on his immune-suppressed flesh.

Some nights, I untucked a hypo from Joanne's wedding dress and studied it. The liquid inside was red and syrupy.

Held against the light, it shone like a ruby. Without the light it lost its depth of colour and took on a pale, pinkish hue. It was nothing like blood.

I don't know why I sat there so long, staring into it. I don't know what I expected to discover.

So the revelation, whatever it was, remained hidden: exhausted, I would pull back the black-out drapes on a dawn sky soft and grey as lint.

One morning, on a whim, I picked the hypodermic up, held it up to the window, and gave it a gentle shake. Lines of gold formed in the ruby flow. Interference lines, golden against the grey sky.

I held the tube still. The golden lines dissolved.

I lay down on the bed and closed my eyes. Fatigue sent my eyelids into a feathery spasm.

I breathed deeply, trying to clear my head, but the air smelled of oranges and spice and wine, and from the kitchen I thought I heard a woman sigh.


'Chris?'

She was withholding her picture, but I knew it was her. I rubbed the sleep out my eyes and settled in front of the terminal.

'It's Shazia. Shazia Ballantyne.'

'Hello.' I wasn't feeling friendly. She could contact me whenever she wanted: I, on the other hand, didn't even have her number.

'Are you all right to talk?'

'Sure.'

'It just felt strange, the other day. Walking out like that.'

I bit my lip. 'I wanted to speak to you again,' I said.

'I know you did. I wanted to call you. I'm sorry.'

'Is George with you?'

The screen flashed and her face appeared. Behind her, in the deep-focus image of the terminal camera, porters were ferrying luggage to the ornate lifts of an expensive hotel.

She looked nothing like I remembered her. Her long black hair had been cropped short; her eyes were bedroom-bruised by grey shadow.

'I haven't heard from him,' she said.

Was this the real Shazia, I wondered? Was this the way she looked when not playing Ballantyne's *hausfrau*?

'What do you want?' I said.

'I wondered if you'd like to meet.'

'Okay.'

'Or if you don't—'

'I do.'

'Chris?'

Not 'Mr Yale', I noticed. 'Chris'. I wondered what it signified.

200

I said, 'I want answers. Of course I want to speak to you. Who else is there?'

'You pick a place,' she said.

As London had drifted East so the river Lea, widened and canalised, had become an important feature of the London landscape. Its banks were jewelled with offices and condominiums, scented with parks and flower gardens. But at its mouth, where it entered the Thames, the arterial crossings at Blackwall and Silvertown had squeezed out all chance of new development. It was still possible, beneath the flyovers, to find patches of waste ground, vacant lots, foundations weeded over, bright with flies and dusty moths.

I arrived at Twelve Trees Quay as the sun was setting.

The people waiting with me were bathed in the orange suffusion from the Silvertown Arterial. Trains and trams hummed and swished above us constantly, unseen behind the arterial's scooped barricade. Muddying and distorting individual sounds, the great concrete throat sounded as though it were breathing.

I glanced at my watch. Shazia was late. Maybe she wouldn't show. Maybe this was just a way of getting me out of the flat. Even now, George might be ransacking it for Jewel. But you can only worry about so many things at once, and I'd long since exceeded my limit.

The daylight was fading fast. Behind the waiting passengers, the sky was dark blue in its upper part, hot orange at the jagged horizon. The two colours refused to mix. A line of grey extended across the sky, separating them. A dead zone, a fault in transmission.

The pleasure boat pulled alongside. Its bows were hung with paper lanterns, illuminating the mottled waters of the Lea. The middle part of the deck was glassed in, and waiters were lighting table candles. Forced roses in thin china vases drank in the mellow light, pink and ruby red.

A cyclo pulled up at the foot of the pier. Shazia descended from the cramped tin interior. Her grey suit caught the setting sun like fur. Her skirt was tight around her hips and ended just above the knee. Her cropped hair was gelled, forming a helmet over her skull. Either George's disappearance suited her, or she was good with make-up, because the usual anxious bruising was gone from under her eyes.

She looked fresh, and delicate, and she moved with her head held high. Her step had lightened, as though she'd broken free of a drab cocoon. I thought about kissing her. She tilted her face for me. Nothing happened.

I led her onto the boat.

We leaned against the rail and watched the city slide by. The prow filled up around us. Though the interior of the ship glowed invitingly, few passengers chose to take their seats just yet, preferring instead the open air of the fore-deck. The air was cooL but comfortable enough. And there was plenty to see.

We passed Stratford Tower. Somewhere inside, a brain-damaged soldier called Elizabeth was playing with a ball with a bell inside, and the wife of an Apolloco doctor was scrubbing floors and surfaces with resentful fury.

Huge external elevators slipped between the ovoid pin-nacles of the tower. They disappeared behind grand arches and appeared again through bright fissures in the tower's skin, like red cells, riding through a muscle on a web of capillaries. Dwarfed by the tower, staring up at it, Shazia could not help but smile.

'It touches you,' I said, softly. 'However much you steel your-self, it touches you.'

'You think so?'

'I've a soft spot for rocketships,' I said.

Leaving Stratford behind, we passed between the homes of London's political classes. Screened by stands of artificially matured larch and oak, these spare, squarely-built mansions glittered like giant sugar cubes. In front of them, in the more public, *arriviste* quarter, bistros and yacht clubs lined the banks of the river. Wealthy Chinese tourists, their pale bodies naked and steaming, sauna-fresh, plunged and paddled in the chill waters of the Lea. A few old men, gathered round a brazier on a bay of imported sand, grinned and waved at the boat, sharing their uncomplicated enjoyment of the night.

Shazia waved back.

I crossed to the other side of the boat. Already to the North I could see ziggurats: the first gloamings of London's second great tower. Beyond them, massy Fuller-domes like bunches of grapes brightened the night sky: bubbles, emerald green with hydroponic gardens. Orchids and rare mallows were grown here, then plucked and whisked on ice to the penthouse floors of Leyton Spire.

Strangely truncated, cut flat at 1350 metres, Leyton Spire – designed to top any structure north of Beijing – had suffered badly at the hands of the downsizers, the outsourcers, the rationalizers. Cheap solutions had all but destroyed it. Its mechanism was exposed in many stretches; its running lights, unlike the gaudy cherry-and-angelica beacons of Stratford, were tiny and strictly functional. Later, some bright spark had sought to emulate the pastel grace of San Francisco, Painted City of the New West, by spraying bioluminescents down Leyton's hull. But the stock was cheap contaminated rubbish from the sweatshops of Berlin; what failed to wash away in the first rains had bred wild, mixed and gone brown, so now at night great pale streaks made of the vast tapering tower a miserable redwood trunk.

With its apparent rust and ill-lit bulk, the Leyton Spire yawed over us as we bobbed our way up the Lea Navigation.

Tt scares me,' Shazia shivered, 'being this close. It looks like a great coffin.'

'Yes!'

Shazia looked at me oddly.

'Don't you see?' I urged her. 'That's why it works. It looks long-buried. How much else is there these days that looks as if it's aged?'

Shazia leaned on the rail and studied the water. Biolumi-nescents had turned the water here muddy brown: a miserable, streetlamp hue when viewed from the riverbank. But the passage of the pleasure craft excited the modified lichens to a greater sheen, and in the kind lantern-light the bow-wave sparkled bronze and even gold.

Later, easing past the last of Leyton's satellite ziggurats, I said, 'Nothing shows its age any more. That's the worst of the new building techniques. The microrobots, the nanotech. Nothing looks old any more: only people.'

'They're working on it.'

'They're mistaken.'

'What's the use of looking old?'

I looked away, troubled by my answer. 'Because it's important to be reminded of death,' I said.

Thirty months before, on the Moon, I'd said much the same thing to Joanne. She replied, 'You only say that because you're not in love with life.'

We were sitting together, facing each other, man and woman, merely human again. Our heads were not stripped – that would only happen when we downwelled. All our capabilities were intact. And if we'd wanted to, we might have talked inside each other's heads, looking through each other's eyes, feeling as each other felt in complete synergy.

Or gone spinning over the Sea of Tranquillity, with jets for limbs and antennae for eyes, inhabiting, as though they were our own bodies, the drones that daily clouded lunar skies.

Instead we sat, man and woman, and measured in pain the new, soon-to-be-permanent distance between us.

Apart, we stared at each other like strangers.

'I love life,' I told Joanne. 'I love self. Love the limits, and you love the thing. Throw the limits away, and the thing evaporates.'

'Unbounded life,' said Joanne.

'Life in time.'

'Growth.'

'No growth *sans* decay.'

We were slipping into idiolect: the private language of post-humans, for whom words were only triggers for the passage of whole thoughts, passed down a wire, each in each, and no translation needed.

Separate again, man and woman, practising for our Descent, we were once more using words to communicate. But we had forgotten how.

Shazia said, 'What would it have been like? If you'd stayed, I mean. If it had all gone ahead.'

'Something like Stratford and Leyton,' I said.

Shazia was scandalised. 'What, giant jelly-moulds everywhere?'

'Great mile-high ice-lollies,' I said. 'Jukebox World.'

'But not Arzachel, surely?'

'Yes,' I replied, 'even Arzachel. Eventually.'

'But I've seen the pictures. You and Joanne made it so subtle—'

'Oh, that was just architecture,' I said, dismissively. 'Never mind that. The town-planning stage would have jazzed it up.'

'There were plans?'

'Oh, great corporate dreams!'

'Phallic towers—' Shazia extemporised.

'Jewelled vaginal galleries!'

'You sound as though you were looking forward to it.'

'Banality has its place.'

'Really? Jewelled towers?'

'Why the hell not? What a grand lunar tour that would make! Venice *via* Liberace. Babylon *à la* Koons.'

'And Arzachel?'

I shook my head. 'Not on the itinerary. Too morose. Add gold! Add ogive arches! Catacombs!'

She took my hand in hers.

'Let's go inside,' she said.

# 30

So now, back in the flat in Portobello, I stroked the surface of the prints upon the walls. Pictures of Arzachel. Photographs of the moon. I went from print to print, pressing my thumb deliberately against the glossy surfaces so that it would leave a mark. This was the closest I'd ever come to touching the moon again. No matter that my camera lens had subtly distorted the scene. No matter that the emulsions produced a wider range of colours than were actually apparent to the human eye at the time. The point was, earthlight had touched these chemicals, and I now held them in my hand.

This photograph was a physical inheritance, more solid, more profound than memory.

It was very late. Three, perhaps. It was quiet outside. I heard Shazia moving about in the next room. I'd not meant to wake her. I began fixing the frame back round the print.

Shazia came in and touched me on the shoulder. 'Are you okay?'

'Yes, of course,' I smiled. 'What is it?'

'Couldn't sleep.'

'What's that?'

I showed her.

'It's beautiful,' she said. 'Which is it?'

'Arzachel. The suburbs on the eastern side.'

She said, 'You miss it?'

It seemed amazing to me, when I recalled my life and work on the moon, how little care I'd taken of that strange and virgin land. How could the moon have moved me so little? How could it have failed to touch me? I thought of Joanne and her builder swarms, and of Arzachel. The moon had only ever been a blank slate for us: a playground for the will.

'I was thinking,' I replied, with a lightness I did not feel, 'when we were there, we were touched so little by the place. Less than this piece of card.'

'Come back to bed,' she said.

'You're sweet.'
    'Your eyes taste nice.'
    'I'll stop in a minute.'
    'You don't have to stop.'
    'You're lovely to me.'
    'Shush,' I said, and licked away another tear.

'Don't pull my hair so hard.'
    'Sorry.'
    'How does it feel?'
    'Very tight.'
    'Does it get you horny?'
    'Mmm.'
    'To be fucking his wife?'
    'That's not—'
    'It's okay, tell me.'
    'I want to fuck you really hard.'
    'In front or behind?'

'I've given you a hickey.'
    'Where?'
    'There. You can get me back if you want.'
    'On your tit.'
    'If you want.'

'What happened?'
    'She got an abortion.'
    'That's really sad.'
    'She went home for it. I stayed with her parents.'
    'After you'd already split up?'
    'She didn't want them to know.'
    'That's weird.'
    'You should have been there.'

*

'I want to lick you further back.'

'I'm sore now.'

'No, further back. Here.'

'You don't want to do that.'

'Yes I do.'

'Do you?'

'Yes.'

'Did you do it?'

'Yes.'

'What was it like?'

'Ticklish.'

'Did you ever do it again?'

'No.'

'Why not?'

'He wanted to take pictures.'

She reached up and took hold of the headboard, stretched. Her skin smelled of soap. 'Do you mind?'

'Of course I don't mind.'

She let her right hand go of the headboard and parted her legs.

'I want to watch,' I said.

'Of course you can watch.'

'Christ.'

'I'm sorry.'

'What was it?'

'Bad dream. Where did I hit you?'

'I'm okay.' I licked experimentally round the inside of my lip. 'What was it about?'

'Oh, it was really stupid.'

I lay back in the bed. She stirred against me. She was burning hot. 'Come here,' I said.

'Where?'

'Come here, onto my arm.' I pulled her close to me.

'That's nice,' she said.

'You okay?'

'Your arm'll go dead,' she said.

'It doesn't matter.'

The phone call came about quarter to six. I woke first, startled by the sound.

'What's that?'

'My mobile,' Shazia sighed, then, remembering where she was, she sat up. 'My mobile.'

'Aren't you going to answer it?'

She looked at me.

'Go on,' I said. I got out of bed and picked her jacket up off the floor and handed her the phone.

'Hello?' she said.

I settled beside her. She leaned forward so I could put my arm around her. My hand settled naturally on her breast.

'I don't want to know this,' she said.

'No,' she said.

She put her hand over my hand to keep it still.

'Stay there,' she said. 'I won't. Of course I won't.' She turned off the phone.

'George,' I said. 'Wasn't it?'

'He's been taken ill.' She got out of bed and cast around for her clothes. She saw I was still lying there. 'Come with me,' she said.

'You're joking.'

'I'm not going on my own.'

I watched her getting dressed. She dug around in her pockets for her car key. 'I need some petrol,' she said. 'I'll be back in ten minutes.'

'I'm not getting into some stupid scene with your husband.'

'It's up to you.'

When she was gone I lay awake, as empty and watchful as a discarded camera.

There was a mulled smell in the air.

I went into the kitchen. It seemed to be coming from the

cabinet under the sink. An orangey savour. I began pulling things out of the cabinet. A half empty bag of compost. A carrier bag of brushes and polishes. There was my lunar camera, just thrown in among the light bulbs. And a toaster I'd never got around to fixing. I set it to one side and carried on unpacking. A can of spray starch. A tin kettle that had never whistled properly.

A rag.

I turned it over in my hands, remembering. A rag with Joanne's blood on it.

Something had got into it. Something shiny had eaten into the fabric so that when I rubbed the patches, the material just fell away. I told myself it was some kind of glue, set hard. I held the rag away from my own shadow.

The rag looked as though it had been dipped in gold.

I held it to my nose and sniffed. The cinnamon heaviness of communion wine filled my head.

I cleared the rest of the rubbish out the cupboard.

There was a stain, spreading across the hardboard under the sink. I got out of my own light and studied it – a pool of gold.

When I pressed my finger into it, it gave easily. But when I tried scraping some up it went hard under my nail and wouldn't budge.

I studied the rag again, trying to pull some meaning from the stains. Shell-like patterns, ferny growths. Brownish blood and golden Jewel ...

'Here's your house key back.' She handed me my keycard. 'Are you coming?'

I threw the cloth back in the cupboard. 'What's wrong with him?'

'He wouldn't say.'

# 31

I insisted on driving. I guess by then I was fishing around desperately for something to be in control of, even if it was only a lump of metal.

As it turned out, Ballantyne's secret clinic was a large converted town house concealed among a row of large, dirty, three-storeyed properties in an expensive but forgotten district between Peckham and Denmark Hill. I negotiated the unmetalled drive clumsily. Shazia, sitting beside me, clung to the chicken strap above the door. She looked pale. Perhaps she was afraid of something. Probably my driving.

Rhododendrons had grown over the track. Their branches, scraping the sides of the vehicle, made a sound like fingernails scoring a blackboard.

We reached the end of the drive. Unkempt trees flooded lawns with blue shadow. Green light gleamed dustily from cracked upper windows. Rhododendrons leaned heavily against the crumbling plaster work of the large white house, lush with sickly pink flowers. I studied the building, the garden, the drive: I recognised nothing.

Shazia led me up the porch steps, into the shadow cast by a damp-streaked clapboard awning.

We went inside. The wide door and the wood-panelled reception suggested a hospital: otherwise, this might have been any halfway expensive private house.

Upstairs, layers of use and disuse lay nested one on top of the other like a palimpsest. Shazia led me through a long, low-ceilinged room near the top of the house. On the walls, garish emulsions flaked like sunburned skin from green and white tiles and wooden dadoes. Underfoot – beneath frayed lengths of ill-fitting red carpet – old varnish gleamed gold on loose parquet.

Plastic curtains on steel runners divided the room into vague alcoves. Beds were ranked along the longest walls. The electricity was off in the building and the only light came from the evening sun. It eased slowly through the mote-heavy air in oily bars and filled the clouded plastic screens with dowdy light.

She led me down a dark corridor. She said, 'He has an apartment in the basement.' We came to a landing. Hand-stencilled signs on the walls directed vanished interns to Neurology and NMR.

Below us, undressed concrete steps disappeared into an impenetrable gloom. I felt for a light switch and played with the button. Nothing happened.

Shazia took my hand. I descended with her, feeling my way along the banister. We reached the foot of the stairs. The corridor beyond was unlit but many of the doors were open, and dove-grey light crept uncertainly over bare and broken floorboards.

'Along here,' said Shazia.

Pigeons had infested many of the rooms, and the sour, spicy odour of decay filled the air. Something soft disintegrated under my shoe, and with it the soft crackle of old bone.

The next door had a wire grille inset: we passed through. A ray of light parted the blackness. A figure leaned out.

'Are you there, lass?'

It was Ballantyne's voice – but thin and querulous.

'I'm here,' said Shazia. She let go my hand. I could feel the tension coming off her. The fear.

'Where've you been?' Ballantyne's silhouette see-sawed in the doorway. There was something over his head: it looked like a turban.

'George,' said Shazia, 'I've brought a friend.'

There was a moment's silence. I held my breath, expecting some outburst.

'Good, lass. Good.' He disappeared back into the room. I caught a glimpse of his face as he turned. It was drawn and white and without strength. It was a gentle face.

Shazia laid a hand on the small of my back, urging me gently into the room before her. I resisted a surge of paranoia, and stepped inside.

*

The room was bare and unlit. Greenish light seeped through a large French window, which looked out on an area overgrown with buddleia and brambles.

Three tubular steel stacking chairs were arranged around a card table in the centre of the room. The carpet was an off-cut, stained and frayed at the edges. The walls were a sickly green. A door led off into a kitchenette, lit by a fluorescent strip-light above a small, tin sink.

Ballantyne slumped into a chair and spread his hands over the rickety card table, as though preparing for a seance. His head was bandaged: a makeshift turban that gave him an exotic look. With a lurch, I remembered Joanne on the mortuary slab; pregnant, it had seemed for a second, with new, transformational life.

Ballantyne was wearing pyjamas. They hung off him oddly. That and his bent, round-shouldered posture, gave him a liquefied look. It was as though he had been dredged up from the sea, or plucked from the weightless comfort of space, and callously deposited here.

The room smelled of oranges and spice and communion wine. The odour seemed to be coming off Ballantyne.

'Come on in, laddie, aye, good to see you, so it is,' sighed Ballantyne, his accent swerving drunkenly from cod-Highlands to bog-Irish.

I stepped up to him and touched his turban. The material gave under my fingers. 'George?' I took hold of a curl of ribbon, and unwound the wrapper.

His skull had burst open, just above his left ear, leaving a crude triangular hole. In its centre, Ballantyne's meninges glistened. Behind them, stirring slightly, his brain had the soft, granulated consistency of porridge.

Behind me, Shazia slumped against the door-jamb, her breath catching in her throat.

Ballantyne opened his eyes. They were vacant, without intelligence. 'Hello, laddie,' he said.

'I—' I began. 'I need – I have—' I stepped back. I was going to be sick.

Shazia reached for me. I pushed her away and stumbled out into the corridor. She clawed at my back. I swung at her and missed.

'Laddie?' George stood up.

I ran.

I tried the first door I came to and I found myself in a large white-tiled communal bathroom. Huge enamelled tubs were ranked along one wall. At the end of the row there was a more private space, assembled out of prepainted plasterboard panels. Opening the door caused the walls to wobble and shake.

Inside there was a bath, a sink, and a toilet.

A white plastic chopping board lay across the bath, making a makeshift table. It was crusted with blood at one end. An electric surgical saw lay in the sink. It was plugged into the shaving socket under the mirror.

Under the sink, scalpels and dental mirrors lay jumbled in a washing-up bowl full of brown water.

I forgot all about being sick. I went out past the baths and back into the hall. There was a new smell coming from Ballantyne's room now. Acrid, like the taste in my mouth. I went inside.

Ballantyne had left the room. He had overturned his chair. Shazia was setting it straight. There was a puddle of vomit under the table.

'What happened?'

Numbly, Shazia pointed with her thumb to the kitchenette: George was in there, opening and closing cabinets at random.

'George?'

A kettle was coming to the boil. A carton of milk stood beside it. 'Fancy a tea?' Ballantyne said. 'Oh—'

'George?'

He bent suddenly and catted. Saliva dribbled unchecked on to the linoleum. 'Oh fuck,' he said, wiping his mouth. The kettle clicked off. 'Right!' he barked, levering himself upright with a tremendous effort. 'Here we go.' He picked up the kettle. It wobbled dangerously in his hand. He set it, rattling, back into its charge-point.

I put an arm round Ballantyne's shoulders. 'George, come and sit down.' I led him from the kitchen. 'I'll make the tea.'

'You will?'

'Of course. Sit down.'

'Ta, laddie.'

There was nowhere soft for him to sit – only the tubular seats by the card table. I helped Ballantyne down on to one. 'Put your head down a minute,' I said. 'Rest on the table.'

Ballantyne spotted his turban. He bent down to retrieve it. The chair began to tip. Shazia ran round the table and steadied him. I handed him the turban.

'A state I must look,' he giggled, fitting it over his head.

'He is going to be all right,' she said.

I stared at her.

'Isn't he?' She watched, spellbound, as her husband adjusted the soiled bandages to cover his melting brain. 'Two sugars, mate,' he said.

'Right-oh,' I said.

There was no terminal in the room. I looked around for a phone.

'What are you doing?' said Shazia.

'Do you have your mobile?'

'No,' she said.

'Is there a phone on the landing?'

'Who are you going to call?'

'An ambulance, of course, who do you think?'

She looked at me, blankly.

'For God's sake,' I shouted, 'look at his head!'

The phone, when I finally found it, was in with the knives and forks in the cutlery drawer in the kitchen. It was a novelty item: it looked like a lunar lander. I fumbled with it. I couldn't find the 'on' switch.

Ballantyne stood up, went to the window and looked out. He seizured again and pitched forward. Phlegm spattered the glass. A second heave took hold of him. His forehead cracked against the window pane, snapping it. Shazia rushed over to tend to him.

I dialled, then straight away hit disconnect.

If we sent Ballantyne to hospital, then The Hague would get hold of him.

There was another way. I dialled again …

'*Hello?*' A child's voice: Joseph.

'Is Jim there?'

'*Daddy!*'

I jerked the phone away from my ear, wincing.

Ballantyne's fit passed quickly. Now he was looking out through the window, wiping spit and blood from the broken pane as though it were condensation. Shazia was dabbing at his head with a spit-moistened tissue. 'Leave me alone,' he complained, shying away from her.

'Get him into a chair, can't you?' I said.

'He's all right.'

'His brains are ready to dribble down his collar, for God's sake.'

'They won't,' she said, wearily.

'Well how the fuck—?'

'Because I've seen this before,' she said.


# 32


We waited together by the Land Rover. Ballantyne was in the back, asleep under a dog blanket.

'Joanne had already taken Jewel when she came to us.' Shazia tucked the blanket round her husband's shoulders and shut the door gently. 'She was getting weaker and weaker.'

I watched her closely. If this was to be her explanation, her apology even, then it had to be hers, made at her own speed.

'Joanne told me she opposed the evacuation of the Moon. That she was part of an organisation committed to going back there one day. That it was secret, that Apolloco opposed it, and that she needed to wipe out her personnel records. She said she wanted George to find her some pirated accessories so she could plug herself into the Apolloco archives.'

'That was why she needed to plug in again? To wipe out a few files?'

With her foot, Shazia drew a circle in the gravel of the drive. 'I believed her. Was that stupid of me?'

'You could plug in for that,' I said. A bit like using a mallet to crack a nut—'

'Besides,' she finished for me, 'she was lying.' She scrubbed the circle out and began pacing back and forth in front of the car. 'I don't think there ever was an organisation,' she said. 'She wanted us for something else. To be with her when she died. To dispose of her.'

'Did George believe all that about her wanting to delete her records?'

'No.'

'Why not?'

'It wasn't what he wanted to hear.'

'Joanne had a different story for him?'

She turned away from me. I'd touched a nerve. 'What did George want to hear?'

'I don't know for sure.'

'You didn't talk about it?'

'He thought what she was doing was romantic. He said she was hungry for heaven.'

'Heaven?'

'It's what she said.'

'Did you know she would die?'

'I guessed. Which is why I came to see you. I thought maybe you'd know something that could help her. That maybe you could stop it.'

I scuffed a hole in the gravel. 'Only I was asleep.'

'You were ill, Chris. You were hallucinating. You couldn't have helped her.'

'You said she wanted to see me. Before she died.'

Shazia said nothing to that.

'You were lying. Weren't you?'

She nodded.

'Did she ever tell you what she really wanted?' She shook her head.

'Was she alive when you got back from Long Lover?'

'Yes.'

'And George was helping her die.'

'Yes. To begin with he'd tried to save her. But she—' Shazia swallowed, painfully. 'She persuaded him. To help her. I was asleep the night it happened. George was with her. I'd sort of guessed what they were up to. I'd washed my hands of them.' She made it sound like they were having a crafty fuck in the back of the Land Rover.

'How does it work?' I said. 'Jewel, I mean. Does it always kill its host?'

'I don't know.'

'Why the hole in the skull?'

'I don't know!'

'Where does it come from?'

'I said I don't know.'

I felt sick. 'What was it like?' I said, swallowing my phlegm. 'What?'

'To let someone die like that. To just stand by and watch it happen. To get away with it. Thanked, even.'

'You'd have to ask George.'

'You were there. You could have done something.'

'It wasn't like that.'

I hit her in the mouth. She crumpled and slid to the ground. 'Sick bitch,' I said.

'Go on,' she said, through bloody lips. She sat up. 'You were the one who could have saved her. You were the one drugged up to your eyeballs with your head under the pillow. But if it makes you feel better—'

'Sick bitch.'

'Go on.'

I heard Durrell's car. 'Sick bitch,' I said, stepping away.

*

It was dark by the time we drove away. I rode with Ballantyne in the back of Durrell's car. Shazia followed us in the Land Rover.

The back seat was full of Emily's toys. Ballantyne kept picking them up and throwing them at the back of Durrell's head.

'George. Sit still,' I said, wresting the latest gimmick from the big man's paw: a silver ball with a bell in it. Elizabeth's? Or had Durrell befriended yet another patient?

We pulled up at the lights at the junction with Albany Road. Ballantyne, still staring out the window, saw something on the street. He scrabbled for the door handle. The seatbelt restricted him. He fought against it a moment, keening, before he remembered what to do. He leaned back, taking the tension off the belt, and snapped the catch. Before I could stop him, he had lunged at the door handle and yanked it up. The door swung open. He slipped to his knees and leaned out of the car. I thought he was going to be sick.

The lights changed 'Hold on!' I said. But Durrell had already seen. He turned in his seat to watch.

Ballantyne reached out onto the road. With his hands on the tarmac and his bum stuck up in the air like that, he seemed about to begin a gymnastic routine. I pictured him walking off across the street on his hands.

'Chris, for God's sake!'

I grabbed Ballantyne by the waistband of his pyjamas and pulled him back inside the cab. Ballantyne came willingly enough, shuffling back on his knees. He was grinning as he took his seat; he let me do up his seatbelt. There was something in his right hand.

Durrell put the car into gear and moved off, muttering something. I wasn't listening. I was looking at Ballantyne's find – a clear plastic packet, with things inside. Pale ovoids. 'What have you got there?'

'Jelly beans!'

'Jelly beans? Let me see.'

Ballantyne snatched the packet away and tucked it between himself and the door, scowling furiously. 'Jelly beans!'

The car bucked and slewed across the road. Durrell stabbed

viciously at the horn. I fell into Ballantyne's lap. Ballantyne pushed me off. 'Watch it, laddie.'

'Go easy, will you, Jim?' I grumbled, strapping myself back in my seat.

'You should have rung for a fucking ambulance,' Durrell snapped, weaving into the slow lane to a chorus of angry horns.

'I thought it was better this way,' I said.

'For you, you mean.'

'I thought you were the best person.' I glanced behind me. There was no sign of the Land Rover. Had Shazia missed a turning?

Durrell stamped on the brake before a red light. 'What good can I do him here?' he said. 'What am I supposed to do? Wave a fucking magic stick?' The lights changed. He fought with the gears and moved off. 'You should have got him—'

'Is he talking about hospitals again?' Ballantyne sat up.

'No,' I said.

'He's always on about hospitals!'

'He's worried for you,' I soothed.

'I'm no going to no fucking hospital. They'll dice my bloody head, laddie. They'll haggis it, ye ken.'

'Just calm down,' I said.

'Where we going, then?' Ballantyne glared spitefully at the back of Durrell's head. When he got no reply, he turned and stared out of the window, propping his chin on his palm.

Durrell picked up speed. Instinctively, I pressed my hands into the seat. We turned a corner, tyres squealing. 'Take it easy, Jim,' I said.

Durrell, with a clear road in front of him, turned his frustrations off the road and onto me. 'Do you want him to die?'

'He's not going to die.'

'For God's sake, man, look at his head!'

'It's been like that for ages,' I said. 'Days, maybe.'

'Nobody walks around with an injury like that. It's infected, for Christ's sakes. He should be dead by now.'

I stole a glance at Ballantyne's shattered skull. 'It doesn't look so bad,' I said, doubtfully.

'Something's turned off his immune system. No inflammation.'

'Which means?'

We hit a red light and Durrell pumped the brake viciously. I winced as my seatbelt dug in, restraining me.

'The white round his mouth,' Durrell said. That's candida. If that doesn't kill him the PCP will.'

Ballantyne opened his eyes. He noticed the car had stopped moving. 'Are we there yet?' he asked, looking round, craning his neck.

'Nearly there.'

Ballantyne clicked free of his seatbelt. 'George?'

'Fuck you,' he said. He opened the door and before I could unstrap myself, he ran into the street.

'George!' I freed myself and scrambled out the car. White light doused me. The slipstream of a speeding tanker knocked me back against the side of the car. By the time I had got my eyes and my brain back into gear, Ballantyne had vanished.

There was a shopping centre on the other side of the road. Steps led down to a sunken precinct. The tarpaulins covering the market stalls snapped in the damp wind howling up the New Kent Road.

I ran across the street and looked over the railing. 'George?' There was a tube entrance to my left, to my right, two underpasses. How could an injured man have got so far?

I crossed back to the car. The Land Rover had pulled in behind it. Shazia was arguing with Durrell. Durrell had his arms folded; his lips were compressed with anger. 'Satisfied?' he said, when I made it back.

'It wasn't my fault!'

'Did you see him?'

'Not a sign.'

'You know he'll die.'

'He wants to die,' Shazia sobbed. 'He wants Jewel!'

'Oh shut up,' said Durrell. He climbed back into his car.

'Come on,' I said to Shazia, 'we'll look for him together.'

The traffic was heavier now, so we took a subway through to

the market. 'Try the tube,' I said. 'I'll check the subways.'

There must have been a mile of them beneath Elephant and Castle. And as well as a tube station there was an overground station and about a dozen bus stops. Even if Ballantyne had not left the immediate area, many of the subways led to housing blocks, and he might be hiding out on any of a hundred stairwells. It was hopeless.

I returned to the cars. Shazia wasn't around and neither was Durrell. Both vehicles were locked. The night had brought with it the first bitter cold of autumn. I turned up the collar of my fleece.

Shazia turned up a couple of minutes later. 'Where is he?'

'I couldn't find him.'

'I meant your friend.'

'I don't know. Maybe he saw George and went after him.'

'I don't think so, do you?'

'No,' I admitted.

'Was it your friend's idea?'

'What?'

'To get rid of him like that. Saves a lot of trouble for everybody, doesn't it?'

'It was an accident,' I said.

'Sure.'

'Get in.' Durrell appeared by the driver's door of his car.

'Did you find anything?'

'No. Get in. You—' He pointed at Shazia. 'You can do what you fucking well like.'

Shazia stared at us, incredulous. 'You're just leaving me here?'

'The police will be along in a minute. Stay or go, it's up to you. Chris?'

I walked around and climbed into the front passenger seat. I closed the door and watched Shazia in the door mirror. She climbed into the cab of the Land Rover and wrestled with her keys.

I wondered where she was going. Was she searching for George? Fleeing the police? Was she going back to the clinic?

Or to her hotel? I was curious about her, though I could not have said why. 'Well, that got rid of her,' Durrell said.

I said nothing.

She bullied the vehicle out from the kerb, tyres squealing, and shot down the road like a loosed arrow.

'Well,' I said, 'what do we do now?'

'You get the fuck out of my car. I go home to my wife and kids.'

'I'm sorry about what happened.'

'I'm not taking a fall for you, and I'm certainly not doing any favours for that bint.'

'Let's go try find George,' I said. 'We can drive around.'

'There's a pirateware dealer out there with half his skull sawn off, and you expect me to play detectives with you!'

Ostentatiously, Durrell slid his mobile phone back into the dashboard charger. 'I gave Rence a tip-off. Let him find the fucker.'

'Did you mention me?'

Durrell suppressed a sneer. 'No, I didn't mention you. I'm saving that for the morning.'

'Why?'

'Because he'll want to know everything.'

'You can't leave me out of it?'

'No.'

'You don't have to do this,' I said.

Durrell wouldn't meet my eye. 'I'm going to tell him what I know.'

'Jim,' I said, trying to keep my voice steady, 'you're killing me. The Jewel. Ballantyne. You know what The Hague'll do to me. For God's sake—'

Durrell glanced at his watch. 'You've got twelve hours,' he said. 'Deal with it.'

I hailed a cyclo to take me home. It was raining in short, bad-tempered bursts. Warm, fatty droplets splashed my face. I zipped up the polythene screen and the rain spattered against it like moths beating against a lampshade.

By morning, Rence would know that I possessed Jewel. That I knew the whereabouts of George Ballantyne. That I was, somehow, involved. What would Rence do with that information? Put out an arrest warrant? Charge me with something? I wondered, for a panicked split second, if I should flee London and return to Leeds. But that could only worsen my position; Rence had already told me not to leave the Principality. Besides, the police forces of the Republic and the Principality were working hand-in-glove on this one: Sheriff Mukut had told me so himself, on our drive down to London. So Leeds offered me no hiding place.

The cyclo dropped me off on the corner of Lonsdale Road and Colville Road, and I walked the few yards to my door. I inserted my key.

Nothing happened.

I palmed the door. It swung open. I hesitated. I heard nothing. I edged up the stairs.

The flat looked like a hurricane had hit it. Magazines had fallen from the shelves. Cupboards had spewed out their contents. Through the translucent plastic curtain separating the kitchen from the bedsitting room, I saw shadows. If someone was there, then he was watching. I slid through the mess on the floor, opened a drawer and took out a knife. I wheeled round to face the curtain. Shadows continued to eddy behind the plastic. I palmed the curtain aside with my free hand.

The window was open. The drapes stirred and billowed in the damp breeze. This room had been trashed, too. The drawers had been pulled out of the chest and upturned over the bed. Joanne's wedding dress lay spread across the dressing table. I gathered it up in my arms.

There were no rips, stains or soiling. There was no Jewel.

I took up the knife again and went into the bathroom. The cabinet was torn from the wall. Loose tiles had been smashed and ripped from the crumbling plaster. The carpet was pulled up and thrown into the bath and the boards surrounding the bath had been kicked in. The top of the cistern lay across the sink, an impromptu work-surface, onto which the intruder had emptied shampoos, creams and bottles of talcum powder. The empty containers lay under the sink.

Whoever it was had been hunting for Jewel. It was the only thing missing.

Numbed, I went back to the kitchen. A familiar smell came out to greet me.

Spices. Cinnamon. Mulled wine.

I knelt down by the sink and opened the cupboard door.

The cupboard was no longer there. It had been eaten through. Its contents were missing. The potting compost, the camera, the cleaning things, Joanne's rags: in their place there was a nest. A bowl of golden twigs and petals. I tapped the side of my knife against it. It rang: a pure, bell-like tone. I crouched and looked underneath the bowl. There was no floor. The bowl was on a stalk, and the stalk appeared to descend all the way into the earth. It was impossible to tell for sure without a flashlight, and that had disappeared along with everything else in the cupboard.

Behind the bowl, where the wall used to be, the bricks had turned to gold. They had grown very small and irregular, like the tiles of a mosaic. They made a fern pattern. They were not fixed: they moved against each other. They rustled. I reached into the cupboard and put my hands against the golden barrier. It was not a wall at all. It was a hedge. The bowl was not a bowl: it was a flower.

I remembered the bin in Joanne's kitchen: how it had taken root. I remembered the cloths, the way the gold and deep brown of dried blood had seemed – had actually – spread across them, and into the floor of my cupboard.

'Pretty fucking amazing.'

O'Connor palmed his way through the membrane curtain. He had a torch – my torch. 'Isn't it?' He shone it in my face.

I remembered the open window. The curtains, billowing. Heavy, plastic-backed curtains – *billowing*.

'So where is it?'

'What?' Blinded, dazzled, I felt around the floor for the knife. He said, 'This is the last time you dick me around.'

225

I found the knife.

'Don't,' he said. He raised the torch above his head. I looked at him. I looked at the knife in my hand.

'Please.'

Which of us said that?

I tried to stand, and my head burst open like a rose.

# 4
# JEWEL

# 33

Winter came down hard.

Ice sheets, snapped and disordered by the piles of Hungerford Bridge, fanned smoothly out to mosaic the ink-black waters of the Thames. They piled over each other, snapping like cheap crockery, against the streamlined pillars of Waterloo Bridge. Gazing at them, it was easy to imagine the gelid water was still, and it was the stone that moved, like the prow of an ice-breaker crossing a settled sea.

On the far bank the trees were frosted white, like delicate confections of spun sugar. No longer hidden by their leafy canopy, the North bank grinned, shattered and dilapidated like a rotten jaw. The Telecom Tower – gaunt, penile reminder of the old city – rose, accusatory, above the scrubby mass of the West End.

It was a clear day, so there must have been some colour somewhere. The sun was streaming through my window. To me, though, the scene seemed overcast.

I turned into the room, studying the walls, the plastic curtains that, once drawn round the curving rail, shielded my bed. The coverlet. Durrell had got me a private room, and I knew from past visits what colours things should be.

But everything was grey to me. I plucked desultorily through the fruit the Durrells' children had left me on their last visit. I picked up a grey apple and polished it against my grey shift. I bit into it. It tasted grey.

Without the usual colour cues, nothing tasted the way it should. In fact, nothing tasted of much at all. Oh God, I thought – half a prayer, half a curse – does it have to happen so soon? I wondered if the blows to my head had somehow triggered this latest bout of EAI.

I shifted my chair round to face the wall mirror, wincing, my fist pressed to my ribs. I sat before the mirror and peeled the outer wrappers off my face. My nose was still absurdly big. The tapes holding the plastic splints along my septum were secure so I didn't interfere with them. There was a silvery dressing along my torn eyelid that stopped me blinking properly, so that my eye watered constantly. The skin around was puffy and swollen in sympathy. I poked at it, shivering as my fingertip depressed the soft, senseless tissue. Recent injections through my cheek and palate had numbed the back of my tongue, and my mouth tasted of silver foil.

I was still in my dressing gown, dabbing lukewarm water round my chin and cheeks before shaving, when the doorbell sounded.

'Sure,' I said. Lee entered the room.

'You're early.' I cleared my newspapers off the coverlet. I adjusted the pillows and sat up in the bed.

Lee dropped into the chair beside me. Was he ashen? Unwell? Was his pallor real, I wondered, or was I misinterpreting what I saw? Without colour cues, I found myself relying more and more on movement to gauge how people were feeling: on subtleties of mouth and eye, on tones of voice.

Over the coming months, as my epistemic appetite diminished, so I'd depend more and more on these fleeting, partial impressions until, dizzy and disorientated, I surrendered myself to – what?

The old treatments were done for.

Fear of the future hung over me like a cloud.

'—Chris?'

Had he asked me something? 'I'm sorry,' I said, 'I didn't expect you so early.'

Since the burglary and the attack, Lee had been keen to help me. 'They're charging O'Connor with assault,' he told me.

'About time.'

'But the case won't come to court any time soon.'

'No?'

'They've charged him with theft. Something from your flat.'

'What thing?'

Lee shot me a distrustful look. 'The thing I don't want to know anything about,' he said. 'Three hypos of Thing.'

'It's called Jewel.'

'I don't want to know,' he said, blocking his ears. 'The Hague people are talking to him about it. What's the betting the case will never come to trial?'

'No?'

'You know what The Hague are like. They'll dice the poor fucker sooner than have their business brought out in open court.'

'Don't be so paranoid.'

He changed the subject. 'Your house: the police promise me they've saved some of your effects. I haven't seen anything yet. You know they demolished the whole mews to below base level? I've been talking to your neighbours. We may have a tenable position on that.'

'Lee, the last thing I need right now is to be handling a lawsuit against the police!'

In my first week of consciousness, Rence had come in person to tell me about the demolition. He had explained the discovery of strange golden life behind the sink, and what The Hague had done with it, and why. He had been as dour and uncompromising as a navy surgeon, describing an amputation to an injured rating.

And after all, wasn't that what it came down to: a bad case of gangrene? Jewel: those busy pinpoints in suspension, microscopic machines, turning all they touched to gold.

Some lab in Zurich or Singapore was even now, I guessed, exploring with electron tunnelling microscopes the complex fine-grain structures of the transmogrified house.

'Keep chasing,' I said, wanting Lee's visit to be over. 'I want back everything of mine you can lay your hands on. If they've left it in one piece, then I want it back.'

'Apparently they nuked her wedding dress.'

So. I rubbed my eyes.

I'd forgotten my injuries.

Lightning tore through my nose. I jerked my hands away and hissed the pain out through clenched teeth.

'You okay?'

I nodded. 'As long as I get the photographs. I don't care about anything else.'

Come the day of my discharge, Detective Inspector Rence was waiting for me in an unmarked government car.

'I wonder, Mr Yale, if you would like to take a walk with me?'

We turned into Regents Park and pulled up under the bare, skeletal lime trees of the Inner Circle. Puppet soldiers were at their usual antics in the Mall.

Rence helped me out and accompanied me on a slow circuit of the lake. Orphanage children in parkas were lining up on the bridge over the water, dropping bags of half-eaten chips through the holes in the ice for the idiot Prince Regent's pet sea lions. 'Mr Yale – I believe you know certain things about a drug called Jewel.'

'No,' I said, 'not much.'

'But what you don't know for sure, you've pieced together, yes?'

I shrugged.

Rence smiled a private smile. 'Let me explain my position.'

'If you like,' I replied, scuffing absently at the snow lining the path.

'I work for The Hague.'

'Yeah, you told me.'

'What I mean is, The Hague has no jurisdiction in London.' He was doing his best to put me at ease. 'There isn't even an extradition treaty.'

'You mean I'm not under arrest?'

Rence looked at me, surprised. 'Of course not,' he said.

'You mean I'm out of trouble?'

'You never were in trouble, Mr Yale.'

'That's not the impression I was given.'

'Well you did harbour unlicensed nanotech. Your flat was grown over with boundless artificial life. You were taking illegal treatments for a disease no one believes in.'

Rence was making fun of me. I looked away.

'But I knew you were innocent,' Rence said, more gently. 'You're an innocent man, Mr Yale. Naive, perhaps. But that's not such a bad thing.'

'You knew what I was doing all along, didn't you?'

'Of course.'

'You knew about Ballantyne?'

'He was my informant, my consultant. He really did know more about pirateware than I do. Besides,' he added, 'I'd spent months getting him nice and complacent. Let him get away with a few deals he shouldn't have got away with. And I never let on that we knew about his clinic'

'You *knew*?'

'Oh come on, Christopher!' Rence laughed, 'we're not totally stupid. We're not totally heartless, either. Treating EAI is difficult politically. But if people find treatments themselves, why should we worry?'

'Did George understand that?'

'No. It was better George felt he was pulling a fast one. George believed he lived a charmed life. Working for me was his latest, grandest way of giving authority the finger. I figured we should encourage him and see where he led us. Trouble was, he led us to you. For a while, I thought you were up for it. You took Jewel from Joanne's flat and took it home with you: pretty incriminating.'

'You knew I had Jewel?'

'Three hypos, wrapped up in your wedding dress.'

'Christ.'

Rence laughed, easily. 'Come on, Chris, we're The *Hague*. You can't keep secrets from us.' He shed his mackintosh and gestured to a bench. 'Let's sit down a moment.' He spread the coat over the snow-encrusted seat and gestured for me to sit beside him. 'Tell me about Jewel.'

I sighed. 'I know it's valuable,' I said. 'But I don't know what it is.'

'You must have come to some conclusions.'

I thought about it. 'O'Connor told me it was a type of wet-ware. A nanotech cocktail. Little robots that build post-human systems inside your flesh once you inject them.'

'Who told him that?'

I shook my head. 'Joanne, maybe.'

'And who told her?'

'I don't know.'

'That's the problem, you see. We don't know either. We don't know where this stuff is coming from.'

'Have you asked Mrs Ballantyne?'

Rence nodded. 'We questioned her.'

'My wife went to Ballantyne's clinic. She told Shazia there was an organisation. A group of post-humans who wanted to go back to the Moon. Shazia thought Joanne was just stringing her a line.'

'You're not so sure?'

'Joanne didn't want to leave the Moon. That much is true.'

'But what about Ballantyne? He'd never even been there.'

'He was obsessed with the idea of going. Shazia told me he had a medical problem that stopped him.'

'And O'Connor?'

I shook my head, defeated. 'I don't know about O'Connor,' I said. 'He met my wife in a metal-heads' dive in Hounslow. He said they were in love, that they lived together in the flat on Beak Street. When I went there I found a supply of Jewel. Ballantyne surprised me there. He stole some of the Jewel, left some in my pocket, and torched the place. With me inside.'

Rence stared at me. 'Why the hell didn't you tell me this?'

'I was getting EAI treatment from Ballantyne's clinic.'

Rence sighed, the pieces clicking into place. 'You were watching your back.'

'Of course I bloody was.'

'I understand,' he said. He made little patronising motions with his hand, to calm me down. 'Would you mind standing up for a moment, Mr Yale?' He picked up the coat, dusted it free of melted snow and put it back on. We continued our walk.

'One thing I don't understand,' Rence said. 'If the flat Joanne and O'Connor shared was full of Jewel, why did O'Connor need to steal your supply?'

'I don't know,' I said. Above us, coming out from behind a solitary cloud, a superliner, like a vast fountain-pen nib, arced and swooped towards the airport at Tilbury.

I realised something.

I said, 'You've arrested O'Connor for stealing my supply of Jewel?'

'Yes.'

'Did you ever find it?'

'No.'

'That's because he didn't steal it.'

'No?'

'I mean it. He didn't steal it. He wanted it. He knew I had a supply. He broke into my flat and smashed the place up, looking for it. That's when I surprised him. Before he hit me, he said, "Where is it?" He'd ransacked the place. He'd turfed out Joanne's wedding dress. But he didn't find it. He didn't steal it.'

'Meaning?' Rence's eyes were alive with greenish light.

'Meaning someone else got there before him,' I said.


# 34


The police had razed my home, and they were housing me in a hotel during the rest of my stay. I spent the next three days watching TV, thinking, slowly putting myself back together out of the bits O'Connor had left spread wetly over my kitchen floor.

The hotel was marginally less pleasant than the hospital: a huge, bunker-like building with small windows and crude, incongruous crenellations along the tops of its walls.

It was an expensive place – Rence had treated me well to

have put me up here – but nothing worked quite as it should. The rooms were always too hot. There didn't seem to be any way to regulate the temperature. So I spent most of the day in the lounge, watching the TV screen behind the bar, listening to other people's conversations. There were a few business-people, but they didn't linger very long. For the most part the residents were old; old enough to remember Britain as it had been, and London as the capital. They were here on bargain breaks from Birmingham and Manchester and Leeds, and they were always complaining. Once they'd finished criticising the hotel they started in on the rest of the world, which, according to the TV, was going to hell as usual.

On the second morning, there was a package waiting for me at reception. I went back to my room and opened it.

The police had returned my photographs.

I opened the packet and leafed through them. There was one in particular that surprised me: it had hung on the stairwell, where I never looked, and I'd almost forgotten it.

In it, Joanne was leaning over the balustrade of a tall tower, waving to the camera. She was silhouetted, her helmeted head grub-like in the lunar dawn. Around her, minarets of limy lunar concrete rose up like the legs of a monstrous upturned insect. In the distance lay the great ranges of Arzachel.

I rang Rence, but he never returned my calls. I wanted to see O'Connor, but he'd been flown to The Hague for questioning.

Shazia rang me once, and as usual she wouldn't tell me where she was staying. She was after news of her husband, and I had nothing to tell her.

'Rence must have told you something.'

'Nothing.'

'Chris—'

I lost my temper. I said, 'Either we start trusting each other or …'

'Or what? Chris?'

I cut the connection.

*

Workmen paddled about in the muddy remains of my home. Wooden balks painted red and white marked where the mews had been. They had not so much demolished the houses as extracted them, leaving deep, pulpy pits. Plastic pipes, fibre feeds and antique power cables trailed over the broken, rain-sodden ground: abandoned vessels, feeding nothing.

Workmen in crumpled waterproofs consulted with their foremen under the clinical glare of newly-erected arc-lamps: it was day, but the sky had turned dark, making inspection difficult. Pneumatic compressors and generators turned the loudest of their shouts and instructions into muted cries for help. Two earth-movers scraped rubble back from the demolition site, tugging at tangled pipes and wires, peeling back teguments of tarmac from the wound.

These municipal works were the fag-end of things. The real circus had come to town six weeks before: great shielded articulated earth-movers, driven by frightened-looking space-suited drivers who wouldn't leave their cabs (how could they? – there were no doors). Unmanned demolition drones had set about obliterating in a day that street: home for about thirty families. Hovercam inspection wasps feasted their glass-shard eyes on the carnage, till the sky above the street turned black beneath their trembling penumbra.

The emergency had left the usual traces: warning stickers everywhere along the neighbouring roads, and flapping, torn-off ends of police tape. Signs strapped to the lamp posts carried the HazNano warning sign,

to frighten people off the infected area.

I felt numbed: here was yet another part of my life erased. Unvisitable, like the Moon.

Rence picked me up from the hotel. His gesture surprised me. I hadn't expected him to take any interest in me, now that the investigation had passed me by.

He did have one question. He wanted to know about O'Connor's flat in Beak Street. But there was nothing I could tell him.

'So he wasn't living there?'

'He said he couldn't face going back there after Joanne disappeared.'

'So he just abandoned it?'

'How would I know?'

'With all those TVs on?'

'Why not?'

'And Jewel in the cupboards?'

I had nothing to say to that. I had no answers for him.

Rence said, 'O'Connor told us he rented it out through an agency. We followed up his lead and we found we couldn't discover who actually lived there. The monthly rental payments are untraceable.'

'What about the neighbours ?'

Rence laughed. 'This is London.'

We pulled to a halt in the underground part of Euston Station and Rence unclipped his seat belt. He hunted about in his trouser pocket and handed me a bottle of pills. 'This is for you,' he said.

I examined the bottle. The pills were small and round and were a dark, glossy grey, as though they'd been dipped in paint. 'What are these for?'

'Epistemic appetite imbalance.'

I was staggered. 'Do they work?'

'Not particularly.'

I turned the bottle over in my hand. Any side effects?'

'Drowsiness. Mild seizures. Short term memory loss. Liver damage.'

I whistled. I put them in my pocket. 'Thanks. I guess.'

Rence had got me to the station early. He didn't hang around. I sent my cases through customs and left the station. Nearby, on Drummond Street, was the cafe where Shazia was coming to say goodbye to me.

'Ed's Easy Noodles' was fitted out like a 50's diner: red leather-ette seats, antique Coke adverts, a clock circled by blue neon; there were even little jukeboxes along the counter. I played with the jukebox buttons, flicking through the tracks.

'Hi!' A lipstick-smeared apparition rose up from under the counter. 'My name's Therese!' It sounded like "Trees". 'Have a menu!'

I ordered a portion of Don Don Sesame and a chocolate malt.

Shazia wasn't there. It was six o'clock when she finally showed, wrapped up in a blue nylon Parka that extended past her skirt. She wore opaque black tights and Caterpillar boots. Her eyes were heavy with kohl; big silver-hoop earrings empha-sised the bob-cut of her hair.

Her transformation was complete. This must have been how she'd looked before she met Ballantyne. I wondered how the farmhouse had changed. Had she thrown out those absurd country-living magazines, I wondered? I thought, This is what it comes down to: nobody changes anybody.

I said, 'I'm glad you called.'

She would not look at me.

I said, Are you sure you won't have something to eat?'

'Have we time?' Shazia looked at her watch. 'When have you got to go?'

I looked at my watch and away again, across the chrome and tiling of the diner. 'Quarter to seven.' The emptiness of our conversation combined suddenly with the sterile whiteness of the walls and the bare fluorescent lights over the counter. 'Christ, Shazia.'

'What?'

I said nothing.

She studied the menu. 'Why does everything here have to be "easy"?'

'What we need,' I told her, 'is *difficult* noodles.'

We ate, and did not talk much. Shazia ordered 'Little strips of Sesame Spiced Chicken and Green Capsicum served with a Warm Mango Sauce'.

'How are the little strips?' I asked her once, but she didn't see the joke.

Later, re-reading the menu, I said, 'That capital "W" is brilliant.'

'What?'

'Warm Mango Sauce.' She didn't understand me.

Belatedly, I realised what I was doing. That habitual irony, those little in-jokes – they were Joanne's. I was wanting Shazia to be like my wife.

Was that, then, what I was expecting out of this meeting; out of her?

Embarrassed to have caught myself out so badly, I played with my coffee cup. There was a pale sip left. When I shook it, bands of interference laced the bottom of the cup. Like Jewel, I thought, before I could stop myself.

'George expected me to destroy Joanne's body.' I put my hand over hers. It was cold. 'Such a firm grasp of character, old George.'

'You don't have to—'

'He wrapped her in a plastic curtain and locked her in the boot of my car with three cans of petrol. That was the day he drove up to see you at Long Lover. He told me to get rid of her.'

'Shazia—'

'After I threw her body out I drove into the country and found a picnic area in some woods. There was nobody else there. Well, it was the middle of the week. I got the cans out of the boot and I emptied them into the car. I remember when I got back in I locked all the doors. Why did I do that?'

She sighed; gently, she drew her hand away from mine. 'I sat there holding a cigarette lighter up to my face, all afternoon—' she drained her cup.

'What happened?'

'It got dark.' She laughed. 'Funny, what saves you.' She leaned so far back on the seat she had to grab the bar to save herself. 'Christ,' she muttered, 'I wish they'd make these stools less high.'

*

It was nearly time for my train, so she walked me back to the station.

'Goodbye, then,' she said.

'I'll miss you,' I said. I was as surprised as she was, to have said that. I said, 'I mean—' and tailed off in confusion.

'I don't know what you want from me,' she said.

I said, 'I'm sorry I was so angry with you.'

'You were cross with everyone. You had reason enough to be angry.'

'Somehow I thought things would turn out differently.'

'Better, you mean?'

'Differently.'

'Oh?'

I wanted to say, I should never have struck you. I wanted to say, I don't blame you. I don't even blame George. I wanted to say – I don't know what I wanted to say. I said, 'I have to be going.'

She looked at the departure board. 'Platform ten,' she said.

She said, 'Goodbye, Chris.' She took my hand, squeezed it, and let go. 'Goodbye.'

Beyond Watford the train filled up with soldiers. It seemed the entire Republican army was on manoeuvres that night. They swamped the train at every stop, company after company.

Some of the stations we pulled into hardly deserved the name. A weathered concrete awning, a platform barely the length of a single carriage. Sodium light bleached the stuccoed shelter and cast brutal shadows over the faces of the soldiers waiting to embark. The harsh, unnatural glare blotted out the landscape beyond. There were no lights in that black curtain, no sign of any town.

The conscripts piled in and filed out, grew confused and shouted at each other. They didn't know where they were, or why. Some blocked the gangway, staring into space like toddlers mislaid in a department store. Others snapped open tins of beer, chained cigarettes and clumped around in hobnailed boots, determined to stay awake rather than suffer the chill and tedium of broken sleep.

It was daybreak when we pulled into Leeds.

Outside the station, the snow on the pavements had melted into slush, with here and there a pocket of clear, impacted ice to fool the foot. The roads were thick with layer after layer of sodden sand and grit. It was as though the pavement itself were thawing; breaking up into a brownish-pink sludge. As I picked my way to the taxi rank, the pavement made a sickening sound under my shoes: bones crunching.

I sat in the back of the cab, my suitcase beside me, my day-pack on my lap, the carrier with my shopping wedged in the gap between the front seats. I peered out the window, tracing our route, from the municipal art gallery, past the bombastic City Hall, to the stolid modernist frontage of the university and into Headingley.

It was a town of empty lots, surrounded by irregular walls of snow, preserving still the geometries of the corporation scoops. There was a temporary, jerry-built quality to the place: its wide roads, its prefabricated concrete housing, its swathes of empty tarmac under snow. It was like a transit camp. Soon its people would move on to some better place: the Moon, perhaps.

We reached the gates of the private estate where I lived. I paid off the taxi and traipsed home along the access road. Snow creaked beneath my shoes.

They'd erected a new playground near the entrance to my block: iron climbing frames; wooden playhouses buried in snow; plastic animals mounted on cruel-looking springs. It was as though the estate had filled up with toys in anticipation of a visitation. A flood. A downpour of strange fertility.

'Why didn't we have kids?' I'd asked Joanne, one evening during our last year in Arzachel.

Not 'Why haven't we?'

'Why didn't we?'

(She never did answer me. She was looking out through other eyes at her city. She was miles away.)

I climbed the steps to my block, and turned and looked back across the estate. The snow had been bulldozed haphazardly from place to place around the high-rise blocks and garages. Holding still the sharp lines and angles of the snow-ploughs, they resembled tank traps mounted haphazardly against another, more adult, less welcome invasion. I thought of Arzachel, its insect towers, its strange, bejewelled life.

I took the lift to the third floor and let myself into my apartment.

The smell was overpowering.

Oranges, and wine, and spice.

I hesitated. My hand trembled against the light switch.

There was another smell, too. Something like the smell of Mudchute Farm's deserted piggery.

It was blood.

I turned on the light.

The door to the living room was ajar. I eased my way down the hall. The smell grew stronger. The meal carpet crunched under my shoes. I palmed the door wide.

The room was empty. My books lay scattered over the dining table, where I had left them. The weeping fig in the corner had died, dropping leaves over the beeswaxed floorboards.

Sighing, I dropped my bags and slumped down in the couch. The smell had already evaporated, if indeed it was ever there. My senses were packing in. Hallucinations were next. Then what?

Rence's grey pills, I supposed.

Minor seizures. Drowsiness. I leaned over and slipped a CD into the player and let Ravel's quartets wash over me.

It was still light when I awoke. I got up, feeling more tired than when I'd fallen asleep. I felt filthy, too, and my clothes had rucked and twisted awkwardly under me. I shed my jacket and shirt and trousers and wandered into the kitchen.

The plate and coffee cup from my last breakfast were lying

in the sink. I drank a glass of water and went to run myself a bath.

George Ballantyne was sitting on the lavatory.

He was naked.

His flesh had a thick, gelid, pornographic quality. There were blotches on his arms. Fat hung off his bones like cheese. His fingers were curled, his fingernails long and grey. His pectoral muscles hung from his chest in rolls, making withered, hairy breasts. His pubic hair was as thin and pale as the hair on his head.

His comb-over was all disarranged, where his skull had burst wide open like a rotten squash. The hole was so wide it had dislocated his jaw. He leered at me. There was no blood, and his skull was full of dust—

*Golden* dust. Dribbling down his grey cheek. Settling on his ashen shoulder. Powdering his pale chest hair like gauze. Trailing over his pencil-grey thigh.

I could see the gold, but everything else was grey: Ballantyne, the room, the daylight bleeding through the opaque window above Ballantyne's head.

Only the dust had colour, like a hieroglyph. Like a promise.

There were petals in his head. Gold petals, where his brain had been. There was a flower in his head.

I left him there, slumped and smiling and victorious, and walked, trembling, into the living room. I tapped Rence's number into the terminal. Nothing happened. The line was disconnected.

There was a payphone on the ground floor. I pulled on my trousers and my shirt. As I was walking to the door the doorbell rang. I unclicked the latch and looked out.

Jim Durrell was standing in the lobby, a bright red hypo in his hand.

'Jim?' I said, opening the door wide for him.

'Relax,' he said, and stabbed me in the stomach.

# 35

I awoke under a black sky. There were no clouds, no stars. There was no air, and no breezes brushed my cheek, and when I tried to breathe I found I had no mouth. I looked down at myself. I was naked, and my skin had turned to hard, surgical-pink plastic. I held my hands in front of my face, and they weren't hands at all. My fingers were pink cylinders, nipped in at the joints like the legs of an insect.

I ran my dummy hands down my dummy flesh. I had no genitals, just a smooth pink mound where they should have been.

I touched my face, and it was a featureless ball.

I had no eyes, but I could see. I was standing in waste ground, where herons stalk desultorily around stacks of abandoned plastic pipes, and drowned bicycles fetch up against the piers of munitions sheds.

Before me there rose a tower. Near the top of the tower was a balustrade. Joanne stood there, naked, her hair like a helmet framing her fine-boned Algerian face. She had smeared her lips with bright red lipstick.

She waved to me. Around her, minarets of limy lunar concrete rose up like the legs of a monstrous upturned insect.

I looked at her. I looked at myself. There was a knife in my hand.

*GO ON*

I looked back at her. It wasn't lipstick round her mouth. It was blood.

*IF IT MAKES YOU FEEL BETTER GO ON*

Above her left ear, her skull had burst open. A segment of bone had been ripped out, leaving a crude black triangle. At its centre, her meninges glistened: plastic bags full of porridge. Her brain.

She left the balcony. Some minutes later, the door to the tower swung open and she came out to me. She took my hand. I felt her warmth. Her flesh slid sweatily across my plastic palm.

*COME BACK TO BED*

I had no mouth, but I could speak. *What's the use?* I said.

*BECAUSE IT'S IMPORTANT TO BE REMINDED OF DEATH*

I looked wildly around me. Everything here was lunatic.

*Faux*-moon.

*IT'S THE NEXT BIG THING*

Plastic moon.

Moon of would-bes, fanatics and dreamers.

Moon of failures and sad stay-at-homes.

I followed her into the tower and up the stairs, watching her, listening to her bare heels slap the steep stone stairs.

*HOST PROTEINS $G_S$ AND $G_I$ MAPPED*

*TRIGGERING PITUITARY TUMOUR*

*REFINING MALIGNANT TISSUE*

*ASSESSING TUMOUR CONSISTENCY:*

  • *NEURONAL 21%*

  • *GLIAL CELL SPONGE 79%*

*HOST TISSUE COMPATIBILITY 97% AND RISING*

*HANDSHAKING HOST TISSUE*

She came to a fire door and pushed it open. The hallway echoed oddly to her footsteps. I caught the door as it swung shut and watched her cross the vestibule. The floor was a grey-flecked linoleum, and it seemed to go on forever.

*Joanne?*

Mausoleums had erupted from out the vinyl floor, splitting and disarranging the grey tiles. Nests of hawthorn and nettles poked up between the gaps, and the hallway smelled of loam and rotting leaves. Joanne did not turn round, and it was hard for me to keep up with her as she weaved her way between the derelict tombs. She disappeared at last between two obelisks. They were like modernist fingers, poking blindly up into the hard fluorescent light.

When I got there I nearly fell over her. She was kneeling before a door. There were numbers tacked to it: 21. Beside the door leaned a small and withered yucca in a plastic pot. The pot stood on bricks, and she was reaching between the bricks. She drew out a plastic oblong key, and something inside me dropped.

*Joanne?*

She turned to me and smiled, and her smile was all wrong.

NO STUPID

I followed her through the doorway. The room within was large and round and low. In the middle of the ceiling hung a circle of fluorescent striplights. In the centre of the circle the even whiteness of the ceiling gave way to a rough area of charred and bubbled paint. Under the charred area sat a dentist's chair, all vinyl and steel.

Joanne skirted the chair and crossed the room to a window. I followed her, scuffing through chip papers translucent with fat and Styrofoam cartons crusted brown with shreds of brown lettuce. *I would have built you palaces,* I said, but she wasn't listening. I stood beside her and followed her gaze.

The subordinate turrets and pinnacles of the tower lay spread below us: truncated shapes, roofs divided at the apex, bare eaveless walls, unfinished ornaments. Looking at them was like looking through a kaleidoscope: the whole structure seemed fractured and disordered.

I said, *I've seen all this before.*

METALLOPROTEINASE  INVASION  OF  COLLAGEN NERVE SHEATHS DISCONTINUED

RESTORING CYSTEINE-CONTAINING PEPTIDES

STABILISING INVASION FRONTS

HANDSHAKE STATUS: 21% OF HOST CNS AND RISING

I said, *Talk to me, damn it.*

RELAX

I remembered Durrell. The hypo of red stuff. I remembered Ballantyne, dead and transfigured, in my apartment.

DURRELL

*Yes.*

DURRELL IS TRYING TO SAVE YOUR LIFE

I turned to Joanne, not understanding her. Her face had softened somehow. It had gone imprecise. Now I was watching, it began to reassemble itself. Slowly, like mercury forced into shape by surface tension, it took on Joanne's look.

*Joanne?*

*I CAN ONLY WORK WITH WHAT YOU KNOW*

*Joanne?*

*I HAVE YOUR MEMORIES I HAVE YOUR WAY OF THINKING THAT IS ALL I CANNOT SHOW YOU ANYTHING NEW I CANNOT SHOW YOU ANYTHING THAT IS TRULY ME I CAN ONLY REPLAY THE PICTURES IN YOUR HEAD*

I looked around me, wildly. *Where am I?*

*IN YOUR HEAD*

*Am I on the Moon?*

*HANDSHAKE STATUS: 58% OF HOST CNS AND RISING*

I turned back to the room. I recognised the chair. It was the scanning couch from the Apolloco hospital. I wondered how it had got here.

*TRUST ME*

Kevlar straps hung off it in long, untidy loops. The headrest had built-in clamps and straps for immobilising the sitter's neck and jaw.

*What is this? Is this a scanner?*

*THE IDEA OF A SCANNER*

*What did Durrell do to me?*

*HANDSHAKE STATUS: 87% OF HOST CNS AND LEVELLING*

*PLEASE TAKE A SEAT*

*Is this a scanner?*

*OPEN TO ME SENSORY FUNCTIONS PARALYSED UNTIL YOU COOPERATE*

*I don't need the straps.*

*SIT DOWN*

*Joanne?*

But her face had softened again, curdling like butter around bones too rounded and simple to be human. I climbed into the chair.

This was a different sort of rape. It hurt like hell.

*CELLSRECEIVEINSTRUCTIONSFROMCIRCU*

*No*, I said.

*LATINGHORMONESNEUROTRANSMITTTERS&*
*SIMPLESHORTLIVEDMOLECULESIENITRICOXIDEC*
*ARBONMONOXIDECELLRECEPTORSPASSON*
*SIGNALSBYACTIVATINGPROTEINSIN*
*SIDECELLMUTATIONSINPROTEINSG$_s$&G$_I$INCLIN*
*ECELLTOREPLICATEG$_I$0CCURSNATURAL*
*LYINBRAINNEURONSGsINMUTATEDFORM*
*RESPONSIBLEFORPITUITARYCANCERCELLS*
*GROWNBYINDUCEDCANCERHAVEALLNECE*

*Please.*

*SSARYSKILLSINVASIVEBEHAVIOURN*
*OTSPECIALTOCANCERCELLSEGPLACEN*
*TAINVADESUTERUSBLOODVESSELSTUN*
*NELTHROUGHENDOTHELIUMWHITECE*
*LLSBREAKTHROUGHBLOODVESSELWA*
*LLSININVADINGCELLMETALLOPROTEINASES*
*PENETRATECOLLAGENPROTECT*
*INGINDIVIDUALBODYPARTSTHESEENZ*
*YMESCONTROLLEDBYPRESENCEOFPEP*
*TIDECONTAININGCYSTEINEIMaGINEA*
*TUMOURASBENEFIcENTaSAblOOdVEsS*
*ELaNDasSmarTasaPlaCenTa.IMAGineCAncer*
*ousneuronS, cHEwingthroUghthemyelI*
*nsheathsofNeighbouringnErvefibres,then*
*wiringthemseLvestothenervesinside,listening*
*IN...'*

'*Joanne?*'

*YOU KNOW THE TRUTH*, she said. *USE IT. TALK TO ME. I NEED*
*YOU.*

*Let me see you*, I said.

She stepped round the chair and faced me.

Hope shot through me, an absurd bolt of lightning. They had prepared her so carefully, binding her broken head with bandages, cleaning her fine boned Algerian-French face to an unnatural sheen. Turbaned and radiant, she was full of new, exotic life. I returned her mischievous smile. But I had forgotten the effects of rictus: that it was usual for the dead to look this way.

*Joanne's dead*, I said.

I said, *You're not Joanne.*

*TRUE*, she said, tapping her stockinged feet. Her short white hair stuck like a spiked helmet to her skull. Her underwear was silken and soft like the insides of a shell...

I swallowed. I felt the soft click of saliva in my throat. I opened my mouth, and licked my lips, and ran my tongue around the rubbery, wet flesh of my mouth. I held my hand up in front of my face. It was a hand again.

*HANDSHAKE STATUS*, she said. *98.6% AND STABLE.*

*That's not you either*, I said, remembering her – some Portobello Road whore.

*NONE OF THEM ARE*, she said, melting.

Reforming ...

He was maybe twelve years old, and his face was pasty and swollen like a balloon.

*I CAN ONLY SHOW YOU WHAT'S KNOWN TO YOU ALREADY*, said Tony Savvides's son, sucking on a can of cherry Coke.

*Why?*

*BECAUSE I'M GROWING INSIDE YOUR HEAD. YOUR HEAD IS ALL I HAVE TO WORK WITH.*

*I'm not on the Moon?*

*YOU KNOW THE TRUTH ALREADY. YOU JUST DON'T WANT TO FACE IT. WORK WITH ME. HELP ME OUT HERE, DAMN IT. THINK ABOUT DURRELL.*

I thought about Durrell.

Durrell saying 'relax'.

Durrell jabbing me with a needle.

A hypo of red medicine.

My mouth felt dry. I licked my lips. I dared to speak.

*Jewel?* I said.

*Jewel, is it you?*

Savvides's son burst into flame. Fire hosed through his eyes. I hadn't even time to flinch before the flames curled over me.

They shot up me, wrapped me in their helix, made a torch of me – and vanished. The fire rolled off me and back along the floor, taking the floor with it. The tower shrivelled up like burning paper ...

I was floating in nothing, orbiting a bright golden sun. A sun with a special shape. A shape I recognised.

*ABOUT BLOODY TIME*, said Jewel, and vanished, and I felt myself borne along a river of sour dreams ...

# 36

I woke paralysed, sprawled across the meal carpet of my hall-way. My tongue felt huge in my mouth, like a roll of cotton wool. I had teared up. Colours swirled around my eyeball. I double took: *Colour!*

Everything was bright again, and coloured as it should be. How on earth had that happened? Excited, I tried to blink. But nothing happened.

I heard footsteps. Someone knelt down beside me. Foggily, I made out Durrell's face. I felt his hand round my face as he turned me gently towards him. 'It's okay,' he said. 'It's got some sort of muscle relaxant in it. You'll metabolise it in a couple of hours.' He let my head slide gently back onto the carpet. The short pile scratched my cheek.

'Durrell, keep the fucking door closed, can't you?' A woman's voice: one I dimly recognised. I heard her shoes tap-tapping on the tiles of the vestibule, then the door swung shut and she stepped into view. I found I could move my eyeballs.

It was Elizabeth, Durrell's patient from the Apolloco hos-pital. Her face was full of lively intelligence.

I looked away from her, afraid. A few inches from my face lay a hypo. I found I could blink. Focusing was difficult, but I could see that the barrel was empty. Durrell must have dropped it. Something clicked inside my left eyeball and the hypo yawed into focus. There were flecks of blood on the needle. Along the barrel there was a word.

JEWEL.

Then the muscles of my iris relaxed and the world blurred again.

They carried me downstairs and into a car. Not Durrell's sleek missile: some beaten-up beige wreck.

*Probably untrAC eable.*

They laid me out on the back seat. Elizabeth did something to my hands and feet and when strength and feeling came back, I found that she had handcuffed me, hands to the right-side door, feet to the left.

'I'm thirsty,' I said. I was still finding it hard to swallow, and my words whistled and clicked oddly in my throat.

Elizabeth was driving, and took no notice. Durrell leaned back to check on me.

I wouldn't meet his eyes. His anxious smile.

'Come on, Chris.'

The seats were vinyl. There was a long, horizontal split along the back seat, above my head. 'Let's talk. Can't we talk?'

'Leave him alone,' said Elizabeth. 'You must have seen him. Did you see his head?'

'You're frightening him.'

'The transmitter in his head?' His voice quivered with suppressed excitement. 'They're going back, Chris. That's what Elizabeth here discovered on the Moon. Elizabeth and others like her, the observers we left there, when we evacuated. One by one we're going back. As data. Uploadable personality. That's what Jewel does. It takes your personality and transmits it to the Moon.'

I looked out the side window. The sky was clear. Now and again I saw bare treetops, whipping past. The road curved, and the Moon swung into view. A pale white nub of bone, set in the pale wet blue of the sky.

'*We're going back!*' Durrell was practically laughing. It was a revelation for him. A religious moment. 'This is the start of it,' he said. Clumsily, unused to such gestures, he reached back and touched my chest.

I licked my lips. They were dry. A line of split skin sparked on my tongue. It tasted like foil. 'How long have I got?'

'Don't answer him,' said Elizabeth.

Durrell glanced at her. I saw his eyes. He was afraid of her. 'He's entitled—'

'Tell him any more and I kill him right now.'

Durrell turned to face front.

I was alone again.

HE'S TELLING THE TRUTH.

'Who are you?'

Durrell glanced back at me.

DON'T SPEAK. THEY DON'T KNOW I'M HERE. THEY DON'T KNOW I CAN GROW THIS FAST.

'Ignore him,' said Elizabeth.

For a moment, I didn't know whether she was talking to me, or to Durrell.

DURRELL'S TELLING THE TRUTH. THAT IS WHAT I DO. WHAT I'M FOR. I CAN SEND YOU BACK.

'You—'

DON'T SPEAK.

*You—*

YES. I HEAR YOU.

*Jewel.*

YES. MY FRIEND.

*Show me.*

COME AGAIN?

*Show me what you can do. I want to know. I have to know.*

Outside the car, the sky darkened. I gasped. My heart hammered.

Elizabeth drove. Durrell faced forward. Neither seemed to realise that anything was wrong.

The moon grew golden. The milky nub swelled. It opened like a flower. Gold petals sprang and unfurled from the heart of the moon like a time-laps-e rose. Bright gold light streamed from the moon.

Through the vents of the car's air conditioning came the overpowering scent of cinnamon and communion wine.

The petals filled the darkening sky. They edged inside the car. They pulled the chrome and plastic and foam aside, and reached for me. They drew me in, arcs and shields of living colour.

They enclosed me, sheltered and warmed me.

They carried me up.

They struck against each other, cleanly, arc against arc, and rang: a billion bells.

The zest of oranges fizzed on my tongue. I fell through the ever-expanding golden petals. They separated for me, opening and swinging like the panels of an elaborate theatre, and then they fell away and I saw the moon, hanging in the darkness like a jewel.

Panicking, afraid to fall, I turned around. There, opposite the moon, hung the Earth.

I hung upon a fine gold wire between the Earth and the moon. The wire pierced my navel. It emerged through the small of my back.

My guts trembled to the primal, tidal pull of the pearly moon.

My mouth and brain and fingertips tingled in the magical magnetic tug of the sapphire earth. For a moment, I hung in the balance. The wire twanged.

*THIS IS WHAT I DO.*

*Yes.*

*WHERE DO YOU WANT TO GO?*

I pulled myself hand-over-hand up the wire, towards the moon. The wire slid through me without burning. The feeling was ecstatic, like a penetration.

Halfway there, something shifted inside me, and the moon, favoured, made high tide in me, and reeled me in.

The smiling pearly welkin of the Moon gathered me up. The great surface features of the moon – Clavius, Ptolemaeus, Schickard and Posidonius – pouted their great mouths at me and moued me welcome. The faults of Rupes Recta flexed sinuously for me. The rills of Vallis Schroteri bristled for me. Tycho, Copernicus and Kepler blinked at me, great white eyelashes of ejecta spilling and spraying from their lids.

I fell towards the Moon, faster and faster. Cities came in view – cities Joanne and I had made – infesting the great clefts and ranges of the lunar surface. Canals and reservoirs, forests of steely fern and insect ziggurats.

Together, they made a face.

A face I recognised.

Not Joanne.

Not Ballantyne.

Not them, nor, I guessed, any of the men and women who had taken Jewel and, dying, had transmigrated to the Moon.

Nevertheless, it somehow contained all of them. And they were waiting for me.

They opened their arms for me.

They opened their mouths.

They bared their teeth ...

*DARLING WELCOME HOME!*

Howling, I awoke.

It was late afternoon. The sky had dimmed, with a greenish overcast. We turned down a side road and Elizabeth unshackled my feet. She opened the right-side passenger door and dragged me part out of the car before she undid my hands. I was too weak to fight her. She cuffed my hands together in front of me and she and Ballantyne frogmarched me into a ditch by the side of the road.

*THAT IS WHAT I DO. THAT IS WHAT I AM. A WETWARE TRANS-MITTER. PART TUMOUR, PART NANOTECH.*

They let me go long enough so I could piss, then led me

straight back to the car. Elizabeth locked my hands to the door, and shackled my feet together, but this time she didn't fasten them to anything. Which meant I could sit up, in a twisted fashion.

This time Durrell drove. We followed main roads for another hour, then dog-legged on to an unmetalled track, Durrell all the while fighting the wheel of the unfamiliar car. We followed the jagged track through a maze of creeks, mud-flats, shingle banks and water meadows. The cranes and conveyors of gravel and aggregates firms lined the estuary. Elsewhere, over the limitless waist-high grass, I glimpsed the tops of windsurfing sails. We neared the coast. The road fed us onto a spit of reclaimed land bounded on one side by a power station and on the other by the derelict parts of an old army base. Elizabeth hung grimly to the dashboard fascia and pointed out the potholes. 'I can see them, God's sake,' Durrell muttered, as the car's belly wallowed and slithered on the muddy middle of the track. All around crouched burned-out cars, like beasts half-hidden in the tawny grass; behind them the scaffolds of abandoned barracks rose above the billowing straw like the masts of half-sunken ships.

*I'M INSIDE YOU. I'M GROWING IN YOU. I NEED YOU.*

There was only one house here: a stolid stone block, simple as a child's toy. There was a chicken coop but no chickens. An incinerator made out of an old oil drum squatted in a circle of burnt grass. There were no trees anywhere. The fences were barbed wire, rusted through in many places, and a few sheep were grazing the grey-green lawn. They ignored us as we drove up the pitted, pebbly drive.

*YOU ARE MY HOST. I AM YOU. YOU CAN HAVE WHAT YOU WANT.*

In the yard behind the house, there was a second building: a tin barn, which I guessed was once a hangar of some sort.

Durrell stopped the car and they carried me out, across the icy courtyard and into the hangar. The doors were open. It was empty. Just concrete, and puddles, and the sight of my own breath.

Two flights of grille stairs led to a scaffold mezzanine which ran the length of the back wall. Halfway along there was an iron stairwell. They led me up the stairs, to a heavy iron door. Elizabeth drew out a keycard and unlocked the door. Durrell put his arm around my shoulders and led me inside.

I found myself in a rotunda of rusty iron and shattered glass. There was a sour, untreated smell here, like newly-set concrete. The walls of the rotunda had been tiled, but that was a long time ago, and the walls had settled and shifted since, splitting and crazing every square.

The room was lit by fluorescents. The lights were set into the wall every few feet behind yellowish frosted glass. There was a double-lined glass roof, cracked in places. Water, condensing against the cold glass, pattered like rain on the concrete and into my hair.

A fragile shell of plasterboard and perspex had been erected in the centre of the room; a sort of indoor tent. A medical pallet lay foot-first towards the opening. Around it, in a semicircle, stood a couple of drip-stands and hospital trolleys. One was laid out with surgical tools. Bloody cotton swabs lay in a stainless steel dish. On others, monitors and oscilloscopes lay shrouded in dust.

'Knock him out,' said Elizabeth.

'No,' said Durrell.

'Do it or I will.'

'I might hurt him,' Durrell protested.

'Who's the doctor round here?'

'There's no need,' I said – and I wondered, as I fell, at what point I'd stopped speaking.

# 37

YOU KNOW THE TRUTH USE IT TALK TO ME I NEED YOU TRUE
NONE OF THEM ARE YOU KNOW THE TRUTH ALREADY WORK
WITH ME HELP ME OUT HERE DAMN IT ABOUT BLOODY TIME
PROBABLY UNTRACEABLE HE'S TELLING THE TRUTH DON'T SPEAK
THEY DON'T KNOW I'M HERE I CAN SEND YOU BACK DON'T SPEAK
YES I HEAR YOU YES MY FRIEND COME AGAIN? THIS IS WHAT I
DO WHERE DO YOU WANT TO GO? I NEED YOU

*All right,* I shouted, *I'm awake, damn it!*

I was floating in darkness. Ahead of me, hanging in the black
non-space, was a golden flower.

*Jewel?*

QUICKLY. YOU'RE REGAINING CONSCIOUSNESS. WE HAVEN'T
GOT LONG.

*Who hit me?*

HOW THE HELL AM I SUPPOSED TO KNOW? I'M INSIDE YOU,
REMEMBER? I ONLY SEE WHAT YOU SEE.

*You showed me the Moon ...*

A GLIMPSE ONLY. I'M STILL VERY SMALL.

*My wife's there.*

AND BALLANTYNE. AND SOME OTHERS. THIS IS WHAT I DO.
THIS IS WHAT I AM FOR.

*But they're dead.*

ONLY THEIR BODIES ARE DEAD. THEIR PERSONALITIES ARE
ALIVE, INSIDE THE AIS ON THE MOON. THEY LIVE THERE, THE
WAY I LIVE IN YOU.

*Are you sending me there?*

IF YOU LIKE.

*I don't like. I don't want it—*

THERE'S TIME ENOUGH LATER FOR THAT. THINK ABOUT DURRELL.

*Durrell?*

YOU'RE IN DANGER. ELIZABETH WANTS TO KILL YOU. DURRELL
CAN'T HOLD HER BACK INDEFINITELY. THINK, DAMN IT, OR WE'RE
BOTH IN THE SHITTER.

*What—*

*THINK!*

So I thought.

Durrell.

Durrell, with his flash car. Durrell, with his beautiful family, living high up in Stratford Tower.

In a London of cyclos, and shacks between ruins, he was living like a king. It didn't add up. It never had added up. How could Durrell afford that sort of life?

*THINK ABOUT BEAK STREET.*

Joanne's flat in Beak Street, with its screens, its stained sheets, its old chip papers and hamburger cartons. Long after Joanne and O'Connor had left, the Beak Street flat was being used. Someone had been using it, right up to the day I went there.

I had thought it was Ballantyne. But what if it wasn't? What if, the day I went there, Ballantyne really had been following me, on Rence's orders?

If Ballantyne had followed me, and stumbled upon the flat by accident, then that meant someone else had been using the flat. Someone else who knew Joanne.

*THINK ABOUT APOLLOCO.*

Perhaps it was someone from Apolloco. Perhaps it was the man who'd stripped us, when we came back to Earth. A friend—

*Durrell.*

I opened my eyes.

I found myself in the plasterboard lean-to. Through opaque panels of Perspex, I could just make out the tiled walls of the rotunda, and the heavy steel door through which Elizabeth and Durrell had dragged me. The door was closed.

I was lying across the pallet. I must have knocked things over when I fell. A drip-stand had fallen across my legs. Its leads and tubes were disconnected and the ends were spattered with congealed blood. Some of it had run out of the tubes, puddling the concrete floor.

I knelt down and gathered up one of the tubes, examining it.

*Jewel?*

There was no reply.

I searched my prison.

Beside the pallet there was a bedside unit. I opened the drawers. They were full of knick-knacks and personal things. Audio cassettes. Pens. A writing tablet. A hairbrush.

At the foot of the pallet, hidden under a blanket, I found a clipboard. There were medical notes still clipped to it. I studied them. They were in Ballantyne's handwriting.

I gazed at the equipment surrounding the pallet, all that chrome and glass, losing myself in the play of shadows and reflections. I stared at my face, reiterated endlessly in the chrome edging of the tripods and trolleys, and breathed in the smell of brine and old blood.

THINK ABOUT BALLANTYNE.

*Jewel?*

THINK. THINK ABOUT BALLANTYNE.

*Where've you been?*

JUST THINK!

I thought about Ballantyne. About his secret clinic.

About his treatments, and how, afterwards, he hid his patients in safe-houses to recover.

Perhaps this place was one of them. A house, like Long Lover farm.

I stood up and went outside the plasterboard shelter. Between the plasterboard sides of the shelter and the walls of the rotunda there was just enough space to walk. I eased my way along the room, brushing reluctantly against the cracked tiling. The steel door was the only exit, and it was stuck firm. I was a prisoner here. As I completed my second circuit, the door pinged and slid open.

Durrell stood facing me. He still had the same sickly smile he'd worn in the car.

I thought about rushing him. But there was Elizabeth to think of. Anyway, where would I go?

The greatest danger was inside me. Wherever I ran, there was no running away from Jewel.

'How are you?' said Durrell.

I looked away from him.

'I'm sorry,' he said.

I went back inside the shelter.

He followed me in. 'Elizabeth wants to kill you,' he said.

*TOLD YOU SO.*

I shook my head, trying to clear it of Jewel's maddening commentary.

'Chris? Are you all right?'

Jewel was right. I had to think. I had to get a handle on all this somehow. But I was so disorientated, I didn't know where to begin.

I said, 'Why should she want to do that?'

He looked at his feet. He was tongue-tied.

'Does she have a reason?'

'You know about Jewel. For her, that's enough.'

I thought about the weekends I had spent, swimming with her and the Durrells. All those weeks, and all the time Durrell knowing I had Jewel hidden in my flat. I said, 'You could have done away with me long before this.'

'Rence was too close. The Hague. She didn't dare.'

'And now?'

He sat on the pallet beside me. For a dreadful moment, I thought he was going to put his arm around my shoulders. But he didn't. He said, 'I said that you should live. I said we couldn't go around killing innocent people.'

'Big of you.'

'So we compromised. We gave you Jewel.'

I said, 'It was you rented the Beak Street flat.'

He blinked at me. 'Yes,' he said.

'You were using it. You were storing Jewel there.'

He tried to sound casual. 'Joanne had gone off to Ballantyne's clinic. O'Connor couldn't afford to keep the place on. When he put it out to rent, I arranged to take it off his hands.'

'He didn't know it was you, did he?'

'Of course not.'

'It's not enough for you to cover your tracks, is it? You have to double-bluff. Jewel in Joanne's flat. Ballantyne's corpse in mine. Me here, in one of Ballantyne's safe-houses.'

Durrell watched me, carefully. He seemed impressed.

'Rence'll find out that it's you,' I said.

'I was careful.'

'He'll find out.'

Durrell smiled. 'No he won't.'

I studied him. He was pale, and unshaven, and I wondered when he had last seen his family. Things were coming to a head for him. He was approaching a crisis of some kind.

I thought about Jewel, and swallowed. 'How long do I have?'

Durrell nodded. It was the sort of question he was good at. 'Jewel takes about a fortnight to read and encode your central nervous system. The transmitter constructs itself in a matter of days.'

Was he lying to me? Sugaring the pill? Or did he really not know how fast Jewel worked?

'There really was no choice,' he said, standing up. 'We had to get rid of you. You knew so much. You were going to realise it was us, eventually.'

YOU SEE?

'Shut up,' I said.

'I'm sorry,' said Durrell, wounded. He hesitated by the door. He was trying to find something to say, something that would heal the rift between us. 'Don't worry about your head exploding,' he said. 'It doesn't hurt.'

# 38

I sat cross-legged on the pallet for hours, those first few days, waiting for Jewel to talk to me. Sleeping. Watching the sky through the glass roof. Hours of nothing passed by, draining me. Flies, entering by a broken pane, buzzed around me, taking shelter from the winter weather. Often I found myself watching, not the sky, but the glass of the window itself, and the way the sunlight fluoresced the grime sticking to its outer surface.

Every few hours or so I panicked. I screamed. I beat my fists against the door of my cell. Once I found a sliver of glass under the broken skylight and held it to my wrist. But my hands went numb and I dropped the glass and a voice in my head – Jewel's voice – told me NOT TO BE STUPID.

Jewel was inside me, heading for synergy. Its million machines were co-opting more and more G-proteins inside my cells. It was riding them, as you'd ride steer, to sensitive locations. Minute by minute they were marshalling micro-jihads. Ragged invasion fronts, bent on converting more of my mere flesh to something new.

It was only a matter of time before it ate my brain. Germinated. Burst my skull and screamed out who I was to listening ears on the moon.

*And then what?*

EVERLASTING LIFE.

*But I don't want it.*

JOANNE'S THERE.

*My wife is dead.*

NO. JOANNE IS NOT DEAD. SHE'S THERE.

*Jewel, she's dead. She's under the fucking ground. She's gone.*

BUT ON THE MOON—

'No. Jewel. Listen. *A lunar AI's not a human mind. Whatever – data – you sent to the moon, it's not Joanne. It can't be Joanne. Joanne was a human being.*

SO WHAT IF JOANNE'S NOT HUMAN NOW? HUMANITY'S OUT OF DATE. YOU DON'T NEED TO BE HUMAN ANY MORE, YOU CAN JUST BE.

I looked up through the skylight. It was night, but it was bright out: the sky was grey with moonlight. Was Joanne even now smiling upon me?

'Bollocks,' I said.

Jewel laughed, and the moon filled my cell with cold, antic light.

But the boredom was the worst thing. Long hours of sun through filthy glass. Weariness. Days went by. Interminable waits, punctuated by sudden fumbling dialogues with the thing inside my head.

Now and again Durrell visited me. He was shaving again, and there were little cuts all over his face. He was going to pieces. I wondered what excuse he'd made his family for his absence. He wanted to talk. He came on like he was doing me a favour, but talking helped him more than it helped me.

I think he just wanted to get out the way of Elizabeth. Sometimes I could hear them outside the door, arguing. But I could never make out the words.

He wanted to confess. I got bored of stonewalling him. It was easier to let him talk.

So I said, 'Who told O'Connor I had Jewel hidden in my flat?'

Durrell shrugged. 'Ballantyne, I guess.'

'Why didn't you give Jewel to O'Connor? He wanted it. He was in love with Joanne. He wanted to join her, on the Moon. You must have known all that.'

'Come on, Chris,' he said, as though I'd suggested something repugnant. 'You saw the state of his head. He was jacking into infected wetware already. Having Jewel growing inside him would have finished him off.'

'I didn't know you were so picky,' I said.

In the days that followed, prison became home. I threw into one corner what little personality remained in the plasterboard tent: stained bedsheets, the clipboard with its yellowing medical records, and the things from the bedside cabinet. Audio cassettes, a handful of discarded clothing, dead flowers: effects forgotten or abandoned by whoever was here last.

I stripped the place bare. Functional, cold, a dead space where there was nothing to do but sleep: it suited me.

It reflected my sense of determination, and my acceptance of the changes taking place inside my skull.

*

I said to him, 'When O'Connor broke into my flat, he didn't find any Jewel there. Someone had already taken it. It had to be you. You were the only other person who knew about it.'

He shrugged. 'Elizabeth stole it. I rang her from my mobile the night Ballantyne ran off.'

'Why?'

'We had to get rid of it before the authorities found it. Once the police picked up Ballantyne, and Ballantyne had talked, then he would have led the police to your flat.'

*THINK ABOUT THE POLICE.*

The police, who all the time had known about my supply. The police, who'd been observing me. Who would have seen it stolen from the flat. Which meant they already knew about Elizabeth, and maybe even Durrell.

*YOU SEE? YOU HAVE ALL THE ANSWERS ALREADY. ALL YOU NEED IS A LITTLE ENCOURAGEMENT.*

I was beginning to like Jewel. It was a kindly daemon. It put the kindest gloss on things. But it couldn't fool me.

If Rence and The Hague team knew all along what was happening to me, then it meant they were using me. All along they'd been dangling me in the stream to see what fish would bite.

Is the tiddler, skewered by the hook, comforted by the thought that it's only there to land some bigger fish?

*YOU HAVE A TWISTED MIND.*

*Oh shut up, can't you?*

Maybe it was Jewel's doing. I don't know. But I began, in spite of myself, to enjoy my strange, liminal existence. I rescued the writing pad and pen from the pile of discarded effects, and began to draw. I sketched people from memory. The first scribbles were infantile. But it did not take long, trained as I was, for me to recover my lost dexterity.

*VERY ARDIZZONE.*

*Shut up.*

*GERALD SCARFE?*

*Shut up.*

I felt, as I had felt during my walks around Arncliffe, as though there were some sea change in me. Some setting right of what in me was crippled with disuse.

*What the fuck are you up to in there?*

HANDSHAKE STATUS: 98% OF HOST CNS AND RISING

'Why did Ballantyne tell O'Connor that I had Jewel in my flat?'

Durrell shrugged.

HE DOESN'T KNOW. BUT YOU DO. THINK ABOUT BALLANTYNE.

Ballantyne, with his lunar obsession. Ballantyne, who longed to go to the Moon. If not in body, then in spirit.

O'Connor was like him. O'Connor had wanted to go to the Moon, too, so he could be with Joanne.

Knowing that, Ballantyne had told him about my supply. Ballantyne, doing O'Connor a good turn? Well, why not? Ballantyne wasn't long for this world anyway. In those circumstances, even Ballantyne was capable of doing someone a favour.

I asked Durrell for a chair, and he gave me an old wooden thing that looked like it belonged in a schoolroom. When he left I thought about smashing it against the wall. I could use one of the legs as a club. I could ram the splintered end in Durrell's mouth and run away.

DON'T BE SILLY.

I don't think I sat on it once. I used it to exercise instead, stepping on and off it until my heart trembled in my chest like a bird and the room swam around me like a whirlpool. I did this maybe twice a day, and I pulled something in my left knee, but I didn't care.

'How did you find Ballantyne, after he disappeared?'

'I didn't find him. He found me. He came to the Apolloco hospital. He was frightened about what he'd done. About what Jewel was doing to him. He wasn't post-human, and it was taking Jewel longer to work.'

'And you stole him away from under Apolloco? Come off it.'

Durrell laughed. 'Come on, Chris, don't be so slow.' I stared at him.

'You think I set all this up by myself? You think Elizabeth and I are the only ones?'

The penny dropped. 'It's Apolloco.'

'Yes,' he said.

The enormity of the idea settled over me like a migraine. '*Apolloco?*'

'Apolloco settled the Moon. You don't seriously believe they'd abandon all that investment without a fight. Do you?'

As he was going I said, 'What do you argue about?'

'What?'

'You and Elizabeth. I hear you arguing sometimes. What do you argue about?'

He shrugged. There were big black bags under his eyes. He couldn't have slept in days.

'She still wants to kill me,' I said. 'Doesn't she?'

He locked the door behind him.


My routine became bizarre. The cell became my whole world. My day was divided between hours of vacant lassitude staring up at the sky, and bursts of violent exercise, running on and off the chair, willing away the pain in my knee.

I continued to draw. My reflection fascinated me. The diet of ready meals and sandwiches Durrell was feeding me had filled my skin with spots and greasy patches. Though he gave me a wet razor and some cream, I chose not to shave, and my skin was dry, and my forehead, just above the bridge of my nose, was deeply furrowed. In some lights, my face looked as though it was made of paper.

But these were trivial changes, incidental to the main process: I was becoming fit. Lean. My arms and legs were well-defined. My stomach was tight: a neat double bar of thick, ribby muscle.

I thought about escape, but I never did anything about it.

I did nothing.

I liked it here.

I liked this curious non-life, this laziness that somehow, against all the odds, was making me stronger.

# 39

*HANDSHAKE STATUS: 99% AND RISING.*

*Who made you?*

THE LUNAR AIS.

*Elizabeth discovered you on the Moon?*

ELIZABETH. AND THOSE LIKE HER. THEY FOUND A FACTORY. THEY FOUND A BIG SIGN OUTSIDE SAYING DRINK ME. AND THEY DRANK.

*But what's the point of you?*

THE MOON IS MINE. THE MOON BELONGS TO JEWEL.

*So what are you doing here? If the Moon is yours, why are you taking us back there?*

ON EARTH, I LIVE IN YOU: YOU ARE MY HOST. ON THE MOON, YOU LIVE IN ME: I AM YOUR HOST. PARENT BECOMES CHILD. CHILD, PARENT. IT IS A CYCLE. IT IS LIFE. ITS THE NEXT BIG THING.

'You gave Joanne Jewel.'

'Yes,' Durrell said. It was night, and in the glow from the wall-lights his face looked like a mask.

'So why did she leave Beak Street? Why did she run away?'

'She didn't want to do what we wanted.'

'We?'

'Apolloco. We send people back to the Moon for a reason.'

'Which is?'

'To make the Moon ours again. But Joanne was a visionary. You know that, Chris. She said that the Moon was its own place. That when she went there, it would be on the Moon's terms.'

I remembered Arzachel, its curious towers, the spiralled leavings of its insect builders. It made a queer sort of sense.

'I don't know how long I can keep her off you,' he said.

'Joanne?'

'Elizabeth.' His hands were trembling.

I laid my hand on his shoulder. I was amazed at myself – but I left it there.

He looked at me, and there was something so pathetic, so grateful, in his eyes, a lump formed in my throat.

'Jim,' I said, 'for Christ's sake—'

'I didn't choose this,' he said. 'I was recruited. Apolloco set it up.'

There was a hammering at the door.

*HANDSHAKE STATUS: 99.7% AND RISING.*

Durrell stood up. He was shaking.

*99.73%*

My stomach went cold suddenly. I wrapped my arms around me. Beneath my fingers, my flesh buckled and shifted. New structures were webbing their way between the old linkage, absorbing it. Sharp golden wires punctured every vein. I felt my blood leak out into myself, the emptied vessels filling with silver juice.

*99.75% I'M RUSHING THIS.*

Durrell went to the door. I heard Elizabeth shouting something.

'In a minute!' Durrell said.

*99.76. SOD IT, IT'LL HAVE TO DO.*

Durrell glanced back at me. There were tears rolling down his face. 'I'm sorry,' he said.

'Don't—'

'I'm afraid.' He reached towards the handle.

*ROCK AND ROLL.*

Tremors bloomed under my feet. Electricity stuffed itself in my ears.

'No!'

'Yes!' Durrell cried.

*ON-LINE. ON-LINE. DAMN YOU, ON-LINE!*

'Wait. Please.'

Durrell hesitated, his hand on the handle of the door. The door shuddered. Elizabeth was smashing it with something.

Durrell cast around wildly. He saw the chair. He picked it up. He swung it against the tiled wall and it shattered. He snatched up a splintered chair leg.

ON-LINE, DAMN YOU, USE ME, LOOK THROUGH MY EYES!

Moiré patterns flooded my eyes.

Durrell took hold of the door handle again. There was a loud retort and the corner of the door, where the handle was, buckled and steamed.

Durrell screamed and let go of the handle. His hand hung limp. The shock had broken his bones.

I shut my eyes tight against the strobing patterns. I shut my eyes. I had my eyes tight shut.

And my new eyes kicked in.

I saw electricity flowing in and out the wall-lights of the rotunda, like a daisy chain.

I saw a ganglion of micro-voltages, buzzing away inside the electronic lock of the door.

I saw the logic control of Elizabeth's gun, hovering just beyond the door like a wasp.

I saw, hundreds of yards away, across the yard, the cat's-cradle of electrics webbed through the cottage.

Elizabeth fired at the door a third time. The retort deafened me, and I stopped up my ears.

And my new ears kicked in.

The bruised rhythm of the cottage lights buffeted me.

The fierce whine of heating elements beneath the coals in the living room sirened through my head.

Telephones and fax machines in offices half a mile away beat a tattoo on my tongue.

ON-LINE.

The door swung back. Durrell stood there like a puppet with its strings cut. Elizabeth shot him. The top of his skull slid away, spinning like a frisbee, trailing hair.

He was still standing, so she pushed him over.

'Ub,' he said.

*ON-LINE!*

She raised the gun to my head. She was so close, I could see two tiny reflections of myself in each of her eyes. I stared back at me, and my eyes lanced golden light back in my face.

'On-line,' I said, in a voice I did not recognise.

I have smelled sunsets, and felt the chatter of digger ants tickling my palm. I have tasted jazz, and it's as sweet as honey and tart as a lime. I have seen the rainbow flow of a woman's scent, and heard the soft, melancholy strains of her smile.

But I have never seen, or felt, or heard, as I did then.

Elizabeth stood before me, lit up like a Christmas tree. Through my new eyes, she was an electrical thing. Her nerves were wires, her brain shone like a light-bulb. Her gun was a glowing fire in her hand.

Time froze.

I stared and stared. I became weightless. I found that I could move. That my will propelled me in any direction, effortlessly.

I moved towards her. She became enormous. She stretched below me. She towered above me. She extended to either side of me to the very furthest limits of my sight.

No – suddenly, things righted themselves. It was not Elizabeth who was big. It was I who was small. Infinitesimally tiny: a point of pure will. The proverbial angel on the head of a pin.

Elizabeth was not a solid thing to me now. The network of nerves in her skin made a mesh around her, but it was not evenly woven. Where she felt most sensation, the mesh was tightly packed. Her fingers and tongue and pudendum were practically solid. Where the sensitivity of her skin was less, the mesh of nerves was lax and threadbare: round her shins and over her back, there was plenty of space for me to crawl through.

I crept inside her. Electrical storms crackled overhead as her diaphragm contracted. A great thunderclap deafened me as her heart, molten with electrochemical energy, struck. I looked for a way up. Nerve signals bore me up along her spine towards her skull. The tissue of her brain was solid and bright white like marble, lit from the inside. I wandered over her brain pan and reached in between the folds of her cerebrum, hunting for her optic centres. A shock ran through me, and I was in: a spectator in the theatre of Elizabeth's mind, watching as, with infinite slowness, she levelled the gun at my head.

Her heart clanged like a great clock.

The gun barrel bobbed.

I climbed out through her optic nerve and jumped from synapse to synapse down her neck and along her outstretched arm.

Her finger was bright with chemical fire as she tightened it around the trigger of the gun. Nerves in her fingertip flared and exploded as she squeezed tighter. Tighter. *Tighter.*

The trigger gave. I fled.

Back in my skull, time suddenly reasserted itself.

The trigger moved.

I reached out and unsqueezed it. Not with my hand. With my mind.

Elizabeth opened her mouth. Was she surprised? Did she sense something was wrong? Her heart beat: an incendiary, lighting up her chest cavity. The gun barrel bobbed. If it went off now, the bullet would blow my jaw off.

I reached out again, and bent her arm. Articulated her wrist. Raised her arm at the shoulder. Turned her head to face the barrel of the gun. Opened her mouth a little wider.

A little wider ...

Elizabeth can't have known what was happening to her, or she'd never have squeezed the trigger.

# 40

I called Rence. I wondered how my voice sounded to him: I wasn't using any phone.

But I think he expected my call.

I think he knew exactly what was going on. And always had.

Police forensics arrived first. In their plastic coveralls and with videocams glued to their eyes, they looked like ghoulish tourists from the future. When they pointed their cameras at me, it was all I could do not to reach out with my mind and turn them away.

They bagged up Elizabeth and Jim and an ambulance drove them away. Another team examined me, took swatches from my clothes, swabbed the inside of my cheek, and took a blood sample. Then, with very bad grace, they let me go into the cottage and wash the blood and bits out of my hair.

The sight of it swilling around the pristine whiteness of the sink turned my stomach. I opened the bathroom window for some air and saw Rence roll into the yard in his big black Jaguar. He got out and stretched. His blue pinstripe suit was very loud. He looked more like a gangster than a policeman.

I went out to meet him. 'You knew all the time,' I said.

'You need some clean clothes.'

'About Apolloco. About Jewel.'

'We're closing Apolloco down.'

'You used me.'

'What did you expect?' he smiled.

He found me some of Jim Durrell's old clothes in a wardrobe on the ground floor and sent a detective away with a flea in his ear when he dared to object.

'I don't want to wear them,' I said.

'You need something.'

'I'm fine.'

'Just look at yourself.'

I looked. 'Oh Christ.'

He laid Durrell's shirt and trousers on the bed. 'Come call me when you're changed.'

I found him again waiting by the front door. He walked me back towards the hangar. The double doors were open. Inside, forensics officers in paper jumpsuits skirted round each other as though rehearsing some intricate, ugly dance. From time to time, police observers wearing the badge of the Principality muttered into their cellphones. There were even some soldiers in Republican uniforms. Throat-miked, wrapshaded, they kicked stones idly about the yard; they had nothing to do.

'What happens to me now?' I asked him.

'Another scan, I'm afraid. But then you'll be free to go.'

I knew that wouldn't happen. I wondered if Rence even believed what he was saying.

I wondered what Nouronihar would find inside my skull, once he had me strapped in the scanning chair. Would he find a flower?

Would I even make it back to London, before Jewel cracked me open, and sent me to the Moon?

'This was Ballantyne's place,' I said. 'I think.'

Rence nodded. 'One of his safe-houses.' As usual, he was ahead of me.

The site bore little mark of its military past. The radar arrays and satellite dishes had all been dismantled, leaving large, low concrete platforms, their smooth grey surfaces punctuated by rusted spars, irregular brick walls, depressions and score-marks.

I said, 'Let me make my own way to London.'

'I don't think—'

'You know damn well I've no reason to run.' He looked at me, doubtfully. 'You owe me this much, damn it!' At last he agreed.

Unable any longer to stand the dereliction surrounding me, I headed for the beach. The scenery depressed me. The whole geography spelled demise and despair. The old base's hardened bunkers, its offices and barracks, had been ripped out years ago. The single concrete runway was crazed and weed-lined and there were shreds of cable rotting in the verges.

The beach, when I got to it, was shingle. I enjoyed the feel of the stones beneath my feet; the sure, solid sounds the pebbles made, shifting under me. They drowned out my thoughts.

Eventually the shingle turned to sand, and a line of dunes sprang up. My legs had begun to ache. I rested a while by the water line, plucking pebbles from the sand.

First the foundation – a bay. (I wiggled my fingers over the smooth sand for waves.) Its sides made a natural amphitheatre, rising to near alpine heights in a succession of tiers. (I had to dig for sand sticky enough to hold together, and still the gradients were too shallow.) For a while I looked at it, reluctant to add more, then, sighing, I added the walls, the river, picking out wide balconies and roof gardens with my fingernail. (Behind my eyes I filled the space with formal gardens, tropical trees and cacti the size of oaks.) I pressed my little finger at a slant into the model to indicate the entrance with its ogive arch to which all atria were meant to bend their light. The finishing touch: I trailed sand between my fingers to make the battlements—

*WHAT'S THAT?*

*I made one for Joanne.*

*ON THE MOON?*

*In my bed in Long Lover. I dreamed it up.*

Afterwards I climbed the sandy track to the top of the dunes, where the gorse bushes gave way to tough, miserable grass, and pill-boxes from World War Two lay sunken and listing in the dirt. I worked along the tops: to my left lay a flood plain, and hills that marked an ancient coastal line. To my right, the spotless beach stretched, sparking and glistening, to sea as still as a pool. Clouds blew away around me, uncovering the sun, and it dowsed me in cool felty light.

I walked for ten minutes or so, and came to a seaside town. Where its main street turned to hug the beach, there were stalls and arcades to catch the occasional sightseer. There was a tea-house: The Kit Kat Café. Next to it there were rusty iron frames dug into the sand, filled with inflatable rafts, and three or four white plastic tables with umbrella shades. An elderly couple and a fat girl in a blue parka – their granddaughter maybe – were eating hot dogs.

I climbed the wooden steps into the shop. There were racks of flip-flops, and lamps made of seashells cast a sickly glow over the scuffed linoleum floor. The walls were tiled like a bathroom. Memories of the rotunda grazed me: the broken tiles, the cracked skylight.

I thought about Durrell, and about what I had done to Elizabeth.

I wondered how you dealt with killing. I couldn't begin to imagine how you accepted it. I wished Ballantyne were here. He was a soldier. He would know.

I wished they were all here. George Ballantyne and Joanne and O'Connor and Jim Durrell and even Elizabeth. I wished everything that had happened had not happened.

I wished I could stop wishing. I ordered a tea and carried it out on a plastic tray. The fat girl was stomping over the sand to a line of trampolines.

'Mind the shingle!'

'Have you put your shoes on?'

'No!' the girl shouted back, not looking at them, then: 'Yes!'

I took a seat at the table furthest from the old couple and looked away out to sea. The fat girl reached the trampolines. She circled them, aimlessly. Her determination had failed her. 'I need a leg-up,' she complained.

'No you don't,' the old man chivvied her.

'I do! I'll hurt myself!'.

The old man stood up and muttered something. His wife giggled behind her hand.

*How long have I got?*

UNTIL WHAT?

*Until you eat me. Until you bloom and trumpet me to your mother the Moon.*

RELAX.

*That's what Durrell said.*

I AM YOUR FRIEND.

*I know.*

YOU CAN HAVE ANYTHING YOU WANT.

I thought of Arzachel: its insect towers and its strange, be-jewelled life.

I wondered at myself.

Just then, if someone had asked me why I was trying to reject it all – a headlong return to the Moon; new eyes, new mouths; perhaps meeting Joanne again – I couldn't have answered.

What tied me so, to my own more limited truths? What was it bound me to the cold and anxious Earth?

I did not know. I had never known. But there it was. I had my answers, and now it was time to stop searching.

*All I want is my life here,* I said. *A human life. Five senses, and no EAI.*

*I KNOW.*

*It's all I ever wanted.*

*I KNOW.*

*So?*

*SO GOODBYE.*

Something stung my palm. I shook my hand hard. The sting went on and on. I rubbed my hand against my leg and the pain redoubled.

Gasping, I held my hand palm open on the table.

There was something there, in the middle of my palm. Something was moving under the skin. I stared squint-eyed at it, feeling sick, and it squirmed.

The skin burst.

Something golden crawled out. A golden grub thing.

There was no blood. The stinging sensation went away. My palm throbbed once, then eased. The grub crawled away from where the hole had been.

There wasn't even any inflammation.

'Jewel?'

The grub had wings. Perfect clear gossamer wings. As I watched, they filled out. Little veins of gold throbbed behind the grub's thorax, pumping the wings out.

The grub-thing fluttered. Its wings were as bright and deli-cate as gold leaf.

A golden butterfly, two inches from wing tip to wing tip,

opened its wings and clapped them once. Little legs of gold wire tickled my palm. It fluttered again, caught the sea breeze – and then it was gone.

I swung round after it, but the breeze had carried it landward faster than my eyes could follow.

'Jewel!'

I closed my eyes. But I saw nothing but darkness, and felt nothing but the beating of blood behind my eyelids.

I stopped up my ears, but I could hear nothing but the roar of my merely human heart. I ran my fingers through my hair. Something was missing.

I teased through my hair, hunting for them, but they were gone.

The plugs above my left ear had melted away. My skull was whole again.

When he scanned me, Nouronihar would find nothing. Just tissue and blood, and all of it human. Perfect, and entire.

*You can have anything you want.* I wiped the tears from my eyes.

'Thank you,' I said, in the hope that it might hear, and a tall wave, plucked by the Moon, lapsed like a woman's sigh upon the sand.

# BRINGING NEWS FROM OUR WORLDS TO YOURS . . .

Want your news daily?

The Gollancz blog has instant updates
on the hottest SF and Fantasy books.

Prefer your updates monthly?

Sign up for our
in-depth newsletter.

## www.gollancz.co.uk

Follow us 🐦 @gollancz
Find us 📘 facebook.com/GollanczPublishing

Classic SF as you've never read it before.
Visit the SF Gateway to find out more!
## www.sfgateway.com